I've travelled the world twice over,
Met the famous: saints and sinners,
Poets and artists, kings and queens,
Old stars and hopeful beginners,
I've been where no-one's been before,
Learned secrets from writers and cooks
All with one library ticket
To the wonderful world of books.

© Janice James.

The wisdom of the ages
Is there for you and me,
The wisdom of the ages,
In your local library.

There's large print books
And talking books,
For those who cannot see,
The wisdom of the ages,
It's fantastic, and it's free.

Written by Sam Wood, aged 92

MIND KILL

Reality has become a nightmare for ex-policeman Bill Fogarty. His sleep is haunted by terrifying visions. Bill's friend, medical examiner Josef Tanaka, has a difficult problem — he can find no apparent cause for Maura Allan's death. As Tanaka encounters more mysterious deaths, he makes a connection — all the deceased played a part in the imprisonment of Julian Gabriel: a man who can re-shape his energy, enter the heads of others and then destroy them. Bill Fogarty had a role in Gabriel's arrest and so, by association, did Tanaka. Now Gabriel is exacting his revenge — with his mind.

RICHARD LA PLANTE

MIND KILL

Complete and Unabridged

ULVERSCROFT
Leicester

First published in Great Britain in 1997 by
Little, Brown and Company
London

First Large Print Edition
published 1998
by arrangement with
Little, Brown & Company (UK)
London

British Library CIP Data

La Plante, Richard
    Mind kill.—Large print ed.—
    Ulverscroft large print series: adventure & suspense
    1. Detective and mystery stories
    2. Large type books
    I. Title
    823.9'14 [F]

    ISBN 0–7089–3954–6   *00 – 807539*

Published by
F. A. Thorpe (Publishing) Ltd.
Anstey, Leicestershire
Set by Words & Graphics Ltd.
Anstey, Leicestershire
Printed and bound in Great Britain by
T. J. International Ltd., Padstow, Cornwall

This book is printed on acid-free paper

To Peter, Jennie,
Terence and Lenny,
the best friends a man can have.

Acknowledgements

Lt Martin Taylor and
Sergeant Steve Norton
of the Philadelphia Police Department
Doctor Horacio Preval
Julie Robinson
Steve Renzin MD
Richard Sullivan, Ph.D.
Bettina Bullrich
Alice Forner
Nat Sobel
Abner Stein
and
My wife Betina

Catch the vigorous horse of your mind
— Zen saying

Prologue

April 5, 1997
Las Vegas, Nevada

He had already lost four thousand dollars on roulette, a couple of hundred in the slots, a grand on the dice and now he was three thousand down at blackjack. He'd been fifty hours without sleep and his hands were trembling, his mouth dry and sour. Everything had begun to look sinister, from the cruel lips of the croupier to the stockinged caricature with platinum hair and blood-red lipstick who brought him the gin and tonic. Half the cold liquid missed his mouth and slid down his chin before he steadied his hand and sucked the glass dry.

His next card was an ace. "Twenty-one." He'd beaten the house but that didn't matter. He wasn't there to win; he was there to stay awake, but now after five hours at the table, the alcohol and exhaustion had conspired to misalign his senses; the voices of people and the sounds of the machines had homogenised

1

to become a low ominous roar. He needed to get out.

★ ★ ★

She was standing at the front of the casino, just where the half-moon of the entrance drive intersected with the macadam of the strip. Bathed in flashing neon and perched on platformed heels, she didn't look much older than his daughter. He pulled the rented Le Baron convertible to the curb and waited for her to saunter to the window.

"Hi, are you lost?" Her voice was sweet and girlish.

"Yes," he replied and told her the name of his hotel.

"I know where that is," she answered, then coy. "I can get you there for three hundred bucks. It'll take about an hour." A hundred and fifty would have done it but she always started high.

"Please, get in." He didn't quibble.

He felt awkward taking her through the lobby, a man his age with a young woman, but nobody seemed to pay any attention. Besides he welcomed the nerves; it was reassuring to feel the butterflies in his belly.

He triple locked the door and handed her the money before she could ask.

2

"I've got some cocaine," he said.

"Well don't sound so embarrassed about it."

He went to the bedside table and lifted the Gideon's bible from the drawer. As she watched he opened it to the middle section and removed the small rectangle of white folded paper. "There's supposed to be two grams inside here." He handed her the wrap.

"Do you want me to cut it?"

He looked uncertain.

"You know, like into lines," she added.

"Yes please."

Sitting down on the bed he looked at her for what was really the first time; he'd been too self-conscious in the car and too nervous in the lobby. She was actually beautiful, like the actress Julia Roberts, with deep brown eyes, a wide mouth with full pouty lips and auburn hair. As he studied her she bent and removed her shoes. Her feet were small and thin and her toenails were painted the same crimson color as the nails of her fingers.

"By the way, my name is Melanie," she said, opening her handbag to pull out a Gold American Express card.

"I'm Howard, how do you do?"

"Just fine," she answered, placing the fake crocodile bag on the floor before dumping the contents of the wrap on to the glass top of the night table. "I think you got beat on this, Howard. There's only a 'g' in here." She squatted down and used the edge of the card to dice the tiny white crystals into six lines, each about two inches long, then licked the plastic before dropping it back into her handbag. Next she rolled up one of the hundred-dollar bills that he'd given her and presented it to him. "It's your party," she said, smiling.

He took the bill, placed it on the table top beside the lines and hesitated. By the time he looked up again Melanie had taken off her sleeveless dress and laid it on the chair. She wasn't wearing a bra and her body was as close as he'd ever come to the centerfold of *Playboy*. Her breasts were white and so full that they seemed to cover her ribcage and her nipples were delicate and pink. He could see her pubic hair through the sheer crotch of her panties. It looked as if it had been shaved into the shape of a heart, a dark heart. Suddenly he felt old and frail. He didn't want her sex; he wanted her youth and her energy, like a transfusion. He was a dead man staring at life, trying to buy a final minute or two.

"My meter's running," she said. "Is there something wrong with the coke?"

4

"I don't know." His words sounded vague, as if he was giving an answer to life in general.

She'd been with a lot of older guys, knew all about their hang-ups, wives and children, guilt and fear of disease. She could handle it. They paid and they weren't that demanding. Sometimes they took a long time to come but aside from that she didn't mind the soft cocks and flabby pecs.

"Here." She took the rolled hundred, bent over and tooted two lines, sat back up and handed him the bill. "All yours, Howard."

He tried to imitate her and blew a line right off the table. She laughed. "You've never done this before, have you?"

"No, I haven't."

She laughed again. "It goes in, not out. Listen, if you don't want to toot it then rub it under your tongue with the tip of your finger. Works just as good." She licked her index finger, touched it to the mirror and pulled up half a line. "Open up." He did as he was told and she massaged it beneath his tongue.

He sat back and stared at her. Her eyes seemed to sparkle.

"Now what do you want to do?" she asked, easing down between his opened legs. He pulled back against the bed. "What's the matter, Howard?"

5

"How much for the whole night?" His voice was as rigid as his body.

She laughed again, but it was a different kind of laugh, forced. He'd begun to worry her. There was something wrong. Not dangerous, just wrong. "I'd need another five hundred."

"It's in my wallet on the desk."

Cautiously she walked to the desk by the window, as if she was expecting a trick. She picked up the old leather billfold and opened it. It was full of crisp hundred-dollar notes, pressed tightly together.

"Take it," he said.

"What have I got to do for this?" she asked, slipping out seven bills. She would have gone for more but he was watching and she didn't want her wad to look too thick.

"I want you to talk to me. Don't let me go to sleep. Keep me awake. Tell me your life story. I don't care."

"No sex?" This was too good to be true. There had to be a catch, a kink.

"No."

"OK if I put my clothes back on?" If he was some kind of pervert she didn't want to run into the corridor of the hotel naked.

"That's fine," he replied, rubbing his powder-coated finger against the underside of his tongue before lying back against the pillow. The stuff tasted bitter and numbed the gums below his teeth.

"You want my life story?"

"Yes."

She banged up another line of the coke and began, awkwardly at first, still uncertain as to what was required. Recalling Asbury Park, New Jersey, the beach and the boardwalk. She'd lost her virginity there, at midnight on the 4th of July in 1979, underneath an upturned lifeboat. The guy had been a lifeguard, a college kid from Princeton, slumming it with a local. She added some details, fantasised a bit, rambled. All the time studying the strange ashen-faced man who lay with his eyes focused on the ceiling, their lids fighting gravity. She talked till four a.m. Making up stuff, all kinds of crap. Finally it didn't matter; he kept thanking her for talking. Until finally his eyes closed and he began to snore, not loud, just a whimper. She waited a minute and stood up from the chair, put her heels back on and walked to him. He hadn't even taken off his shoes. She searched his face. Even asleep he looked worried, his mouth was drawn tight and his forehead was furrowed, as if he was waiting for bad news. Then he began to twitch, his head jerking from side to side. "Get away!" His words were surprisingly clear and she jumped back, frightened. He'd seemed like such a tired, beaten man but now, asleep, he appeared full of rage and energy. He jerked again, his hands clenching into fists as his eyes opened wide, pupils buried in their sockets so that only the whites were visible, making them appear huge and glaring.

"Jesus!" she said, stepping further away and fighting an urge to run for the door. "Howard, are you OK?"

He opened his mouth and gasped before heaving a deep breath inwards. As he exhaled he appeared to sink lower into the quilt, as if he was being pushed down by a tremendous but invisible weight against his chest.

"Howard?"

There was no response.

She kept her eyes on him as she walked to the desk and picked up his billfold, her hands trembling as she slid out the remaining notes. She wiped down the wallet with a Kleenex and stuffed the money into her purse. Then she headed for the exit.

"No you don't! Oh no!"

Her hand froze on the doorknob.

"Please." The energy evaporated from his tone.

She turned. He was still lying on the bed, but he'd changed position.

"Plea — " It was more a discharge of

oxygen than a word. His knees were bent and his feet planted flat, pushing against the mattress, using all the strength in his thighs to force his back up, into a high arch. So high that it resembled a bow, taut and quivering, while his head was thrown back, away from his chest, his jaw jutting out and his mouth open, scooping air. He was turning blue.

"Don't panic. Think. Think," she told herself. What was happening? Was it some kind of reaction to the cocaine? She could see it sitting there beside the bed. How about the wallet? Maybe she should put a couple of hundred back inside. Don't want it to look like he was robbed.

He grunted, wheezed and arched higher; the bed shook and she was too terrified to move. She was witnessing a crime. That's how it felt. Some kind of beating, or execution, and the violence was spilling towards her.

He gasped again and it sounded like the rattle of a snake. After that she was in the corridor, slamming the door behind her, fighting for self-control as she walked quickly to the elevator, passing people en route to their rooms, keeping her eyes down and hugging her handbag to her body. Maybe she should call 911? But why? Why get involved?

9

She didn't owe Howard whatever-his-name-was anything. Not a damn thing. "Howard. Howard." Pushing the memory away. "Fuck you, Howard."

★ ★ ★

They were the most horrible eyes he had ever seen. Jet black and much larger than his own, so large in fact that their sockets met in the middle of the skull. And the pupils. There were no pupils, instead there was a pit-like hollow at the core of each iris. It was hovering directly above him.

He tried to arch higher, to throw it off but its talons had gripped the flesh above his nipples and were digging in. He could hear himself breathing, the sound was like a rasping bellows between his ears. His arms and legs felt thick and heavy, as if the blood from his pounding heart had engorged them beyond mobility.

Where was the girl? What was her name? Melody? Melanie? He couldn't hear her voice but that didn't matter anymore. He had slipped between the crack in the worlds. No one could save him.

"I'm going to hell," he thought. The black eyes agreed.

He struggled for breath. His ribcage

rose and fell and with it the pressure increased. It was like an iron strap across his chest, its circumference tightening with each respiration. His mouth was parched. He gasped and the pressure intensified, sucking the last of his strength, his body collapsing from the inside out, piece by piece, muscle fiber tearing, organs leaking blood. He wanted to die but the eyes wouldn't let him go. They anchored him to the pain, extracting their vengeance. He could smell it. The rot and decay, as if his bowels and bladder had burst and he was afloat in a cesspool of his own filth. Then it lowered its head. The horned beak was hot as it dug into him, eating through flesh and bone, entering his body through his sternum, probing the cavity that held his heart. It was big, too big to fit inside but that's exactly what it was doing. Crawling in, dragging its rough feathered bulk through the hole in his chest. He could smell it and taste it and feel it. Filling him. Choking him. He struggled to move his right arm. It was numb but he found his fingers. Straining, he lifted. His hand moved, then his arm. Up. Above his head. He hoisted his left. Bunched both fists and punched down, hard enough to break two of his own ribs.

The thing responded by flexing and

growing inside of him, snapping tendons and ligaments as it found form and took shape.

"I'm going to hell."

There was a grinding sound, like gravel against gravel, and movement. Agonising movement as the wings spread, pumping in awkward syncopation, unused to the confines of mortal flesh, forcing his joints to pop and dislocate. Against his will. Everything was against his will. He was a hostage. To another mind, a mind that he had known and studied. A mind that was without remorse or conscience. A mind that was superior and stronger than his own, and relentless. He couldn't fight it. It hurt too much to fight.

Then he was looking down. At a man's body on a king-sized bed. At a face contorted with pain. A face he had known intimately but that had somehow changed without his knowledge. Aged and hardened, its nose grown prominent and its hair receded to reveal the fear ingrained in its brow. There was a stubble of beard and a wide gaping mouth and eyes that stared up and past him, as if they knew something he did not. Some terrible secret.

He did not like the face, not particularly, but still he held on to it because it was familiar.

A tearing sound, like cloth ripping and he began to feel himself being pulled away from the man with the familiar face. Away from anything and everything that was familiar, into a vortex of confusion.

"I'm going to hell."

★ ★ ★

It was two o'clock in the afternoon and the temperature was ninety-seven degrees. It was sunblock weather, factor fifteen at least.

Inside, the curtains were drawn and the room was dark and cold from the air conditioning. There was nothing unusual about that. A lot of guests gambled throughout the night and slept most of the day. What was unusual was the smell. Like a baby's diapers. Rosario Martinez didn't remember there being any babies on the floor, but that's what it smelled like. Caca. Shit. She'd had six kids in Juarez. She knew all about diapers. She walked very softly across the room, without stopping by the door to switch on the overhead lights. She'd knocked three times, but if the people were still asleep, and if the baby was asleep, she'd sneak out and come back later. She got a few feet from the bed. There was definitely someone there. The smell was stronger, a stink. A person was

13

lying on top of the covers, a man, wearing a suit, his legs spread-eagled and his arms folded so that his hands rested on top of his chest.

"*Senhor?*"

Maybe he'd been drunk and passed out.

"*Senhor. Permiso?*"

There was no answer and no sound of breathing. No sound at all. His head was tilted way back and she couldn't make out the features of his face.

"*Sir?*"

There was something wrong here, very wrong. She reached out and found the switch to the bedside lamp, high up beneath the bulb. She pressed it and pearl light exploded on the hardened mask.

"Santa Maria, mother of God!"

That's what it was, a mask. Swollen and blue, eyeballs like white marbles, mouth gaping.

"*A visto el diablo!*"

The fingernails of his fat purple hands had torn inwards, through the fabric of his shirt and ripped the flesh above his breasts. The blood was thick and congealed. Dark against the white of the cloth.

"He has seen the devil," she repeated, making the sign of the cross before she turned and ran from the room.

14

1

Graterford Prison, in Collegeville, Pennsylvania was constructed in 1929. It is a single gray stone building. Inside, three thousand five hundred prisoners live in the shadow of the thirty-foot wall which surrounds and contains their bleak existence. Two hundred of these are segregated from the rest. They are the hard-time drug traffickers, the sex offenders and the murderers.

★ ★ ★

Justin Gabriel's prison cell measured eight foot from the steel bars to the small single window, and six foot from the gray-white wall behind the cot to the similarly colored wall behind the steel-bowled toilet and wash basin. The ceiling height was approximately ten foot. It was hard to imagine a man living in this confined space, yet he had lived within its concrete boundaries for sixteen years. His skin was the same gray-white as the walls and his beard extended from his chin to the cold stone floor upon which he sat, legs folded, eyes closed, like some psychedelic buddha, his waist-length hair fanning down the back of his state-issued overalls. There were stacks of books behind him, ranging from the King James version of the English Bible to *The Tibetan Book Of The Dead*.

"He's been like that half the night," the first voice said.

"It's best not to disturb him," the second voice answered.

"Why?"

"Just let him be."

"It's eleven o'clock. He ought to be in his bed asleep, like everybody else."

"Justin Gabriel's not like everybody else."

"What?"

"Forget it, leave him alone. C'mon let's go."

Gabriel recognised Art Weller's voice but not the other man's, then he listened to their footsteps as they faded down the corridor. He knew each of the prison guards by the rhythm of their gaits and the smells of their clothes and bodies. Each had a signature, some sound or odor that preceded him. Weller's flesh reeked of nicotine, animal fats and salty food, and his feet smelled of vinegar, right through the cracked leather and rubber soles of his working shoes. The Old Spice aftershave that he splashed behind his neck and on to his cheeks did nothing to disguise

16

his physical fermentation. He ate badly, slept badly, and his footsteps were a dead shuffle. The other voice and footsteps, however, possessed a certain vitality and the man's smell had been of Ivory soap and starched cotton. Gabriel knew, as he listened to the weight and cadence of the steps and the interval between the right and the left, that the new guard was large framed, physically strong and, to some degree, disciplined. He was also young, arrogant, and insecure, his insecurity marked by the click of his boot heels against the paved walkway, as if the smack of a metal cleat could reinforce his presence.

Gabriel listened for another few seconds, like an animal listens when his lair is disturbed, his spine straight and his senses heightened.

His body, from the neck downwards, was numb. It had begun with his toes; the way it had when as a child he had slept in an awkward position, cutting off the blood supply to a leg or arm, causing first a heaviness, then a complete loss of feeling in the limb. Now, the only physical sensation he had was a tightness in the center of his forehead, above his eyes, as if the point had become compressed by the concentration of his mind. The Tibetan mystics referred to this area as the 'third eye' while the Indian sorcerers had called it the 'assemblage point'. The nomenclature may have differed but the meaning was identical. It was the place in which all external stimulus was received and processed to create consciousness, projecting recognisable forms outwards like a gigantic hologram, a dreamlike illusion that the unenlightened termed 'reality'.

Once, nearly thirty years ago, when Gabriel had lived in Mexico and studied black magic with a 'diablero' it had required pscilocybe mexicana, an hallucinogenic mushroom, and the mental manipulations of his teacher to force him to this place beyond form, where there was only energy. His introduction was, at first, an impossible test of his sanity, until he realised that sanity, like the rest of humankind's constraints, was no more than a definition, an agreement to boundaries, solid and reassuring. In truth, there were no boundaries, no sanity, or insanity, there was only energy and the phenomena that the mind assembled.

Gabriel's eyes were open and focused on the wall, but it was not the scrubbed stone that he saw; it was a blue-gray sky, stretching outwards.

He began to blink, slowly, over and over again causing a feeling of contraction in his forehead, as if the physical act was shortening the distance between his hairline and his nose. As he did this he straightened his spine and forced his lower jaw outwards, imagining legs and claws forming, forcing their way through his bones and flesh. He imagined a tail growing slowly from the back of his neck; he could feel it falling like his long hair, tickling his skin. Feeling. That was the important thing; feeling was the key to transformation.

He looked into the sky and listened. He could hear the cries of other birds, every note a song unto itself, round and full with nuance and melody, calling him to flight. His heart was beating rapidly as his taloned feet pushed against the hard ground. He bounced up and down, using the muscles of his legs, rebounding on razored claws, until the sensation of bouncing became that of springing, lighter and lighter, higher and higher. Finally he spread his wings and pushed down against a pillow of air. Two, three more times, and he was rising, moving forward. Stronger now, his talons and legs tucked beneath him, eyes focused as he flew through the concrete sky, soaring to freedom.

* * *

"Look at him. Still hasn't moved a muscle. He's like a statue."

"Leave'm alone."

The young inexperienced guard lifted his ring of keys towards the lock on the cell.

"I said leave him," the older man commanded. This time he cupped his hand hard down against the other's wrist, gripping him.

"Just move along!"

The new guard was named Phillip Harrison. He was twenty-five years old and didn't like being shoved around by a guy old enough to be his father.

"I want to check on the prisoner," he said, standing firm.

"Then do it when my shift is over," Art Weller answered.

Harrison met Weller's eyes.

"If you and me are gonna be working together, there's a couple things we ought to get straight," Weller continued.

Harrison looked down at the hand that was gripping his wrist. "How about letting go of me?"

Weller released his grip, then, changing tack, he smiled. His teeth were stained yellow and his gray eyes glowed with religious conviction. He reached into the top pocket of his shirt and pulled out a crumpled pack of Marlboros.

"You smoke?" he asked.

"No."

"Bad habit but it relaxes me," Weller said, jerking the pack upwards so that a cigarette emerged to meet his lips. Then, stuffing the Marlboros back in his pocket, he walked forward, nudging Harrison away from Gabriel's cell.

"Things go on around here that don't get talked about. It's strictly on a need-to-know basis," he said, pulling a stick match out from the pocket of his trousers.

It was Weller's conspiratorial tone that made Harrison feel uneasy and suddenly he was aware of the unnatural stillness that seemed to have fallen on the cell block. It was too quiet and Weller was standing too close to him, in his face. He didn't want anything to do with this man. No shared secrets.

"Maybe you won't believe what I'm gonna tell you but you should listen anyway, for your own sake." Weller struck the head of the match against the edge of his thumbnail and the sound seemed magnified in the hollow of the hallway. Harrison was about to turn and walk away when Weller spoke again.

"Justin Gabriel controls this place. You. Me. Everybody here. He's not like us; he has special powers, he can do things that normal people just dream about," he began, the flare from the raised match adding to the glint of his eyes.

"Is that why's he in here?" Harrison asked sarcastically.

"That's just his physical body."

"Yeah, right."

"I'm warning you." Weller's voice lowered. "You go easy on him and it'll make it a lot easier on all of us. You'll be able to go home peaceful at night. You fuck with him and he'll get you right here." He lifted his index finger to his temple and tapped. "Justin Gabriel is the most dangerous man who ever lived."

Phillip Harrison shook his head and began to walk away.

"I'm asking you to listen to me, son. For your own good." Harrison stopped and turned.

2

Bill Fogarty rarely remembered his dreams, but this one was different; it was particularly vivid. He had dreamed of a bird, a great black bird that had been flying gracefully through a clear blue sky, the sunlight adding an aura to the silhouette of its wings. At first the dream had been peaceful and the great bird a thing of beauty and wonder, but as the dream progressed and the bird circled and descended, its dark eyes fixed and penetrating, the feeling had changed and Fogarty had become frightened.

He had tried to run but was unable to move, his feet and legs buried in wet heavy sand and by the time the bird had begun its final dive, with its spreading horned jaws eclipsing the sun, Fogarty was petrified, jolting awake with the image clinging to his eyes, until finally, the light from the rising sun, glowing warm through the curtained window of the bedroom, burned it away.

Diane Genero was sleeping beside him. He lay still a moment, taking solace from her gentle breathing, before settling back against his pillow and lifting the duvet to his shoulders. He thought again of the great bird, but the image was less threatening, further away, just a thought.

★ ★ ★

After a year living together in Santa Fe, New Mexico, it had become obvious to Diane that Fogarty missed his roots on the East Coast. He spoke often of Philadelphia, and of Josef Tanaka, the city's Japanese-American

23

medical examiner. He and the doctor had worked many cases together, had grown to respect and trust each other, and Josef and Rachel Tanaka's son Billy was Fogarty's godchild.

It had been Diane's idea to rent the house on Long Island. The place they had chosen was in Springs, on the shore of Gardiner's Bay in the township of East Hampton. It had been the first project of a young architect and was an ambitious sculpture cast in cedar wood, a pyramid of windows and skylights with dramatically slanting roofs and panoramic views of the water.

Fogarty loved the house and he loved Springs. It was a year-round place, a working community, free from tourists and day-trippers, a hundred miles from Manhattan and a four-and-a-half-hour drive from Philadelphia. It was the kind of peaceful environment he had needed after a lifetime of pounding city pavements as a police officer. White sand and blue water, and wild life, deer and birds.

Birds.

The dream recurred, until finally he found it difficult to sleep. The bird seemed to enter his mind the moment he drifted off, becoming more aggressive and more terrifying with each encounter, until one day, while driving home from the village,

24

he thought he saw it, circling in the sky above the car.

"Look up there, Diane. Right there, to the left?"

"What am I supposed to be looking at?"

"That bird, that big black thing."

"Where?"

He pointed. "Follow my finger."

"That's a cloud."

"No. No way. It's moving in circles."

Diane looked over at him. He was driving very slowly, his head pushed forward, eyes focused through the tinted window of the Chevy Blazer.

"I'm sorry, Bill, I don't see anything but a thin cloud."

"Damn thing's looking at me."

"Oh, come on . . ." She laughed as she said it.

He glanced angrily at her. "The goddamn thing is circling the car."

"You're joking, aren't you?"

It wasn't Fogarty's style of humor but there was definitely no bird and, by now, he had slowed the Blazer to a crawl. There was a pick-up truck a few feet behind them and the road was too narrow for it to pass. Diane turned and saw the driver's face. He was saying something and shaking his head. Finally he honked his horn. Fogarty paid no attention and continued at less than ten miles an hour.

The man honked again and Fogarty erupted. "Shut up!"

Another blast from the horn and Fogarty slammed on his brakes. The pick-up truck missed him by inches as it skidded to his side.

"Asshole!" Fogarty shouted.

"Stop it, Bill, you're acting like a child!"

Fogarty raised his fist to the window as the other man glared at him. He was wearing a baseball hat with the peak turned backwards.

"I hate guys in baseball hats," Fogarty hissed as the pick-up continued along the road.

"What's the matter with you?" Diane demanded.

Fogarty ignored her question and opened his door.

"I want us both to get out of this car right now."

"Why? Why are you acting this way?"

"Just do it."

"All right," Diane replied, opening her door.

She joined Fogarty at the driver's side of the car.

"It's up there, towards the east."

26

They walked across the road and looked out over the bay. The water was smooth and Gardiner's Island sat long and low to the horizon directly in front of them. Above the sky was a patchwork of white and blue.

"Bill, all I see are clouds. That's it. There is no bird, not even a seagull. Not then and not now."

Fogarty looked up. His face was stern and for a few moments he remained still. "Goddamn it, do you know something? You're right." He was so relieved that he felt like dancing a jig in the middle of the road.

3

The kayak, or baidarka, was first used by the Eskimo; they were canoe-like boats with wooden frames and seal skin coverings. The modern versions are constructed from plastic, fiberglass, or even kevlar and range anywhere from nine to nineteen feet in length, weighing between thirty and sixty pounds, and can be less than twenty-four inches in width.

There was a plastic kayak in the garage and Fogarty became fascinated with it, finally asking the real estate agent who rented them the house if it would be all right if he tried it out. The agent came back with a warning about strong currents and a consent form, clearing the owners of liability in case of an accident.

The first step in mastering the art of kayaking is getting into the boat. The cockpit is narrow, more oblong than circular and the legs must be positioned flat against the downside of the hull, feet forward. Fogarty was over six feet tall and weighed close to two hundred pounds, plus, in the past year he'd put a few inches on his own beam, which made the maneuver even more difficult.

Diane watched silently from the decked porch as the retired police captain hauled the red torpedo-shaped vessel to the water's edge.

"I hope you know what you're doing," she said.

He held his double-bladed wood paddle in one hand and wore a yellow life-vest, which made him feel like a clown. In fact, Bill Fogarty was not a great swimmer; he hadn't had much opportunity to learn as a kid and he had never completely mastered breathing while doing the crawl. He preferred to keep his head above water.

"I'll be fine," he assured her.

There was something about getting out on the water that lured him. It was a search for peace, a serenity the bay held, with its morning mists and gentle tides. He didn't really want to paddle the boat; it wasn't exertion he was looking for, it was relaxation. He often sat in one of the wooden deck chairs on the porch, a glass of whiskey in hand, and gazed out over Gardiner's Bay. The water soothed him, bringing him in tune with something deep inside himself.

Josef Tanaka had once presented him with a book written by the Ancient Chinese philosopher Lao Tsu, the founder of Taoism. Fogarty had glanced through it, looked at the etched illustrations and placed it aside. There was only one bit of writing which, at that time, had caught his attention. 'What others teach, I also teach. A violent man will die a violent death.' The message was clear and simple and, even then, when he had been in the middle of a murder investigation, the words had stuck. He understood that his life had been filled with violence, from the urban streets of his childhood to the business of law enforcement, to the road accident which had cost him his family. He had lived with violence and now he wanted something else.

29

To float on the water, feel its undulations and swells beneath him, travel with the currents, become part of something that was greater than himself. Josef had spoken of meditation, of the need to find a quiet place within one's self, a place where the mind relaxed and the tension of thought dissolved. He used to speak of karate as a moving meditation, and said that if there was any one secret to the martial arts, beyond practice and perseverance, it was the ability to relax. Relaxation spawned spontaneity. Fogarty had boxed as a schoolboy, and for a while he'd coached for the Police Athletic League. He knew that you couldn't box three rounds without relaxing. On that level he'd understood Josef, but lately, as he walked the sandy beaches around Louse Point, he'd pondered their conversations again. It was more than a relaxation of the physical body that Josef had implied, it was a relaxation of the self, a loosening of the confines of the personality, a relaxation that fostered change and growth.

Fogarty dragged the kayak to the edge of the water, pointing the bow seaward so that the gentle surf washed halfway up the hull. He laid the paddle to the side of the boat and got his right leg inside the cockpit. The boat tipped and he lost balance, his left foot slipping backwards in the sand as his legs spread, leaving him in a near full split.

"Are you sure you should be doing this?" Diane called from the porch.

He shot her a disgruntled look, pulling himself clear of the boat in preparation for a second attempt. This time he got both feet inside the hull before it rolled sideways and he pitched head first into the shallow surf.

"Shit!" Thoughts of Zen oneness deserted him.

"Are you all right, captain?" Diane asked, muffling a laugh.

"There's got to be some kind of trick to this," he retorted.

"Put the paddle behind you!" Fogarty turned and saw a tall, red-haired man, in his mid-thirties, wearing blue jeans, a plaid shirt and high fishing boots walking towards him.

"Howdy, Rick," Fogarty said.

Rick Slater was their next-door neighbor. He was a local, a Bonacker, as those people who had been born on the Accabonic Harbor side of Gardiner's Bay were termed. A carpenter by trade, he also worked as a volunteer fireman.

It had taken Slater a while to accept his new neighbors. He was always suspicious of renters; they were often city folks with lots of money and no manners, but, gradually, and over the course of several iced margaritas, Diane had won him over.

Slater had a fleet of kayaks, racked one on top of the other against the bulkhead which divided his lawn from the beach.

"What do you mean?" Fogarty asked. He felt like a kid trying to ride a bicycle for the first time.

Slater laughed and picked up the paddle.

"Like this," he instructed, placing it perpendicular to the stern end of the cockpit, then, using the paddle as a balance pole, he climbed into the boat. The kayak tipped to the right and the blade held the boat steady in the sand.

"You get out the same way," Slater instructed, reversing his original technique.

Fogarty nodded, accepted the extended paddle and successfully imitated the procedure as Diane Genero applauded from the porch.

"Now place the paddle in front of you, and use your hands to push yourself out into the water," Slater continued.

Fogarty followed instructions. The kayak slid effortlessly into the bay, bobbing up and down on the gentle swells. Fogarty felt strangely weightless, low to the water.

"I feel like a duck," he said.

"You look like a duck," Slater answered. "I think it's the yellow vest."

Fogarty laughed, then attempted to paddle. The kayak dipped to the left and he thought he was going over.

"No, no, no, you're digging too deep. You've got to pull long, shallow strokes. Go ahead, hunch forward a little and use the big muscles in your back."

Fogarty obeyed Slater's commands and got the boat in a nice steady line seawards.

"Now, when you want to turn, stick one blade in the water and it will bring the boat around."

Fogarty turned towards him and saluted.

"That's right, now stay close to the shore," Slater ordered.

"Are these things easy to tip over?"

"Relax and go with the rhythm of the water and you'll be fine," Slater answered.

Relax, Fogarty thought. There was that magic word, again. He placed the blade in the water and began paddling.

"That's good. Big, long strokes."

Fogarty laughed. "I owe you a pitcher full of margaritas, Rick."

"That's fair enough," Slater answered.

Diane walked from the porch and joined Slater.

"Is he going to be all right?" she asked.

Fogarty was, by now, about twenty-five yards offshore.

"It's low tide and if he does go over he can stand up. The water is only a few feet deep."

"Do you want that margarita?"

"Nah, thanks. It's too early in the day, maybe a glass of water though?"

Rick Slater and Diane Genero walked back to the porch, sat down and watched Bill Fogarty navigate the coastline.

At first his strokes were tentative but, as he grew accustomed to the shifting of the kayak, more confident that it was simply rolling with the slight swells, he pulled harder on the paddle and gathered speed. He turned the boat away from shore, towards Gardiner's Island and the sea beyond, paddled a few more strokes then drifted, settling back in the contoured seat. He closed his eyes and felt the water rise and fall beneath him.

Relax, he thought, *hell I could go to sleep like this, it's rocking me like a baby.* He drifted a few more seconds then opened his eyes to check his bearings, noticing that he had turned sideways with the incoming tide. He looked up and down the sand and tree-lined coastline, dotted with wood-framed houses, each individual in architecture and style, and, whether simple or grand, designed with respect to the land and the water.

The sun was warm behind him and reflected off the huge glass windows that invariably featured on the bay-fronted homes, giving some the appearance of a rainbowed iridescence. He could see Rick Slater and Diane seated on the porch of the Gerard Drive house; they were facing each other, talking. Diane was in profile; she was wearing a white cotton dress, low on her shoulders, and her dark hair fell long and loose beyond the line of the fabric, framing a face that had improved with age. She had never been 'pretty', but there was an aristocracy to her slightly aquiline nose and wide, full lips and now, in her mid-forties, her features had become, somehow, more refined, her skin smoother, almost translucent against the bones of her face. And then there were her eyes, wonderful pale blue eyes. In their reflection Fogarty felt clean and full of hope. Able to forget the scars that criss-crossed half his face, and the guilt to which they were testimony. He had been drunk at the wheel; the car had crashed, his wife and daughter had died. He had wanted to die with them, but he had been sentenced to life, instead, with that single screeching moment repeating over and over again in a time-looped memory.

Diane Genero and Bill Fogarty had been joined by tragedy. He had headed the investigation into the murder of her only child, her daughter Gina. The case had nearly destroyed him; he'd put himself on the line, acted recklessly against his own judgment and paid the price. He'd caught the killer but ended in a hospital bed, broken inside and out, not caring if he lived or died, until Diane Genero had come to visit him. That had changed everything. He had been reborn.

God, I love you, he thought, watching her laugh as she raised the glass to her lips. She looked once in his direction and waved. He waved back, then, strangely self-conscious at the honesty of his thoughts, he picked up the paddle, and turned the kayak seaward. He counted his strokes, trying to affect the correct posture, allowing the blades to pull high in the water, propelling the boat. By his fiftieth stroke he could feel a tightness in his upper back. *Another six*, he told himself, *one for every year I've been alive*. After that, he stopped paddling and drifted, allowing the tide to turn him again, towards the shore. He could still see Diane and Rick on the porch, smaller now. He estimated that he was about a hundred yards out; the sand bottom of the bay was no longer visible beneath him and a brisk breeze had begun to blow, causing small white caps on the water. He caught a bit of spray over his port side and decided to paddle closer to land. No panic, he just felt better when he could see the bottom. The coastline curved to his left and once inside the arc, protected by the rise of the dunes and the tree line, the wind subsided and the water calmed. He was getting tired, not exhausted, but good tired, his muscles satiated from their exercise, and he was in the shallows. If he had wanted to he could have rolled out of the boat and walked to shore. He laid the paddle in front of him, on the lip of the cockpit, closed his eyes again and relaxed. A wonderful sensation of well-being filled him. His head was tilted forward, chin resting on his chest, and the salt air was heavy and clean. The kayak rocked gently and, for a moment, he drifted on the threshold of sleep.

At first it was not graphic, more a kaleidoscope of color, swirling and shaping, emerging like liquid mercury, silver turning to black as the wings formed against the sky. Clearer now, he could see the obsidian eyes and ivory beak as the creature circled, wings beating a hollowed rhythm, powerful like thunder. Searching for him. Searching.

Fogarty jolted upright, forgetting in that

instant where he was and what he was doing. The kayak bobbed, then, caught by a swell, rolled to the left as Fogarty reached for the paddle and dipped the blade, pulling too deep and too hard, tipping the boat in the direction of the oar. The shrill cry came from above his head. The boat righted itself as he looked up. The bird was diving towards him, wings spread, jaws open.

"No! Get away from me. Get away!" he shouted.

Lower it came, looming larger, legs stretched downwards, talons extended.

"Get the fuck out of here!"

Fogarty raised his paddle, attempting to force the blade into the underside of the creature. The bird shifted laterally, striking down with its corresponding claw and the paddle was wrenched from his grasp, landing in the water, as Fogarty covered his head with his hands, cowering down into the cockpit of the boat as the sharp beak ripped a patch of hair from his head. The second attack tore into the side of his throat, then the bird was on him, its weight smothering, as the horned jaws pushed inwards against his cheek. He fought back, rearing up, trying to get a grip on the straddling legs, attempting to throw the creature off, but its strength was irrepressible, and, all the while, its beak, hot

38

and sharp, was drilling forward, towards his eyes. He punched, but the punches felt light and ineffective.

"Oh God, no, no!" He could hear his own voice, garbled and pleading as he heaved for breath, hyperventilating, his heart pounding inside his chest.

He tried to pull himself lower into the cockpit, wanting to fold his body in two, head flat on his thighs, in an effort to hide inside the hull of the boat. He leaned hard to his right and the kayak tipped, spilling him into the water. The creature followed him down, below the surface, as he punched and kicked.

"Stop it, Bill! Stop it!"

It was Diane's voice.

"Stop it!"

He stopped fighting.

"Come on, Bill, stand up. That's right. Stand up." The man's voice was soft but firm.

Rick Slater was cradling him like a baby, one arm beneath his back, the other under his thighs. Diane Genero stood behind, her eyes red from tears.

"It's shallow here; you're safe. You're not going to drown," Slater continued, as, gently, he placed Fogarty on his feet.

Fogarty stood. The water came only to his

hips and the sand was firm beneath him. He stared at Rick Slater and it was as if he was seeing him for the first time. Slater's plaid shirt, which hung soaked and heavy against his heaving chest, was a brilliant patchwork of red, gold and blue. His hair, which he always combed backwards, was wet and fell forward, across his forehead, revealing the shining bald crown of his head. Fogarty had never really been conscious of Slater's age; he was one of those men whose manner belied his youth, but now Fogarty was aware of the smooth, unlined skin of his face, lightly tanned and unmarred except for the red marks on his cheeks where Fogarty's fists had connected. He looked from Slater to Diane. Her face was very distinct, like a sculpture in bronzed clay, features clean and precise, lips full and pink, while her neck, shoulders and bared arms glistened with beads of water. She seemed to sparkle, yet there was a different, almost surreal quality to his vision, as if everything had been drawn into a cleaner, sharper focus. There was also something unnerving about what he saw. His perception of depth had altered. Diane and Slater stood out like cardboard cut-outs. Behind them, the beach houses were two-dimensional against the landscape and the sun above was perfectly flat and white gold in color, hanging like an ornament in the sky.

"You all right, Bill?" Slater's voice had a deep, hollow sound.

Fogarty rubbed his eyes and shivered. The water felt like ice around his legs.

"Come on, let's go home," Diane said, taking hold of his arm as Rick Slater reached beneath the hull of the overturned kayak, gripped the edge and righted the boat. Then he retrieved the paddle and stowed it inside the cockpit.

Fogarty appeared stunned, his eyes vacant. He hesitated, turning to look behind him, then skywards.

"Did you chase it away?" There was bewilderment in his tone, something childlike and vulnerable.

Slater looked at him.

"How did you get it off me?" Fogarty continued.

Slater held Fogarty's eyes and shook his head.

"What are you talking about, Bill?" Diane asked.

"I'm talking about the bird."

Diane searched Fogarty's eyes. There was something wrong inside them, a strange glint, an unfamiliar flicker.

"We saw you go over," Slater replied, wading towards the bow of the kayak.

"You didn't see the bird?"

"Bird?" Slater repeated calmly, getting a grip on the tow rope.

"I thought it was going to tear out my eyes," Fogarty said and, even as he remembered, his fear returned. He froze up, immobile.

Diane tugged against his arm but Slater caught her attention and shook his head. "He's in shock," he mouthed the words to Diane then turned back to Fogarty. "We heard you shout, then we saw you lose the paddle. After that the kayak flipped and you went in," he explained slowly.

Fogarty looked from Slater to Diane. She nodded her agreement. Fogarty felt as if he was in the middle of a bad joke, some kind of terrible conspiracy, betrayed.

"What the fuck do you mean!" he shouted. "The damn thing tore a chunk out of my neck." He reached to the side of his throat, expecting to feel the bleeding wound. There was nothing but flesh, made smooth by the salt water.

"Come on, Bill, let's get inside," Diane insisted, pulling again against his arm.

He shrugged her loose.

"What the hell's going on?"

"We can talk about it in the house," Diane said.

"What do you think you're doing to me?"

The three of them stood for a few seconds in silence.

"Hey, Bill, take it easy, nobody's doing anything to anybody. Everything's fine," Slater assured him.

Fogarty stood and shook his head.

"All right," he began again, glowering at Diane. "Let's stop playing games. You tell me what's going on."

She returned his stare, angry for a second at his obstinance, then, seeing the angst in his expression, she softened.

"There's nothing going on, Bill." She spoke slowly and with great calm. "You turned the boat over and fell in the water, that's all."

"You didn't see a bird?"

"No. I didn't."

"Like an eagle. Do you have eagles around here?"

Diane was reminded of the incident in the car a week before. She looked at him, shaking her head, for the first time truly fearful for his state of mind.

"I don't know," she replied, turning to Slater.

"Eagles are rare, Bill, but there are osprey, and they nest right behind there." Slater

43

pointed west, in the direction of Wood Tick Island. "But it's pretty late in the season for osprey."

"How big's an osprey?"

"It's a fair-sized bird, maybe a wing span of three feet."

"This was way bigger than that."

"Well, I don't know what it could have been," Slater replied. He was humoring Fogarty, trying to get him to relax and come out of the water. In his years as a fireman Slater had handled a few cases of shock. The best remedy was always observation and patience.

"This fucker must've been seven or eight feet across."

"That's a big bird," Slater agreed.

"Have you ever heard of an osprey attacking a man?" Fogarty asked. He was beginning to feel weak in the knees.

"It could happen, if you were to disturb its nest," Slater answered, moving closer.

"Strong, are they strong, really strong?" Fogarty was beginning to ramble.

"Yes, they're strong," Slater replied, getting his free hand on Fogarty's back and his arm below Fogarty's armpit. He motioned for Diane to get the other side.

"I'm talking about something the size of a man. Nearly killed me," Fogarty continued.

He could feel tears welling behind his eyes and his legs were going slack. "Damn it, didn't you see it?"

They had him now, one under each arm, walking him towards the shore.

"Came at me from inside a dream," he mumbled, but neither Rick Slater nor Diane were paying attention to his words.

4

"I can't find anything wrong with her heart," Josef Tanaka said, holding the phone close to his mouth and speaking quietly. There was no one else in his office but he felt mildly embarrassed at what felt like a confession of incompetence.

"There's no history of disease, no sign of scar tissue, and very little arteriosclerosis."

"How about blood tests?" Bob Moor asked. He was sitting in the living room of his three-storied house on Pine Street and hoped that Tanaka could not hear the television that was tuned to a cable re-run of *Saturday Night Fever*. The song 'Staying Alive' was blaring in the background and Moyer considered it a testimony to the boredom he had been

45

suffering since retiring as the city's chief medical examiner.

"All the lab work came up clean. I mean, Bob, this is a health-food junkie, a regular exerciser with a minimum-stress lifestyle," Tanaka answered. He'd taken over Moyer's position five months ago but still considered the older man his teacher and mentor.

"Then how did she wind up with you?"

"Her husband woke up at three o'clock this morning and found her gasping for air. He called 911. She was dead by the time the ambulance arrived."

"Sounds like the heart."

"Yes, but it's perfect."

"It could have been a sudden blow to the sternum, something that would have caused her heart to fibrillate and go into spasm."

"There's no bruising on the sternum."

"Did you meet her husband?" Moyer asked. He was thinking of some type of domestic situation, maybe a poison, something that could have been administered in small enough doses to beat the initial blood tests.

"Yes. He was devastated. Tomorrow was their wedding anniversary; they were flying to San Francisco for a long weekend. I didn't get any sense that the guy was covering for anything."

"Get some detailed blood work done anyway."

"OK."

"How about medication? Was she taking anything?"

"Nothing that's showed up so far."

"Painkillers, anti-inflamants, anti-depressants . . ."

"None of those."

"How about her fingernails?"

"They were long and recently manicured. Clean as a whistle, no breaks, no blood and no flesh. Absolutely no sign of violence."

"OK. OK. This isn't the first time I've heard of something like this. Hell, I remember a case in 'seventy-seven, an eighteen-year-old girl. There was no apparent cause. Nothing. Turned out her boyfriend, during sex, had taken a straw and blown into her vagina, causing an air bubble in her Fallopian tube. Don't ask me what the hell kind of sex they were having. Anyway, the bubble reached her heart, caused an embolism, and killed her." Moyer hesitated. He was rambling on again and he knew it. "The answer is, Josef, keep looking, just keep looking, 'cause you never know."

Tanaka smiled, replied, "I will," then waited for what he was certain would come next.

"Want me to come down there and give you a hand?"

The ex-ME had been a frequent visitor to the medical building since his retirement and Tanaka could hear the excitement in his voice.

"I wouldn't mind," he answered. It was almost a pat routine they had down. Tanaka welcomed the visits as much as Moyer liked making them.

"Norma's out grocery shopping and she'll raise hell if I'm not here to carry the bags in, so give me an hour."

"I'll look forward to seeing you."

"And, Josef. Everybody dies because of something. Don't worry, we'll find it."

* * *

"Her name is Maura Allan," Tanaka said.

Moyer looked down at the face of the body on the table.

"Jesus Christ," he whispered.

"What is it?" Tanaka asked.

"I know her."

"Maura Allan?"

"Yes." As if it was incomprehensible.

"I'm sorry, I had no idea."

Moyer continued to stare, shaking his head.

48

"Did you know the family?" Tanaka asked gently.

"I knew her," Moyer answered. There was a finality in his voice and something else. Maybe it was apprehension. Tanaka couldn't be sure but he wondered what their relationship had been. Friends? Lovers? The latter seemed out of context with the rather staid character of the ex-ME, but there was something.

"It was a long time ago," Moyer added, shaking his head again, as if to clear it.

"Well, I'm sorry I got you down here," Tanaka apologised.

"Nonsense. Let's get on with it."

"Bob, you don't have to do this."

"Yes I do."

★ ★ ★

"The myocardium's a good color," Moyer observed, referring to the wall of muscle that comprised almost the entirety of Maura Allan's heart. "None of the yellow-brown that would indicate oxygen deprivation, front wall of the left ventricle is fine, no scarring, there's certainly been no previous infarctions," he continued, using his scalpel as a fine artist might use his brush, with sure, purposeful strokes. He seemed better

49

now, more distanced, as if the act of being a doctor had removed him from whatever feelings he'd had before.

Tanaka stood to Moyer's side and watched him repeat the exact procedures that he himself had performed earlier in the afternoon, half expecting the older man to stumble on something that he had missed. They'd worked this way many times in the past years and there was no friction between them, no rivalry and no ego. Tanaka respected Bob Moyer and that respect was mutual.

Physically, they made a strange combination. Tanaka was six feet two inches tall, which put him a half foot taller than the former ME, and while Josef was a combination of the big strong bones of his American mother and the fine, chiselled facial features of his Japanese father, Moyer appeared the epitome of the American academic, pale and bespectacled, with a prim red goatee and a bald head.

"Here's something." Moyer lifted his scalpel towards one of the overhead spotlights. A tiny bit of plaque, less than a quarter of the size of a short grain of rice was balanced on the edge of the blade. "Hardly enough to cause an occlusion," he said dismissively, flicking the hardened piece of fat to the floor.

Three hours later and they had made a

thorough reinspection of the heart, lungs, liver, kidneys, brain and pelvis.

"It beats me, Josef," Moyer said, his eyes red rimmed behind his glasses and his voice tired.

"There's nothing wrong with her is there?"

"Aside from the fact that she's dead," Moyer answered, glancing back towards Maura Allan's naked body. "I doubt if *I* look that good inside."

"So what do I do?"

"Wait until the final lab results. Maybe they'll show a trace of something, a food allergy, a poison, something that could have stopped her heart. There's always a reason for death."

Tanaka pulled off his surgical gloves and tossed them into the disposal bin while Moyer looked again at Maura Allan. She was positioned on her back, her face illuminated by an overhead beam; they had shaved her head to facilitate the cranial examination and the effect had been to accentuate her features. The mole in the very center of her forehead seemed larger now and her eyes appeared to dominate her face. Moyer bent lower; it looked as though he meant to whisper something to her.

Tanaka had the same feeling he'd had earlier. It was as if something was being

51

withheld, some secret. "Bob?" He kept his voice soft. "Do you know something that might help me with this? Anything personal about her, anything at all?"

"She's seen a lot, maybe too much," Moyer said, but it wasn't an answer. It was as if he was talking to himself. He reached out and stroked his gloved fingers across the lids, closing Maura Allan's eyes.

"Anything?" Tanaka repeated.

"No. It's a mystery," Moyer answered, turning away.

★ ★ ★

It was like waking from a dream, a dream in which every detail was recalled. Gabriel could still see the sky, wide and blue, with its storybook sun and white vaporous clouds. And his spirit guides, the birds? Yes, they were there, he could sense them, hear their far-away calls, but they were gone from his field of vision. It was the smells that finally brought him around, the sickly sweet odor of body sweat, too many people in too small a space, and the heavy mildew of cots made moist from urine and semen. Then the sounds of men awakening, groaning and farting, coughing up phlegm and spitting, toilets flushing, tap water running. Bodies protesting against another day of monotony.

He could still see the sky, even as he heard the muffled prayers of the recently 'born again' multiple murderer in the cell next to him.

"Dear Lord Jesus, give me the strength and courage to live inside your light, to face these four walls with dignity — " The man had been raised in Tennessee and his voice had a thin, southern rasp.

"Shut up!" another prisoner shouted.

" . . . and to love my fellow man as — "

"I said shut up!"

"I love you, Lord Jesus, ahmen."

Their voices were draining the atmosphere of energy and the sky was becoming less blue, more a flat, silver-gray, without depth. "Fuck you and fuck Jesus!"

"Blasphemy will be punished!" the southern 'born again' retorted.

"Silence!" Gabriel pushed the single word from the pit of his stomach. After that the corridor of cells grew quiet, because every man in the segregated housing unit was afraid of Justin Gabriel.

He listened another few seconds, until satisfied that peace had been restored, then returned his gaze to the wall, but the cold stone had, by now, completely lost its magic and the fine, wispy clouds

53

were just smudge marks in the faded paint, while the sun was a circular patch of bare white plaster. He breathed in, squaring his shoulders, then rotated them gently on the out breath, increasing the blood flow to his upper torso, experiencing a melancholia as his mind flashed on images of roof tops, deserted beaches, and white cresting waves. He began to unfold his legs, lifting his right thigh with his hands, pulling his foot across from his left and laying the limb down straight in front of him, massaging the muscles until he could feel the nerves tingle and the blood surge, repeating the process with his other side, until he had disengaged from the full lotus posture. He was very careful, kneading and stretching every muscle from his neck to his feet, and it took him many minutes to stand.

He was both psychically and physically drained, and after removing his clothing he lay down on his cot. He was asleep within seconds.

★ ★ ★

Phillip Harrison walked alone along the corridor, peering in at each prisoner.

'Supernatural powers, mind voodoo, telepathy', by the end of Weller's talk,

54

Harrison had decided that the older man was deranged. Still, his stories had been interesting enough to warrant Harrison's request for a look at the prison records of Justin Seers Gabriel. What he'd read had made him curious. Gabriel was a doctor, not a medical doctor but a Ph.D. His field had been clinical psychology, and he was doing fifty to a hundred years for conspiracy to murder.

★ ★ ★

Harrison stopped outside the cell. He stood there for several seconds thinking of his keys but his better judgment told him to be patient, after all, as Weller had informed him, he was observing the 'most dangerous man who ever lived'.

He looked through the bars.

Inside, Gabriel lay on his back, overalls neatly folded and placed on the floor beside his cot. His eyes appeared open but it was difficult to be sure from Harrison's vantage point.

The first thing that struck Harrison was just how tiny the doctor was. Judging by the six-foot cot and the amount of space remaining below Gabriel's feet, Harrison figured he was about five feet three inches in height. On top of which, naked, Justin Gabriel reminded Harrison of a chimpanzee. His chest, abdomen, and legs were covered by a quilt of dark, coarse hair, his penis was uncircumcised and his body had a compact muscularity. The soles of his feet were thick with yellowed callus and his hands, which were positioned palms upward to his sides, were square in shape, the fingers short, and without taper.

'The most dangerous man who ever lived', Harrison recalled Weller's words. "Pig ignorant," Harrison thought, "Weller's just pig ignorant." If he was going to work here he was going to establish dominance and 'the most dangerous man' was a good place to start.

"Hey, you!"

There was no response from the cot.

"I'm talking to you, Gabriel!" Harrison raised his voice. At the mention of the doctor's name, the rest of the prison block grew silent.

The little man remained motionless.

"Stand up," Harrison ordered.

Still, no movement.

Harrison reached to the side of his belt and detached his key ring. The sound of it turning in the lock was magnified by the hush inside the building.

Once inside, Harrison felt less sure of himself. There was something deeply disturbing about the atmosphere of the cell. Perhaps, Harrison told himself, it was the musky smell coming from the small man's body, thick and heavy in the air. It was an animal's smell. Then there was the lack of movement in Gabriel's chest and lower abdomen, as if he was not breathing. Harrison had a moment of fear, deep and irrational. "Gabriel's angels murdered four people, a minister — a Reverend Paisley — his wife and two children. Made a real mess of them, cut'm to pieces while they were still alive. Their hearts were never found." Weller's words repeated.

"When I give you an order I want you to obey it," Harrison said, but his voice lacked the authority it had had from the other side of the door.

He stepped closer, staring down into Gabriel's face, aware of the potential of some sort of sudden attack. He thought of retreat, and the thought brought feelings of inferiority. He had come from a military family. His father was a Colonel in the Marine Corps, a combat veteran, first in Vietnam, then in the Gulf War. Harrison had been in the Gulf too, as a Marine Lieutenant, just long enough to see two of his closest friends blown away by a misguided air attack from their own side. That and three months as an out-patient in a veteran's psychiatric unit had changed his mind about a life in the military. He got out with an honorable discharge and GI grant that paid for a bachelor of arts degree in psychology, neither of which were much help in civilian life. It had taken some pull to get him the job with the prison system. He wanted to get into the corrections department's educational system and his uncle had suggested this as a place to start.

"Come on, Gabriel, I'm doing a room check. Get up."

Justin Gabriel was aware of the smell of soap and starched cotton. He could hear a man's voice but the words were coming from the other side of a wall that separated his dream consciousness from his waking state.

Harrison bent over, closer to Gabriel's face, realising that his prisoner was fast asleep. It was the first time he'd seen a man sleeping with his eyes open.

"He looks really young — he couldn't possibly be fifty-seven years old," Harrison thought, remembering 11/28/40 as the birth date given in the prison records and comparing Gabriel's unlined skin to that of his uncle, who had just turned sixty. Then he noticed Gabriel's eyes. Harrison had never seen eyes like Gabriel's; they were a blue-gray and appeared in constant motion, liquid and rippling, shifting from side to side like pools of water. They began to draw Harrison in.

"Never look directly into his eyes. Never." Weller's warning flashed as he broke contact, looking away.

"Stand up," Harrison repeated.

Harrison's voice penetrated the dividing wall and Gabriel's dream body reacted to it by standing up. He was in a large, wood-panelled room, shackled, hands and feet, and he was staring into a sea of faces; every face was distinct, but there were only four that were important to him.

"I'm talking to you," Harrison said. He wanted to reach down and shake the little man but instinct stopped him.

Justin Gabriel looked down at his hands, the restraints were tight and the veins bulged from above and below the steel bracelets. 'Hands', they were the key to his control. His diablero had begun his 'dream' teachings with instruction as to the awareness of his hands. They were his orientation point. Many times during the day Gabriel had been instructed to study his hands, then to close his eyes and visualise them. As he drifted off at night, sweating with the heat of the

59

Mexican desert, he had endeavored to keep that image clear in his mind. Finally, after several months, he was able to retain it, even as he entered REM, or dreaming sleep. That had been his first exercise in remaining lucid, or conscious, while asleep.

"Get up, that's an order."

Gabriel took a last look. He had seen each of the faces many times since his incarceration, because his dream was recurrent and, for many years, each dream had remained identical in every detail to the last. Only in the past year had it begun to change. Perhaps that was because the urgency of his situation had enhanced his need to channel his thoughts, motivating him to become stronger and more focused. In any case there were fewer faces in his dream mind.

Gabriel focused on one face in particular. "You should be gone," he said.

"What did you say?" Harrison asked, this time nudging the side of the doctor's cot.

"You should be gone," Gabriel repeated, staring at the face in his dream.

"Wake up," Harrison ordered.

Gabriel's eyes lost their rippling movement and settled as the dream face transposed with the face of Phillip Harrison. He looked up at him. "How nice of you to drop by."

"Cut the crap and stand away from the bed," Harrison ordered.

Gabriel lay still and smiled. "You have just interrupted the most interesting dream." His voice was very soft.

"I'm doing a room check. I want you to stand and move away from the bed and place your hands against the wall."

"Do you remember your dreams?" Gabriel continued.

"Shut up and do as you're told."

"I'm going to tell you a secret. What you think of as reality is really just another dream," Gabriel said, getting to his feet. "Can you comprehend that, Phillip? Are you ready for that?"

The sound of his own name caught Harrison off guard. How had Gabriel learned his name? It had to have come from Weller. They must have talked about him.

Harrison studied Gabriel. He felt no malice from him, instead a gentleness.

"Phillip, do you believe a man can fly?"

Harrison looked down and met the doctor's eyes. It may have been the angle but they no longer looked blue-gray. Now they seemed very dark.

"Haven't you ever had a dream where you were flying?" Gabriel continued. "I do all the

61

time. Straight through these walls and into the sky. I can go anywhere I want to. Do you follow me?"

"What the hell are you talking about?"

"It's just a simple question," Gabriel replied.

"I'm not in here to answer questions."

"No, you're here to assert yourself, to show me who's boss. But, Phillip, why should I threaten you?"

"You don't."

"Is it because we've been sleeping together lately and you don't want anyone to find out?" Gabriel asked.

"You sick little fuck."

"Well I won't tell," Gabriel promised.

"Walk to the far wall."

Gabriel walked slowly. "How's your uncle?"

"My uncle?"

"Yes, I haven't seen him in ages. He's a friend of Warden Simms, isn't he?"

The question completely threw Harrison. Now he knew that Weller had been talking because only Weller had known about his uncle.

"Can you imagine if he found out? His nephew and Justin Gabriel sharing the same bed."

"You're in the wrong place, Gabriel, you should be in an asylum."

Gabriel laughed. It was a light laugh, almost a giggle.

"You don't remember, do you?" He flapped his arms and bounced from foot to foot. "You got up and opened the window of your bedroom and there I was, all warm and feathery. But your uncle, now he's a problem. He keeps his windows locked."

Harrison shoved him towards the wall. "Cut it out, turn around and place your hands above your head, spread your legs."

"Oh really, Phillip, aren't you taking this a bit far? I know how important it is for you to be macho, but this is harassment."

"Shut up and do as you're told," Harrison continued.

Gabriel turned towards the wall and raised his hands. "I'm his worst fear."

"What did you say?"

"He hates birds."

"What is it with you?" Harrison asked.

"It's just that you're so close. He's really been like a father to you, hasn't he? Getting you this job and everything." Gabriel persisted. "It's a shame about his heart."

Heart? There was nothing wrong with his uncle's heart. Nothing that he knew of. He'd seen him only last weekend, but coincidentally he hadn't thought he'd looked too good, something in the pallor of his skin. He'd even cautioned him about his diet, the fried foods and the red meat.

"I don't see him surviving the encounter," Gabriel concluded.

"That's enough!" Harrison snapped, walking to the entrance to the cell. "I don't want to hear any more of your bullshit." He stepped into the corridor, closing and locking the door behind him. He was confused and angry. He'd been set up. That was the only explanation. Fucking Art Weller had been talking to Gabriel. They were trying to get a handle on him.

"Phillip?" Gabriel called from the darkness.

Harrison kept walking.

"I'll see you tonight."

"Fuck you," Harrison answered.

"Kiaw." It sounded like the cry of a wild bird.

* * *

Phillip Harrison woke up covered in sweat. He turned to his side and there it was, soft and warm, reaching towards him. He shouted and pushed it away.

"You're dreaming again," Patty Harrison said, withdrawing her hand. "Was it Connelly?"

64

James Connelly had been one of his friends who had died in the Gulf and Phillip often dreamt of him.

"No," he replied.

She waited for him to say more but he lay in silence beside her and after a few minutes she thought that he'd gone back to sleep. She had just rolled on to her side, away from him, when he switched on the light.

"You son of a bitch," he said.

Patty turned to see him sitting up against the pillow, his eyes fixed on the window.

"Phillip?"

He turned towards her.

"What's the matter?"

"He was in here." His voice was flat. "I can still see his eyes. The way he was looking at me."

"See who?"

"That little bastard psyched me out."

"Phillip, I don't have any idea what you're talking about."

"Give me the phone."

"What?"

"The phone. I need to call Uncle Rob."

"At three o'clock in the morning?"

"It's important," he snapped.

She moved closer to him and touched his hand. It was ice cold. "Before you call anybody, why don't we talk about what's upsetting you?"

He withdrew his hand.

"Come on," she urged. They'd met in Virginia, at the VA hospital, where Patty had counseled lots of combat veterans. "You were dreaming. That's all. Now tell me about it."

"This wasn't a dream. It was too real to be a dream. I mean I was there. I saw it."

"What?"

"A bird. I let it in the window. It's not after me, it's after Uncle Rob. I've got to warn him. This is serious." He sounded on the verge of hysteria.

"Phillip, calm down. Your uncle is probably sound asleep."

Harrison shook his head. "That little bastard." He could still hear that wispy voice, thin and insinuating, as if it had remained inside his head.

"Who?"

He recalled Art Weller's warning. Maybe there was something to it, maybe Gabriel had some kind of power. He wiped his hands across his closed eyes as if to scrub the thought away.

"Phillip, who are you talking about?" Patty insisted.

66

"Justin Gabriel," Harrison answered. His breath stank of bile.

"Who is Justin Gabriel?" She kept her voice soft and even.

"Some kind of voodoo man."

"What do you mean by that?"

"He got to me."

"Phillip, calm down. You were dreaming. That's all."

"You don't understand."

"No, I don't."

"He's a prisoner in the segregated unit. I saw him today. I talked to him. He hypnotised me. It's his eyes. He does it with his eyes. Goddamned bird had the same eyes. I'll kill the little bastard — "

"Phillip, I want you to relax."

"Get Uncle Rob on the phone for me."

"Honey, it's three — "

"Get him on the fucking phone!"

"Phillip! Stop it. Please!"

"I'm sorry, I'm sorry. Give me the phone, I'll do it. I've got to. You don't understand," he said, trying to pull himself together. He felt compelled. "All right." She handed him the portable phone and watched as he dialed the number. It seemed a very long time before anyone answered.

"Hello, Auntie N, is that you? It's Phillip. Yes, I know it's the middle of the night, I

67

know, but I need to talk to Uncle Rob."

In the background he could hear his uncle's voice, groggy, asking what was going on. Another few seconds passed and a male voice came on the phone.

"What's happened?"

Phillip stopped. It was his uncle. Talking to him. Alive.

"Nothing," Phillip answered, then he laughed from sheer relief.

"Nothing? What do you mean 'nothing'?" His uncle sounded irritated.

"I'm sorry, Uncle Rob, I really am. I was just checking to see if you were all right."

"Why wouldn't I be all right?"

"It was something that somebody said at work, and then I had this dream."

"What?"

Phillip Harrison was beginning to feel embarrassed. He shot a glance at his wife; she was shaking her head, a faint smile of relief on her lips.

"It was a very bad dream."

"Goddamn it, Phil, have you been drinking?"

"No, no, nothing like that . . ."

Harrison was about to apologise and call it a night when something happened that hadn't happened since his stay at the Veterans' hospital. He started to cry. The tears came without warning, rolling down his face.

"I'm sorry, Uncle Rob. I'm really sorry." He was blubbering now and he hated himself for it. "I don't want anything to happen to you."

"Well nothing has."

"It's your heart."

A heart attack was something that Harrison's uncle feared. His father's heart had gone at fifty-five years old, and his older brother's a year ago. He didn't want to talk about a heart attack.

"Goodnight Phillip."

"I feel like a fool," Harrison continued. "I let some guy at work twist my head." He wanted to get it off his chest. "Justin Gabriel. You ever heard of — "

"That's enough!" His uncle's voice was loud enough that Patty could hear it.

"Come on, Phillip," she said, moving closer to him.

Harrison choked back a fresh rush of tears.

"Just go back to sleep," his uncle said, controlling himself. "Do you want a transfer out of there? I can talk to Jimmy Simms." He was suddenly very anxious.

"I really am sorry, Uncle Rob."

"There's no need to apologise. These things happen. It's all right."

69

"Will you tell Auntie N that I'm sorry for waking her up."

"She's forgiven you. In fact, she's already gone back to sleep."

"That's good."

"Phil. Don't dwell on this incident. Just put it out of your mind, and Phil, stay away from Justin Gabriel. Do you understand me?"

"Yes, sure." Suddenly his uncle's tone of voice reminded him of Art Weller's.

"I'm serious Phil, very serious. The man is sick."

"I understand."

"All right." His tone simmered. "Goodnight, Phil."

"Uncle Rob?"

"Yes?" Impatient now.

"Do you believe that a man could change his shape, that he could become something other than a man? Do you believe a man can fly?"

There was a long silence as the fear trickled through the telephone wires, awakening something that had been coiled beneath layers of denial.

"Uncle Rob?"

"The answer is no. Goddamn it. No," his uncle said, as he placed the receiver down and lay staring at the ceiling.

5

With Billy's birth, Rachel Tanaka had cut back on her office hours, and today, with only four scheduled appointments and two visits with post-ops she had managed to get home by two o'clock.

★ ★ ★

Billy was sitting in his high-chair when she entered the apartment and the new nanny was feeding him.

"He loves his vanilla pudding," the nineteen-year-old said. Her name was Beska. She was Swedish and looked enough like Rachel, blond and fair, to be her younger sister. "He's got his father's sweet tooth," Rachel replied, noting that most of the jar seemed to be running down the front of her son's bib.

"Yes. I think he called," Beska replied. "We hear his voice on the machine. And a lady. She sounded very upset."

Rachel walked to the side table by the sofa and pressed the play button on the

71

Panasonic. Josef's voice came out of the speaker, saying that he would be working late, then going straight on to teach his class at the dojo before coming home. He said hello to Billy before signing off. The next two messages were from Diane Genero, leaving her Long Island phone number. Beska was right; Diane sounded shaky.

"I'm going to the other room for a few minutes, are you OK here?" Rachel asked.

Beska nodded and Billy burped.

Rachel walked to the bedroom, closed the door, picked up the phone and dialed. Diane Genero answered on the first ring.

"Diane, it's Rachel."

"Oh God, it's good to hear your voice," she replied.

"You didn't sound so good on the machine, is everything OK up there?"

"No. It's Bill."

Rachel felt her stomach tighten.

There was a long silence.

"He's sick," Diane said.

Rachel relaxed slightly.

"What is it?"

"I don't know," Diane replied. Then she began to cry. "Hold on a second, hold on."

Rachel could hear the other woman choking back her sobs.

"He's in the other room, I don't want him

to hear me. That's all he needs, me breaking down."

"Tell me what's going on," Rachel repeated, her voice taking on a more professional, calming tone.

"He's been talking about getting a gun. I thought maybe Josef could say something to him. He trusts Josef. Josef knows him better than anybody."

"Well Josef's not here right now. Have you tried his work number?"

"I left a message at his office."

"Then don't worry, he'll call you."

"Oh, Rachel, I'm in such a mess."

"What kind of mess?"

Diane hesitated.

"Come on, Diane, maybe I can help," Rachel continued.

"Bill hasn't slept in days," she began. "He hasn't even come into the bedroom. He just sits in the chair that looks out over the bay and stares up at the sky. He's not eating, just drinks coffee, pots and pots of coffee to stay awake, and he wants a gun. He keeps asking me to go out and get him a gun. I can't do that. I don't even know where — "

"*Is* Bill sick?"

"It's his mind."

"I don't understand."

"He's paranoid, totally paranoid. Every

73

time there's a wind, every time the house creaks, he thinks it's coming for him."

"What's coming for him?"

"Oh, Rachel," Diane Genero's voice was easier now, the edges smoothing. "It all sounds so crazy."

"That's OK, just tell me about it."

"It started two months ago, when he began having these dreams. They were very vivid. He kept talking about them, saying everything was in incredible color, very detailed and very real. There was a bird. He describes it as an eagle, or something like an eagle, big and predatory. In his dreams the bird was circling above his head, looking down."

Diane stopped talking and listened. She could hear the wind beat against the windows and the sound of small waves breaking against the shore. There was no sound from the other room.

"Diane?"

"A few days ago," she continued, "Bill was by himself, in a kayak. He was out on the bay, just learning how to use it. I was sitting on the porch, talking to a neighbor. I mean it was all such fun, we were laughing and Bill was really enjoying himself. He'd never been in a kayak before and we were watching him, just to make sure he was all right. He couldn't have been more than fifty

74

feet offshore and he looked like he was really getting into it, relaxing. Then suddenly he started shouting. It was like he was going crazy, smacking the air with the paddle, jerking around in the boat, until it tipped over. He was only in about three feet of water but by the time we got to him he was hysterical, ranting about this giant bird, saying it had attacked him. I didn't put it all together till we got back inside the house. Not until he told me that it was the same bird that he'd been dreaming about. That it had finally found him, that it had come from inside his mind. That it would find him again if he went to sleep. Oh, Rachel, he's so frightened. I've never seen Bill frightened before. I'm so used to him being in control. He's like a child. He thinks the bird is real, Rachel, he actually believes it."

Rachel thought for a moment.

"Who is your local doctor?" she asked.

"There's a guy in the village but we've never needed to see him."

"Ask him to come to the house, Bill might need some sedation. The longer he's sleep deprived, the more intense his paranoia is going to become, so, somehow, you've got to get him to relax."

"I've thought about dissolving some Valium in his coffee."

75

"I think the town doctor is a better idea."

"But Bill's such a private person; I don't want anyone to know about what happened."

"Diane. Forget about that right now, just get the doctor to have a look at him. And if for some reason Josef misses your message at the medical building, I'll get him to call you as soon as he walks through the door. It's one of his karate nights so it might be after eight before you hear from him. In the meantime, I want you to call me if you have any problems getting the doctor to come, or for any other reason, even if you just need to talk. I've got a hunch that as soon as Bill has some sleep this whole thing will look a lot less threatening."

"OK." Diane answered. "I'll call right now."

"Don't worry, we're not going to let anything happen to Billy's godfather," Rachel assured her.

"No, we're not," Diane replied. She felt stronger for Rachel's call.

"I'll talk to you soon," Rachel promised, said goodbye and placed the receiver down. She'd seen Bill and Josef go through some real ordeals, cases that had taken the pair of them to breaking point, and Fogarty had always come through. He had a core of steel.

It was almost impossible to imagine him in the situation that Diane had just described. Fogarty was not the kind of person who would become victim to his own mind.

* * *

Amagansett was the closest town to Springs and the local doctor was away on holiday, leaving two visiting doctors, both straight out of medical school, to look after his practice. The man that Diane spoke to identified himself as David Stryker and sounded concerned when Diane described Bill Fogarty's condition. She purposefully left out the details of the predatory bird and concentrated on the acute insomnia. Stryker suggested that she drive Bill into town and offered a three o'clock appointment. When Diane explained that Bill wouldn't leave the house and that, in fact, she was worried for his personal safety, implying that he was potentially suicidal, Stryker volunteered to drive out to Springs at the close of his working day. He sounded young, but his voice radiated reassurance. Diane thanked him, then, with her confidence bolstered, she walked into the main room of the house.

Bill Fogarty was sitting on the same wooden chair that he had occupied for three days and nights. It was a high-backed, pine chair with no arm rests and a hard seat. One of six that had surrounded the dinner table. He had turned the chair sideways so that its seat ran parallel with the far end of the table and afforded him an unobstructed view through the bay window. It was a picture-postcard view, of a white, sandy beach bordering a vast expanse of blue water. The water was alive with delicate, white-capped waves, and the evergreen shores of Gardiner's Island beckoned in the distance. To the right of Gardiner's Island was open sea and the horizon beyond. Diane Genero loved horizons. They were without confinement, places without constriction, where her mind could wander and her imagination rule. Seeing Bill sitting on the hard chair, his shoulders squared against the frame, one hand on either thigh, his hair matted and his face fallen from fatigue, staring at a view that had given them both such happiness and tranquility, produced in her a terrible feeling of helplessness and inadequacy. She needed to be close to him now, to be able to tell him that this time would pass, to be able to make him believe that it would pass. She stood watching him for a few seconds, willing him to turn towards her, to accept her energy, to feed from it, but he seemed in a vacuum, sitting there in front of her, but not there at all, a shell without animation.

"Bill?"

He continued to stare upwards, towards the clear blue sky.

"Bill, you've got to stop this."

Still, he did not respond.

"You're making yourself sick, Bill."

"Go away, just leave me," he answered without turning around, or blinking.

"I'm not going to leave you, I'm your friend and I'm not going anywhere. I want to be with you."

"Get me a gun."

"I don't know where to get a gun."

"A thirty-eight."

"Why do you need a gun?"

He offered no answer as she walked closer to him, stepping around the table so that she could see his eyes.

"Any coffee? I need coffee."

His eyes had the same glint that they had had that day on the bay, the day that he claimed the bird had attacked him.

"You need rest, Bill, sleep."

"I've read about people who don't sleep, don't need it. They go their entire lifetime without sleeping. It's a fact, I've read about them."

"Yes, maybe, but somehow I don't think

79

you're one of them." She tried to add levity to her tone, moving closer to him.

"I can train myself," he said flatly.

"Bill, you're not making sense."

He turned towards her angrily. "You know I can be very violent. I've put men in hospital. I know how to defend myself — "

"Stop it!" She spoke as if she was admonishing a child.

He stopped and stared at her. The terrified look in his eyes evoked her pity.

"I'm sorry, Diane. Oh, Jesus, I don't know what I'm saying," he replied, and for a few moments he felt whole again, as if the pieces that formed his personality had regrouped and were standing together. "I don't know what the hell's been going on with me."

She reached forward and touched his face. "You've got to trust me. We're going to get through this."

"You don't believe me, do you?"

She looked at him, a question in her eyes.

"I'm talking about what happened out there on the bay."

It was the first time in two days that he had communicated with her, other than to ask for coffee or refuse food.

Diane bent down and kissed him on his forehead. "I believe in you."

"You didn't see anything, did you?"

"I didn't see a bird, if that's what you mean."

"Remember in the car, that day going home from town? There wasn't any bird up there either, was there?"

"No," she replied softly. There was a delicacy to her voice; she was making an effort not to upset him yet at the same time to be truthful.

"I'm going nuts, aren't I?"

"You're having a bad time, but you're going to get through it."

"Do you understand how real this is to me? I mean I could see it, I could feel it on me. Yet part of my mind is saying that it never happened, that it was all my imagination. I just can't make that part stronger than the part that tells me it's for real."

"You need rest."

"The damn thing won't let me rest. That's the hold it has over me, as soon as I fall asleep it's there. I can't control it."

She pulled another chair from the side of the table and positioned it next to him, then she sat down and removed his right hand from his thigh, holding it in her own.

"Talk to me about it."

"Is this what going nuts is like? It's real,

you know, the damn thing seems as real as you are."

"Have you seen it since that day?"

"It's around." Motioning with his head towards the bay.

"Have you seen it?"

"I can feel it."

"I don't understand."

"If I close my eyes, I can feel it moving inside my head. I can feel the wings spreading, pushing outwards against my skull. Oh, Diane, I don't want to talk this way."

"So it's not out there?" Diane motioned towards the sky.

"It is if I let it escape. The only way I can keep it under control is to stay alert. When I sleep my brain relaxes and I can't control it." He looked at her. "Listen to me, I sound like a fucking lunatic."

She shook her head slowly, and held his eyes. "So what you're saying is that the bird is only a thought?"

"Yes, but it's a thought that becomes a reality." He looked at her. "The bird's as real as you are, I swear it."

"Bill, it sounds like you're talking about an hallucination."

"No, this is real."

"Hallucinations seem very real to the

people who are experiencing them."

"You mean to people who are insane. I'm going crazy, aren't I? Tell me that that's what's happening." He started to cry.

She had never seen him cry before. He looked broken.

The phone had begun to ring in the adjoining room.

"Bill, I should answer that." She hoped it was Josef Tanaka but as she attempted to remove her hand from his, he tightened his grip.

"Stay with me, Diane, I'm very frightened. Stay with me."

She relaxed and settled back into the chair as the answer machine caught the call, then she listened to Bill's voice give their number and advise that the caller could either leave a message or send a fax. She recalled how they had laughed as they'd recorded the outgoing message, trying to get a welcoming tone to Fogarty's gravelly voice.

The bleep sounded and Josef Tanaka echoed from the speaker.

"Hi, Diane and Bill, it's Josef. It's about two-thirty in the afternoon. I've got some work to finish outside the office so if I miss you today I'll try you again from home tonight. Hope you're both well. Bye, bye."

"If I call him back right now, I can catch

him before he goes out," Diane said.

"I don't want you to leave me," Fogarty said.

"If I stay, will you try to sleep?"

"I don't want to sleep."

"Well then, just rest."

"I'm afraid to close my eyes."

"Here, lean your head against my shoulder." She pulled his head down gently until he was nestled against her. "Nothing's going to happen to you, nothing. I promise."

Her voice was a caress and he felt himself falling softly into a black abyss. He caught himself on the threshold, his body jerking.

"Can't do that, oh no," he muttered.

"Can't do what?"

"Sleep."

"Rest then, just rest."

"Keep talking to me, please. I don't care what you say, just keep talking. Tell me about when you were a little girl in California. Tell me about your mother and father. What did your father do? He was a college professor wasn't he? Tell me about him. I need to hold on to your voice. I'm holding on."

* * *

Phillip Harrison and Art Weller were standing in the small office reserved for the guards on duty, a fortified, glass-plated room that offered both privacy and security in case of trouble.

"What's the game?" Harrison asked, watching the other guard light his tenth cigarette of the morning.

Weller shook his head as if to say he didn't understand the question. His nonchalance made Harrison angry.

"Is it some kind of initiation for working here or are you just sick?"

"What are you talking about?" Weller asked defensively.

"I'm talking about Justin Gabriel."

Weller stared at him. "I don't know what you mean."

Phillip Harrison eyed the other man suspiciously.

"What did you tell Gabriel about me?"

"Nothing, I don't talk to the guy."

"He knew my name."

"All right, he asked me your name."

"And what else?"

"Nothing."

"Did you tell him who my uncle is?" Harrison asked, edging towards Weller and causing him to back into the metal table that sat against the wall.

"Ease up, man. What's your problem?"

"You are."

"I told you not to go near him. I told you he'd get into your head."

"That's bullshit," Harrison answered. He wanted to hit Weller, just one smack would do it but he knew that one smack would cost him his job. He could imagine what his uncle would say then. He backed off. "Now I'm warning you. The game's over. No more."

Weller exhaled and a pillow of smoke left his lips.

"You don't get it, do you?"

Harrison stood in silence.

"When I tell you the man's dangerous, I mean he's dangerous. Like in ways you can't imagine. We've had government guys in here to study him. A few years back when the FBI was experimenting with mind control, who do you think they came to talk to?"

"You don't quit, do you?" Harrison said.

"Justin Gabriel doesn't need me to tell him about you," Weller continued. "He can tune into you like a TV set. Find out anything he wants to know. You want my advice, stay on his good side. You get him pissed off and he'll take you to pieces."

Phillip Harrison felt foolish. He was standing in front of an ignorant man, allowing himself to be threatened. Yet, something had happened to him last night. His dream may have been the result of auto suggestion or it may have been sheer coincidence, but something had happened. "The only way to overcome your fear is to look it straight in the eyes", that's what his father had preached to him when he was growing up. He no longer agreed with all his father's macho philosophies but his old man's principle on the control of fear had stood the test of time.

"How late are you working today?" he asked Weller.

"Six o'clock. Why?"

"Just curious," he answered. He didn't trust Weller. In fact he was next to certain that he had talked to Gabriel about him. There was nothing that the little man had said that couldn't have been gathered from a conversation with the guard.

"You ain't thinking of going in there again?"

"Where?"

"Into Gabriel's cell. I'm warning you, he's trouble."

"No, I'm not," Harrison lied.

★ ★ ★

Several small groups of people stood near the sandy tip of Louse Point. The locals had arrived in their 4 × 4s and pickup trucks

87

and the visitors in their rented cars. All had gathered to watch the sun set. It was like a ritual and on this particular fall evening, with the air temperature still in the low fifties and a thin band of cloud rimming the western sky, the sun cast a fiery incandescence.

Only a few of the sun-watchers heard the man's shout from the other side of the inlet. It was like a short, convulsive slap against the bay and so out of context with the tranquility of the evening that those that did turned only briefly in the direction of the secluded house on Gerard Drive.

★ ★ ★

"It's all right, Bill, I'm with you," Diane assured him, turning to see the wall-mounted kitchen clock, praying that the doctor would arrive soon.

"You can't protect me. Nobody can protect me." He had a strange sensation as he spoke. It was as if he was listening to his own words, as if someone else was speaking them.

Diane looked up.

"Bill, there's nothing up there. Trust me." She could feel his hand trembling in her grasp. "You're exhausted and your mind is playing tricks on you. You've got to calm down."

"I'm telling you, it's come back. It's sitting on the roof of this house. It's waiting. Listen, dammit, can't you hear it? Listen!"

Diane lifted her head and listened, more to satisfy him than anything else.

"You hear it scratching? Can you hear the claws, listen, right above your head?"

There was in fact a sound, but it could have been the scraping of branches against the shingles.

"It's the limb of a tree, blowing in the wind, rustling against the roof," she explained.

"I'm not imagining it, it's up there," he said, his voice low.

She felt the hairs stand rigid along the nape of her neck.

"Please, Bill, you're frightening me."

"Don't let me go to sleep. That's how it gets in, you've got to believe me. I make it happen with my mind."

"That's not possible." She kept her voice gentle and steady. The scratching intensified. "It's probably a squirrel. I think I should go outside and see."

"No. Stay here."

She didn't move and within a few seconds, the scratching above them had stopped.

"You see?" he asked.

She met his eyes.

"I made it stop."

His entire demeanor was one of exhaustion, as if every drop of blood had been drained from his body.

"I'm containing it. Here, inside here," he said, touching the side of his head. "I'm going to kill it!" He shouted suddenly, ramming his fist into his forehead. Once, twice, until Diane reached for his wrist and held it. It took all her strength to restrain him.

"Stop it, Bill, please. Oh, please," Diane pleaded. "I don't know what to do for you, I don't know what to do."

She had tried to be strong but she was losing her strength to desperation, her body trembling as her tears came in bursts.

"Please. Please."

"You want to know what you can do for me?" Fogarty ranted, "You can leave, clear off, that's what you can do! You think I'm making this up? You think I'm crazy?"

Diane barely heard the sound of David Stryker's car, the engine being turned off and the door slamming shut.

"No, I don't think you're crazy," she said, "I promise I don't."

He calmed.

"I hear someone outside, footsteps," he said. He sat straighter in his chair.

There was a knock on the door.

"Who is it?" Fogarty asked, looking at Diane as if she had somehow betrayed him.

"I called a doctor."

"I don't want to see a doctor."

Another series of knocks on the door.

"I'm going to let him in, Bill."

"I don't need a doctor, I need a gun. I can end it with a gun," he said, his tone taut, then he turned back to the window.

The man at the door was in his late twenties, tall and lean with short blond hair and hazel eyes.

"Hi, I'm David Stryker," he said.

Diane introduced herself and stepped back as Stryker carried his black leather medical bag into the small entrance hall at the lip of the main room. He was wearing a brown corduroy suit, with a striped maroon silk tie that had been loosened to allow him to open the top button of his shirt. He was also wrapped in the largest leg brace that Diane Genero had ever seen. It was a blue cylindrical device that covered his right leg from mid thigh to mid-calf with a hole cut out at the knee.

"ACL," he said when he saw Diane's eyes linger on it.

She nodded her head.

Stryker was nervous. He'd only finished interning three months ago and this was his first house-call, so developing a good bedside manner was important to him. He forced a confident smile.

"I tore the ligament playing basketball. I only got the repair a month ago, but the brace comes off in a couple of weeks," he explained, walking forward and trying not to limp.

Diane was actually more concerned with Stryker's apparent youth than his sports injury. She had expected a much older, more experienced man.

Stryker interpreted the question in her eyes as a need for further elaboration.

"Anterior cruciate ligament surgery." He pronounced the words carefully and his voice reached across the room where Fogarty had withdrawn to a safer place inside his mind. He was seated at his desk at the old Roundhouse Building in Philadelphia. He was a cop again, and he was in control. He'd cracked a lot of tough cases from his old beat-up desk and this one wasn't going to stop him.

"Anterior cruciate ligament." He repeated Stryker's words.

"Oh, you know about ACL?" Stryker said, looking at the back of Fogarty's head as he made his way towards him.

"I've had the operation." Fogarty's voice

was flat and far away.

"Have you really?" Stryker answered.

"My knee's never been right since," Fogarty added.

Diane Genero looked at Fogarty. His knee surgery had taken place during the investigation into her daughter's homicide. It was part of an episode that Fogarty rarely mentioned and she was surprised he was talking about it now, particularly in front of a stranger.

"How long ago was that?" Stryker asked.

"A long time," Fogarty replied.

"Well, the procedure's a little different now," Stryker said, loosening up, working on his rapport, "They use grafts from muscle, when they did yours they may have still been working with synthetics." He was standing in front of Fogarty, looking down at him. He extended his hand, "My name's David."

Fogarty continued to stare straight ahead, his mind disconnected from the here and now.

"That bastard nearly killed me. I was curled up on the floor, praying. That's right, praying. He tore out half my throat, crippled my leg, but I took him down in the end, put five bullets in his head. Five bullets, thirty-eight caliber, hollow points. Leaves an exit wound the size of your fist. He didn't get

93

away with it, believe me, I took him down. Ugly bastard but he was only a man, flesh and blood, nothing unnatural."

Stryker withdrew his hand and turned towards Diane Genero.

"He was a police officer. He's talking about an old case. I don't understand why he's bringing it up now," she said.

"How long did you say that it's been since he slept?" Stryker asked.

"Three days."

"That's a long time, he could be delusional. What's his first name?"

"Why don't you ask me, son, there's nothing wrong with my hearing," Fogarty said. He was back in the room now, staring up into Stryker's eyes.

"I'm sorry, sir," Stryker said.

"My name is Bill Fogarty."

"Bill?" Stryker said. "Your wife tells me you haven't been sleeping."

"My wife's dead. I killed her, killed my kid too. Automobile crash, Route 70, on the way back from the Jersey shore."

Stryker held Fogarty's eyes and nodded his head.

"There's no need to talk about that, Bill," Diane said gently.

Inside Fogarty's mind, the walls were crumbling.

"I was drunk. Killed'm both, watched them burn."

"Bill, please," Diane said, moving to place her hands on his shoulders.

"Don't touch me," Fogarty said, jerking away. He suddenly felt raw and vulnerable, naked amongst strangers.

"What the hell are you doing here anyway?" he asked, looking at Stryker. There was the hint of aggression in his tone. Stryker was stepping into waters beyond his depth and he knew it.

"Your w — " he hesitated, looking at Diane. "Your friend thought maybe I should come out and take a look at you."

"Did she tell you I was cracking up?" Fogarty asked. Things were coming in and out of focus, Stryker's voice, his face. He looked like an awkward kid. Was he really a doctor? What the hell was he doing at the Roundhouse? The cry of a seagull pulled Fogarty back through the looking glass. "What are you doing here, son?" he repeated.

"Ms Genero said that you were having a hard time sleeping."

"You mean Diane? Are you talking about Diane?"

"I asked Dr Stryker to come," Diane replied.

95

"Did you tell him about the bird?" Fogarty asked.

"No," she replied.

The question aroused Stryker's curiosity but he sensed it was not the time to push any buttons.

"Good," Fogarty replied and the fissure inside his head, the one that contained the bird, sealed. Maybe he wasn't cracking up, maybe he had been dreaming. Maybe he was dreaming now? Maybe the whole damned thing was a dream. He pinched the skin above his left wrist.

"I can feel my skin so I'm not dreaming, am I?"

"No," Stryker answered, "but it sounds as if you are very, very tired."

Diane placed her hand on Fogarty's shoulder, then bent over and hugged him.

"Does that feel real enough?"

Fogarty's emotions shifted again. He found a delicate sense of equilibrium, as if the two people above him were holding him in a psychological safety net. His sense of panic ebbed.

Stryker felt the moment.

"Bill, would you mind if I checked your blood pressure?"

"No, I wouldn't mind."

Stryker opened his medical bag and took

out a gauge and cuff. He pushed up the sleeve of Fogarty's denim shirt, wrapped his arm and pumped the mercury to 260 before releasing the valve. The gauge read 220 over 100.

Stryker was alarmed but kept his voice matter-of-fact.

"Your diastolic pressure is running high."

"What does that mean?" Fogarty asked.

"It means the pressure when your heart is at rest is quite a bit outside the normal range."

"Why would that be?"

"It's probably due to anxiety."

"Yeah, I've had a bit of that."

"Let's check your pulse." Stryker said, reaching forward to grip Fogarty's wrist. He timed it with the sweep hand on his wrist watch.

"You're around a hundred and ten."

"Jesus, I'm usually under seventy."

"As I said, it's probably anxiety."

The sun had set behind the house and the room was growing dark. Diane walked to the wall nearest the entrance door and turned on an overhead light.

"Could you just keep that off for a second?" Stryker asked.

Diane switched the light back off as Stryker lifted an ophthalmoscope from his bag.

"I don't want your eyes reacting to any external light," he explained. "Now, I'm going to need you to turn towards the wall behind me, pick a spot and focus on it with both eyes."

Fogarty did as Stryker requested. It was making him feel much better now that someone else was in control. He felt safe for the first time in three days.

Stryker bent over Fogarty, gently held the back of his head, positioned the scope and peered into his right eye.

"What are you looking for?"

"I want to see if there's any swelling inside your eye, broken blood vessels, that kind of thing."

"And if there is?"

"It would indicate that there's been pressure on your brain. It's possible that you've had a minor hemorrhage; that would explain your loss of direct sensitivity, you know, that feeling you described earlier, of being here, but not here."

"A stroke?" Fogarty asked.

"So far it looks pretty good," Stryker reassured, repositioning the scope above Fogarty's left eye. "No, there's nothing of any significance here," he acknowledged. He'd had a hunch that he'd see some sign of papilloedema, something that would indicate a trauma or tumor in the brain.

"So, what's going on with me?"

"I'm not sure," Stryker said, returning the instrument to his bag. "I need to know more about what you've been experiencing. What's causing the anxiety?"

Fogarty looked at Diane.

"Please, Bill, tell the doctor what's been happening," she urged.

Fogarty turned back to Stryker.

"I'm seeing things," he replied.

"What kind of things?"

"A bird," Fogarty answered, then began to laugh.

"Is there something funny about the bird?" Stryker asked.

"I'm sorry," Fogarty said. "It's just that, for a moment, the whole situation seemed ridiculous."

"I understand," Stryker replied. In the growing darkness of the room, the scarred side of Fogarty's face was cast in shadow. Earlier, Stryker had assumed the damage to be the result of burns; he had noted where the skin had been grafted. Now, with the play of light, and the sallowed color of Fogarty's skin, it was as if he was looking at a dead man. The sensation made him uneasy. "You could turn the light on now, Ms Genero," he suggested.

"It started with a dream," Fogarty continued.

"Are you talking about the bird?"

"Yes, that's exactly what I'm talking about."

Stryker rubbed his hands along the side of his trousers, as if his palms were sweating. It was a move that Fogarty had seen many times during interrogations. He sensed that Stryker was nervous.

"What did you say your name was?"

"David Stryker."

Fogarty stared up into the young face. The overhead spot clicked on and the yellowed beam emphasised the tiny flecks of dandruff on the shoulders of Stryker's jacket. What kind of a doctor had dandruff?

"You don't look like a doctor. What are you doing here, anyway?" Fogarty asked and the connection between them was broken.

"Come on, Bill, you know why Doctor Stryker's here," Diane interjected.

Fogarty nodded his head.

"Well, you see, son, I've got an eagle living in my brain and I don't know what to do about it. How about you? Have you got any ideas?" His voice was clipped and as he laughed again, there was an edge to his laughter.

For the first time, Stryker wondered if Fogarty could be violent. The man had been a cop, and cops were tough. With his knee still in a brace, Stryker felt particularly vulnerable. He concocted a smile. "I'd like to see you a little more comfortable," he said, thinking of the Valium that he'd taken from the supplies in the office and added to his medical bag.

"Damn thing gets loose and we're all in a lot of trouble," Fogarty stated. It sounded like a threat.

"Stop it, Bill," Diane said.

"Stop what? What are telling me to stop?" Fogarty snapped back.

"Bill, we want to help you," Diane said. Her voice was soft and her words sincere and Fogarty's paranoia faded beneath them. He sat back against the chair and breathed deeply, willing himself to relax.

"Sorry," he said, "I'm just kind of nervous."

"That's perfectly understandable," Stryker said. Then, bending down to remove a plastic-wrapped syringe and a box containing a small vial from his bag, he asked: "How long has this thing with the bird been going on?"

"A few weeks," Fogarty answered.

"That's a long time," Stryker replied. "I really think you need to talk to somebody about it."

"Like a shrink?" Fogarty asked.

Stryker nodded his head. "Somebody who's a lot more qualified in these sort of things than I am."

"Does it sound like I'm losing it?"

"It sounds like you're confused about whatever it is that is taking place. There could be a very logical reason; it might even be a chemical imbalance, some kind of food allergy, but, as I said, I'm not the man to tell you." He tore the lip of the plastic wrapper and removed the syringe. "What are you giving me?"

"With your permission, I'd like to give you something that may make you feel a bit better," he said.

Fogarty studied Stryker's face.

"What have you got in mind?"

"It's a relaxant," Stryker answered, sliding the vial from the cardboard box.

"You're not going to put me to sleep, are you?"

"You don't have to sleep," Stryker answered, inserting the needle through the rubber cap of the 10 ml vial.

Fogarty watched the fluid fill half the barrel of the syringe.

"What is it?"

"Valium."

Fogarty relaxed. "Fine, Valium's OK. I

used to use it when my back went into spasm. I've probably got some pills lying around here somewhere."

"This will be a lot faster."

Fogarty nodded, watching Stryker's hand as he depressed the plunger enough to force a drop of liquid out the end of the needle. "You sure that's Valium? I don't want anything heavy, I don't need to sleep — "

"Bill, please, trust us," Diane said, placing her hand on his shoulder.

"It will take the edge off that anxiety," Stryker promised.

"I don't want to sleep."

"That's your choice," Stryker said. "How about rolling up your sleeve for me?"

Fogarty unbuttoned the cuff of his denim shirt.

"Push it right up and make a fist so I can get a vein." Fogarty complied.

"That's great," Stryker said, sliding the needle in and emptying the barrel.

"Never even felt that," Fogarty said.

"Good. Now, I'd appreciate it if you would lie down."

Fogarty looked at Diane.

"It's all right. You don't have to sleep, just rest," she said.

"I'm not going to bed."

"How about the sofa along the window?" Diane suggested.

"All right," Fogarty agreed. He tried to stand up but his legs felt soft and wobbly. "That stuff works quick," he said, sitting back down.

"Ms Genero, maybe you could give him a hand," Stryker suggested, "I'm not much good with this brace on." His confidence was returning now that his patient was effectively sedated.

Diane got a grip on Fogarty's arm, then guided him to the sofa. Fogarty lay down and Diane propped his head up on one of the hard cushions. "Let me take off your shoes," she offered.

"No, my shoes stay on. I don't want to get too comfortable," he answered.

She nodded her head and backed away as Stryker motioned for her to follow him to the far side of the room.

"Why is he so terrified of falling asleep?" Diane glanced at Fogarty.

His eyes were half open and he felt as if he was floating, barely aware of the voices on the other side of the room. He was only mildly conscious of the supine position of his body and of his head against the pillow. The white painted ceiling above him looked porous and alive, as if it were made of smoke, billows that shaped and shifted, opening and closing in time with his breath.

Diane turned back to the young doctor.

"He dreams of the bird," she replied, hesitating.

Stryker sensed her indecision. "I can't be of much use unless you tell me about it," he urged. He was considering a call to Mark Segal, a friend from medical school who was currently practising psychiatry in Southampton. Stryker had his phone number in his Filofax.

"It's a recurrent dream and it terrifies him. It's been going on for weeks," Diane said. "And then there was the incident out on the bay."

She stopped abruptly and studied Stryker's face. She felt as if she was betraying Fogarty by discussing it.

The doctor remained impassive. Inside, he was dying of curiosity. "Go on," he said.

"He believes that the bird from his dream materialised and that it attacked him. I don't know what actually happened or what he saw but Bill doesn't scare easily. I mean he was a cop, he saw all kinds of things . . ."

"There's no need to justify anything," Stryker assured her.

"Well, whatever happened traumatised him."

"And this was four days ago?"

"Yes, and he hasn't slept since." She looked over at Fogarty as he shifted position, his eyes still open. "He's petrified it's going to come back."

"Has Bill experienced any emotional trauma lately, a loss or bereavement, anything that could have manifested in the symptoms you are describing?"

Diane didn't answer.

"The delusions, the broken sleep, the severe anxiety," Stryker coaxed.

"I can't think of anything," she replied.

"Earlier, he said something about his wife and daughter. An automobile accident? Did that happen recently?"

"That was years ago, before we met."

"It obviously still troubles him."

"Yes, it does."

"Has he ever seen anyone about it?"

"He saw a psychiatrist in Philadelphia."

"Did he have a good relationship with the psychiatrist?"

"He and Stan Leibowitz, that was the psychiatrist's name, became personal friends."

"Have you thought of seeing Dr Leibowitz?"

"Stan is based in Philadelphia and I didn't think I could get Bill out of the house, let alone into a car or on to a train."

"Well, I really think he needs to talk to somebody. I would say that that's an imperative."

There was a sound from the sofa and both Diane and Stryker turned. Fogarty had begun to snore.

"I thought you said he wasn't going to sleep?" Again, she felt as if she had participated in some form of betrayal.

Stryker shrugged his shoulders and smiled. His face displayed a cockiness that she hadn't noticed before.

"You say he's been awake three nights?"

"Yes."

"Don't you think he deserves some rest?"

"Yes, but you told him he didn't have to sleep."

"I said it was his choice."

"But he was so frightened of going to sleep," she insisted angrily.

"Don't worry, he'll be fine. Besides, I'm going to be right here with you, at least long enough to call a colleague of mine in Southampton. He's a psychiatrist and I'd like you to take Bill to meet him. He's very good."

Stryker carried his black bag towards the kitchen table. He was feeling professional, having taken what could have been a difficult situation and containing it. His first house call had been a success. Even his injured knee felt stronger.

6

Justin Gabriel was sitting in a half-lotus position with his hands resting on his thighs and his eyes closed when Phillip Harrison stopped outside his cell. He could barely detect his breathing but behind the beard he thought he could see the hint of a smile on Gabriel's lips. That angered Harrison; it was as if he was mocking him.

"I could go in there and bash his head in," he thought, fingering the top of his baton. He'd seen that kind of stuff in movies; in real life he'd never actually had a one-on-one fight with another man.

Gabriel opened his eyes.

"You look a bit ragged today, Phillip, did you have a hard night?"

"If you fuck with my family, you're dead," Harrison said. He hadn't intended to come on so strong but Gabriel's demeanor antagonised him. He seemed so confident and self-contained, it was as if Harrison was the prisoner, not the man in the cell.

"Those are very strong words," Gabriel replied, smiling and opening his arms with his palms out.

"You know what I'm talking about."

Gabriel smiled and shook his head.

"I don't want to find out that you and Art Weller have been discussing me, ever again, do you understand?"

"Art Weller?" Gabriel repeated. There was a playful quality to his voice.

"I've got some connections in here. I could make it pretty rough on you," Harrison continued.

"Phillip, are you threatening me?"

Harrison remained silent.

"I take threats very seriously," Gabriel stated.

"I take my family very seriously," Harrison replied.

"Then I think we should talk about this," Gabriel said, unfolding his legs and getting to his feet. "Do you want to come in and lie down on the bed? You see, I don't have a couch."

"Why don't we stop the bullshit," Harrison said. "I don't know what you and Art Weller have going on but leave me out of it."

"Phillip, please," Gabriel said, walking towards him.

Harrison met the strange vapid eyes. Nothing in them except a reflection of his own anger and confusion, all contained behind a smiling façade.

"You had that dream again, didn't you?" Gabriel continued, his voice taking on a concerned, fatherly tone.

Harrison didn't answer. He didn't want to give Gabriel anything else to work on and manipulate.

"The dream doesn't stop because we don't talk about it. Once it starts, it won't stop. Not until it's over."

Harrison felt his anger rising but kept his mouth shut. "Why do you keep opening the window?"

"I'm warning you," Harrison said flatly.

"You're warning me?" Gabriel's voice was lower and more menacing.

"Yes I am."

"That's so silly." He stopped walking, his head even with Harrison's sternum. "Are you going to beat me up?"

Harrison considered it.

"What else can you possibly do to me, Phillip?" Gabriel asked. Then, as quickly, he relaxed and smiled, raising his hands peacefully. "What can anyone do to me?" His smile faded and he stood still. "Do you know the reason I'm here?"

"Yes, I do."

"The truth is, I was framed."

This time it was Harrison who smiled.

"I'm not a criminal," Gabriel stated. "I'm a liberator."

"I think that's enough," Harrison said. Their physical proximity was uncomfortable to him and he knew that his absence from the wing would be conspicuous.

"Some people require death to truly awaken from the dream and even then enlightenment can be momentary. What do you think, Phillip, are we dreaming now, or are we awake?" As he finished speaking he reached up and pushed his index finger through the bars, touching the spot on Harrison's forehead between his eyes.

Harrison saw a flash of light and heard a sharp cracking sound. Then he saw his uncle's face, it was swollen and blue and his eyes looked as if they'd exploded from their sockets. "He's dead. Uncle Rob's dead."

"Do you know what that was?"

Harrison swallowed and shook his head. He wanted to reach for his baton but felt vacant, without strength or will.

"A spontaneous transmission of energy," Gabriel said. His voice sounded hollow and Harrison had a sense of vertigo.

"It's not a trick. It's an exercise in

communication. The energy was the catalyst. The thought was there. The energy awakened it. You know, Phillip. You know what's going to happen. We all know. We're all just one big mind."

Harrison felt dazed and confused, then he had the sensation of falling. He hit bottom as Gabriel turned, walked back to his cot and sat down. He was smiling beatifically.

"Thank you, Phillip. Thank you so much for dropping by." After that Gabriel folded his legs and shut his eyes. Harrison continued to stare as Gabriel's body assumed a rigidity and the feeling inside the cell changed. He was alone and Justin Gabriel was somewhere else. Gone. Phillip Harrison didn't know where, but Justin Gabriel was no longer present.

★ ★ ★

Fogarty watched the great bird circle in the pale sky. There was majesty in the creature's movement, and there was power, deep and primeval, as if the bird, with its satin feathers, had been born from the merging of the sun and the wind.

Fogarty lay on his back, his arms spread wide, his feet close together, mesmerised by the poetry above his head, so caught within

112

the mystery of the mighty animal that his fear retreated, replaced by wonder and awe. He watched as the great bird descended until he could see its eyes. Feel their weight upon his mind, as if they were demanding entrance, pulling him into a dream within a dream.

At first he didn't recognise himself, not the young, scrubbed face, without scars or wear, nor the ease with which his body moved, but it was him, Bill Fogarty. Yes, he remembered the suit, khaki colored and made of linen, always wrinkled. He'd bought it at Brooks Brothers, to celebrate his promotion to plain-clothed detective. Bill Fogarty. God, he looked good. Life hadn't touched him at all, not yet. His corn yellow hair was full and cropped to frame the angular bones of his cheeks and jaw.

There was another man beside him, a tall man with dark, shaggy hair spilling from a red baseball cap; he had a handlebar mustache and wore blue jeans, a light leather jacket and training shoes. They were running through an alleyway, littered with garbage cans and spilled refuse, walls of gray stone to either side, fire escapes and blackened windows. Stopping in front of a white wooden door with a uniformed police officer standing to one side of it. "It's unlocked, sir," the officer said, addressing the man beside Fogarty.

113

Fogarty turned to the taller man, confused. "Welcome to the Church of Human Consciousness." There was the hint of irony on the smile behind the mustache and the voice was a hoarse but familiar whisper. 'Church of Human Consciousness'. The words triggered intense fear and suddenly everything linked. Mac. Mac Parkinson. That was the man's name. He was Fogarty's partner and they were on a bust, Fogarty's first since he'd made detective.

"You ready, Bill?"

Ready? No. He'd never be ready to go back inside that house.

"Ready?" the voice repeated.

He wanted to wake up, to swim to the surface, to crawl into the light. "Yes," he thought he heard his own voice respond but perhaps it was just a thought, then he watched himself slip his hand inside his jacket to draw a thirty-eight snub-nosed revolver.

Parkinson lifted a walkie-talkie. "Rick . . . .? The count will be one, two, and go. You copy?"

"I copy that," a tinny voice crackled in reply.

Fogarty stood to the side of the door. He looked at Parkinson and a sadness filled him. He liked Mac Parkinson. Trusted him.

114

Something was about to happen. He could almost remember what it was but his thoughts seemed out of sync, a moment behind the action.

"Go ahead, Bill."

He wanted to stall, to resist, but that seemed as impossible as clear recall.

"Open it. Just a little."

He gripped the doorknob, twisted it and pushed. A shaft of light illuminated the polished wood floor of the inner room. He gave his eyes a few seconds to adjust then pushed some more. His fear heightened and with the intensity of the sensation his dream body grew closer in alignment to the part of him that resisted what was taking place. He needed to tell Mac Parkinson not to go inside but he couldn't speak. He couldn't change a thing.

Parkinson lifted the walkie-talkie. "No movement inside. No sound."

The tin voice replied. "Should be nine people in there, three of them kids."

"I copy that."

"We're standing by."

"One, two — "

Fogarty wanted to wake up. Wanted to stop the dream but it was like swimming against the tide.

"Go!"

115

He lowered his weapon to a centered position, waited a moment then entered the room, one step behind Parkinson, taking the left side while his partner swept to the right. Time became a vacuum.

Inside, the place resembled a religious shrine or pagan temple; there was a wooden altar with tall candles burning to either side and the bleached skull of a goat resting on the mantle between them.

"Oh man," Parkinson uttered.

Fogarty turned and followed his partner's gaze to the congealed blood that filled two of the bowls at the base of the altar and the third, larger bowl which contained the remains of a dismembered pig, its thick snout aimed upwards, pink nostrils staring like sockets without eyes. Something was going to happen. Something bad. If he could only remember it; it wouldn't need to take place. He could stop it. He could wake up. His terror mounted.

"These are some sick fucks," Parkinson said, then motioned for Fogarty to follow him through the dim light to the entrance of the corridor. There was a fetid smell all around them as they walked the hallway towards the front of the house and fear and nerves conspired to magnify everything within Fogarty's field of vision. No detail

116

escaped scrutiny, even the matted clumps of dog hair that had been trampled into the worn green carpet.

The walls were tight to either side and there were prints of human hands on them, as if someone with bleeding palms had tried to climb to the banister of the staircase above. Ahead, as if coming towards them through the fish-eye lens of a camera, Fogarty saw Rick Romano; he was wearing his regulation blues and a trooper's hat with 'Stakeout Unit' printed on the brim. His dark eyes flashed as he spat the words, "Clear in front."

There were two other men behind him and Fogarty knew that the fourth would be securing the front of the house.

"Back room's clear," Parkinson answered.

Romano motioned his men towards the staircase. "Go!" he ordered. Then, to Fogarty and Parkinson, "There're two dead dogs by the door, big ones, look like German shepherds. Their throats have been cut and there's a lot of blood around. It looks pretty fresh."

Fogarty's mind was racing. He thought of the palm prints. Dog's blood? But why kill the dogs? The dogs were security, unless security was no longer required. He fought for recall but the dream kept pulling him deeper, sweeping him along.

"I'll go topside," Romano said, then turned and followed his men up the stairs.

Fogarty and Parkinson continued along the hallway. They'd studied layouts of the house in the operations room, but under pressure nothing ever looked the same.

The first door led into a closet. It contained sheets and towels and what appeared to be an assortment of musical instruments, primitive drums made of skin and gourd, and several rattles.

The next was the basement. Fogarty stood to the side of the opened door and listened. Silence. He reached along the inner wall, found a light switch, then turned, nodded and hit the lights. Again they waited and listened. Nothing. Then Fogarty descended into the dank of the tiny room. The ceiling was only inches above his head and the cement block walls were covered in the same, blood-colored hand prints as the hallway above. Piles of books and magazines were stacked at the base of the stairs — psychology journals, medical texts, and crudely printed manuals with mandalas and other geometrically patterned symbols painted across their covers; there was also a wooden crate containing bundles of bound sticks of incense, and several sealed jars of dried leaves or herb. The place was oppressive and time seemed sealed inside its walls.

"Clear down here," he called.

"They've got something above," Parkinson answered. "Let's go."

The fetid smell was stronger on the third floor of the house, emanating from the crack between the floor and the edge of a door that had been painted black. "It's bolt locked from the inside," Romano said. Then, turning to the man carrying the pick axe, "Whack it."

Fogarty wanted to shout for them to halt. But why? Why?

The door had been reinforced with sheets of steel and the first blows of the axe did little more than shred its wood veneer. Five strikes later, the hinges gave and a sweet gray smoke drifted from the room. As it dissipated, its aroma was overpowered by the stink of rotting flesh.

Fogarty felt like a prisoner, on a journey he did not want to make.

He stumbled as he entered. Looking down he glimpsed something wrapped in a blanket. About the size of a small child. He stepped over it, his weapon held in front of him, moving left, along the perimeter of the room. Mac Parkinson followed the same pattern to the right, getting halfway around the large, squared space before Romano and a second man from the stakeout entered.

The bare wood floor was littered with the dead bodies of men, women and children.

"Oh sweet Jesus," someone uttered.

"Stay alert," Parkinson snapped. "Give me some light here."

Some were clothed, wearing red and black cotton robes, while two were naked, the woman on her back, the man on top, her slack legs wrapped round the back of his thighs as if their dying act was of procreation. The children were swathed in blankets, their faces pale, fresh, and innocent. Fogarty kept returning to the faces of the children.

"I'm counting eight bodies," Romano said.

"These are the angels, that's what they called themselves, Gabriel's angels," Fogarty replied. It was coming back now.

"Aside from the kids, these are the freaks that butchered a man, his wife and two kids," Parkinson added, his tone dry. He was bending down beside a large bowl in the center of the room. "Looks like some kind of suicide pact. They turned on one last time and checked out." He placed his finger alongside the bowl. "It's still warm." He looked at Fogarty. "Whatever's in that bowl might've been seeped in poison."

"How about the children?" Romano asked.

Fogarty stared at the carnage. "The smoke

120

was blown in their faces," he answered. He knew. The pieces were jigging into place.

"Stay away from the pipe. Don't inhale that shit," Parkinson warned. "Let's look through the bodies and hope that little son of a bitch is one of them."

Fogarty turned towards the door. That's when he saw it.

7

"He's saying something."

Stryker walked towards the sofa and looked down at his patient.

Fogarty groaned.

"His eyes are open. I don't understand why his eyes are open," Diane said.

Fogarty's eyes widened, his pupils dilating and contracting in rapid rhythm.

"It's all right, you see his pupils, the way they're moving? It's called rapid eye movement; it means he's dreaming. Nothing to worry about," Stryker announced. His tone was not convincing. He'd phoned Mark Segal less than ten minutes before and had been told that Segal was with a patient. The psychiatrist's secretary had taken Fogarty's

121

home number and promised that she'd get Segal to phone between appointments.

"Hands above your head," Fogarty said suddenly, his words garbled.

Diane bent over him, closer.

"Bill?"

"Don't fucking move!"

★ ★ ★

Standing inside the room, just beyond the doorway, back lit by the light from the stairwell. It had the shape of a man, arms and legs, but its head. It was the head of a wild bird, with features exaggerated and blown out of proportion, its beak so long and pointed that it seemed only inches from Fogarty's face, feathers slicked backwards across a hard angular skull. Its eyes were like small dark beads of glass. The arms of the creature were short and muscular, but the hands. Not hands, but claws, with long razor-edged talons and metal joints, reaching out.

"Shoot the fucking thing!" Parkinson shouted.

Fogarty steadied his gun, aiming straight between the black eyes. Concentrating on the eyes. They were staring straight at him. Entering him, gripping his mind. He tried to pull the trigger but his fingers would not obey his commands.

It shrieked as it flew towards him.

Someone fired from behind; the bullet went wide, tearing a patch of plaster from the wall. Another flash of light and Fogarty turned in time to see Mac Parkinson's head explode.

"Man down!"

After that there were gun shots and people tripping over bodies. Fogarty tried to run but he couldn't move. He was rooted to the floor, grunting and gasping with the thing right on top of him.

"Bill, you're dreaming. You're dreaming."

It was so heavy he could hardly draw breath.

"It's a dream. A nightmare!" The words broke through. Feminine and throaty, coming from another plane of reality, a much safer, more ordered place.

"Bill, wake up!"

He heaved a breath and the pain receded, the fear with it. The connection was weakening.

"Bill."

He focused on the voice.

"That's it, Bill, come on."

There were feelings inside the voice, love and concern. "Wake up."

123

The words were like the rungs of a ladder leading from the darkness to the light above. He could climb the words.

★ ★ ★

"Wake up, Bill, wake up. It's OK, everything is OK."

Climbing. Climbing. Up the ladder of light.

"That's it."

Almost there, nearly free when Stryker bent over and took hold of his wrist to feel his pulse. Breaking his balance. He fell. Back down into the dark room. He wrenched away from Stryker's grasp. That was his gun hand. He didn't want to lose his gun. His protection. Stryker grabbed his wrist again and Fogarty fought, punching as Stryker reeled backwards. Then the sharp pain in his thigh as a fresh syringe of Valium discharged through the leg of his pants. He rolled and grabbed Stryker by the collar of his jacket, his hands tightening against his throat.

"He was coming through on his own. He didn't need that!" Diane shouted, gripping Fogarty from behind as Stryker broke loose, found his feet, and got to the phone. Diane could hear him giving the Gerard Drive address and saying over and over again that

124

it was an emergency.

"Diane?" Fogarty's voice was thick and slurred. "He won't let me go. I can't escape."

"Who won't let you go?"

He looked at her and closed his eyes. By the time Stryker had walked back across the room Fogarty was unconscious.

"I'm going to get him to Stony Brook. It's the nearest psychiatric facility."

Diane stared at him.

"Mr Fogarty needs help," Stryker concluded. His throat felt swollen and he was worried that the struggle had caused more damage to his knee.

"I don't want him hurt and I don't want him humiliated," Diane said.

"Hurt? Humiliated? That man nearly killed me," Stryker thought, holding back the words.

Suddenly Fogarty gasped, clenched both fists and hammered them into his chest. "Can't breathe. I can't breathe," he stammered.

Stryker knelt awkwardly and placed his hand on Fogarty's chest. "It may be his heart. Or it may be a reaction to the Valium." His words sounded like a confession. "Call an ambulance."

Diane rushed to the phone and made the call as Fogarty's eyes opened. He panicked again, striking out.

"Help me!" Stryker shouted.

Then it was Stryker, Fogarty, and Diane Genero rolling on the floor.

The town cops entered through the unlocked door, saw the commotion and tried to separate them.

"I'm a doctor, this man is my patient. My patient! He's out of control!"

Fogarty fought harder until one of the cops wrapped his arm around his neck and applied a choke while dragging him clear. A second officer cuffed Fogarty's hands behind him, then the two men hauled him to his feet.

The young doctor considered his alternatives as the ambulance arrived at the front of the house. Two paramedics entered carrying a stretcher and portable oxygen unit.

Fogarty was standing between the police officers, his eyes wide and vacant. The thin divide between his dreams and waking reality had collapsed. He looked at the cop on his right and gave his name, rank and badge number.

The policeman answered with a nod of his head and a puzzled look at Diane Genero.

"He was a police officer," she said.

The cop looked more puzzled.

Fogarty remembered a room, children's

126

bodies, and Mac Parkinson, but the memory was confused and out of context with what was happening around him.

"Where's Mac?" he asked.

Again the young officer looked at Diane and again she shook her head.

"I'm sorry, sir, I don't know who you're referring to," the cop answered.

The cuffs were tight to Fogarty's wrists, their steel edges digging into his flesh and the pain triggered a disjointed memory. "Mac Parkinson, my senior officer. I want to see Mac. What happened to Mac?"

The cop looked back at Diane.

She felt useless and said: "I don't know what he's talking about. I'm sorry."

"Am I under arrest?" Fogarty asked.

"No, sir," the policeman answered.

"Then why have you cuffed me?"

Fogarty's legs were going slack.

"You were reported as being violent, sir."

"Violent?" he repeated. There was irony in his tone. Then his legs gave way and the two officers were supporting him.

Stryker stepped forward and checked Fogarty's pulse. It was stronger now, enough to satisfy Stryker that the respiratory reaction had been a result of the medication, not his heart. He walked over to the paramedics who had remained on the periphery of the action and introduced himself.

"It's a psychiatric problem," he said. "I'm going to have the police officers take him to Stony Brook."

The men spoke with Stryker for a minute or so and during that time the cops carried Fogarty to the sofa. He sat with his body slumped forward.

Diane looked at Stryker. "I want to go with him," she said.

"You won't be able to ride in the police car, you'll have to come with me."

"Then that's what I'll do."

"Am I under arrest?" Fogarty repeated as the officers removed his handcuffs then re-cuffed him to the front of his body in preparation for the long ride.

He remembered struggling with two men; he remembered that there had been dead bodies everywhere and he remembered being more frightened than he had ever been in his life. There were other memories, but they were shrouded, playing in the world of shadows.

★ ★ ★

The patrol car felt warm and had the familiar smell of disinfectant and take-away food. Fogarty had spent many hours in similar cars and he felt strangely secure with his knees wedged tight between the seats and the doors closed and locked like a metal cocoon around him. His head seemed extremely heavy and fell forward. He heard voices and car engines starting, looked up once as the ambulance drifted by, lights blinking in slow motion sequence. Then he was moving, down Gerard Drive, water on either side, the road rough with loose rock and potholes, the car's suspension hard and the two uniformed men in front of him, shoulders broad against the back of the seat. He was with his own kind now, cops, and nothing was going to get him.

They drove at forty miles an hour down Springs Fireplace Road, slowed down as they went through the village of East Hampton, then accelerated as they turned right on to West 27, driving through the small storybook towns and continuing along the highway towards the distant neon of shopping malls and Big Macs.

Stryker followed the patrol car with his cellular phone held tight to his ear. He had Mark Segal on the line and he was talking. "Delusional," was a term he used over and over again. Then he was listening, nodding his head and making "mmmm" sounds while glancing over at Diane Genero as if it was all too sensitive or confidential for her to hear. Finally he finished.

"Dr Segal says it's likely to be some kind of stress disorder," he said, slipping the small phone into the pocket of his jacket. "Maybe something brought on by Mr Fogarty's former employment."

"Yes," Diane replied and left it at that. She had tried to put herself in Stryker's position and knew that he'd done his best but he was young and there was an annoying arrogance to him that persisted even though he was clearly out of his depth.

"The symptoms can be treated," he added. "Good."

The police car left Route 27 at the Manorville exit and continued on the link road to the Long Island Expressway.

Diane could make out the back of Fogarty's head through the Chevrolet's rear window, bobbing and rolling as his body shifted with the banked surface of the entrance ramp. Then they joined the stream of cars and trucks on the highway, the police car slipping out from the traffic, into the left lane, top lights flashing as it disappeared down the asphalt.

Stryker was in the middle lane, a long way back, and for a moment Diane was afraid she'd lose sight of the white Chevrolet. That it would vanish, taking Bill Fogarty with it. She needed to protect him now, more than ever.

"They're losing us. Can't you go any faster?"

"I know where Stony Brook is, don't worry," Stryker replied.

They drove on, and with every mile Diane felt as if she and Bill Fogarty were being drawn further and further apart, both of them traveling headlong into some dark place in which they could never truly find each other again. She fought the feeling.

"How long will it take?" she asked.

"About another forty-five minutes," Stryker answered.

She'd meant something else. She'd wanted reassurance, to know how long it would take to make Bill Fogarty well, to turn him back into the man she had known. She remembered the first time they'd met, in a hotel room in Philadelphia. Her daughter, Gina, had been brutally murdered and Bill Fogarty was the police lieutenant in charge of the investigation. She remembered opening the door to him. He had worn a coffee-colored suit and maroon tie, his body turned slightly away from her. He had seemed tall and broad at the shoulder and he'd smelled vaguely of lime, or some citrus aftershave. It was only as he entered the room that she'd noticed his scars, like a mask, covering half his face, clouding its expression. The other half had once been handsome, All-American handsome, like the football captain in a high school yearbook, but something had happened to alter it, draining the light from its eyes and furrowing its brow. She observed all these things in the time it took him to introduce himself. Bill Fogarty. Not Lieutenant, not officer. He was obviously uncomfortable with his duty of escorting the mother of the deceased to the morgue for the purpose of identifying her child's body and his voice had been clipped and gruff, nerves coming through like thread through worn fabric, but there had been something else about him. He'd worn it as decidedly as he had worn his aftershave, his clothing, and the scars on his face. It was the scent of loneliness. It was a nuance that most would have missed, but Diane Genero knew it well. She had lived with it and studied it, and there, back in that room, it had been standing in front of her. Bill Fogarty, raw and honest and alone. Loneliness had been their connection. It was something sensed, quick and instinctual. It was the reason that she had trusted him, enough to do what she had needed to do but had not allowed herself. To break down and sob like a baby.

* * *

Fogarty drifted off to sleep in starts and stops, each time jolting himself awake, still frightened of what waited in the shadows of his mind. Occasionally the passenger-side officer would turn and look at him.

"Are you all right?"

Fogarty didn't answer, he simply stared at the young face and tried to place it. Since he'd made detective he'd lost touch with the uniforms. He should have known this guy. Who the hell was he?

They pulled off the LIE at Exit 62, followed the ramp to Nichols Road, turned right and continued to drive. It wasn't until the Chevrolet's headlights flashed on the square blue sign with the letter 'H' on it that he had the first inkling of where they were headed.

"You taking me to a hospital?" His words were still slurred.

"Yes, sir."

"Why?"

"Those are our orders."

"Have I been shot?" He was thinking of the death room again.

"No, sir."

"Then what's the matter?"

"You've been violent."

"Am I under arrest?"

"No, sir."

"Then pull over, officer. Stop the car. I'm getting out."

"We can't do that, sir."

"I don't like hospitals."

No answer.

"What kind of hospital is this?"

"It's a state hospital."

They had slowed to take the left into the driveway of Stony Brook. The hospital loomed ahead like an architect's nightmare, something dreamed up in the late sixties when minimalism reigned and the environment was an inconvenience, two blackened-glass towers, each eleven stories high, joined in the middle and supported by giant steel girders. It was a dark, foreboding monolith.

"I'm not going in there," Fogarty said, frightened by the look of it. He twisted in the seat, straining to see through the rear window of the patrol car.

"Where's Diane?" Even as he said her name, fragments of the evening returned in memory. He remembered a struggle. He and another man. Diane Genero screaming for him to stop.

"Diane's OK, isn't she?"

The officer on the passenger side turned and watched him closely. "She'll be here soon. She's with the doctor."

Fogarty locked on to the cop's eyes and, for a moment, he was totally lucid. He remembered the young doctor, the injection of Valium.

"Stryker? Dr Stryker?"

"That's right."

Fogarty hesitated, yearning for things to slow down, reverse. He didn't want to be here, in this car, with these men, at this hospital.

"I'm crazy. Is that what you think? That I'm crazy?"

The cop looked at him. "Settle down."

They stopped in front of the big glass doors. 'Psychiatry Outpatient' was printed above them. Fogarty read the sign and froze. He had a terrible, hollow feeling.

"Hold on a second," he said as the sound of the Chevy's engine died.

The officer turned in the seat and looked at him.

"This is a mistake. I've been having trouble sleeping, that's all. I don't need a hospital."

The officer at the wheel appeared slightly older than the second man and his eyes were less forgiving.

"Sir, we were called because you were violent and your doctor — "

"I don't even know the guy."

"Dr Stryker called us and reported that you were out of control," the policeman stated. "That means you get a trip to Stony Brook. That's just the way it works. We don't make the rules."

"I'm not moving till Diane gets here."

The older cop exchanged a sideways glance with the policeman on the passenger side.

"Come on, you don't want to make it tough on yourself. Let us take you in and register you. Your wife should be here by then."

"She's not my wife."

The man was clearly losing patience.

"Now listen, Mr Fogarty. One way or the other you are going into the hospital. We'd prefer it if it was under your own volition, but if we have to assist you, we will. Do you understand?" Without waiting for his answer they got out of the car and opened Fogarty's door.

★ ★ ★

It was the smell of fried butter from the kitchen that first assailed his nostrils as Fogarty entered the Triage area of the

136

Psychiatric Outpatient wing. It was the kind of aroma that was more akin to the popcorn machine at a movie theater than to the reception area of a hospital, thick and heavy. Fogarty found it nauseating.

"I don't like it here," he said, looking nervously towards the entrance door.

"Come on," the older cop said, taking a hold of his cuffed wrists and leading him to the reception desk.

The Triage nurse looked up. Fogarty had been in the same clothes for four days; he was unshaven, his face scarred, and his eyes had the wild, frightened quality that she had seen often. He looked like a street person, and although she couldn't smell any alcohol, she guessed he may have been coming off a binge.

"Name?" she asked.

Fogarty looked at her, then lowered his head silently. He felt a mixture of confusion and shame.

"Fogarty," he mumbled.

"Pardon me, sir?"

He stared into her eyes and willed himself to concentrate, but his mind had begun to skip like a faulty record. He was losing track of where he was and the thin divide that had formed the threshold between sleeping and waking consciousness was breaking up again.

"My name is Captain William F. Fogarty and I'm not sure what happened. There were bodies everywhere, dogs, kids, somebody's weapon discharged and hit Parkinson. Then Diane grabbed me — " He stopped abruptly, sensing he was in trouble.

"His name is William F. Fogarty," Diane Genero cut in, stepping forward from behind them. Stryker was a few steps in back of her.

"Sorry, I'm sorry," Fogarty apologised, trying to harness his thoughts.

The nurse went on to take Fogarty's address, religion and insurance details then instructed the two officers to guide him towards the corridor at the far right of the Triage.

There was a closed white door with small reinforced glass windows directly in front of them, the letters CPEP printed above its frame and the words Comprehensive Psychiatric Emergency Program printed beneath the letters.

The door opened as they approached.

Fogarty stopped walking. He was about ten feet from the tall man who walked from the opened door. The man was wearing a dark suit and tie and had a thin, angular face, accentuated by black, receding hair. A pair of glasses hung by a cord around his neck. He was followed by a stocky man wearing white hospital overalls. There were no smiles.

Stryker walked to the man in the suit and exchanged a handshake and a few words, then turned and signaled for the police officers to bring Fogarty forward.

Fogarty turned to the younger of the officers.

"Don't do this to me, son."

"I'm sorry, sir."

"I don't want to go in there," Fogarty said, beginning to resist.

The officers dragged him forward.

Fogarty looked ahead. He could see the room beyond the opened door. There were people in there, more white coats and solemn faces. Another opened door, another room beyond that. Through the second door he could see a long, flat table, two men standing beside it, adjusting the leather restraints that were attached to each of its corners. The table. The restraints. His mind snapped and he was staring at a similar table. He'd seen it in a doctor's office. The doctor had done terrible things to people on that table. Sick, ugly images flashed, frame by frame, pain and torture. He'd seen it all; the doctor had made videos. It had been Fogarty's final murder investigation. The one that had caused him to retire. He knew all about restraints and tables.

"I'm not going in there!" he shouted, kicking out with his left foot and catching the older cop in the shin. After that he was hoisted in the air, the younger officer to his left while the psychiatric orderly wrapped a thick arm around his ankles and kept him off the ground. He struggled but they were too strong. The man in the suit stepped to the side as they carried him through the first door. He could hear it snap shut behind him.

"Diane, Diane!" His shouts were muffled against the sleeve of the cop's uniform.

Through the second door and he was inside the small white room. He tried to kick a few more times as they lowered him down on the table. There seemed to be people all around him, faces, eyes, staring, watching. He felt his legs being spread then a tightness on his ankles and he couldn't kick any more.

"Ready?"

"Yep." Gruff, quick voices. Men who had performed this operation often and were sure of themselves.

Someone rolled his upper body to the side and his hands were free, but only for an instant, after that they were pulled outwards, his arms stretched in crucifix position as his wrists were shackled, hard leather restraints replacing the steel cuffs. He thought he could hear Diane's voice, but it was far away, then the door was closed and he couldn't hear her at all. He was alone, staring at the cracks in a flat white ceiling. His feeling was one of utter loneliness, as if he had slipped past a point of no return and arrived at a place where nothing was familiar and there was no one to rescue or redeem him. He pulled against the restraints on his wrists. There was give, but not much. Where was he anyway? His thoughts were coming in waves. "How the hell did I get here?" He recalled a police car and the smell of buttered popcorn. "Here. Here. Where is here?"

"My name is Bill Fogarty and I'm in a hospital in New York," he said out loud. His voice sounded small and far away. "Bill Fogarty. Bill Fogarty." He repeated his own name and closed his eyes.

He could see the bird against his eyelids, circling, searching for him.

"You're imagining this, it's all in your mind," he said. Order it to stop and it will stop. "Stop."

He experienced a sound, metal slamming against metal. It was synchronous with the feeling that his mind had divided cleanly into two halves and that he, Bill Fogarty, had remained in the secure half, the half in which reality was sure and safe.

"Everything's going to be fine," he told himself. He could control this situation, learn from it, all he needed to do was to stay out of that other compartment in his mind, the one that was reserved for dreams. It was the dreams that had tricked him, distorting his senses to the point that they had become real, frightening and confusing. He was sane and rational. There was no need for him to be shackled to a bed in a loony bin. He was in control. He wasn't going to slip again and wind up in that other place. He didn't need to fight; he wasn't crazy. They'd see that soon enough.

"Mr Fogarty, I'm Dr Parnelli."

It was the tall man with the slick, receding hair. His eyes were brown, calm and objective.

"How are you feeling?"

"I'm fine," Fogarty answered.

Parnelli smiled. "Good." The CPEP unit could house only four patients and there were already three inside. Upstairs in the Tower, as the tenth-floor psychiatric ward was known, they had room for thirty and they were nearly full. He'd hoped Fogarty could be treated as an outpatient.

Fogarty laughed. He felt almost giddy.

"Would you care to tell me what's so funny?" Parnelli asked.

"There's a bird directly above your head."

Parnelli recalled the conversation he'd had with the young doctor. He hadn't particularly liked David Stryker, had found him too eager to impress and, in his opinion, too quick with his second injection of Valium and too high on the dose, but Stryker had termed Fogarty as 'delusional' and that seemed accurate. He was obviously hallucinating.

"Would you care to describe the bird to me?"

Fogarty stared. The bird seemed to be taking its time up there, circling lazily. He searched for the correct words. Words were important now. He had to let Parnelli know that he was firmly in control.

"It's not really a bird, it's a dream."

"That's interesting."

Parnelli's patronising reply angered Fogarty. After all, Parnelli was a doctor, surely he should understand what he was talking about? He concentrated beyond Parnelli's head and focused on the bird. "Now, how about unbuckling me, I'm getting tired of lying here."

The bird was sitting on Parnelli's shoulder. Parnelli smiled without showing teeth, then

143

studied Fogarty and considered how best to deny his request.

The delay rekindled Fogarty's anger. He glared into Parnelli's brown eyes as the bird began to nibble on his earlobe. "Doesn't that hurt?" he asked, his voice barely veiling his hostility.

Parnelli looked at him very closely, then said, "I think you should rest another few minutes."

Fogarty was about to protest when the bird opened its beak and engulfed Parnelli's head.

"Jesus Christ!" Fogarty shouted. When he looked up he was staring at a creature with a man's body and a bird's head. The creature lifted its arm. Something shining where a human hand should have been. A flash of light.

Fogarty struggled, pulling downwards with his hands and buckling up with his knees, forcing his pelvis into a raised position on the table.

"No, goddamn it. No!"

A pain shot through his right shoulder.

Gradually, the bird disappeared and Fogarty settled back against the table. He was still trembling as he stared up at the ceiling. Seconds, minutes, hours.

His mind had slowed and he felt a deadness

144

inside him. It was not a peaceful feeling; instead, it was as if every thought, every memory of his life had been compressed and stuck together with a thick glue and the bundle, bound and tied, was sinking into the mire of his consciousness. It required his last reserves to remember Diane Genero, to conjure her image. She was standing on the back porch of the house on the bay, wearing her white cotton dress, long hair fanning in the breeze. There were tears in her eyes and she was waving goodbye.

He was going to miss her.

His heart grew still as the thought hit the soft bottom and disappeared.

★ ★ ★

Parnelli tossed the used syringe in the waste bin and walked from the restraining room.

He had injected Fogarty with droperidol, a mixture of the anti-psychotic drug, Haldol, and a strong anesthetic. The drug would keep a man of Fogarty's size and weight sedated from four to six hours.

Parnelli crossed the linoleum floor and pushed open the second steel door, then continued towards the small office which was positioned to the right of the entrance. He hadn't slept well last night and his mood was black. Two divorces in ten years and the recent loss of the custody battle for his nine-year-old son. He put it down to his job, the hours and the stress. He was terminally tired. "Thank you, God, for pharmaceuticals," Parnelli said to himself. A little liquid through the sharp end of his syringe and the ex-police captain was trussed up as tight as a strait jacket. Another shot in a few hours and he'd keep till morning, then the shrink could sit down, talk, evaluate and decide what to do with him. "Hell of a place for a guy like that to wind up," he thought, glancing through the wired glass that separated CPEP from the outside world. He saw the two cops, huddled together talking. Parnelli stopped and unlocked the door, then stepped into the hallway long enough to thank them for their services and tell them that Mr Fogarty wouldn't be going home with them tonight. After that Parnelli straightened his tie and pulled down the sleeves of his jacket, then popped a breath mint into his mouth before entering the small office that served as a place to interview the families and relatives of the recently admitted.

★ ★ ★

David Stryker and Diane Genero sat on opposing plastic-covered chairs. Parnelli acknowledged Stryker with a curt nod of his head then looked at Diane. He hadn't really paid much attention to her in the reception hall of the Triage but now, up close, he noted a disturbing resemblance to his last wife. Diane Genero was older but the look was similar — earthy and sensual. His pretence of a smile faded as he thought of his son, tightening his lips as he extended his hand. It had always been curious to him that after spending more than a decade working with the problems of others he couldn't reconcile his own.

"I'm Robert Parnelli and I'll be looking after Mr Fogarty."

Diane took Parnelli's hand and began to stand.

"No, please, stay seated. I'm going to need to talk to you. It would be useful for me to have a little background on Mr Fogarty."

"Is he going to be all right?" Diane asked.

Parnelli evaded the question. "Right now, he's sleeping, which is exactly what he needs." The word sleeping always sounded better than 'sedated'.

Diane settled back into the chair. "What is it, Doctor? What's the matter with him?"

"That's what I'm going to find out,"

Parnelli assured her, observing the tears welling in Diane Genero's eyes.

"Thank you," she said, barely controling herself.

Her voice and manner bore no resemblance to his 'ex', which relaxed Parnelli. Diane Genero felt well centered and had intelligent eyes. She was also much easier to look at than the pompous young man who sat by her side, clearing his throat and trying to catch Parnelli's attention. Finally, Parnelli turned towards David Stryker.

"How much Valium did you say you'd given Mr Fogarty?" His voice was clipped.

Stryker looked startled.

"Ten milligrams."

"I believe it states in Mr Fogarty's admission report that it was more."

"Yes, yes, of course," Stryker said, correcting himself. "The first injection was ten milligrams, then there was a second injection. That was also ten mils."

"Which seems excessive considering that Mr Fogarty was not a regular patient of yours and you were unclear as to his physical condition," Parnelli replied.

"Well, uh," Styker stopped and cleared his throat again. "Considering that Mr Fogarty was so highly agitated, I thought the dosage was warranted."

Parnelli allowed the young doctor's words to die in midair, then, shaking his head, he turned to Diane Genero. "Some of the questions I'll need to ask are going to be rather personal, so if you'd prefer, there is no need for Dr Stryker to remain in the room."

Diane nodded.

"If you'll excuse us, Doctor," Parnelli said, "we shouldn't be long."

Stryker hobbled to the door as if he'd been expelled from class.

★ ★ ★

"Post traumatic stress syndrome." Parnelli used the term many times during their conversation. According to the psychiatrist, a lot of police officers suffered the illness following a particularly traumatic situation, months, even years after it had occurred. It was his hunch that Bill Fogarty's delusional state was being triggered by some past trauma that had been repressed and was now trickling back into his consciousness. "This bird he keeps talking about is probably an embodiment of something he doesn't want to consciously face. It's his personal bogey man. The fact that it initially manifested in a dream is common, since the underlying cause has been so successfully suppressed. The bottom line is, we've had a good success rate with these type of cases and I'm hopeful that we can work him through it." When she'd asked how long a 'cure' would take, the doctor had been promising but vague and when Diane had requested to spend the night in the unit he'd said that unfortunately CPEP had no facilities for overnight visitors, but perhaps she could use the general waiting room which was part of the Triage complex.

* * *

Diane turned as the door was locked behind her and looked a last time through the mesh of wires. The door to the inner room was also closed. Behind it, Bill Fogarty was sleeping peacefully. At least that's what the doctor had told her. She wanted to believe him.

She spotted Stryker pressed against the wall closest to the reception desk; he was concluding a second call to Mark Segal on his cellular phone and he was feeling better, having been assured that a malpractice suit was unlikely. He was very relieved when Diane shook his hand and thanked him for his assistance, then surprised when she told him that she'd be spending the night at Stony Brook. He accompanied her to the waiting room, wished her luck and asked her to keep him informed as to Mr Fogarty's condition. Then he said goodbye and walked as quickly from the hospital as his injured leg would allow.

The waiting room housed a cluster of green plastic chairs, pointed in the direction of a wall-mounted TV, which was tuned to the Jay Leno show. The sound had been switched off and Diane, alone in the room, watched a muted Jay interview a woman wearing a twenties style dress with her hair cropped short and gelled back. An actress, a singer? Diane couldn't place her and as the screen flickered above, she lowered her head and closed her eyes, surrendering to the negative thoughts that flowed from exhaustion. "What's going to become of us? What if he never gets well? What if he never gets out of here? What if he kills himself? What if . . . ?" She struggled against them but they kept coming, swamping her, each more depleting than the last until she was slumped forward in the chair, cradling her head with her hands. She didn't hear the rubber-soled footsteps until they were right on top of her.

"Mrs Genero?"

She looked up, worried that the thin, gray-haired nurse had come to tell her that she could no longer spend the night.

"Dr Parnelli said that you might be staying with us, so maybe you'd like these."

Diane accepted the pillow and blanket with only the glimmer of a smile. She was too tired to speak.

"If you want to stretch out, please, go ahead, I don't think you'll have much company in here tonight."

This time Diane managed a faint smile, placed her head on the pillow, pulled her feet up on to the adjoining chairs and wrapped the blanket around her legs, tucking it in tight to her body. She was asleep by the time the nurse left the room.

Minutes later she woke with a start and didn't know where she was. When she looked up Jay Leno was grinning like a jack-o'-lantern and the starlet with the gelled hair was convulsed with silent laughter. From somewhere she could hear the sound of the metal wheels of a food trolley against a hard floor and thought she smelled buttered popcorn. "Bill? Oh God, where's Bill?" Then the whole thing came back to her in one desperate, lonely rush. It was going to be a long night. She got up and walked towards the pay phone that she'd seen in the lobby.

The room was small, without windows and the walls and ceiling were a faded green. The floor had been covered with a soft rubber-covered mat and the single reinforced door had only an observation slot through which Dr Parnelli or one of his aides would look every half-hour or so. There were no sharp objects in the room, no lamps or tables, not even a bed.

Bill Fogarty lay on the floor, on his back, his feet close together and his arms stretched out to his sides. His mouth was wide open. When he breathed he made a low, whining sound, somewhere between a snore and a slow gasp for oxygen. Two hours earlier he had been stripped naked then placed in a gray-green gown with three ties in the back. The ties had come loose as they had carried him from the restraining room to the seclusion room and the gown was now open, covering him like a sheet.

He was lying still, floating on the surface of a dark abyss. Below him, beneath numbed layers of sensation, emotion, volition and thought, there were monsters, swimming and flying, crawling and writhing. The monsters wanted him, but, for the moment, he had been spared. The droperidol, like a thick liquid life preserver, had wrapped itself around his mind and prevented him from sinking.

Bill Fogarty could sleep, but he could not dream.

8

Josef Tanaka arrived at the medical building at eight thirty the following morning to begin one of the worst days of his life. He'd hardly slept following Diane Genero's midnight call. As soon as he'd finished with her, he'd called Dr Parnelli. The psychiatrist, having had two more visitors to the restraining room since Bill Fogarty, was tired and hesitant to talk but Tanaka had insisted and because of his professional credentials Parnelli had briefed him. He had reported Fogarty as delusional and said that his initial diagnosis was that the delusions were being caused by some form of stress disorder. However, Parnelli was adamant that he would not have a firm picture till he had stabilised Fogarty's mental condition enough to talk to him.

"I've got him on a fairly high dose of droperidol," the psychiatrist had explained.

"It seems to have settled him down."

"Yes, and turned him into a zombie," Tanaka thought. Through his involvement with police work, he knew a fair bit about the anti-psychotic drugs; he'd seen situations in which the 'liquid baton', as certain of them had been termed, had been the only alternative to a bullet. They were the nearest thing to embalming fluid, taking the fight out of even the most violent offenders, but having been raised on martial arts, acupuncture and herbal medicine, Tanaka had strong feelings against them.

His mind was preoccupied with his phone conversation with Parnelli as he walked up the stone steps and into the building.

"Dr Tanaka?"

He turned. The Chinese-American woman was new to her job at reception. Her name was Angela, or Annie, Tanaka wasn't sure.

"I have a message for you."

He walked to her desk and took the slip of yellow paper with 'Memo' stenciled at the top then glanced quickly at her name tag.

"Thank you, Angie," he said.

He didn't look at the message till he was inside his office.

"Please call Moyer. Urgent."

Tanaka wondered whether Bob had come up with something on the Maura Allan post mortem, something that may have initially slipped both their minds. That was the way the ex-ME was — persistent. Sooner or later he'd crack it.

As he dialed the number he wondered how he'd tell Bob about what was going on in Stony Brook. Moyer and Fogarty went back a long way. They'd worked their first cases together. The news was going to upset him.

A male voice answered, low and throaty and, for a moment, Tanaka wondered if he had misdialed.

"Hello, this is Josef Tanaka at the medical building; I've got an urgent message here to call Dr Moyer. May I speak to him, please?"

Silence. Then, "Hello, Josef, this is Steve Moyer. The message was from me."

"Sorry, I didn't recognise your voice. I thought you were up at State College. Is everything all right?"

"Dad died last night."

Now it was Tanaka who was silent.

"Just before midnight."

Josef sank back into his cushioned desk chair. He felt short of breath.

"How?" he asked.

"It was his heart."

"I'm so sorry," Tanaka said, but his words

seemed lost down the line.

"He thought the world of you, Josef." Suddenly the teenager sounded old and bedraggled.

"I thought the world of him, too."

"Yeah, well . . . "

"How's your mother?" Tanaka asked.

"She was with him when it happened. It must have been awful. She says his face turned blue."

"That's what a massive coronary does," Tanaka answered. "I'm sorry she had to see him like that."

"She's still pretty bad."

"I can imagine."

"It was just so unexpected," Moyer said.

"Steve, I'd like to come and see Norma. What do you think?"

"I think it would be good for her. I think it would be really good. We've got some family flying in over the weekend and my brother Andrew is on his way down from New York, but right now, it's just me and Mom in the house."

Josef looked at his wristwatch. He could delay the start of his scheduled autopsy for an hour.

"I can come over now. Why don't you go and ask her if that's OK? If she doesn't feel like seeing anyone, that's OK too."

"Hold on." Steve Moyer placed the phone down and Tanaka waited. He felt as if he had just lost his own father. Bob Moyer had meant that much to him. He recalled how Moyer had fought to get him hired, 'because I believe you've got talent, simple as that', then drilled him in practical technique, encouraged and corrected him, but, more than that, Moyer had stood by Tanaka during a period of great personal doubt, a time in which Josef had questioned his entire being, his relationship with Rachel, his choice of career, his loyalty to his Japanese family, and his decision to remain in America. The mixture of uncertainty and guilt had nearly broken him, but Bob Moyer had been there, helping and guiding. Bob Moyer, Bill Fogarty, and Josef Tanaka, they'd formed a strong triangle, been great friends, and now that triangle was broken. For ever.

"Josef?"

"Yes, Steve."

"Mom says she'd love to see you."

"I'm on my way now."

★ ★ ★

Norma had always been Tanaka's idea of a gypsy, or what a gypsy should look like. She had big brown eyes and long black hair that had been streaked with silver since she'd been thirty, and always wore dangling silver earrings. She also had a sharp mind and a wry sense of humor, which made the Moyer house a warm place to visit, a refuge from the medical building with its cold metal tables, surgical instruments and the smell of disinfectant that barely covered the smell of death.

Tanaka walked up the three steps that led to the small front porch, sensing a stillness inside the house that had never been there before. He looked at the entry buzzer and decided to knock.

Steve Moyer opened the door.

Josef remembered him as a chubby teenager with his father's red hair and freckles, more interested in spending his afternoons surfing the computer net than becoming the mathematical genius than Bob claimed his son could be if he 'applied' himself. Now he looked like a man, as tall as Josef, with angular features and a stubble of beard.

"Steve, you've lost weight," Josef said, forcing a smile.

Steve extended his hand and Tanaka shook it.

"I'm trying one of those diets you used to give Dad," he answered. "Mostly rice and water, it works well with my allowance at school."

Josef's smile became more relaxed. "Don't forget your protein," he replied, entering the house.

"Do you want something from the kitchen, orange juice or coffee?" Steve asked.

"No thanks."

"Mom'll be down in a minute. Here, please, sit down," Steve motioned towards the sofa. There were the faded remnants of a wine stain on the beige cotton covering. Tanaka remembered the night that Bob had spilled the Merlot, then tried quickly to wipe it off before Norma caught him. "Kill me, she'll kill me," he'd repeated, while making the stain worse.

Josef sat down on the sofa just as Norma Moyer entered the room. As she did, Steve walked to the kitchen, leaving them alone. Josef stood and faced her. They remained still a moment. Norma was dressed in a dark silk blouse, woollen slacks and low-heeled shoes. She was a small woman and when she finally crossed the room and entered Josef's open arms she seemed to have no weight at all.

"Thank you for coming," she said.

"I'm sorry, Norma."

"You never know, do you?"

160

He didn't answer as they sat down together on the sofa.

"I always thought I'd go first. Bob had such life in him. You just never know."

Josef watched the tears roll from her eyes. He felt his own welling and held them in check as he reached out and took her hand. "Norma, tell me what I can do for you."

"Just being here. That's enough," she replied. "Do you know that Bob thought of you as one of his sons?"

"That's how he made me feel."

"He was proud of you. I think he got more joy out of going to the medical building after he retired than he did when he ran the place. He loved to watch you work. He was talking about it last night."

Josef smiled.

"I think he was going to go and see you today," she said. "It was about some case you were working on. He said he had the answer."

Tanaka thought of Maura Allan. "Do you know what it was?" Tanaka asked without urgency.

She shook her head. "He hadn't talked to me about it but I knew he was working on something. It was like in the old days, he'd say, 'Let me sleep on it', then lie there awake for hours, thinking. He'd been

161

that way lately. Until last night. He was so exhausted he went right off . . . " she hesitated and her voice choked, "and never woke up." Her tears came in a rush. "I felt his whole body jump when it happened. I was right there beside him and there was nothing I could do. Nothing to help him. He was struggling to breathe, gasping, and he looked so frightened, like he knew he was dying and he was fighting it. I never thought of death as something ugly, but this was ugly."

Tanaka held her till she'd stopped sobbing. When he looked up Steve Moyer was standing in the doorway.

"You OK, Mom?" he said.

Norma nodded her head and found her composure.

"Yes. I think I need a little more time on my own. I'll just go back upstairs and sit a while in the bedroom. They only took him away this morning but I can still feel him in there, more than anywhere else in the house. I can still talk to him, as if he's lying in the bed, waiting for me to get in, just lying there, watching me put my hair back, asking why it takes me so damn long. I guess I still have a few things left to say to my husband." She looked at Josef. "I don't know if I'm making sense? I don't sound as if I am," she apologised.

162

"You're making perfect sense, Norma, believe me," Josef said, standing up. He helped her to her feet and kissed her goodbye, then waited for her to leave the room before turning to Steve.

"Is there anything I can do?"

Steve shook his head. "We'll be fine."

"I loved your dad."

"He loved you too."

Tanaka held Steve Moyer's eyes.

"Andy's on his way and I can keep an eye on Mom for now. Don't worry."

"I'm not worried," Josef said. "How about funeral arrangements?"

"Dad wanted to be cremated."

Josef nodded.

"We're going to have a memorial service on Monday. It's just going to be a family thing. I don't know if the city will want to do anything."

"I'm sure they will," Josef said.

"Well, the one on Monday is just for family and a few close friends. We'd like it if you and your wife could come."

"Of course we will."

"It's at six o'clock at Doherty's, just off Pine, on — "

"I know where it is."

"We'll see you then."

"Between now and Monday if you need

me for anything, you know, like to come to talk to your mother, anything like that, you can reach me on one of these."

Tanaka gave him his personal card; it contained his home phone number and the number of his answering service.

"I've got to be out of town for a little while, but my service always knows how to get a hold of me."

"Thanks."

"I don't have to give you the number at the medical building?" he asked, extending his hand.

Steve Moyer shook his hand and smiled. "No, I know that one by heart."

★ ★ ★

Josef, Rachel and William left for New York at seven o'clock in the evening, Josef at the wheel of the Jeep that had replaced Rachel's Mercedes after the birth of their son.

He caught a fleeting glimpse of his Harley, just a flash of black and chrome in the rear-view mirror as he turned to drive up the ramp and out of the underground park. Rachel had given him the bike as a birthday present two years ago. He hadn't been riding much lately and he missed it.

It wasn't just the pressure of his new

position as medical examiner that had caused him to slow down, it was William. With William's birth came a different understanding of his own mortality. Tanaka was just forty but William had made him stop and count the years he had left. Time was precious; it was everything. He wanted to see William grow up and become a man. He calculated that he'd be older that Bob Moyer by the time his son left college. "It can all end so quickly, so unexpectedly. Anytime. For any of us," he thought, looking across at Rachel and his son. It was a truth he'd learned to live with over the past years. Death. It was his business. He attended to it each day, observed and dissected it, calculated and measured it, cold and blue with glassy eyes and ridged fingers. He thought again of Bob Moyer. How many times had the two of them stood side by side above that metal table, surrounded by white walls and bathed in the unforgiving glow of fluorescent lights, staring down at another human? Not human, not exactly. A corpse was never really human, not until the corpse was someone you once loved.

"How are you doing?" Rachel asked, reaching out to touch his shoulder.

"Thinking about Bob," Tanaka replied.

"He wasn't old, was he?"

"Sixty."

"That's not old."

"No, and he was one of those people who didn't really have an age, he had an energy. His mind was so active."

Rachel hadn't known Moyer the way that Josef had but she had spent enough evenings in Bob and Norma's company to know that she liked him very much. He made her laugh, and he was an expert at making Tanaka see the light side of himself.

"I never knew he had heart trouble," she said.

"Neither did I," Tanaka answered.

"They're certain it was a coronary?"

"I don't know who the family doctor is, but Norma said that's what it was."

"No warning?"

"I don't know," Tanaka said. There was a finality to his tone and Rachel let the subject drop.

They got on the expressway at the 30th Street station entrance and entered a gridlock of traffic, commuters headed to the suburbs.

"We're going to be here a while," Tanaka said as the Jeep inched along.

"Relax, William's enjoying it."

Tanaka looked back to the car seat and saw that his son was fast asleep, his head

166

nestled against the big soft teddy that Bill Fogarty had given him during his visit. Billy's lips were pursed and he was making soft gurgling sounds.

"He's beautiful," Tanaka said.

Rachel smiled, soft and reassuring, ice-blue eyes framed by blond hair that had been pulled back and tied behind her head. That had been the first thing that Josef had noticed about her, almost ten years ago. She had been standing in the corridor of Jefferson hospital, turned away from him, long hair braided and falling down the back of her surgical gown. He'd nearly done a pirouette to get a look at her face.

"You're beautiful, too," he added.

★ ★ ★

They arrived at the hospital at ten o'clock and Diane was in the waiting room, preparing for a second night on the green chairs. She had napped restlessly during the day, eaten once in the cafeteria, surrounded by medical students and hospital personnel, and spoken again to Parnelli and one of his social workers, but she had received little information about Fogarty and had not been back behind the locked CPEP door. The Stony Brook staff had been kind to her, but her feelings of alienation were mounting as the hours passed. She was a stranger, alone and tolerated, but certainly an unnecessary part of the machine. Seventy-two hours, that was the state-allocated time during which they could hold Fogarty inside the unit. After that he would be either released or committed.

"Am I going to be able to take him home?" she had asked Parnelli.

"I don't know," he'd answered, but there had been a frank solemnity to his voice and expression. "These things can take time."

* * *

She looked up as Josef walked in. He seemed to shine in the dim light of the room, filling the dark space and reconnecting her to a happier, more secure place in her mind. Rachel followed behind, holding Billy in a baby carrier.

"I'd cry but I think I'm all cried out," Diane said. "I'm so glad to see you." Then she was on her feet, hugging Rachel and the child, before turning to Josef. "And I'm so scared."

"Well, don't be. Things are going to get better. I promise," he said, holding her tight.

"I keep hoping the doctor will come in and

168

tell me that Bill's getting well, that he'll be able to come home with me."

"I spoke to Dr Parnelli earlier," Josef replied, "and I know he wants to hold on to Bill for at least another twenty-four hours."

"Well I'm not leaving him alone here," Diane answered.

"We understand how you feel," Rachel said, "but nothing more is going to happen tonight, so why don't you let Josef take over for a while and you come with me and Billy. There's a hotel back up the road and we've booked two rooms. You'll only be a mile away and you can get a bed and a good night's sleep. Besides, I've brought some extra clothes; you can have a bath and wash your hair." She touched Diane on the shoulder. "Come on."

It was the idea of the bath that got to her. Hot and clean. Her body felt permanently kinked from the edges of the green chairs. A soapy bath would be heaven. She looked at Josef.

"We'll get this thing straightened out," he promised.

"OK," Diane said softly.

Josef watched them walk from the room, then went back into the reception area of the Triage and introduced himself to the

169

nurse in charge of admissions. She phoned through to CPEP and asked Josef to wait. A few minutes passed before the door opened and a small, black woman came out. She was dressed in a red, turtle-neck pullover, loose slacks and Reebok training shoes and walked quickly, eyeing the handful of people that occupied the reception area. With her short hair she bore a passing resemblance to Oprah Winfrey. She walked straight to Josef and extended her hand.

"You must be Dr Tanaka?"

"Yes."

"How's that for being psychic?" she asked. "Well, actually you're the only one left but me in civilian clothes. I'm Mary Carpenter. I'm a social worker and I understand that Mr Fogarty is a friend of yours."

"Yes, he is."

"Well, your friend's in good hands. Dr Parnelli is the best in the business. He's overworked but he's the best." Josef walked behind her to the door of CPEP. She unlocked it and led him to the small office.

"Please, sit down. Are you sure I can't get you anything?"

"Yes, I'm certain."

She glanced at her wristwatch. "The doctor shouldn't be much longer."

She was about to elaborate when there

was a loud quacking sound from one of the adjoining rooms. It sounded like a duck.

"Donald's back. He gets brought in about once month."

Again the quacking, this time louder.

"He used to work in the city, in advertising. One day he just started quacking. That was it."

"Quack. Quack."

Josef glanced in the direction of the noise.

"Don't worry, they'll sedate him and he'll shut up. Tomorrow afternoon he'll be out of here and back in Riverhead with his mother."

A long scream came from another section of the unit, dying in a series of groans.

She shrugged her shoulders. "You've got to see the lighter side of life in here, otherwise, it gets very depressing."

They both turned as Robert Parnelli entered the room. Mary leaped to attention.

"Dr Parnelli, this is Dr Tanaka."

Josef stood and they shook hands.

Parnelli had been working since ten o'clock in the morning and wanted nothing more than a large whiskey and his bed, but he had known Tanaka was coming and tomorrow was his day off. Also, he'd hoped to have some positive news about Bill Fogarty. The unit was full and he needed the space.

"I was just telling Dr Tanaka about Donald," Mary said.

"Thank you," Parnelli replied. His voice contained none of her humor or benign amusement.

Mary shifted nervously from Reebok to Reebok.

"I was just on my way home," she said.

"Fine."

"Do you need anything before I go, tea or coffee?"

Parnelli looked at Tanaka who shook his head.

"Not a thing. Thank you, Mary."

She said goodbye and left the room.

"Please sit down," Parnelli said.

Both men sat facing each other.

"How much do you know about Mr Fogarty's condition?"

"Not a lot," Tanaka replied. "The last time I saw him, which was about eight weeks ago, he seemed fine."

Parnelli nodded his head and scratched his chin with his hand. He had a stubble of beard, dark circles below his eyes, and his skin looked yellow beneath the overhead lights. "My best guess is that it's post traumatic stress disorder. I'm basing this on the information I received from Ms Genero, regarding the automobile accident that killed his wife and child, and also on the demands placed upon him by his work in the police department."

"Bill retired over a year ago; I don't think he's been doing much other than playing golf since then," Tanaka replied. He was a self-taught expert on stress disorders, Rachel had suffered one following her abduction during the Mantis case. Intellectually, Parnelli's diagnosis made sense but Tanaka's intuition was saying something else. He really needed to get to Bill.

"These things can come on years after the event which triggers them," Parnelli said.

"I know that," Tanaka answered. There was no edge to his voice, simply concern.

"I've managed to get him talking a couple of times in the past twenty-four hours," the psychiatrist explained, "but he's physically and mentally exhausted and his speech isn't always coherent, plus there's this anxiety about going to sleep."

"I don't follow you."

"Mr Fogarty is petrified of dreaming."

Tanaka shook his head.

"According to Ms Genero, whatever is disturbing him first manifested itself in a dream. I believe in the form of a bird."

There was a muted quack from behind the wall and Parnelli turned a second, listened, then returned to Tanaka. There was a trace of irony on his lips.

"One thing for certain is that Mr Fogarty is delusional."

"How about the anti-psychotics?"

"They settle him down, but they interfere with the sleep pattern; there's no REM phase, so while he's not dreaming, he's also not physically or mentally recovering."

"Would it be possible for me to see him?"

Parnelli had anticipated the request. He nodded his head. "I'm going to have to be there with you."

"I would prefer to be alone with him."

"I can't do that."

"Bill and I go back a long way, he trusts me, he may open up."

"I understand but I can't allow it. Mr Fogarty has been aggressive and I want to have some medication available."

Parnelli read the resistance in Tanaka's eyes.

"I'm sorry but it's hospital policy."

Tanaka nodded his head. "I understand."

★ ★ ★

The door clicked and locked. Parnelli remained behind Tanaka, a psychiatric aide

174

at his side. The aide was a short stocky man with butcher's hands, a shaved head, and a earlobe that had once been adorned with a gold ring but was now bare and divided cleanly in half as a result of an attack by a former patient.

Bill Fogarty sat on the floor of the square room with his back propped against the wall. He was unshaven and the thin gown barely covered his body. He was looking straight ahead, but his eyes were not focused and the lids drooped giving them a heavy, hooded appearance. He looked old and defeated.

"How are you doing, Bill?" Tanaka asked, walking towards him, attempting to keep a professional handle on his feelings while, inside, his sense of sorrow was tremendous.

"Bill?" Tanaka repeated.

Fogarty looked at Tanaka, his eyes blank. He experienced a sense of something familiar, but the sensation was distant.

Tanaka turned back to Parnelli.

"When was his last medication?"

"About six hours ago."

"How much did you give him?" He tried to keep the accusation out of his voice but he had begun to feel angry.

"Ten mils. It shouldn't be affecting him now, at least not like this."

Parnelli walked forward and joined Tanaka.

"Bill?" Josef gripped Fogarty's shoulder.

This time the voice was more assertive, demanding entrance. "Bill. Can you hear me?"

Tanaka shook him. "It's me, Josef."

Tanaka thought he observed a flicker in Fogarty's eyes.

"Josef?" Fogarty repeated the name, and with it a cascade of feeling threatened the walls that protected him.

"Josef Tanaka."

The words triggered a sensation of warmth and trust and the feeling dragged him back from the barren void. Yet, even then, in the world of form and flesh Fogarty was mistrusting, as if, perhaps, the man he saw in front of him was an illusion, no more or less real than the great bird had been. His eyes focused. "Josef, Josef. What are you doing here?"

"I came to see you," Tanaka answered, maintaining his grip on Fogarty's shoulder. He had the feeling that if he let go Fogarty would slip away from him.

Fogarty laughed, but the laugh ended abruptly.

"Is this a dream?"

"No, it's not a dream," Tanaka replied.

"I don't believe that."

Tanaka squeezed harder.

"Hey, that hurts," Fogarty winced.

"You're in a state hospital, Bill. You were brought here yesterday. Diane called me last night. The man beside me is Dr Parnelli; he's looking after you."

Fogarty looked at Parnelli then back at Tanaka. It took him a while to assemble the pieces. Finally he spoke. "I remember some of it, but not everything. I'm all confused up here." He touched his fingertips to his forehead, then stared at Tanaka. "Josef, let me ask you something."

"Go ahead."

"Do you believe that dreams could be like doors in your mind? I mean do you think it's possible that something could come through a dream, something tangible, something you could touch. Something that could touch you?"

Tanaka studied Fogarty's eyes and shook his head. "No, I don't think that's possible."

"Well, Josef, that's what happened to me."

"Maybe we should talk about it," Tanaka replied.

Fogarty looked at Parnelli. "It's private."

Tanaka turned. "Do you mind if I speak to him alone, just for a minute?"

Parnelli nodded and backed off, joining his aide against the far wall.

177

"Okay, Bill, tell me about it."

Fogarty looked hesitant. He felt like retreating to the other place, the darker place, the place where he could hide.

"We don't have long, Bill," Tanaka urged.

"It's a bird. It comes from a dream, flies right through my head and out my eyes. Starts inside and ends up in front of me. I can't stop it. If I relax for a second it's there," Fogarty said. "I mean it's more than a bird. That's just the shape it takes. The shape the energy takes. It's an energy. It's not mine. It's not my dream. Do you follow me? I don't know if you follow me." His effort to communicate was becoming frustrating. When he spoke again, his voice was low so as not to be overheard. "He's going to kill me, Josef." After that, he pushed himself further back against the wall, as if to distance himself from his own words. "He's going to kill me." He turned his head toward Parnelli and raised his voice. "You think I'm crazy, don't you?"

Parnelli remained silent.

"I thought you said it was a bird, Bill?" Tanaka answered, trying to hold his attention.

"I'm telling you the truth and you think I'm crazy," Fogarty insisted, staring at Parnelli and becoming agitated. "You think I'm the

178

kind of guy who sees things? Listen, I was a cop, I saw all kinds of things when I was a cop. Joey will tell you." Then, back to Tanaka, his voice hush. "Son of a bitch thinks I'm hallucinating. Let me tell you something, this hallucination has got claws. He'll tear your eyes out." His voice got louder. "Damn thing comes at me from inside a dream, and I'll tell you something else. It's as real as what's happening now. What's that mean? What's that say? Are we all dreaming?" He stopped talking and turned back to Tanaka. "You got to get me out of this place."

"I'll do everything I can," Tanaka answered. He thought he heard Parnelli sigh in the background.

"Then help me. I don't want my mind to slip any more. I want to stay in this dream, where we all agree what's what. I want to go home with Diane, to the house on the bay. I want to wake up there."

"I understand that, Bill, but we've got to straighten a few things out first."

Fogarty's body tensed as his eyes hardened. "Like what? Parkinson?"

"Parkinson?" Tanaka repeated. He had no idea what 'Parkinson' meant.

"It was a mistake. I tried to tell'm what I saw. They said it was the drugs. Said I was hallucinating. A man can't fucking do that. It couldn't have been a man. It was a bad dream, very bad. You watch out for that little bastard."

"Who? Parkinson?" Tanaka wanted to pursue it but Fogarty's laugh cut the connection. The sound was hard and his teeth were clenched; it was more a growl than a laugh.

"He'll tear your eyes out."

"Who?"

"Bob knows. He picked up the pieces. Bob Moyer knows."

"Bob Moyer," Tanaka thought. "All he needs now is to find out that Bob's dead. That would finish him."

Fogarty lowered his head and shook it slowly. When he stopped and looked up again his eyes appeared very clear and very blue. "I've lost control of my dreams, that's all. That's what the fucking bird's about. Do you understand me? It's somebody else's dream. Am I making sense?"

"I'm with you, Bill."

"Good, good," Fogarty said, relieved. Tanaka's presence was calming and reassuring. "Come on, Josef, sit down here beside me."

Tanaka sat next to Fogarty against the wall.

"Don't think it's strange if I lean my head

against your shoulder," Fogarty said.

"Go ahead," Tanaka replied, smiling.

Fogarty let his head roll to the side, touching the corduroy of Tanaka's jacket.

"Oh yeah, nothing going to happen to me now. You could kick anybody's ass." He sounded like a kid talking to his father. "I'm just so tired. Never knew I could get so tired."

"You go to sleep, Bill."

"You're not leaving me?"

"I'm right here."

"That's good to know."

He was snoring within seconds. Tanaka looked up at Parnelli and nodded his head, then he moved carefully away from Fogarty, leaving him asleep against the wall.

"Sounds like acute paranoia," Parnelli said softly as the three men walked quietly from the room.

They were just outside the door when Fogarty awakened with a loud gut-wrenching shout. Tanaka turned to see him flailing with his hands, his eyes wide open.

"Goddamn thing! Go away!"

"Chucky!" Parnelli shouted for his aide as he pushed the door open. Tanaka ran to Fogarty's side and knelt over him.

Fogarty grabbed hold of Tanaka's collar and pulled him down. "It's broken through.

Right there. Above your head." Fogarty stared past Tanaka and towards the ceiling.

Tanaka held him down and looked up, following the line of Fogarty's eyes. For a second he thought he saw a shadow, as if the air had darkened above him and he felt a coldness and a weight. It was all very quick, a fleeting perception, then the psychiatric aide was beside him, helping to restrain Fogarty while Parnelli uncapped his syringe.

"Am I dreaming? Am I dreaming now?"

"No," Tanaka answered.

"Then how come it's here?" Fogarty asked. The droperidol slowed his speech.

"Bill, there's nothing here. You're safe."

"Safe," he repeated then laughed as if he were drunk. "Maybe you ought to wake up. Maybe I'm awake and you're asleep. Maybe I just crossed the big divide." He stared hard at Tanaka. "Have I been a bad guy?"

"No, Bill, you haven't been a bad guy," Tanaka answered.

After that Fogarty's voice slurred and the words ran into one long unintelligible sentence as he sank into the blackness.

"You know more about his past than I do," Parnelli said as they walked from the room. "Is there something that I'm missing?"

Tanaka stopped and watched as the aide

secured the lock on Fogarty's door. Then he turned to Parnelli.

"I don't know. I'd need more time with him. I'm sorry you had to sedate him so quickly."

Parnelli read the disapproval in Tanaka's tone.

"That's the way I work, Doctor. I'm a biological psychiatrist, I use drugs. In this case I thought my patient was in danger of doing harm to himself," Parnelli replied.

"I appreciate that," Tanaka answered, his voice mellowing. They were both tired and he knew it. "I also appreciate you letting me come in here to see him."

The two men shook hands and Parnelli led Tanaka to the CPEP door. "I'm not here tomorrow, but if you call and ask for Mary, she'll tell you how Mr Fogarty is," he said.

Tanaka shook the psychiatrist's hand a final time and walked out. He felt frustrated. As if something was going on that he should have had an answer to, that he should have known about. Something that he should have grasped. Tanaka had studied with many martial arts masters, some of whom had gone far beyond the physical in their training. The concept of reality being akin to a dream, no more than a projection of the mind and ego was not new to him. He had heard it explained many times. "Insanity is the brink of enlightenment." He had heard that too. Fogarty had said things that had triggered questions.

9

Saturday began with Billy waking at six o'clock to stick his finger in his daddy's ear, rousing him from a dream. Bill Fogarty had been in Josef's dream, though he'd looked very much older, his body stooped and his face deeply etched with lines. They had been sitting together by the edge of a stream, surrounded by mountains with the sun peaking through a shroud of trees.

"I'm waiting for mine," Fogarty had said, his head bowed over the water. "You see."

Tanaka looked. There were human bodies in the stream. At first he hadn't seen them because they were floating beneath the surface of the water, propelled by the current, their naked flesh shining and smooth. As he'd stared he'd recognised Bob Moyer and Maura Allan, but there were others and he'd had the feeling that he should know all of these people, or remember them, but as he'd leaned closer he could only see his own face in reflection.

"It's almost time," Fogarty said, his voice weary.

One body was different from the rest, because it was moving, arms and legs flapping like a fish struggling on dry land.

"Help me, Josef, I can't let go."

Tanaka sensed that the body belonged to Fogarty but he could not see him clearly because of his own reflection. Then he realised that he did not want to see him. It was important that he did not. If he did something was going to happen, something bad and irrevocable. Yet he continued to stare, on the point of recognition. Until the tickle inside his ear.

"Billy, leave your father alone," Rachel said softly.

Tanaka awakened with the colors and images from the dream fresh in his mind.

"Stop it," Rachel continued, pulling the small hand down from Tanaka's ear and drawing the child's body closer to her own.

"Your daddy's still asleep."

Tanaka remained silent, his back to Rachel and Billy and his face to the window; he closed his eyes and replayed the dream many times, searching for its significance.

"Was Bill asking me to help him die? Is that why I didn't want to recognise the body? Who were the others?" He stayed that way until he could sense the sun's early light through his closed lids and feel the chill of the morning against his cheeks. Below the covers it was warm from the heat of their bodies, with Billy nestled between them and Rachel's feet touching the back of his calves. The dream retreated, leaving a lonely foreboding.

"Rachel?"

"Yes?" Her voice was soft from sleep.

"You know what I'd like to do if Billy wasn't here?"

"So would I."

"Tonight then?"

"You betcha."

It wasn't sex that he desired, not hard fucking, but a closeness to life. He needed to take the warmth from beneath the covers and spread it through his body, letting it circulate like the blood in his veins.

★ ★ ★

It was a crisp sunny day by the time they'd entered East Hampton. The temperature was in the low fifties and most of the leaves were still on the trees, their colors a golden

186

patchwork, dancing in the morning breeze. Diane instructed Tanaka to take the left turn before the windmill at the east end of the village and to follow the road till it forked, continuing the five miles up Springs Fireplace Road, before turning right on to Gerard Drive. Then they drove across the peninsula that divided the white caps of Gardiner's Bay from the calmer waters of Accabonic Harbor.

"This is beautiful," Rachel said. She was sitting in the back of the Jeep with Billy sleeping beside her in his car seat.

"Yes, we loved it here," Diane replied.

"And you will again," Rachel answered. "This thing with Bill is temporary. I know, trust me."

"I want to believe that."

"Believe it."

Josef remained silent. He had called the hospital before they'd left Stony Brook and found that Bill had required more sedation. On top of that, Mary Carpenter had told him that Fogarty was slated for the Tower. He was being committed. Tanaka had not passed this information on, neither to Rachel nor to Diane, and now, as they drove through paradise, it weighed heavily upon him.

"That's it, there," Diane said as the secluded gravel drive came into view.

Tanaka turned on to the gravel and drove to the house. It sat before them like a sculpture in wood and glass, surrounded by evergreens.

"Bill loves it here," Diane said as he parked. "I think he was actually finding some real peace of mind before all this happened."

★ ★ ★

Later in the day, Tanaka left Rachel, Billy, and Diane alone in the house and walked to Gerard point where he sat down in the sand, facing the open bay. To the west, the sun had begun its descent, leaving a sparkling trail along the water.

There was a chill in the air and he had borrowed one of Bill's jackets. It was suede with a thick lining and Tanaka pulled the collar up tight around his neck as he sat, trying to imagine Bill Fogarty here, in this place, or out on the bay, paddling the small boat that he'd seen in the garage of the house. 'Peace of mind.' What was it? Was it the price of self-knowledge, the state achieved when all pretense was dropped, all desire and ambition quelled, the past reconciled and the present accepted? No more striving, no more guilt. 'Peace of mind.' What was the price?

188

Tanaka looked out on to the water and thought of his friend, locked inside that room with the faded green walls, chemicals inhibiting his mind and deadening his body. What path had led him from this paradise to that hell? What had Fogarty found in his search for 'peace of mind', what part of him had he exhumed? Who was Parkinson? He heard a splashing sound and looked to see a fish jump, then watched it fall, breaking the surface of the water, its body white and shining. The flash of its flesh against the blue triggered the memory of his dream, the details still clear in his mind as was the feeling of loneliness and foreboding; it was as if he had been peering through a window between the world of the living and the world of the dead. Bob Moyer had been on the other side of that window and Bill Fogarty somewhere in between, wretched and tired, a part of him wanting to give up, to let go and drown, while the other, greater part, the part of him that remained the fighter, resisted and suffered the torture of its resistance. The colors in Josef's dream had been vivid, as vivid as the sand and water that shimmered in the light of the setting sun. What had it tried to tell him? What voice was speaking to him through his dream?

"He is petrified of dreaming," Parnelli

had said when explaining his condition. The psychiatrist, in a typically Western approach, had suggested that Fogarty's dreams embodied his guilt, his fears and his anxieties. Tanaka felt this neglected the spirit and soul. Shinto, the old religion of Japan, held purification as its zenith and 'magokura', which translated as a 'bright, pure heart', was the essential requirement for the communion between man and his spiritual nature, a communion often found in dreams. Tanaka wondered if his friend was experiencing a breakdown in this connection, a result of some psychological wedge that had been driven between his mind and his spirit, a fear which blocked his heart and darkened his perception. But what had brought it on, where was the catalyst?

Why did he refer to the bird as a 'he', why give it a gender? And Bob Moyer? Fogarty had said that Bob had picked up the pieces. Pieces of what?

A cold gust of wind blew across the bay and Tanaka drew the collar of Fogarty's jacket higher against his face. He could almost feel his friend beside him, hear his low, gruff voice and his throaty laugh.

"What's going on with you, Bill?" he asked out loud.

A bird flew above his head, casting a

shadow on the sand. It was a big bird, a hawk or a gull, hard to tell because of the way its wings were back-lit against the sun. The bird circled, searching the ground below. Tanaka got to his feet and began to walk in the direction of the house. He glanced again towards the sky and the bird was still there, almost directly above him and, for a moment, Tanaka re-experienced the feeling of deadness that he'd felt in the seclusion room at Stony Brook, the cold weight that seemed to hang in the air above Fogarty's head. He walked another few paces and looked again. The bird was gone.

10

They arrived at Doherty's Funeral Home at 10.45 on Monday morning. There were about thirty people already seated in the main room, family and immediate friends, and Tanaka recognised many of them. He and Rachel walked to the last row of chairs and sat quietly, waiting for the service to begin. It lasted a little over half an hour and afterwards Tanaka and Rachel joined a smaller group that gathered at the Moyer house. They had been there only a few minutes when Phillip Harrison entered. He was dressed in a suit that was too tight in the chest and shoulders and his black engineer boots with their brass buckles looked bulky and out of place beneath the cuffs of his trousers. He hovered nervously in the doorway, then, seeing Norma, walked to her and kissed her awkwardly on the cheek.

Tanaka had met Harrison on several occasions and knew that he'd been a concern to his uncle, and that Bob had pulled strings to get him the prison job that he now had. "The kid's had it hard with that right-wing fascist for a father," Moyer had said. "He's a sensitive boy."

Tanaka watched as he and Norma spoke a few more seconds, then Norma excused herself and walked to another cluster of people, leaving Harrison alone with a cup of coffee in his hand. He looked across the room, eyes searching until they settled on Josef, then he nodded and manufactured a pinched smile.

"Are you all right if I leave you alone for a few minutes?" Tanaka asked Rachel. "Bob's nephew is here and he looks like he could use somebody to talk to."

"Sure, I'm fine," Rachel answered.

Tanaka stood up from the sofa and walked over to Phillip, saying hello to Steve and Andrew Moyer along the way. Harrison's hand was moist and trembling as he shook it.

"Have you seen Stan Leibowitz?" he asked.

It was a strange opening question considering the circumstances.

"I saw him earlier, at the service," Tanaka answered.

"You think he'll be coming?" Harrison was looking past Tanaka and at the front door of the house.

"I don't know."

"I couldn't make the service."

"That's OK, you're here now," Tanaka replied.

"It's not OK. Nothing is OK. I need to speak to Stan."

Up close, Phillip Harrison did not look well, his eyes were puffy, his lips dry and cracked and there was a nervous, edgy quality to his voice and manner.

"He may still come," Tanaka replied, keeping his voice easy.

"Yeah."

"Do you want to talk to me about anything?" Tanaka asked.

"I need Stan."

"Maybe we should try to phone him."

Harrison straightened. "No, this is my problem."

"OK," Josef answered, turning to walk away.

Harrison reached out and touched the shoulder of Tanaka's jacket and Tanaka turned back towards him. "I'm sorry, Josef. I sound like a real asshole and I don't mean to, it's just that Uncle Rob . . . " He hesitated as his eyes welled.

"Your uncle meant a lot to me too," Tanaka said softly.

Phillip stared at Josef. "Yeah, but you didn't kill him."

Tanaka looked into Harrison's eyes.

"I'm sorry, Josef," Harrison said, turning. "I've got to get out of here."

Tanaka followed Harrison to the front door. "Phillip?"

Harrison turned.

"What did you mean by that?"

Harrison shook his head and lowered his eyes and Tanaka sensed it was not the time to push.

"You sure you don't want to talk?" he asked gently.

"You're a doctor, Josef, but you're the wrong kind of doctor," Harrison answered before turning and leaving the house.

★ ★ ★

Later, from the medical building, Tanaka phoned Stan Leibowitz. The doctor was in the middle of a session so Tanaka arranged, through his secretary, to meet him at his office at six o'clock.

He found Leibowitz at his desk, wearing the same dark suit that he'd had on at the service but with the sleeves pushed halfway up his muscular forearms and minus his tie. He was reading *Perfect Health*, a mind-body guide by the Indian medical doctor and spiritual healer, Deepak Chopra.

"If more people read this, I'd be out of a job," he said. "Mind and body, most people don't understand the partnership."

Leibowitz, himself, was very disciplined in terms of physical training and his vitality glowed through the ruddy skin of his face.

Tanaka smiled as the psychiatrist placed the book down, walked from behind his desk and embraced him.

"It's been a sad day," Leibowitz said.

"Yes," Tanaka agreed, knowing he was about to make it sadder. They shared a few seconds of silence before Stan spoke again.

"I expected to see Bill there; he must have known about it."

"No, he doesn't," Tanaka answered.

"Hasn't anybody tried to reach him?"

Tanaka hesitated briefly. "I was with him this weekend."

Leibowitz looked puzzled.

"Bill's in a psychiatric unit in New York. He's been committed."

"What?" Liebowitz sounded stunned.

"That's why I'm here, Stan, I need your advice. Actually, I need more than your advice, I need your ideas on what's wrong with him."

"Anything, just name it."

Stan went back behind his desk and Josef took the high-backed leather chair in front of him. He went over the history of Fogarty's condition as it had been told to him by Diane Genero and Robert Parnelli. Stan listened and nodded his head.

"Yeah, it all sounds reasonable, if Bill had been brought to me and I was in Parnelli's position I'd have put it together the same way and come up with same stress disorder diagnosis and, probably, if he was delusional and I was processing a dozen street cases a day I would have rammed him with Haldol or some other anti-psychotic, just to get him out of my hair. The difference is, Josef, I do know Bill."

"Yes, so do I," Tanaka said, "and this

doesn't make sense."

Stan leaned back in his chair. "Look, I feel as helpless as you do. I love Bill Fogarty, but I just don't know what I can do to help. I've got no jurisdiction in New York and I don't know anybody at Stony Brook. Maybe this Dr Parnelli will talk to me and maybe he won't. He sure as hell isn't under any obligation."

Tanaka put his hands together and lowered his head. He felt about as near to beat as he could remember.

"Yeah, it's a son of a bitch, isn't it?" Stan said.

"There's more to it," Tanaka replied, looking up again. "I can feel it in my gut but I can't get it together in my head. I wish I had a transcript of everything that Bill said. I'm sure I've left stuff out."

"Well, you know where I am if you want to talk, and in the meantime I'll call Stony Brook and see what I can find. If I get anything I'll phone you at home, I promise," Leibowitz said, his voice softening. "I know how you feel. The hardest part is having him so far away."

"I guess that's it," Tanaka agreed, standing up from the chair. "Thanks, Stan. Thanks for your time."

"Come on, Bill's my friend too. We go

back a long way," Leibowitz answered as they shook hands.

Tanaka walked to the door and hesitated. "By the way, earlier, at Bob's house, I ran into Phillip Harrison. Did he manage to get to you?"

"He phoned from work this afternoon," Stan replied.

"Is he OK?"

"I'm going to see him in the morning, first thing. He's very upset about Bob."

"Yes, well like you said, it's been a sad day," Tanaka replied as he left the office.

★ ★ ★

Phillip Harrison walked passed Justin Gabriel's cell. He could see him in the periphery of his vision and he thought that he could feel the warm weight of Gabriel's eyes, but he refused to acknowledge him.

"Hello, Phillip, don't you want to stop and chat?"

Harrison ignored the soft voice and kept walking, listening instead to the cleats of his boot heels as they marked cadence along the cement walkway. He was terrified of Justin Gabriel, but his hatred outweighed his terror. He felt as if he had been raped and used by the little man. It was a feeling that ate

198

into him and demanded a resolve. Harrison had never actually killed a man in combat, not one that he could see, anyway. Maybe one of the rounds from his assault rifle had found a distant mark across the enemy line, but, to his knowledge, he'd never had a kill. A combat soldier without a kill. What would his father have to say about that? It didn't really matter because he'd soon put it right. Justin Gabriel would be his first.

★ ★ ★

Instead of going home, Tanaka drove back to the medical building. It was a little past seven o'clock and the place was quiet. He walked to his office and closed his door. He wanted time to think but a swirl of emotion clouded his clarity; it hurt to see Bill Fogarty beaten. It was as if a part of Tanaka was lying helpless in that padded room; that's how strong their connection had been. There had also been a reversal of roles. He'd seen his father beaten once, by the death of his older brother, Hiro, and it had been the same way. He'd wanted to reach out and by his touch, or his presence, heal the pain, the child playing father to the man, but there had been a barrier then as there was now, something buried and hidden and he'd felt impotent in the face of it. He pushed the feeling away, along with his sense of sadness. This was another case, another body on the table; it had to be. There were clues. There were always clues. He'd learned that from Bob Moyer, and from Bill Fogarty. There was always something, a reason, a way to break through the barrier. He picked up a pencil and began to write on a yellow legal pad. 'Bill Fogarty. Stony Brook. Bob Moyer knew. Knew what? What killed Maura Allan. No. Maura Allan's history. A heart attack killed Maura Allan. Maura Allan. Forget Maura Allan. Bob knew. Bob picked up the pieces. Pieces of what? Parkinson. Pieces of Parkinson? What the fuck is Parkinson? Who is Parkinson?' That was something he'd forgotten to mention to Stan Leibowitz. 'Parkinson.' Tanaka placed the pencil down and picked up his phone. He dialed the Long Island number. By the fourth ring he expected the answering machine to pick up. On the fifth it did. He almost slammed it down in frustration. He wanted an answer not a voice on a machine.

"Diane, this is Josef. Could you please call me — "

"I'm here," Diane Genero replied. "Hold on, let me turn this damned thing off." The phone clicked. "Josef?"

"Yes."

"I'm sorry, I was drying my hair."

"How are you feeling?"

"Wrecked," she replied, but there was no self pity in her voice.

"Well that's understandable."

"I guess so."

There was hesitation and she hoped that he was going to offer something positive. Maybe something had changed in the six hours since she'd spoken to the people at the hospital. After all, Josef was a doctor. They'd tell him things they wouldn't tell her.

"Diane, I'm trying to put this thing together. You know, look for reasons, a cause. Parnelli's talking about a stress disorder and I've been sitting here in my office trying to recall everything that Bill said to me when I last saw him. There must be something, some kind of catalyst to his condition."

"You mean nothing's changed?"

"No, not that I know of." He felt as if he was letting her down.

"Well, I'll help you in any way that I can but I doubt that I know anything you don't," she answered.

"There's only one thing for the moment. When I was with him he used the word 'Parkinson' a couple of times. I mean I think it was 'Parkinson'. They had him pretty well sedated but when he said it there seemed to be a lot of emotion attached. Anyway it's been bothering me."

"I believe he was a police officer," Diane replied.

"Who, Parkinson?"

"Yes, maybe he worked with Bill. Before they took him to the hospital, when he was all confused he mentioned somebody by the name of Mac Parkinson. I'd never heard of him before and the name stuck in my head; I think Bill said he was his commanding officer, or senior officer, or something like that. He kept asking for him. Saying, 'Mac? Where's Mac?' Nothing else made much sense but I definitely remember the name."

"That's terrific," Tanaka answered. "Who knows, we may have hit on something. Let me follow it up. In the meantime I'll keep talking to Dr Parnelli and if I get anything new I'll call you right away."

"I'll do the same," Diane replied. She was learning why Bill trusted Tanaka; there was something about him, even in his voice, that gave her a sense of confidence.

"Get some rest, Diane. We're thinking of you."

"Thank you, Josef. Give my love to Rachel. Bye."

The Roundhouse, when viewed from the air, resembles a pair of police regulation handcuffs. It's a massive gray stone structure, two circles joined by an interconnecting lobby, and takes up the corner of Eighth Street and Race. It is Philadelphia's oldest precinct building.

Police Commissioner Dan McMullon was sitting at his desk on the third floor, directly in front of Henry O'Reilly. The overweight commissioner and the lanky captain, both in their middle fifties, had known each other for many years and although their conversation had begun with a current but not particularly pressing investigation it had digressed to a personal discussion concerning the rejuvenating properties of an over-the-counter wonder pill that reputedly mixed the anti-aging hormones melatonin and DHEA in one glorious concoction.

"I've been taking the shit for about a month and something's definitely happening," O'Reilly said, using a confidential tone that had been refined by luring confessions from murder suspects. "This morning I woke up with a flagpole. First time since I can remember. Pity that Barbara was off visiting her mother in New York; I'd have liked to have had somebody there to verify it."

McMullon laughed just as his bleeper went off. He checked the display and recognised Tanaka's number at the medical building. They weren't working on anything together and he wondered what the doctor wanted.

"Let me use your phone, Hank," he said, reaching across the desk.

Tanaka picked up on the first ring. He knew that McMullon and Fogarty had never been friends and he wanted to avoid any unnecessary discussion. "Thanks for returning my call, Dan," he said.

"No problem. What can I do for you?"

"I need to know something, just a bit of trivia."

McMullon sat a little straighter. Tanaka was not a trivia kind of guy. "Sure. What is it?"

"Have you got a man working in homicide by the name of Parkinson?"

"No, I don't."

"Max, or Mac?"

McMullon tightened up. Sure he knew. He was supposed to have been on the Gabriel bust with Parkinson but Bill Fogarty had gone instead, police politics. "Mac Parkinson?"

"Yes, that's it," Tanaka answered.

"You're a little out of date. Like about twenty-five years."

"I don't follow you."

"Mac Parkinson hasn't been here since the early seventies."

"Do you know where I can find him?"

"In a cemetery in Paoli. He's dead. What do you want to know about Mac Parkinson for?"

Tanaka had anticipated the question. "I was tidying up some of Bob's old paperwork, just trying to get his files in some kind of order, and the name's come up a few times, along with Bill Fogarty's, and I got curious. You know how I am. I think it's called anal retentive."

McMullon made a sound like an aborted laugh. It was an incident that he didn't feel comfortable talking about. Like a bad omen. If Tanaka dug deep enough he'd probably find the autopsy reports but McMullon wasn't inclined to help. "Yeah, well they were partners for a little while, but like I said it was a long time ago."

"Thanks, Dan, I'll just put all this old stuff to bed and forget it."

"Good idea. How's Bill?" McMullon hadn't seen him at the funeral and felt obliged to ask.

"His back's bothering him again. I keep telling him he's got to consider having the lower lumbar fused but he doesn't want

205

to know about surgery. As soon as he's walking he'll be down to pay his respects to Norma."

McMullen remembered Fogarty's back trouble. The car accident that had caused it, killing his wife and child, and the boozing that had followed. He'd once testified against Fogarty to Internal Affairs, claiming he was a liability to the police department. That was something else he didn't want to talk about. "Say hello to him and wish him better."

"I'll do that," Tanaka replied.

"Good."

"Thanks, Dan, sorry to have troubled you."

★ ★ ★

At eight o'clock the next morning Josef Tanaka walked into the Roundhouse and took the elevator to the first floor. The doctor was well known in the precinct building and no one in the records department found it particularly unusual when he asked to use one of the computers to reference some old case reports in order to put his files in order.

He punched in Parkinson, M. and the microfiche delivered a date and case number, naming MacArthur D. Parkinson as the

206

complainant. Tanaka copied the number, thanked the officer in charge and left the building.

His next stop was Broad Street, at the police storage facility. He knew the officer there, explained what he was doing and presented her with the case number. Ten minutes later she brought him three cardboard boxes.

"Sorry, Dr Tanaka, but your number was cross-referenced with another file. I dug them both out for you, thought it might save you some time."

Tanaka thanked her and carried the boxes to a metal table in the adjoining room and sat down on a folding chair. He opened the box marked Parkinson, 1972113a. There was a manilla envelope inside. He slipped it out and opened it, expecting to find a set of scene-of-crime photographs and an incident report. Instead there was a single document citing the case number, the complainant, Parkinson, the location of the crime and naming Justin Seers Gabriel as the suspect under investigation and detective William T. Fogarty as the sole witness. There was an official seal stamped on the yellowed paper: 'Investigation Referred to Internal Affairs'.

Tanaka cursed under his breath. 'Internal Affairs.' The paperwork may as well have been locked in a vault in Fort Knox. He wrote the name 'Justin Seers Gabriel' in his book and placed the document back in its envelope and into the box.

The files marked 'Gabriel, J.S.' were full. The crime stills showed a man, a woman and two children, their bodies positioned on their backs, the woman's head at the man's feet with one child laid horizontally to either side, arms tucked neatly to their bodies, the entire configuration resembling a human crucifix. They had all been gutted, opened from neck to navel, breastbones and ribs broken inwards to expose their internal organs, and their hearts had been torn from their cradles. All naked, with the exception of the man; he was wearing a clerical collar.

Again the suspect in the investigation was Justin Seers Gabriel and the investigating officers were listed as MacArthur D. Parkinson and William T. Fogarty.

Tanaka pored over the report, jotting down the names of the victims, and noting that Bob Moyer had been the medical examiner at the crime scene. After that he opened the last box. It was loaded with surveillance reports, notes regarding Dr Justin Seers Gabriel and his Church of Human Consciousness, and photographs of his 'Angels' as they were termed within the report. One of the names caught Tanaka's attention. 'Maura Rich.' It was the first name that interested him. The name was unusual and he had a feeling, a hunch. He went back through the stack of black and white photographs, showing various members of Gabriel's Church entering and leaving a three-story building on Arch Street. Yes, there she was. 'M. Rich.' The dark-haired woman appeared in several of the photographs. Younger by many years, but the body type and bone structure were similar and in one shot, in which she was wearing her hair pulled back, Tanaka could see the mole in the center of her forehead. 'Maura Rich. Maura Allan.' Bob Moyer had said that he'd known her, and Bill had mentioned Bob Moyer in his ramblings. 'Bob Moyer knew. He picked up the pieces.' Tanaka thought of the mutilated bodies and believed he understood what Bill had meant by 'pieces'.

★ ★ ★

Robert Parnelli did not see an alternative. There was a limit to everything, and he had just hit his limit with Bill Fogarty. The man was not responding to the droperidol and in his delusional state he posed a threat not only to himself but to the other inhabitants of the

Tower. He had already sent one psychiatric nurse to the emergency ward with a broken nose and Parnelli did not have enough staff to continue his twenty-four-hour-a-day watch on the retired policeman.

The elevator bumped to a halt and Parnelli stepped out. He was flanked by the two largest male nurses in the psychiatric division of Stony Brook. Their names were Peter and Paul; their combined bodyweight was somewhere close to six hundred pounds and their tattooed arms hung like sides of illustrated beef from their short-sleeved uniforms. He wasn't taking any chances. Nobody liked going downstairs and if Fogarty resisted, Peter and Paul could be both gentle and persuasive. Parnelli did not enjoy or particularly endorse what he was about to do; it was an admittance that his chemicals had failed.

They walked the linoleum-lined corridor with silent purpose and stopped outside Room 15A.

Bill Fogarty was sitting on his single bed, his back pressed to the wall. He was wearing a light green hospital gown and holding a pillow tight to his body, both his arms crossed over it as if it were some type of shield, his head turned down and his eyes wide and staring. "Fogarty. My name is Bill

Fogarty. I'm a police officer. Bill Fogarty. Bill Fogarty." He had repeated this, or variations of it, for the six hours that he had been awake following his last injection. The most important thing was his name. It kept him whole.

"Bill?"

It was a different voice, not his own.

"Mr Fogarty?" It was insistent.

He tried to focus his eyes.

"Yes," he answered robotically.

"Mr Fogarty, the medication is not doing what I had hoped it would for you, so we're going to try something else."

"I'm Bill Fogarty."

"I know who you are," Parnelli said gently, sitting down on the foot of the bed. He didn't like to admit it, even to himself, but in the past year he had become insensitive to many of his patients. Each seemed an obstruction to something that he wanted to believe. It was something about himself, something that would have given purpose to the hours he spent trying to make sense of the lives that paraded in front of him, naked and raw. He had wanted to be a healer, believed that he could heal, but he wasn't healing, he was patching the casualties up and sending them back to war, like a medic on a battlefield.

"What I want to do is stop your

medication for a while," Parnelli said softly.

Parnelli reached out and touched the sleeve of Fogarty's gown. He was feeling something for this man, and the feeling made him feel guilty. He slipped a syringe from the pocket of his jacket. "Let me have your arm."

Fogarty held his arm forward. The movement had become a reflex.

"This is a little pre-med, just something to relax you," Parnelli continued. "I want to try you on a course of ECT." He preferred the initials to the actual words. Electroconvulsive shock therapy sounded barbaric.

Fogarty looked into Parnelli's face. The psychiatrist's words had been incomprehensible but their feeling had been a transmission of kindness mixed with sorrow and a touch of fear.

Parnelli waited a few minutes, studying Fogarty's eyes, watching his respiration slow and his muscles slacken, then motioned for the boys to wheel the trolley into position beside the bed. The wheels squeaked against the floor as Parnelli kept his eyes on his patient, sensitive to any change in his posture or attitude that could signal violence. The squeaking stopped.

"Now, Bill, you don't have to do a

thing, Peter and Paul are going to lift you from your bed and lay you on the trolley and then we're going to take a ride downstairs."

Fogarty felt a soft rush that started in his head and began working down into his exhausted body. After that two huge hands took hold of his arm and shoulder. He pulled back against the wall and the grip tightened but there was no panic on either side.

Then Fogarty was moving, watching the ceiling roll by, listening to the squeaking of the wheels as steel doors opened in front of them and closed behind. The elevator made him feel nauseous and he belched.

"You OK, not going to get sick on us?"

The elevator stopped and the rolling began again, more doors, deeper into the labyrinth of concrete walls, antiseptic smells, and hushed voices.

"Am I ever getting out of here?" Fogarty asked, but he didn't really know or care where 'here' was.

"Sure you are," one of the aides replied.

"Am I going home?"

"Soon. Soon."

They entered a smaller room with dull white walls. Fogarty tried to sit up but he

213

was woozy and the act of changing position made him dizzy.

A kind face looked down at him, pale blue eyes and a gray-white beard.

"Hello, Bill, I'm Dr Roberts, and I'm going to put you to sleep."

"Don't want to go to sleep," Fogarty mumbled.

"Oh, you'll like this. You'll just float away."

Fogarty felt panic, but it was buried so deep beneath confusion, exhaustion and the mix of chemicals that coursed through him that he closed his eyes and pressed back against the trolley, as if the act itself would create invisibility. He never felt the prick of the needle through the skin above his hand, nor the strong arms that lifted him from the trolley to the operating table. The next injection paralysed the muscles in his body and made it necessary for a respirator to be placed above his mouth and nose in order that he continue to breathe. It was very simple and straightforward from there. Two electrodes were attached to his temples and a hundred and fifty volts of DC current was sent through his body. It took Bill Fogarty approximately five seconds to begin convulsions comparable to an epileptic seizure of the grand mal variety, but because of the general paralysis of his body, the only visible sign was a rapid twitching in the subcutaneous muscles of his face and the release of urine from his bladder.

"I think that will do it," Parnelli said. He always felt strange when overseeing the administration of electric shock, as if he was involved in something primitive and therefore alien to the biochemical science that he practised. The fact remained that ECT produced results when chemicals often failed. It was the ritual itself that made him uneasy.

★ ★ ★

Justin Gabriel vomited into the steel bowl of the toilet that was fixed to the far wall of his room. Another violent spasm and he wretched again, emptying the remains of lunch from his stomach. One more time and he crawled to his cot and pulled himself into a fetal position, cradling his head in his hands. He was pouring sweat and it felt as if a steel band was tightening around his skull. "This is it. I'm dying. Dying inside these bars, like an animal." Justin Gabriel had not been sick in over a decade, in fact he thought that he was impervious to sickness, that by virtue of his physical and mental training he had gone beyond the laws of flesh and blood. He certainly thought that he had risen above the mortal thoughts that plagued him now. He coughed and wheezed. Then it really began, like bees swarming in the pit of his stomach, fanning outwards on razored wings, cutting at every nerve and fiber of his body. The pain terrified him because it was without explanation. "What if it never ends?" He closed his eyes and concentrated on the bird, the great soaring bird. The bird could take him away from the pain. The bird was his transcendence but he could not hold the thought, couldn't fly on the wings of his imagination. Agony kept him grounded. He heard the clank of a lock and the opening and closing door. "I'm dying," he groaned.

"Take it easy, Doctor. I'll call for a stretcher," Art Weller answered.

"It's eating me up."

They carried Gabriel to the infirmary. By the time they'd lifted him from the stretcher to the bed he was vomiting. That made him feel better. Then the sickness passed completely.

"I'm OK now," he announced. "I want to go back to my cell."

11

Tanaka drove uptown to the medical building. He had five pages of notes and another three pages of the names of people involved in the Gabriel case. 'Bill Fogarty, Mac Parkinson, Bob Moyer and Maura Allan', they were the ones that Tanaka could immediately connect, and three of them were dead. 'Sole Witness, William T. Fogarty', that was the key. Sole witness to what? 'Bob Moyer picked up the pieces.' He was assuming that Fogarty was referring to the Gabriel murder case but what about Parkinson; the phrase 'picked up the pieces' had been used in conjunction with Parkinson. What exactly had happened to Parkinson? His case had been dated within a week of the Gabriel case. Bob Moyer must have been the medical examiner on both of them.

Tanaka got up from his desk and walked from his office, stopping at the main desk to get the keys which unlocked the door to the records department of the medical building. He went to the computer and ran a search on Parkinson, M. Seconds later the screen gave him a date and reference number. The date, 11/7/72, corresponded with the date in the police files. He wrote down the number and walked to the storage unit of the medical building. The coroner's report listed Parkinson's death as accidental, caused by a single gunshot wound to the head. The weapon was a Remington 12-gauge shotgun, property of the Philadelphia Police Department. At the bottom of the report was a hand-written notation. Tanaka recognised Bob Moyer's writing, half-print, half-script. 'Pump-action shotguns are used by stakeout. Bill Fogarty would not have used this weapon. See Patterson. Same wounding.' Tanaka put down the file and searched the old metal cabinets for Patterson. He found the coroner's report on Sergeant Fred Patterson, also signed by Moyer. The cause of death was massive bleeding due to a single gunshot wound to the sternum at close range and the weapon listed was a Remington 12-gauge shotgun. Another note was scrawled at the bottom of the page. 'Bill's weapon was never fired.' Tanaka closed the files and went back to his office. He didn't want to disturb Norma Moyer; he had already spoken to her regarding Bill's absence from the funeral service, although he'd held back on the severity of his condition. Now he saw no choice. It was beginning to look like Parnelli was correct. A stress disorder. Caused by an incident that had cost the lives of at least two police officers, an incident that was directly related to the Justin Gabriel case and that had gone to Internal Affairs, an incident to which Bill Fogarty was the sole witness.

He dialed Moyer's number.

"Hello?" Norma's voice sounded strong.

"It's Josef. How are you?" He kept his tone light.

"Josef. I'm fine, just fine. Steve and Andy are taking care of me. They're good boys."

"I know."

"If it's OK with you, Rachel and I will bring Billy over to see you next week."

"I'd love that."

"Listen, Norma," Tanaka said, lowering his tone, "Remember I told you that Bill Fogarty had had a breakdown?"

"Of course I do. How is he?"

"Not so good."

"I'm sorry to hear that."

"His doctor thinks it may be a stress-related illness," Tanaka continued. "Something that happened a long time ago."

"Like the car accident?" Norma asked.

"I thought that at first too, but not any more," Tanaka replied. "It seems more likely it was an incident that took place before that. He spoke about it when I saw him but I couldn't make much sense out of what he was saying. I wasn't around here then; I wasn't even in the United States."

"So what can I do?" Norma asked.

"Listen, I'm sorry to be laying this on you now, it's just that Bill's not responding and I'm getting desperate."

"What can I do?" she repeated.

"Tell me if the name Mac Parkinson rings any bells?"

Norma thought a moment. "I'm sorry, but no, it doesn't."

"He was a police officer," Tanaka primed, "and from what I can get from the old case reports he died in an accidental shooting."

"Was it one of Bob's cases?"

"Yes, the old file's still down here with a few of Bob's hand-written notes on it."

Norma leaned back against the cushion of the sofa. Somehow, talking about him made her feel as if her husband was still alive and it hurt. "Sorry, I just can't — "

"It's all right," Tanaka said. He was pushing now and he knew it. "How about Justin Gabriel?"

There was a lengthy hesitation.

"I shouldn't be troubling you with this

stuff," Tanaka apologised, about to call a halt to their conversation.

"He's a madman," Norma stated, her tone flat. "I haven't really thought of him for years, not till Phillip phoned the house in the middle of the night."

"I don't follow you," Tanaka replied.

"Phillip, Bob's nephew. He's working in the prison where they keep Gabriel. He called here and upset Bob."

"When?"

"Just before Bob died, a week, ten days, something like that."

"Have you got any idea why?" Tanaka asked, remembering the incident with Harrison following the service at the funeral home.

"I don't know exactly what was said but it must have brought back some bad memories." Norma paused. "Justin Gabriel was a bad case. It was hard on all of them, Bob and Bill, all the people who worked on it. I can't give you details. Bob never talked to me about what was going on at the time, he was very protective, but I read some of it in the papers, the way Gabriel's people butchered that family, then the threats he made to the folks who convicted him. And now, all these years later, Phillip is right in there with him. Bob would never have got him that job

221

if he'd have thought that he'd be stuck inside with that lunatic . . . " Her voice was breaking up. "I mean Bob spent a lot of time making sure that monster never got out."

"Norma, that's enough. That's all I need to hear."

"I don't know anything else and I don't like thinking about that phone call. Phillip upset him so much."

"Do you want me to come over there?" Tanaka asked.

"No, no." She seemed to recover as she spoke. "I'll be fine. It's strange what brings the tears on, I'm sorry. I'm really embarrassed."

"Stop it. There's nothing to be embarrassed about. I shouldn't have bothered you with this."

"But I want to help. If Bill needs anything, please let me know."

"Of course I will. Now are you sure you don't want me to drop by?"

"I'm sure."

Tanaka said goodbye and put the phone back on its cradle. After that he organised his staff to take care of the morning's business and left the medical building.

★ ★ ★

He got to Leibowitz's office just before eleven o'clock, rang the buzzer and entered the waiting room.

"Is Phillip Harrison in there with Stan?" he asked the new secretary. His voice was more aggressive than he'd intended it to be.

Her name was Ann Thorne, tall, red haired and an ex-school teacher from Cherry Hill. Very authoritative when she felt the need. "I'm sorry, Dr Tanaka, but is Dr Leibowitz expecting you?"

"Phillip Harrison, is he in there?" Tanaka repeated, looking at the closed door of Leibowitz's office.

Tanaka smiled. "Come on, Ann, this is serious."

The smile warmed her slightly. "If you'll wait . . . " she glanced at her watch, "five minutes, I'm sure Dr Leibowitz will see you."

Tanaka sat down in a beige armchair and stared at the closed door.

A few minutes later Stan Leibowitz ushered out a short fat man wearing a full, badly fitted hairpiece. Tanaka thought he recognised him. Ike Berger, or Ike Berg. Phillie's friendliest diamond merchant, or so his cable TV ads said. One thing for certain, it wasn't Phillip Harrison.

The man shook hands with Leibowitz,

223

took his coat from the rack, made a discreet adjustment to his jet black hair and walked from the room.

Leibowitz turned towards Tanaka "Josef?"

"Doctor, your eleven o'clock is running a few minutes late," Ann Thorne cut in.

"OK, Ann, thanks." Then to Tanaka: "I was just going to phone you." Indicating for Tanaka to follow him into his office.

"The news from Stony Brook isn't good," Leibowitz said as he closed the door. "They've started Bill on a course of ECT."

Tanaka shook his head. "I don't understand. Why?"

"I didn't get a lot from Parnelli but I did get the distinct impression that he's hit some kind of impasse. There's a limit to the chemicals, and if he can't get to the root of whatever's troubling Bill then the electric shock is the next progression."

"That stinks," Tanaka said.

"Yes, well, I'm afraid that's what's happening."

"I've been doing my own digging," Tanaka said, sitting down, "and I've come up with something that might be relevant, particularly in the scenario of a stress disorder."

"Tell me what it is."

"A man by the name of Justin Gabriel."

Leibowitz remained quiet and Tanaka

224

misinterpreted the silence.

"He was the prime suspect in one of Bill's cases about eighteen years ago — "

"Oh I know who he is," Leibowitz replied.

"Then there was something that Phillip Harrison said to me at Bob's house yesterday."

Leibowitz sat a little straighter behind his desk. "And what was that?" he asked.

"He said he'd killed his uncle."

The psychiatrist nodded his head. He made a point of not discussing clients with anyone other than immediate family, and only then when it was necessary, but there was a coincidence here and Leibowitz did not believe in the random definition of coincidence. "Josef, I'm going to break one of my own rules and talk about a patient, and only because I think it may be relevant. Phillip Harrison works in the segregated unit at Graterford Prison. That's where Justin Gabriel is locked up."

"I know that," Tanaka replied.

"How much do you know about Gabriel?"

"Not a lot."

"Well the guy's a master manipulator with no conscience, no moral base. None at all. And he's been laying a very heavy head trip on Phillip," Leibowitz added.

"I don't see how that ties in with Bob's death," Tanaka said.

225

"You don't remember the case?"

"I've read an old police report. I know that Bill was involved, and Bob was the ME, and I've seen some pictures but all the stuff was basically procedural."

"Right, well what Justin Gabriel was really all about was mind control. The police could never place him at the crime scene in the Paisley murders so the essence of their prosecution was that his people were under his power. That they would do virtually whatever he suggested, and what he suggested was murder."

"I'm trying to stay with you but I'm not making all the connections," Tanaka replied.

"Phillip Harrison believes that Gabriel used him to kill Bob."

Tanaka shook his head as if he didn't understand.

"By some form of auto suggestion," Leibowitz explained. "That's the reason I was going to telephone you. There's a definite similarity between what Bob's nephew told me this morning and what you told me yesterday about Bill."

"What's that?"

"The bird. Phillip believes that he opened his uncle's mind to Gabriel through a dream, and the principal component of that dream was a bird. The bird is Gabriel; or, more accurately, an embodiment of him. I guess the closest definition in Western terms would be an alter-ego. In black sorcery, which is what Gabriel studied after he was barred from practising conventional therapy, the bird would be Gabriel's power animal. It's sort of a psychological metaphor. Gabriel would reshape his energy, transmit it psychically, and that energy would attack and destroy his enemies." Leibowitz stopped and considered. "It's a kind of voodoo, a mind fuck on a very primitive but at the same time sophisticated level. Once the victim is open and vulnerable, his or her belief system does the rest."

"How?"

"The fact that all the action takes place in a dream state is incidental to the body, all the emotional and physiological systems, including the heart, react as strongly to an internal stimulus as to an external one."

Tanaka nodded his head.

"It's possible that Bob was frightened to death," Leibowitz concluded.

"But why?"

"I don't know," Leibowitz replied. "I don't know what the connection is."

Tanaka thought of Maura Allan and felt his stomach tighten. Suddenly he was cold.

Leibowitz sat quietly with his hands on the desk in front of him. He stayed that way for

227

what seemed to Tanaka a long time, his eyes far away. Finally he spoke. "I've got some stuff that maybe you should read. It's going to take me a bit of time to dig it out, but I'll find it this afternoon and fax it over to you at the medical building."

"What is it?" Tanaka asked.

"Just read it, then we'll talk."

"OK."

"By then I'll have had a chance to talk to Parnelli again, although I don't think it's a good idea to get into anything with him about dreams and magic."

Tanaka smiled. "That's probably very wise."

Tanaka stood as Leibowitz came from around his desk. They shook hands.

"Don't worry, we'll get through this," Leibowitz said.

"One way or another," Tanaka replied.

12

The fax started at two o'clock and before the seven pages had finished piling in the tray Tanaka was reading an article written by Justin Seers Gabriel, titled 'The Manipulation of Energy and the Interpretation of Dreams'. It had been published in 1967 in the *Journal of American Psychology*.

At first the article struck Tanaka as no more than academic theory, the ramblings of a newcomer to an old profession attempting to shake the established order, an eclectic mix of Eastern and primitive mysticism with Western practice, but as he read further he realised Stan Leibowitz's reason for sending it to him. When he'd finished reading, he picked up the phone and dialed. The doctor was between appointments.

"Hi, Stan. I've read it."

"And I've talked to Stony Brook. The news is not good. Parnelli sounds like a competent guy but he doesn't have a lot of answers when it comes to Bill. He's still talking about stress disorder and sleep deprivation but I could hear between the lines. Bill's got him worried."

Tanaka felt a tightness across his scalp. "Why's that?"

"Because Bill's symptoms don't seem to be letting up. If anything, the delusions are getting stronger."

"What do you think it is, Stan, really?"

"I don't know."

"Then why did you send me this article?"

Leibowitz didn't answer.

"This thing reads like a confession,"

Tanaka continued. "Gabriel is claiming that he manipulated his patients' minds by entering them through their dreams? That he could consciously transfer thought?"

"That's what he claimed," Leibowitz replied.

"Do you believe him?"

"In theory."

"What do you mean by that?"

"It means I'm being cautious. Listen, what he says he was able to do has never been proved in a laboratory. They came close in the eighties out in Stanford, communicating back and forth with sleeping subjects, and apparently the Russians got even closer with their studies on mind control, but Gabriel is talking about working on a much more sophisticated level."

"Which brings us back to what you were saying earlier."

"Yes, I know. Listen, Josef, with regard to this I'm an academic, I understand it intellectually, but I haven't experienced it."

"Well then, intellectually, how - could Justin Gabriel have entered Bob Moyer's consciousness?"

"He would have used someone that Bob cared about as a conduit. Read the article again. The trick, or secret, or whatever you want to call it, is vulnerability. After that comes suggestion. Then that suggestion manifests in thought and that thought, potentially, forms belief. Take the bird for example. The bird is a figment of Gabriel's imagination, but if you want to play head games, consider this; I'm a figment of your imagination, a projection of your consciousness, an interpretation of energy. It all sounds very esoteric but in fact modern neurophysics is finally coming into alignment with what Eastern mysticism has been saying for centuries. Reality is simply an interpretation of energy. A projection, like a hologram. A dream."

"And you're telling me that Justin Gabriel has enough power to impose," Tanaka hesitated, searching for words, "to impose his imagination on other people? To create dreams?"

"He's had nothing to do for the past two and a half decades but sit in a five-by-ten foot room and practice. He may as well be in a cave in Tibet. He probably lives in his dreams. Everything he began in the sixties, all his studies in alternative belief systems, everything from meditation to voodoo, that's all he's got. In theory, I believe it's possible."

"So what you're suggesting is that Gabriel killed Bob through a dream."

"Again, in theory, I think it's possible."

"OK, but how about Bill?"

"Joey, this is just hypothesis."

"I understand that."

Stan hesitated. "OK. Let's just say that Justin Gabriel got to Bob Moyer through Phillip Harrison. Bob's feelings for Phillip were the opening into his consciousness. The fact that Bill is experiencing similar symptoms may be relevant or it may be sheer coincidence or it may mean that, somehow, because of the shared experience, they're all linked up, like some kind of mental circuitry."

"But why? Why would Gabriel want to do this now?"

Leibowitz firmed up. "I don't even know that he *is* doing it. This is all conjecture." He relaxed. "I mean, Christ, if that guy in Stony Brook," he fumbled for a name and looked down at his note pad. "If Parnelli could hear us talking he'd have us both inside with Bill. I've just never discounted the possibilities. And I don't believe in coincidence."

★ ★ ★

The court transcripts of the Gabriel trial were located in a central records depository, in the basement of the District Attorney's office on Arch Street. Tanaka cleared his

232

visit through the mayor's office and began a marathon search through half a dozen boxes of stenographer's reports. The name Maura Rich appeared dozens of times. She had been one of several disciples who had dropped out of the Church of Human Consciousness and the only one who had testified against Gabriel in court. Her testimony was full of inferences to mind control and brain washing and shamanistic practices, but what had been particularly damning to Gabriel was her statement to the effect that the self-created holy man had incited his followers to 'silence by whatever means necessary' those who spoke openly against his quasi-religious cult and had named Reverend Paisley, the minister whose family had been butchered, as a 'test of faith' for those loyal to the Church of Human Consciousness. The name of the DA in charge of the prosecution was recorded as Howard Rossi and before leaving the office Tanaka asked how he could get in touch with him. He was informed that Rossi was retired so he pressed for a contact number and was given a listed phone number with a suburban area code. After that he drove back to the medical building. There, he pulled his own file on Maura Allan, formerly Maura Rich, phoned her husband and asked for a meeting.

Jim Allan agreed to see him at three o'clock. Next he dialed Howard Rossi's number.

"Hello?" The voice was female.

"Is this the home of Howard Rossi?"

"Yes, it is."

"May I speak to Mr Rossi, please?"

"Are you selling something?" The tone was curt.

"No, I'm not. This is Dr Josef Tanaka at the medical building in Philadelphia; I'd like to speak to him about a professional matter."

"This is Barbara Rossi. Howard was my father and he's dead."

"Oh, I'm sorry, I was given this number by the DA's office."

"Is there anything I can do to help you?"

"Could you tell me how he died?" Tanaka asked.

There was hesitation.

"I'm sorry. I don't mean to pry, my reasons are professional."

"Dad had a heart attack."

"Unexpected?"

"Very."

"Were you with your father at all directly before he passed away?"

"I hadn't seen him in months; he lived alone. I spoke to him every week on the phone but I didn't see him. Why? Why are you asking these questions?"

"Would it be convenient if I came to speak to you in person?"

"I don't understand what this is all about."

"I'm conducting an inquiry into a case that Mr Rossi prosecuted."

"Which case was that?"

"It was a murder trial. A man by the name of Justin Gabriel."

Tanaka could feel her bristle down the line and when she spoke again her voice had hardened.

"I'm not comfortable talking about that and actually I'm very busy."

"It's important," Tanaka insisted.

"How do I know that you are who you say you are?"

"I'll give you my phone number here. First confirm the number and then call me back."

He gave her the general number of the medical building, said goodbye and waited anxiously. Several minutes passed and he thought he'd blown it, then his line buzzed.

"I've got a Ms Rossi on the phone for you, doctor. Are you available?"

"Yes."

"Hello, Dr Tanaka?"

"Ms Rossi?"

"I'm sorry, I got paranoid for a minute. I didn't mean to offend you, I just had to be sure. It's just that there were so many strange things surrounding that case."

"I don't follow you?"

"Threats and phone calls."

"Recent?"

"Right up till my father died."

"Ms Rossi, I'd really like to sit down and talk to you."

"Why?"

"I'm a medical examiner and I have a feeling that, maybe, there was more to your father's death than a heart attack. It would mean a great deal to me if we could talk."

There was a long silence and Tanaka worried that she was about to say 'no'.

"I'll be in Philadelphia tomorrow afternoon. I have an appointment at three o'clock on Walnut Street."

"Give me a time and an address and I'll meet you," Tanaka answered, relieved.

13

Jim Allan's Locust Street office was located in a five-story building with a slow, jerky elevator. The sign outside his frosted-glass door read 'J. E. Allan and Associates,

Architectural Design'. Inside there was a good-sized reception with three rooms adjoining it.

Tanaka told the short, red-haired secretary who he was and then took a seat in one of the leather chairs along the wall facing the offices. A minute later Jim Allan opened his door and walked towards him. He looked years older than the last time Tanaka had interviewed him regarding his wife's death, and that was only two weeks ago. Now, there were dark circles beneath his eyes and he'd lost weight, enough to make his neck look drawn and accentuate the deep lines of his face. He was shaved and wore a gray cashmere pullover, gray slacks and Gucci loafers, but there was still something unkempt about him, something lost. It was in his eyes; they were without life.

"Hello, Dr Tanaka," he said, offering his hand.

"Mr Allan," Tanaka replied, standing.

"Please, come into my office."

Tanaka followed him behind the solid wood door, noticing the antiseptic cleanliness of the place and the meticulous way in which the implements of Allan's trade were arranged on his drawing board. Not a speck of dust anywhere. There were two Barcelona chairs in front of Allan's desk, their x-shaped stainless-steel frames supporting flat leather cushions. They looked very stylish and equally uncomfortable.

"Sit down," Allan said.

Tanaka sat in the chair closer to him while Allan walked to the high-backed chair behind his desk. He remained silent while his eyes weighed Tanaka. Finally he asked, "Have you ever lost anyone that you've loved?"

"Yes, I have," Tanaka replied, his mind going instantly to Hiro, his older brother.

"It's the worst feeling in the world, isn't it?"

"Yes."

Allan nodded his head slightly as if to say that he was satisfied with Tanaka's sincerity. "Now, what can I do for you?"

"First of all, I'm sorry to come in here and take up your time . . . "

Allan glanced at his drawing board. "It doesn't matter. I don't have any work on. I'm just here because the kids think it's good that I'm out of the house."

"The reason that I've come," Tanaka said, sitting forward in the chair, "is that I still don't have a cause for your late wife's death and it's troubling me."

Allan looked puzzled. "Maura had a heart attack. You know that."

"I'm sorry," Tanaka replied. "My phrasing

238

wasn't exactly accurate. Let me put it another way. I can't find a reason for Maura's heart to have stopped."

Allan seemed to wince, then recover. "I told you in the beginning; there was nothing wrong with Maura, no medical condition."

"Please, just bear with me," Tanaka continued. "I'm looking for something subtle, something that may have aggravated what happened, maybe something that had not been diagnosed. Was she troubled by anything in the past months?"

Allan tightened his lips and shook his head.

"Was she emotionally stable?" Tanaka pressed.

The architect continued to look reticent but there was a spark kindling in his eyes.

"Please, Mr Allan. This visit is off the record, anything that you might say could be helpful, anything at all."

The spark flared. "How about if I told you that fear killed my wife? Would you tell me that was impossible?"

"No I wouldn't, but I'd ask you to explain it to me," Tanaka replied.

Allan's face dropped and he put his head in his hands.

"I'm sorry but I'm still very upset."

"I understand."

Allan looked up slowly. "How much do you know about Maura's background?"

"Medically?"

"No, no. I'm talking about her past."

Tanaka considered his next words carefully. He didn't want to push too hard. "I suppose the most significant detail is that her unmarried name was Rich and that eighteen years ago she was involved in a big murder trial here in Philadelphia."

"The Justin Gabriel trial," Allan confirmed.

"Yes, but I'm not certain if that's relevant to her death."

"Oh, I think it's relevant. I think it's very relevant," Allan answered, studying Tanaka. "Are you familiar with Justin Gabriel?"

Tanaka stayed cool. "I've read some court transcripts and an article that Gabriel wrote in one of the psychology journals, but, to be honest, I don't know a lot about him."

"Did you know that Maura was one of his patients?"

"No, I didn't," Tanaka answered.

"That's when the little bastard first got his hooks into her."

"What do you mean by that?"

"I mean he got into her through her dreams."

Tanaka started to buzz inside, as if the

circuits were all connecting.

"Doctor, let me ask you a philosophical question," Allan continued. "Do you mind?"

"Not at all."

"Do you believe that everything that has ever happened to you or will ever happen to you is already scripted in your subconscious mind, that you're just acting out a role that has already been written? Even now?"

Tanaka shook his head. "I'm not sure that I'm following you."

"That's what Gabriel was selling. In the beginning anyway. He preached that we're all pre-programmed, functioning without free-will, you know, just going through the paces. He promised that everyone could become totally conscious, that the concept of God and destiny and good and evil was all just a cop-out for the fact that we're sleep-walking. All the time." He hesitated. "Sorry, Doctor, I seem to be going on and on about this — "

"No. Keep talking, I'm interested," Tanaka urged.

"OK. The gateway to this subconscious programming was through dreams, but not in an interpretive Freudian sense. Gabriel treated dreams as a separate reality, every bit as valid as the one we're experiencing now, just more pliable. He taught that by

241

becoming conscious while asleep that you could become aware of all your intentions and therefore not walk into any more self-imposed landmines while you were awake. You could change the course of your dreams and by doing that alter the course of your life. It was all about intention and free-will. It was an interesting theory, it was the way that he tried to make it work that was the problem."

"How was that?"

"He used drugs to break down the concept of waking reality, to show the people that he was working with it was not solid or rigid; that what we see is nothing more than imagination, our minds' reaction to external stimulus. He used LSD, mescaline, all the sixties mind expanders. Then he worked on them while they slept, talking to them, inducing images. Maura told me that he had her at the point where they could communicate while she was sound asleep. She could hear his voice and see him; he was literally in her dreams. Don't forget, these people had come to Gabriel for help, not to be experimental guinea pigs. It all got pretty crazy, and then one of his patients committed suicide and that was it. There was a lawsuit and Justin Gabriel never practiced therapy again. For him that was only the beginning. He went off and lived in Mexico till the heat died down. When he came back he claimed to be a diablero," Allan hesitated. "Do you know what that is?"

Tanaka shook his head.

"A witch doctor or a sorcerer, but one who works on the dark side of magic. Gabriel always preferred the dark side. It generated more fear and gave him more power over people. Anyway, he gathered a group around him. Some of them, like Maura, were former patients and he founded his Church of Human Consciousness. They treated him like a god, but what he was was a megalomaniac."

"And they committed murder for him," Tanaka said.

"Yes. He had them totally under his control."

"It must have taken a lot of strength for Maura to break away," Tanaka said.

"The crazier things got the more she was convinced that it was all about to explode. I think there was tremendous paranoia inside the group, especially when people like Reverend Paisley started to speak out publicly against Gabriel. There was a lot of talk about self-defense and retribution. That's what did it for Maura. She would have never hurt anybody. Then about two months ago it all started again."

"What was that?"

"The dreams."

"Could you tell me about them?"

"After Mexico, Gabriel claimed to be able to change the shape of his body, to take on the form of a bird. That was what he called his power animal, his protector. So when Maura started dreaming about the bird, that's when she believed that Gabriel had found her."

"I don't understand why after all these years?"

"Yes, I've thought about that too. Did you know that he's coming up for parole?"

"No," Tanaka replied.

"Well that would please Gabriel, because he wants this to be real low key, no publicity, no interviews, no opposition. It's his one and only shot."

Tanaka shook his head, indicating that he didn't understand Allan's point.

"He was given fifty to a hundred years for conspiracy to murder. According to the law, unless there are extenuating circumstances, he gets one parole hearing and that comes at the beginning of next year. One hearing, that's it, and Maura was actively opposing that hearing ever taking place."

"Was she working alone?" Tanaka asked.

"No, she had some very influential people with her."

"Can you give me their names?"

Allan thought a moment. "You've got to understand, I know a lot about certain aspects of this thing because I lived with it over the years, through all the therapy and all the nightmares. I needed to understand what I was up against or more to the point, what Maura was up against. I questioned her about Gabriel, about his methods, about what he did to her and how it all worked because she was my wife; I loved her and I wanted to help, but she had her own private agenda regarding the legal stuff and I respected that privacy. She didn't really enjoy talking about any of it."

Tanaka felt close to something and he didn't want to let it go. "I do understand, but right now names could be important," he replied.

"Why?"

"Because maybe Maura wasn't alone in what happened. There might be other people experiencing the same thing. I'm looking for a connection."

"Doctor, I want to help but it wasn't like they were all friends; they didn't see each other socially. They got very close during the trial but that was a long time ago."

Tanaka deflated as he realised the truth in Allan's words. It was a long time ago. Maybe he was grasping at straws.

Allan read the disappointment on Tanaka's face and dug deeper into his memory. "I think there was a lawyer and I think his first name was Howard. I've heard her mention him but I'll be damned right now if I can remember his last name — "

"Rossi? Howard Rossi?"

"Yes, I believe that's it. And there was a doctor but I have no idea of his. He worked for the city."

"Moyer? Bob Moyer?"

Allan shook his head. "I don't know." He met Tanaka's eyes. "I'm sorry, I wish I did."

"That's OK. You've done fine. Maybe it's me. Maybe I'm trying to make too much out of nothing."

"Oh, and there's something else," Allan said, loosening up. "About three weeks before she died somebody sent Maura a postcard."

"I don't follow you."

"It may have even come from Gabriel. I think they can send mail out of prison. I think that's a constitutional right." There was bitterness in his voice.

"Tell me about it."

Allan relaxed, dropping his hands to his desk top.

"It was like something you'd buy in the souvenir shop at the zoo. It was a picture of an eagle perched on a cliff. There was nothing sinister about it. On the message side of the card someone had written: 'Do you believe a man can fly?' The card was addressed to Maura Rich and it was signed, 'Father'."

"Father?"

"'Father' was one of the names that Gabriel used with his followers. He liked them to call him Father. He called them his angels."

"Have you still got the card?"

"No, I tore the goddamned thing up, but that's when the dreams started."

"Did she ever talk about them?"

"Sure, she dreamed of a bird, like the one on the card, circling in the sky above her. As the dream continued it began to attack her and she couldn't move; she couldn't run or fight back. That's when the panic set in. She'd just lie there gasping for breath, choking. It was a very frightening thing, for Maura and for me. I felt so helpless. I couldn't wake her; it was like she was in another world, a million miles away. Finally she didn't want to sleep any more. Ever. Until the night she had the heart attack."

Tanaka felt the buzz return. He was on to something. "Why didn't you tell me all this two weeks ago?"

"Because you're a doctor and I know how this sounds. Unless you'd seen it with your own eyes, it sounds crazy. Maura had seen a lot of shrinks in the past; she'd been analysed and she'd been on medication but there were places in her mind that they couldn't reach. Justin Gabriel could get to those places. Believe me."

"I do," Tanaka replied.

"Justin Gabriel killed my wife," Allan stated. "But how the hell am I going to prove it or do anything about it?"

Tanaka sat in silence.

"How do you get to a man who's protected by the law? He lives in a cage and he's surrounded by guards. How do you ever touch him?"

Tanaka did not have an answer.

★ ★ ★

Fogarty's next attack came at exactly three o'clock Saturday afternoon. He was participating in his first group therapy session.

248

There had been six of them, four men and two women, and they had been given sketch pads and crayons.

"Oh, man, this is too much," a lanky resident in a baseball cap had complained when presented with his coloring kit. He reminded Fogarty of someone but Fogarty couldn't link the face with his memory. It had been like that in the past week following the ECT; sometimes he was lucid and sometimes there was a vagueness to his associations.

The closest that he had come to making art in the past forty years had been line drawings of crime scenes, layouts that usually included a body, or the outline of multiple bodies, in the center of a floor, and that he'd done for himself, a way of ingraining detail in his head. His first attempt with the yellow crayon yielded something similar, a configuration of lines in the shape of a 'v'. He wasn't sure where his creation was headed so he persevered, adding a yellow sun-like circle to the upper-right corner of the paper, then exchanging his yellow crayon for a blue one and going to work on a set of curvy diagonal lines at the base of the drawing.

"That's nice, Mr Fogarty. A seascape?" the nurse commented in passing.

"A seascape? How the hell am I supposed to know?" he thought. Her voice had antagonised him and he suddenly felt silly with his crayons and coloring book.

He looked down at his paper and his eyes became fixated on the 'v'. There was something wrong with it. The shape? The color? His realisation brought a rush of anger that caught him by surprise. "It's the wrong fucking color!" The blue crayon snapped between his fingers as he put it back in the box.

He felt eyes upon him and looked up to see the ward nurse staring in his direction. He forced a smile and lifted another crayon, a silver-gray, waved it at her like a naughty child and went back to work.

"Yes, that's it, that's it." He felt better as he re-outlined the 'v' with the new color, adding lines that extended outwards from the main structure. That made more sense, "that's how it looked". He had gone over it several times before he heard the nurse's voice. At first he could not make out the words because they sounded soft and far away.

"And what have you got there?"

He didn't answer, just kept working.

"Sooooomun."

"I'm sorry, I couldn't understand you."

"Supermaaaa . . . "

Fogarty sneaked a furtive glance to his side and saw the bulky nurse standing above the man in the baseball cap. His mustache looked so long that it seemed to trail on to the white drawing paper.

"Superman. I said Superman." There was frustration in the man's tone.

"Oh, so that's Superman's cape?"

Fogarty watched them. The guy with the mustache. Who the hell was he?

"Yes, that's his cape. What the hell did you think it was? It's a cape."

"Sorry, Max, I just didn't see it."

Mac? Mac? Did she say Mac? Fogarty sat up rigid in his chair and stared at the man in the baseball cap. Mac Parkinson. Was that Mac Parkinson?! And the man, angry with the nurse and self-conscious that Fogarty was staring at them, met his eyes.

"What's the matter, buddy, you got a problem?" After that, the bird that Fogarty had drawn flew right out of its paper cage and hit him between the eyes.

By the time Parnelli arrived, Peter and Paul were holding him so tight to the floor that he never felt the injection. Fifteen minutes later and he was back in the mire, thoughts and emotions held in the soft, sticky clamp.

14

Tanaka stood outside the small, gourmet coffee shop on Walnut and watched the tall, dark-haired woman approach. She was looking directly at him.

"Dr Tanaka?"

It was the same edgy voice that he'd spoken to on the phone.

"Ms Rossi?" He extended his hand. Up close she had a fine face with small pretty features and her handshake was firm and dry.

"May I see some identification?" she asked.

He handed her his ID card from the medical building and his driver's license.

"I'm sorry about all this but I just want to be sure." She looked at the photo on his license. "Not very flattering," she said, returning it to him.

"Shall we go inside?" Tanaka asked.

It was a small walk-in place with a counter and stools and a lot of no-sugar doughnuts and non-fat muffins underneath glass domes. There were two vacancies at the counter with people to either side and it was noisy with chatter.

"It's not that I'm too cheap to buy the cappuccino but I'd prefer it if we could talk somewhere else," Tanaka said.

She looked at him and smiled. "OK."

"Do you trust me for a car ride to my office, it's only a few minutes away?"

"Sure. As long as you get me to the train station by five."

"That's a deal. Now if you wait here I'll go get the car and pick you up."

"That's all right, I don't mind a little walk."

They started talking on the way to the car park and by the time they'd arrived at the medical building their conversation had covered the Gabriel trial and reached the weeks directly preceding Howard Rossi's death.

★ ★ ★

"The strangest thing he did was to go to Las Vegas," Barbara Rossi said, sitting back in the cushioned chair in front of Tanaka's desk. "I mean he'd been there before once or twice but not that I know of since he'd retired. He was never much of a gambler and he hated crowds of people, but I think that

253

was just what attracted him to the place."

"The gambling?" Tanaka asked.

"No, the crowds. In the last weeks he was terrified of being on his own. I would have come and stayed with him but I was at the tail-end of my divorce and fighting for the custody of my two kids, so I couldn't just up and leave Chicago. Otherwise I would have been there."

"Can you tell me why he was so frightened?"

"Over the years there was a lot of hate mail regarding the Gabriel trial, and just before Dad died he had some pretty frightening phone calls."

"Frightening in what way?"

"In that whoever made them knew a lot about the murders, and a lot about my father. It was some crazy who identified himself as Graham Paisley."

"The minister?"

"Yes, the one who spoke out against Gabriel and lost his life for doing it."

"Right. Right. Didn't your dad try to trace the calls?"

"He didn't have any luck with that."

"Why Paisley?"

"I'm not sure, maybe because Dad had known Paisley, or maybe because at the trial the police photos of the Paisley family were the most upsetting to my father. I think it was the children. They'd been very badly mutilated."

"Do you know what the caller said?"

"Yes, I do. He asked: 'Do you believe a man can fly?'"

"Did that mean anything to your father?"

"Sure, it was a headline in one of the big papers."

"I'm sorry, I wasn't in Philadelphia at that time. Would you explain that to me?"

"It was a question that the defense asked the jury. Part of the testimony against Gabriel, from the people who had worked with him and from the one member of his cult — or commune or religion or whatever it was — who testified against him, was that he had the power to fly. Not in a literal sense but in dreams. He could fly between the worlds of waking and sleeping. That's how he kept control of his flock, by controling their dreams. I mean Gabriel was not at the murder scene. He did not physically take part in the Paisleys' deaths. That was what his entire defense was based on. That's why the best they could do was get him for conspiracy. The flying stuff became a joke and his attorneys tried to capitalise on it, although I don't

255

think my father ever considered it a joke."

"Why was that?"

"It was a very frightening time, during that trial. I had just turned fifteen and I can still remember my father locking the doors of the house every night, checking on the windows, walking around in the dark with a loaded gun. He was frightened of Gabriel. And he couldn't sleep. He moved out of the main bedroom and into the spare room because he was keeping my mother awake. She kept saying that he shouldn't let that little guy get to him, but he did. Dad had insomnia for weeks and weeks, and when he did sleep his dreams were poisoned."

"Poisoned?"

"That's what he used to say."

"What did he mean?"

"Dad was a very practical man, and he sure wasn't superstitious, but that trial got to him. First of all Gabriel used to sit there and stare at my father. He would never blink his eyes, just stare. Dad said they were the deadest eyes he'd ever seen and when he did sleep he would see them staring at him, right through his dreams. Whatever he was dreaming he could see those eyes. That's what he meant by poisoned. Finally he started to see them all the time. That's when he had to see a psychiatrist."

"Do you know the psychiatrist's name?"

"No, I don't." Her voice softened. "You said on the phone that you thought maybe there was more to Dad's death than a heart attack. What did you mean by that?"

"I've been involved with two other heart-related deaths in the past two weeks," Tanaka replied. "Both these people were involved in the Gabriel case and I'm looking for some kind of link."

"Then I'd like to ask you something else."

"Go ahead."

"Do you believe a man could be frightened to death?"

"It's possible," Tanaka answered.

"How would it happen?"

"A sudden shock could do it."

"You see, I believe that's what happened to my father."

"Why?"

"Because for weeks before that heart attack he told me he couldn't sleep at night because his dreams were poisoned again."

"Did he mention how they were poisoned?"

"Not really. I think it had something to do with the phone calls; it just brought everything back at once, like it had all

257

happened yesterday. He became obsessed with Justin Gabriel again. He kept saying, 'He's found me, that little bastard's found me.'"

"Have you any idea about the calls? Who could have made them?"

"Gabriel's following was bigger than the few people who died at his house," she answered. "I'm sure some of them are still out there, waiting for their messiah to return. Maybe it was one of them. I don't think Dad had the strength to go through it again, the first time was very traumatic and he was younger. This time I think something inside him just gave up."

"I see," Tanaka replied.

"I think it was fear that killed him," she concluded.

"You may be right."

There was a long silence.

"Is there anything else you need to know?" she asked.

Tanaka shook his head. "Not for now, but you've been incredibly helpful and I appreciate it." He got up from his chair. "Barbara, if there's anything I can do for you, you've got my number here at the medical building." He reached into his pocket and handed her his card. "And my home number's right there."

"You can help keep Justin Gabriel locked up till he rots, that's what my father wanted and that's what you can do for me," Barbara Rossi answered.

"I'll try," Tanaka promised.

* * *

Tanaka dropped by Stan Leibowitz's office on his way home from the medical building.

"Three visits in three days," the psychiatrist quipped. "My secretary's wondering why we're not billing you."

Tanaka smiled and sat down.

"Stan, I think there's something going on here. I said it before and now I'm certain of it." He sounded excited.

"Slow down, you're way ahead of me."

"Justin Gabriel."

"OK. Now I'm catching up."

"I've been to see the relatives of two of the people who were involved in his trial. One was a witness for the prosecution and the other was the assistant DA who actually prosecuted him; both of them are dead. The witness two weeks ago, the DA about eight months ago. Bob Moyer would make three — "

"Hey, Joey. That trial's twenty years old and people do die."

"All of them, including Bob, died from heart attacks and none had a history of heart trouble. Remember, Stan, you're the man who doesn't believe in coincidence."

"How does this tie in to Bill?" Leibowitz asked.

"Fear."

"Are you saying they were frightened to death?"

"That's what their next-of-kin believe and in every case there was some type of message from Gabriel, either a postcard or a phone call, that precipitated a spate of dreams . . ."

Leibowitz rested his chin in his hand. He didn't look at all convinced.

"It's just like he explains it in the article you faxed me," Tanaka continued. "The communication creates the opening, the vulnerability. It gets better though. After Gabriel was barred from practicing therapy he went down to Mexico and came back claiming to be a witch doctor; his power animal was a bird. I know for certain that one of the deceased was having a recurrent nightmare of a bird, to the point where she was terrified of falling asleep."

"Phillip Harrison's dream was about a bird," Leibowitz replied. Suddenly he was very serious.

"Sounds like Bill, doesn't it?" Tanaka asked.

"Yes," Leibowitz agreed.

"I've even got motive."

Leibowitz cocked his head.

"Gabriel's parole hearing," Tanaka said.

"I wasn't aware of any hearing," Leibowitz replied.

"It comes up in three months and it's his only shot at freedom."

"But a parole hearing would be handled by people who were not directly involved in the case," Leibowitz said.

"I'm fairly certain that Howard Rossi and Bob Moyer were actively involved in seeing that that hearing never took place, and I know that Maura Allan was."

"And Bill?"

"I don't know yet."

"Okay, Josef, just two questions."

Tanaka was on a roll. "What are they?"

"How do you prove it and, if you can, what the hell do you do about it?"

"That's why I came to you."

Leibowitz sat quietly for what seemed to Tanaka a very long time. Finally he spoke. "Josef, I've been interested in this alternative belief stuff for most of my life, it's probably what got me into this field to begin with. I've never discounted the power of the mind and

I've never thought that Western medicine or Western psychology ever even scratched the surface of what it's all about, but Western medicine is what I practice." He stopped talking and reached for a black Filofax that sat on his desk.

"You need somebody who's had more experience with this type of thing than me. I read about it and I intellectualise but like I said before, I'm an academic, I don't *know*." He placed particular emphasis on the word 'know'.

Leibowitz opened the Filofax and sifted through the pages until he located the number. "I speak to this guy occasionally. I even send patients to him. He runs a kind of ashram up in the mountains and he's spent a lifetime exploring the kinds of things that this involves. Let me run it by him without being too particular."

★ ★ ★

Three hours later Tanaka was sitting at the dining table across from Rachel. Billy was asleep and the monitor, connecting them to his room, had been quiet for the past half-hour.

They'd eaten mozzarella and dried-tomato

risotto. Made from a recipe that Josef had learned from one of his Italian students at the dojo, it was a radical departure from the Japanese rice and noodle dishes that he usually prepared when he took the helm in the kitchen.

He had not intended to be dramatic. Had no desire or intention to worry Rachel with stories of Justin Gabriel or his discoveries of the past week but there had been no way to be truthful without bringing up his suppositions.

★ ★ ★

"I've listened to everything that you've said and I'm sorry but I just can't buy the idea of a mind killer, or whatever you'd call him," Rachel said, placing her wine glass down. "I remember Justin Gabriel. He was a very sick, very frightening man, but today the guy must be nearly sixty and I just don't see him turning into a bird and flying through concrete walls, all the way up to Long Island."

The way she put it brought a smile to Tanaka's face. "OK, but how about the phone calls to Bill in New Mexico?" He'd spoken to Diane Genero less than an hour ago and when she'd mentioned the calls he'd felt as though he was on the last leg of the race.

"Crank calls. We've had them here," Rachel answered. "Come on, you told me yourself, Diane doesn't know what was said and after they changed their phone number the calls stopped."

"And the dreams started," Tanaka added.

"Coincidence." There a little too much nonchalance in her tone.

"I hate that word," Tanaka snapped.

"Don't get so edgy. I'm being honest with you. What do you want me to say?"

Tanaka looked at her and shook his head.

"I'm a medical doctor, just like you," Rachel said. "I have a hard time with this type of thing. I mean I enjoy watching *The X-Files*, but when it gets down to it I wouldn't call myself a believer."

Tanaka respected his wife's opinion and felt as if he was being gently subdued. He looked at her empty glass and reached for the bottle of Chablis but she shook her head and sat back in her chair.

"I know how you feel about Bill and I'm not trying to be insensitive," she continued. "I just think there's got to be a medical reason for his condition. I mean, maybe you're right about Gabriel, maybe he's the cause of it, but I'm more inclined to think in

264

terms of a stress disorder than of something paranormal."

"Yes, maybe," Tanaka answered. By now he was questioning his own rationale, wondering if he'd been less than objective when listening to Jim Allan and Barbara Rossi. Maybe there was no connection between any of it.

"What's happening to Bill is awful, I know that better than most people," Rachel added. She was referring to the stress disorder that had followed her own abduction. "Before I met Stan Leibowitz, I was a goner. I couldn't function."

"I remember," Tanaka replied. It was after the Mantis case, and had been the first time he and Bill had worked together.

"What does Stan make of all this?" Rachel asked.

"He's not pretending to understand it, but at the same time he's not discounting it."

This time it was Rachel who smiled. She loved and trusted Stan Leibowitz. She also knew him as a frustrated mystic who read everything from Stephen Hawkins to Baba Ram Dass, anything that offered insight into the nature of reality and the universe.

"In fact he's got me hooked up with some people who may be able to shed some light on it," Tanaka added. "I've been invited to a Buddhist retreat."

"I don't understand."

"A lot of Gabriel's writing sounds like the mystical side of Buddhism," Tanaka explained. "There are religious sects that are very close to sorcery, where meditation and dreaming are used to gain power. I don't think it would hurt me to hear the other side of this, the non-medical side, particularly before I meet Gabriel."

"You're going to meet him?" There was surprise in her voice.

"He's in Graterford and the warden's an old friend of Bob Moyer's. I set it up through him."

"Why?"

"Because if all this is coincidence, and nothing more, then I'll know it when I meet him. I'll feel it."

"You really think so?"

"Yes, I do."

Rachel held his eyes until he spoke again. "I know I moved quickly and I know I made some decisions without talking to you, but Bill's in a lot of trouble. I owe him this much."

"I understand," she replied. "I just don't like the idea of you getting close to that man. It gives me the creeps."

Before he could answer the baby's monitor

crackled to life and there was a gurgling of unformed words, a hiccup, and a cry.

Rachel got up from her chair. "Didn't that sound like 'hey, Mom, I'm hungry'?" she asked, her demeanor lifting. "Don't go away, I'll be right back."

When she returned she was carrying Billy. "I think he was just feeling left out."

Tanaka held out his arms and Rachel lowered the boy to his father.

"Don't worry," Tanaka said, hugging his son. "Everything will be fine."

15

Five thirty in the morning and still dark. There was a brittle stillness to the sleeping city, broken only by the sound of milk trucks and street sweepers. The sky was clear and the weather predictions had been good, temperatures in the high fifties, an Indian summer, a perfect day for a ride.

He'd wanted to take the Harley because the bike put him in a certain frame of mind. Riding was like meditation; it required concentration and awareness. His mind rarely wandered when he was riding and his senses were heightened to the sounds of the road and the rush of the wind. He didn't want any negatives today, nothing to creep in and cloud his thoughts, no preconceptions; he was going to learn and he wanted to be receptive and clear. For that reason he'd not eaten at all the preceding day, just water to flush his system. It had been a long time since he had fasted and the sensation of hunger was like a stimulant, energising him. He bent over the bed and kissed Rachel. "I'll phone you when I get there," he promised. After that he slipped into the adjoining room and looked down at Billy. The little boy was asleep on his back, his arms folded in front, hands resting on top of his chest. His face was full and round but beneath the puppy fat Josef could see the formation of bones, the beginning of character. From where he was standing he could see himself in the child's profile but as he bent closer it was Rachel who appeared in the full lips and eyes. Josef's eyes had a slight slant but Billy's were straight and set far apart like his mother's. They were also the same pale blue. Josef had wanted a son. Now, above all else, he wanted to be a good father. He thought of his own life, of the twists and turns, the times he had been close to death, the chances he had taken. "I want to live long enough to see you grow up. Be healthy enough to enjoy things with you, and wise enough to stand back and let you learn your own lessons." He reached out and touched Billy's forehead, just a light touch with his fingertips on the smooth warm skin. "I love you," he whispered.

The Harley sat next to the Jeep in the underground parking space. The saddle was off and a charger was attached to the battery. Josef hadn't ridden in a month and the bike had barely turned over when he'd last tried to start it so after he'd packed his saddlebags he'd hooked up a slow charge and left it over night. Now he disconnected the leads and bolted the saddle back into place. The hundred-horsepower engine fired up on the first try and he let it idle while putting on his helmet and gloves. He was wearing thermals underneath his leather jacket, jeans and engineer boots and his body felt warm as he rode up the ramp and on to the street, the big twin rumbling through town, its straight pipes echoing off the vacant office buildings. By the time he'd hit the expressway he'd begun to relax. It was always that way after a lay-off from the bike, it took him a few miles to get it back together with the machine. After that, with the morning sun rising behind his right shoulder and the fresh breeze batting his cheeks, he remembered why he loved to ride. It was the solitude and the freedom.

The Schulkill was clear and the run to the turnpike was quick and smooth. He paid his toll, accelerated to seventy and forgot about everything but the throb of the engine for the next twenty miles. Then he followed the signs for the Northeast Extension and powered on towards the mountains.

He exited the turnpike at Allentown, took the road through Stroudsburg and started to climb. He was familiar with the mountains, he'd ridden them many times in the past years; they were two and a half hours from Philadelphia and a different world. He concentrated, easing the bike around the bends then twisting the throttle on the straight climbs, past waterfalls and houses made from yellowed stone.

The Retreat was located ten miles north of the town of Summit and Leibowitz had given him the landmarks and the phone number, explaining to him that the place looked like a small farm. Its founder was a writer by the name of Richard James, and Tanaka had read one of his books years ago. It was an occult thriller, set in New York. Tanaka had enjoyed it enough to be curious about the author. He discovered that James had written a string of cult hits in the early seventies, invested his money in land and dropped out of the 'bestseller' race. That was all Tanaka knew till Leibowitz had mentioned the Retreat.

"Two turnings to the right after the saw mill," the doctor had said, and now Tanaka could see a building with a sign that read 'Summit Wood Works' a few hundred feet ahead of him on the left side of the road. He slowed down as he rounded the next bend, then took the second right, past a couple of rundown shingled houses with smoke spiraling from their chimneys, and continued to ride. He had just begun to wonder if he had taken the correct turn when he saw the white farmhouse set back from the road. There was a sign mounted on a post at the foot of the gravel driveway with a six-pointed star inside a circle and the words 'eternal nature' carved into the wood. A mailbox marked 'Retreat' sat below the sign and suddenly Tanaka was conscious of the thunder from the Harley's exhaust. He hardly sounded like a spiritual traveler. He turned into the drive and cut off his engine about fifty yards from the house, leaving the bike half hidden by a tree as he removed his helmet en route to the front door. He knocked and waited but no one answered.

He tried twice more and still no one came. He began to feel awkward and suffered a flashing image of several bearded monks witnessing his arrival and taking cover, then reminded himself that Leibowitz had assured him he was expected. He was about to knock for a fourth time when he heard the sweet sound of a temple gong through the door. It was actually more than a sound; it was a resonance that seemed to penetrate the wood and press gently outward against his body. Another reverberation and the door was opened by a tall, bearded man dressed in a loose muslin shirt and trousers and wearing zori, Japanese rope sandals.

"Josef?"

Tanaka would not have recognised Richard James from the back cover of his book but he remembered the beard and piercing eyes.

"Richard?"

"Yes, we've been expecting you. Then we heard this incredible noise, we thought a helicopter was landing, it was right at the end of morning meditation." James looked down at Tanaka's helmet then behind him in the direction of the Softail.

"I'm very sorry," Tanaka said. He was about to continue his apology when James whisked by him in the direction of the oak tree.

"What is it anyway?"

"A Harley Davidson."

"I can see that, but what have you done to it? It looks stretched."

A minute later and the bearded holy man was seated on Tanaka's bike talking about his love affair with a 1969 Electra Glide. "I gave it up after my third knee operation. Never could ride when I was stoned and I was stoned most of the time by the end the sixties."

Tanaka and James talked motorcycles for a few more minutes before he was invited to the house.

Inside, the smell of incense was like a delicate burning grass. There were several people standing and talking and James introduced Josef to each of them. All were American with the exception of a small, squat Japanese woman. She was very different from the rest and seemed to stand alone in the room, as if she was waiting for something or someone. Her hair was long and thick, fanning down past her hips, and she was dressed in robes of very rough fabric, like a burlap. Her forearms were visible below the sleeves and they were muscular like a man's and covered in tattoos: birds, deer, a cat and what looked to Tanaka like a bear. The tattoos had been done in blue ink and not colored in, leaving only the outlines of the animals. Her face was strongly featured, a mixture of feminine and masculine, her nose large and flat, her mouth full, while her eyes were soft and brown. She bowed when she was introduced to Josef and he sensed a strength and vitality in her that was at once attractive and daunting.

"Josef, this is Akiyo," James said. "Akiyo and I met many years ago when I was researching a book near Lake Biwa."

Josef knew Lake Biwa. It was so named because it was curved like the belly of a musical instrument, a mandolin or balalaika. Hills and mountains surrounded it, and, in Japan, its views were a favorite subject for both painters and poets.

Josef and Akiyo exchanged bows, then Akiyo took hold of Josef's hand and gripped it firmly. Her skin was dry and callused, and the same strength that Josef sensed in her presence exuded from her flesh. She held him that way for a few seconds, looking at him, studying his face and eyes.

"OK, OK, you are strong enough, I will take you," she said in Japanese and before Josef could respond she dropped his hand and walked from the room. Her gesture and her presence were dramatic yet without pretense or self-consciousness. James, who had been watching their exchange, walked to Josef.

"Good, she's accepted you."

"Who is she?" Josef asked.

"A friend," James answered.

Josef looked puzzled and James did nothing to inform or reassure him. "Please, let me show you the house," he said.

The eighteenth-century building was deceptively large, most of its downstairs having been opened to form a single room; the floor was pine, aged and polished to a rich gold, and covered in thick Indian and Tibetan carpets which extended to a raised platform at the far end, adorned by smaller prayer rugs. The meditation gong was mounted inside a wooden frame and sat on the platform. It appeared to be about three feet in diameter and was made from hammered brass.

"I heard that when I was standing outside. It makes a beautiful sound," Tanaka said.

"Yes. I got it in Thailand in 1966. It took me nearly a year to have it shipped home, but it was just one of those things I had to have, at the time I didn't even know why."

"You were in Thailand in 'sixty-six?"

"I was there on r and r."

"From Vietnam?"

"Two tours. I was in the infantry. Sergeant Dickie James."

Tanaka smiled and reappraised his host.

"How did you go from being Sergeant James to this?" he asked.

"I think it was a form of natural progression. Don't forget it was the sixties, but you look a little young to remember."

"It was probably different in Tokyo, anyway," Tanaka said.

James laughed and Tanaka liked his laugh. It was honest and open.

"How about Stan? How did you meet him?" Tanaka asked.

"At a seminar in Esalen, in Big Sur. Stan always did question the science of his profession. He's a free thinker."

Tanaka smiled in agreement.

"He mentioned that you were interested in Justin Gabriel," James continued.

"Yes, I am."

"A very dangerous man."

"Do you know him?" Tanaka asked. It was odd but even the mention of Gabriel had begun to make him feel uncomfortable. He was getting to feel strangely connected to the man.

"Years ago I read a bunch of his essays and saw that we were interested in the same thing, but coming to it from different places," James explained. "He was a practicing psychologist who had studied shamanism and I was an aspiring writer who was fascinated by it. He used to give seminars so I attended several of them, but he was too much of an egomaniac, even then he was all tied up in power games, and that wasn't where I wanted to be."

"So you know why I'm here?"

"You think he may be playing head games with one of your friends. That's what Stan told me."

"I'm looking into it," Tanaka replied. He didn't want to sound too convinced.

"That's the reason I wanted you to meet Akiyo."

"The lady with the tattoos?"

"She's a shugenja."

"A mountain mystic?"

"You know about shugendo?" James asked, impressed by Tanaka's knowledge.

"I had a martial arts teacher who practiced."

James nodded his head. "Akiyo has been visiting with us for about three months. It's the first time I've been able to work out all the arrangements, you know, passports and all, then actually get her into an airplane to make the trip. The hardest part was to convince her to wear shoes. The airlines have a rule about shoes."

Tanaka laughed.

"She's one of the great healers," James

said. "Her methods can be a little radical but she's a genius."

"How did you meet her?"

"As I said, it was years ago, on one of my first trips to Japan. I got sick. I don't know exactly where or how; I suppose it was some sort of viral infection, but it nearly finished me. I went to a lot of doctors and not one of them could diagnose it. Antibiotics didn't work. Nothing worked. Finally I just lay in bed. I figured I'd die. The girl I was staying with was Buddhist and she had heard through the temple of this amazing healer. The trouble was the healer lived in the mountains and rarely came down. Some people didn't believe she existed at all. My friend was desperate and I had pretty well given up — I mean I was actually making plans to ship my body back to America — and that's when Akiyo showed up saying that she'd heard that there was a man in trouble. It was as simple as that and I wasn't about to ask questions. You know, before all this, before I got sick, I wanted to believe in certain things, I understood them intellectually and I thought I believed, but there was a huge gap between my mind and my actual faith. When I was lying there, wasting away, that gap more or less disappeared. It was magic, real magic."

"May I ask you how she did it, how she healed you?"

"It took place inside a dream," James replied.

"Do you remember the dream?" Tanaka asked. Now he knew why Stan Leibowitz had insisted he meet Richard James.

James looked at Tanaka and smiled gently. "I don't usually talk about this. I'm not sure that it's good."

"It's good for me to hear it. To understand it," Tanaka answered.

James nodded. "I was lying in a desert, starved and wasted. The sky was so blue and peaceful, and my only desire was to let go, to leave my body and my pain and drift away, into that beautiful blue. Then I heard a sound, well, more like a melody than a sound, but it was a natural melody, sort of like — have you ever heard wind chimes?"

"Yes," Tanaka replied.

"Like that, but full and absolutely pure. As I heard it I saw this great silver bird circling above me, and the flapping of its wings seemed to be making the music, but it wasn't music any more, it was a vibration, warm and soothing, like a warmth coming down on to my body. As I watched I became aware that the bird had come for me. It was a strange feeling, more relief than fear, because I thought the bird had come to take my soul, to pluck it from my carcass and carry it to heaven. It's difficult even now to describe my feelings, but I was open in a way that I had never been before. I suppose it was because my body was so near death that I accepted what was happening. I surrendered to it, and that's when it landed on my chest. The weight of it surprised me. I mean it was an actual presence, with claws and eyes and wings, an actual living, breathing thing." He hesitated and looked at Tanaka. "Do you know what I did?"

The imagery of the story had captured Tanaka completely. He shook his head.

"I panicked."

The way that James delivered the line caused Tanaka to laugh and James laughed with him.

"It's true. I completely freaked out and started to struggle, pushing it away, fighting for breath. That's when I woke up." His voice became serious again. "It was more than simply waking from a sleep; it was like being born, coming from a darkness into the light. Akiyo was standing above me. She had laid her hands on my chest and when she removed them I had the sensation of being without weight, as if I

280

was floating above my body, and the air, the air was so fresh and clean. It was like pure oxygen and I just wanted to breathe it in, to let it fill me. Akiyo was chanting and I recognised the sound of her voice as the music of the wings. Three days later and I was well."

"That's an incredible story," Tanaka said. "Parts of it sound amazingly similar to what's happening to my friend."

"Yes, that's what Stan told me. The difference is that Akiyo's purpose was to heal. Her projection could have as easily been used to do me harm."

"With no disrespect, Richard, I have a hard time understanding all of this."

"I know."

"I'm a medical doctor and . . . " Tanaka hesitated.

"You've hit your limits as to what makes sense, but somewhere in here," James placed his hand above his heart, "you do know, and that's why you've come. That's why I want you to have some time with Akiyo, but you'll have to be receptive, you'll have to trust her completely. If anyone can help you to see the nature of your friend's illness, she's the one. She understands these things."

★ ★ ★

281

Gabriel lay on his cot, his eyes open, staring at the ceiling. His morning tray of toast, scrambled eggs and green tea lay undisturbed in the slot of his door. He had dreamed of the courtroom again and was now locked into the hypno-pompic hallucinations that occurred between the worlds of sleep and wakefulness. They were vivid seamless visions and he could control them by altering the pattern of his breath, maintaining his body in a sleep mode while remaining conscious.

The jury was 'in' and he could see each of their faces as they re-entered the room and took their seats in the box. The courtroom was different now, different from the place he had sat in nearly twenty years ago and listened with his heart racing and his mouth dry as his life had been taken from him. He had altered the dream in the past years, breaking down its fabric by removing its participants. His intention was to be found 'not guilty'. Not that an 'innocent' verdict could replace the years of his confinement, but it would confirm that his work was complete.

Bill Fogarty stared back at him, his mind reaching out. "Guilty. Guilty. Guilty." His thoughts were like shackles.

Gabriel focused his mind upon the mind of the cop and concentrated, connecting with his energy as he envisioned the bird. The great avenging bird, with its powers of flight and perception. He concentrated and willed the tentacles of his consciousness to unfurl from the dark predatory eyes, reaching out. He was with him now, inside Bill Fogarty's mind. He could sense Fogarty's fear as it evolved, turning to panic, but there was something else happening, threatening their connection.

★ ★ ★

Darkness, then light, like fireworks exploding. After that came the spasm in his gut as his skull felt as if it was splitting open.

The sickness was all over him, twisting and turning him. He convulsed, biting down on his lips, sucking air, frothing from the mouth. For five eternal seconds, then he was unconscious.

He woke up twenty minutes later. He was lying on the floor but what floor? Where? The smell of his own body, a sweet musky smell, and the feeling that he was wearing his skin like a garment and the garment was too tight, stretched fine across his forehead and temples.

"Gabriel?"

The voice came from behind the bars,

two eyes looking inwards. He crawled to his hands and knees.

"You haven't finished your food. I thought you liked your eggs scrambled?"

"Leave me alone."

The sound of the door being opened as Art Weller entered.

"I don't understand what's the matter with you? Do you need to see the medic?"

Gabriel pulled himself to the side of his cot and clung to it. His head ached.

"I don't want anything." He was tired again, incredibly tired but his memory was trickling back.

"What's happening, doc?" Weller asked.

It was Weller's smell that brought it all home, that sickly aroma of Old Spice and Listerine which blanketed his chronic halitosis.

"What time is it?" Gabriel asked.

"Almost nine thirty in the morning."

Nine o'clock. The sickness always came at nine o'clock in the morning and it always took the same pattern.

"Thanks, you can leave now."

Weller hesitated.

"You all right about Tuesday?"

Gabriel thought for a moment and stared blankly at the guard.

"Chief medical examiner. What's he want

284

in here?" Weller continued.

He remembered when there were always new requests to visit his prisoner, newspapers and magazines, doctors and professors, but in the past few years the interest in Justin Gabriel had waned. "Maybe it's got something to do with the parole hearing?"

"I want to know who this man is."

"His name is Dr Josef Tanaka," Weller replied.

Gabriel looked at him and stood up. "I want to know all about him," he said.

★ ★ ★

Phillip Harrison waited on the other side of the cell door. He could smell the food on the tray and the smell disturbed him, particularly the smell of the eggs. He'd gone to a lot of trouble with them.

16

A toothbrush, toothpaste, a razor, a comb, two pairs of socks, two pairs of undershorts, a cotton training suit. Tanaka laid his belongings out on the white duvet that covered the platformed futon. Aside from the bed and night table, with its single reading lamp, the room was purposefully sparse, no pictures or mirrors and no superfluous decoration. The walls were linen white and the curtained window looked out on to fields and valleys. In the distance, a shimmering blue lake floated like a mirage above the landscape.

James had installed only a single telephone in the Retreat and that was kept in his office, away from the main room, and after Tanaka's call to Rachel, to tell her of his safe arrival, James had closed and locked the office door. Silence was everywhere.

Tanaka had dreamed again of the mountains and of the stream flowing with bodies. It was the same dream he'd had at Stony Brook following his visit to Fogarty, but this time the bodies were closer to the surface. "Help me, Josef, help me." Fogarty had asked him in the dream and, again, Tanaka had been too frightened to look beyond the reflection of his own face. He had awakened to the stillness of the room with the dream clinging to him. He'd felt it all around him as he got out of bed and walked to the bathroom at the end of the hall, as if soap and water could wash away his uncertainty.

After he had finished bathing and dressing

he went downstairs. Akiyo was seated in the meditation room. He hadn't seen her since their meeting yesterday and she was wearing the same coarse cotton dress. Her feet were bare and stained brown from the earth, substantial in appearance like her strong arms and hands. She stood as he entered and they greeted each other in Japanese. This time, however, she hugged him and Tanaka was surprised by both the power of her body and the intimacy of the act.

"Ready then?" she asked, looking down. "You should wear tough shoes."

Tanaka retrieved his riding boots from the shoe rack in the entrance hall and carried them with him to the back of the house, stopping a minute to pull them on before trailing Akiyo into the field.

They walked silently for twenty minutes until they reached a plateau overlooking a gorge.

"You must love your friend very much," she said.

"I do," Tanaka replied.

She smiled. It was a big innocent smile, her teeth white and her face like the face of a child, only the lines around her eyes gave any hint of age.

They climbed down along the side of the hill into the gorge.

"First to hell, then to heaven," she said, using her hands to grip the shrubs and roots while her feet held sure and steady against the dirt and stone. Tanaka was an athlete and a sensei, making it his business to maintain a high level of strength and fitness, but after a hundred yards he was lagging behind. He tried to quicken his pace and stumbled, landing on his side. Akiyo turned and watched him regain his feet.

"No injury?"

"No injury," Tanaka confirmed. "Just humiliation."

Akiyo laughed and her laughter echoed into the ravine that lay at the base of the gorge. "No need for that. I have lived in the mountains all my life. I was born in the mountains, it is my natural habitat, my hands, my feet, my whole body are made to climb. Like a cat."

Tanaka inched his way down the hillside towards her. She waited for him, then led him to an area where the shrubs had been worn thin by footsteps. "My path," she said.

It was steep and continued to the base of the gorge where three large rocks, two facing each other with the third joining them in the middle, formed a natural seat. Akiyo stopped and motioned for Tanaka to join her.

"I come here often," she said. "Please, sit down."

Tanaka walked to her and sat on the cold rock.

"Now we begin. You must speak honestly. Everything depends upon that. You must purge yourself of all impurity."

Tanaka looked at her in silence, not certain of what she meant.

"Talk about your life," she said. "Begin with the day that you were born."

Tanaka had not known what to expect and had promised himself that whatever happened he would remain open but Akiyo's request caused him to feel self-conscious and tongue-tied.

"You must speak," she ordered. "You must empty your self." Tanaka began, speaking slowly and quietly at first, about his American mother and Samurai father, explaining that he was his father's only child by his second marriage and that his older half-brother Hironori had been pure Japanese. He spoke for about ten minutes, about his childhood, his Christian education and early schooling, then stopped.

"You are not speaking from your heart," Akiyo said.

Tanaka sat stoically.

"Each of us is burdened," she continued.

"Doubt and guilt, there is not a living soul without these things, but you, you are seeking strength. You must have magokura, pure heart."

Tanaka began to speak again but his words were empty.

"This will not work," Akiyo said, walking from behind to face him. "If you are serious about helping your friend, perhaps you must die for him."

Tanaka met her eyes.

"Come with me; we will try another way."

She led him along the path, to a point a few feet from the edge of the ravine that split the bottom of the gorge.

"Do you believe a man can fly?" she asked.

Tanaka looked down; he estimated the drop to be about two hundred feet.

"No," he answered, looking up.

She was holding a long length of rope in her right hand. One end had been tied and resembled a hangman's noose. She held it towards him.

He hesitated.

"If you cannot fly, then I think it would be a good idea for you to use the rope," she insisted. "Come on, we have no time to waste." She pressed it into his hand. "Put it over your head and down beneath your arms, tight so that it will not slip."

Tanaka looked at the rope. "Why?" he asked.

"It is part of the old custom and it is not without purpose."

Tanaka shook his head. "I don't think so."

"If you no longer wish to continue then our journey is over," Akiyo said. She turned and began to walk. "I cannot help you."

"Hold on," Tanaka called after her.

She turned back.

"Can't you even tell me why we're doing this?"

She looked at him and shook her head. "You are very Western in your thinking. Always needing a reason. Sometimes the reason becomes apparent only after the act."

He felt foolish as he slipped the rope over his head and down to his chest.

"Give the other end to me," Akiyo said.

He handed her the loose end and she pulled, tightening the knot across his chest, then she led him to the edge of the ravine.

"Climb down."

"What!?"

"I am holding you," she replied.

He remained hesitant.

"It is the only way for a person of your temperament."

"The only way for what?"

"There you go again, asking your questions. The reason is to empty the vessel of your self."

The side of the ravine was a sheer drop and Tanaka's initial steps were tentative. He clung on with his hands while his feet found small ledges and indentations in the rock surface. He thought of his friend in Stony Brook. "I don't know who's crazier, Bill, you or me?" He looked up to see Akiyo staring down at him, letting the rope play through her hands. What the hell was he doing? Rachel hadn't even wanted him to take the bike in case the weather turned bad, and now here he was rock climbing. There was an element of black comedy to the whole thing. Oh yeah, Rachel would really love this one. He almost laughed but his right foot slipped and he felt the rope give, changing his mood in an instant; he became angry with himself. What the hell *was* he doing? He owed his wife and son more than a broken neck. It was crazy, it was dangerous and it was over; he would find another way to help Bill. He was going home. He took a firm grip on a piece of jagged rock and pulled himself upwards, pushing with his feet and wedging the fingers of his free hand into a crevice, pulling again.

His forehead was even with the top of the ravine when the rock crumbled and for an instant he was plummeting through space, then the rope dug hard into his armpits and his body swung out and over the drop. He used his hands to cushion his impact against the wall on the return swing, then hung there, catching his breath. The rope had given with his weight and looking up he reckoned he was about twenty feet from the edge of the ravine. He tried to climb, hoisting himself hand over hand, but as he did the rope gave some more. Next he looked up hoping to see Akiyo, intending to tell her to tie the rope to a tree so that he could attempt another climb, but she wasn't there. He called her name.

"Talk to the mountains, not to me," she answered. Her voice sounded far away.

"It's over. I've had enough," Tanaka shouted.

"You have not yet begun."

Her reply angered him and he tried to climb a third time. The rope gave, or was let out, so he hung silently, until his anger simmered and his emotions gave way to thought. "Talk about your life." One thing was for certain; he would never tell anyone how he'd managed to end up down the side of a mountain on the end of a rope. "Talk about your life." But then again, how could he resist. Bob Moyer would have laughed his ass off. And Bill? He'd never let him live this down. Bill would roar.

"It's the kind of thing that used to happen to me as a kid. The kind of thing that Hiro would get me into, telling me that if I wanted to play with the older boys I'd have to pass a test. Then tying me to a tree and leaving me there until I'd figure out they weren't coming back and I'd end up shouting for my mother to rescue me. Yes, Hiro, he could be a real little bastard, the way older brothers can be, but if anybody at school ever called attention to the fact that I was half-caste, that my mother was American and I was 'gajiin', if anyone called me an 'outsider', Hironori would be on them like an avenging angel." Hironori had been Tanaka's first lesson in tragedy. Two half-brothers forced to face each other in the final round of the All-Japan Karate Championship, the 'gajiin' versus the Samurai, the younger brother versus the older. Josef was not supposed to win. Something inside him told him that. He was supposed to lay down in the face of the cameras, the public, his brother and his father. He was not pure. His skin was too fair and his eyes nearly straight. There was too much of his American mother in him. He was inferior. He knew that, and from somewhere deep down he believed it, but he had never known it as acutely as that day in front of ten thousand cheering people. Cheering for his brother, cheering for old Japan. He had been intimidated to the point of rigidity and the kick to Hiro's head had been thrown without control. He recalled the moment, the fear inside of him, the anger, the sound of his instep thudding into Hiro's flesh, the feeling of give as the vertebra snapped.

It had been a public execution, a repayment to Hiro for tying him to the tree, for standing up for him, for loving him, for being pure, for being his brother. And years later when Hiro had died, after a lifetime in a wheelchair, a lifetime in which Josef had tried every means of atonement and finally escaped to America to become a doctor, to heal that which could never be healed inside himself, all those years it was still there, the guilt, gnawing away. How many times had he pushed his own life to the edge? How many relationships had he destroyed because he was not worthy of a relationship? Until Bill Fogarty. It had taken someone with as many scars as himself to lead him through the nightmare, to drag him out the other side. "You think you're the only one with a fucking problem, son? You think you've got the market on guilt cornered? Grow up." Old Fogarty had fathered him when he needed fathering and brothered him when he needed brothering. The old cop had grown him up. So what the hell was he doing now, hanging by a rope, down the side of a ravine? If Fogarty could only see him. "I'm doing this for you, Bill." The whole damn thing was preposterous. Tanaka laughed out loud, then he thought of Bill, huddled in the corner of a padded room in a state hospital, alone and without dignity and he sobbed.

"I'm sorry, Bill. I'm so sorry."

The feelings of sadness emptied with his tears.

After his emotions had steadied he became aware again of his physical distress. The rope was bothering him, digging into the glands beneath his armpits. He shifted position and the rope slipped, dropping him another foot. What was happening up there? Was she letting it out, playing with him, or was she losing strength? She could kill him. He was at her mercy. He'd seen victims of long falls, fourth-story windows and bridges. He and Bob had performed autopsies on bodies with crushed vertebrae and splintered bones, thighs driven into the pelvis, every organ rammed upwards, ribs puncturing lungs and brains spilling.

"Come on. I'm finished. I've talked!" he shouted to the mountains and the sky.

An hour more passed and he was very cold. His anger gave way to a feeling of solitude and desertion. He thought again of Rachel and Billy and was overcome with emotion. It was like the feelings he'd had when he had first held his newborn son in his arms. Until then the child had been somehow abstract, more a promise than a fulfilment, but in that moment he had understood both the inevitability and purpose of all life. It was an intuitive understanding and had simultaneously humbled and exalted him and he had cried with joy as he was crying now — good clean tears, tears that made him whole and well. By the time he'd stopped crying the sun had passed over the lip of the ravine and disappeared. He closed his eyes, grateful for the darkness.

In his dream he was flying, soaring up the side of a mountain towards the sky.

★ ★ ★

"You are clean now. That's good, very good."

Tanaka recognised the sound of Akiyo's voice. It was close to him and very clear. He was back on the ground; he could smell the leaves and the earth. The air was fresh and pure. Akiyo was kneeling above him, plying the muscles of his shoulders and neck and her hands felt sure and strong.

"How did I get here?" he asked.

"You let go of your feelings and flew," she replied.

"Did you pull me up?"

"I told you. You flew."

"But — "

"Stop using your mind to give definition to everything. How do you feel now? That's the important thing."

Tanaka sat up slowly and she backed away from him. He was dressed as he had been before, leather jacket and riding boots, but somehow he felt lighter and less restricted, as if he had shed some sort of heavy armor.

"I feel light."

Akiyo laughed. "Perfect!"

Tanaka thought of Rachel and Billy. They seemed far away, not so much in a physical sense but emotionally. The feeling bothered him.

Akiyo studied his face as if she was reading him. "Passion can be a weakness," she said. "Emptying one's self is a good way to quell it. A warrior should not be too passionate. It causes mistakes."

"I've come to you in order to help my

friend," Tanaka said humbly. "Everything so far has been about me."

"You can only help him by helping yourself. You are the connection. He is a part of you, or I should say, he is a part of your vibratory field, your energy. Everyone that you have ever met or will ever meet is part of that field and every thought or feeling is transmitted through it. Your thoughts affect the object of them. All action and thought creates effect. This is the law of karma." She hesitated. "Think of your friend."

Tanaka envisioned Bill Fogarty as he had last seen him and the thought brought back the sadness and a feeling of sickness in the pit of his stomach.

"When you think of someone who has been close to you, the thought itself causes subtle changes to your vibration. I connect with him through you." Her eyes grew intense. "I sense his isolation and confusion. Things are being willed upon him that he does not understand. Either his mind will break completely or his heart will stop." Akiyo ceased talking and seemed to draw herself inwards, holding her arms tight to her body.

Tanaka thought of the police photographs that he had seen of Justin Gabriel. It was

299

his eyes that distinguished him. Dark and piercing.

Akiyo shuddered. "Your friend's enemy is very strong. I don't like to let him close to me, and you must not let him close to you. This one is treacherous, very bad."

"How can I stop him?" Tanaka asked.

"Only with a pure heart, magokura," she replied. "There must be nothing buried inside of you to be prodded and unearthed and used as a weapon against you. You must become like a mirror, shining and clean. Not a speck of dust. When the polluted soul looks at you, that soul will see only himself and his dark energy will be reflected, turning back on him. He will be consumed by his own malevolence. That is the only way."

Akiyo stopped and looked at Tanaka, then moved closer to him, her voice becoming more intense.

"It is important that you give him nothing in the fabric of your feelings and emotions to grip and tear open. He must have no place to enter you, because if he does, he will grow inside of you until he takes you over. This man is strong." She placed her head in her hands. When she looked up again her face was stern. "You must not face him until you are completely prepared."

"Tuesday at three o'clock," Tanaka thought. "Bill can't wait."

"I am warning you," Akiyo said.

"How do I prepare myself?" Tanaka asked.

"By letting go of everything that you love. By giving up your past and future, by emptying your self, then emptying the self that has remained, over and over again until there is no self. Then the mirror will be without dust."

"I haven't got the time — "

"Time is an illusion," she said sharply. "That's enough talk. Words open doors. Come on. Stand up. We will climb the mountain."

17

"So the doctor has a child, well that's very interesting. Very interesting," Justin Gabriel said, holding the photocopy of the newspaper article at arm's length so that he could read the fine print.

"I got my glasses, doc, you want me to read it to you?" Weller asked. He was always surprised that, in spite of his magic, Gabriel's eyes had weakened with age, just like everybody else's.

"No. I don't need you to read it," Gabriel answered. "I'm doing just fine."

"That was written just over a year old, right after the guy made it to medical examiner," Weller explained. "He's been involved in a lot of police stuff, hey?"

"Please," Gabriel said, motioning for silence. Then he continued to scour the *Sunday Feature* article on Josef Tanaka. One of the smaller pictures that accompanied the piece showed Tanaka holding Billy in his arms with Rachel standing beside him. "Ah, here's what we wanted to know," Gabriel said, eyeing the third paragraph of the article, "Doctor Tanaka and Police Captain William F. Fogarty have worked successfully together on several investigations including the 'Mantis Murders' in 1991 for which Dr Tanaka was awarded the city's citation for valor."

"I found a bunch of stuff on that Mantis thing, too," Weller added. "That's where I thought I'd heard the Japanese guy's name before. It was a big deal on the outside about five or six years back. Stuff's at the bottom of the pile." He was feeling good about his trip to the library archives. He was in for a decent reward from the master.

Gabriel finished the article then picked

up the clippings on the 'Mantis Murders'. Gabriel could read quickly, sometimes two books a day and he did have a pair of reading glasses, they were folded and placed alongside his copy of the *Book of the Dead*, but he didn't like to wear them in front of people. He didn't like anyone to have the idea that he relied on anything artificial.

It was in the last of the three articles on the 'Mantis Murders' that Rachel Saunders was mentioned by name and on the top of the page there was a picture of her with very long blond hair. 'Abducted and held hostage' was printed beneath her picture. There was no mention of a connection between the pretty plastic surgeon and Josef Tanaka but it was clearly the same woman that was standing beside him in the later piece.

"This guy's full of holes," Gabriel said. "I think he could be very helpful."

Weller stood in front of the little man and waited. Finally, Gabriel looked up.

"Thank you, Art. Now what is it that you need from me?"

"I want to win the lottery," Weller blurted. Even for the master he knew this was a big one.

"Oh really?"

"I mean not that it would affect my

position here. I'd still work here and everything."

"I see."

"I've been thinking about this for a long time. With everything you can do, it shouldn't be that hard. Listen, I can enter and we can split the money, no shit."

"That sounds reasonable."

"I just need the winning numbers."

"You'll have to give me a little time to get that together for you, Art," Gabriel replied, making no attempt to conceal the contempt from his tone. He hated ignorance.

"How much time do you think you'll need?"

"Let me see to the doctor first. I'll need to concentrate my energies."

"Sure, I understand."

"Fine, now I want to keep these," Gabriel said, looking down at the photocopies. "And I want to be left alone, no food, no disturbances. Do you understand?"

"But I got the short grain rice. Harrison's bringing it up from the kitchen — "

"Not now."

"Sorry," Weller replied. He was going to be a rich man, he could feel it. He was going to move to Seaside Heights, New Jersey, have a house on the boardwalk and a speedboat with a hundred-horsepower

Evinrude engine in the harbor. It was all going to happen.

★ ★ ★

It had taken Tanaka and Akiyo four hours to climb the last mile. They had stopped several times along the way, at a cave, a lake, and on the lip of a valley. They had seen birds and snakes and deer, sat, meditated and hardly spoken. Not with words anyway. A tremendous peace had developed between them and Tanaka had never felt more in tune with the process of nature. He felt lighter as he walked and experienced no fatigue as they climbed; instead he was relaxed and exhilarated.

"I know a place up ahead, we will stop there," Akiyo said, as they approached the summit.

It was not a tall mountain and the terrain was dense with shrubs and evergreens prohibiting a view ahead but amidst the calls of the birds and the whispering of the falling leaves Tanaka could hear the sound of rushing water. The sound amplified as he followed Akiyo over a rise of jagged rock and on to a plateau. A stream lay in front of them, surrounded by the higher peaks of the other mountains and a shroud of trees, pierced by the setting sun. Tanaka's sense of déjà vu was overwhelming.

"This is it," Akiyo said.

Tanaka walked ahead and sat down on a rock overlooking the water. He wanted to tell her that he knew the place, that he had dreamed of it last night, but before he could speak Akiyo began to chant, her voice merging with the sound of the water. It was the most soothing, lyrical sound that Tanaka had ever heard yet it produced within him a feeling of melancholia, a sense of yearning for something that was intangible and a deep loneliness. He tried to concentrate on Rachel and Billy but they seemed distant, as if he had become detached from them. Then the sound of the stream filled the empty space inside his heart and he was drawn to it.

He was seated with his legs folded beneath him and his hands resting on his thighs, his spine was straight but his head was tilted forward, looking down. He felt his eyes grow heavy and begin to close as Akiyo's chant continued.

★ ★ ★

"I've been here before," he said.

The chant stopped.

306

"Everyone comes here eventually," Akiyo replied.

He turned and she was seated beside him. "This is the place of transition," she added.

"Do you mean from life to death?"

"That is your great fear, isn't it? Dying. But who is dying?"

Tanaka studied the water and, as in his previous dreams, he began to see naked human bodies below the surface.

"Those people. There, in the water."

"Who are they?" Akiyo asked.

Tanaka stared. "I can't see their faces, I don't know," he replied.

"Of course you do."

Tanaka looked and Maura Allan's glassy eyes stared back at him.

"I know one of them," he said.

"You know all of them," Akiyo insisted.

Tanaka concentrated and as he did the faces became more clear, but still there was no recognition.

"Let go," Akiyo said. "You know how to do it, remember the rope, remember the feeling of freedom. Empty your self."

Tanaka leaned closer to the water. He could see the reflection of his own face and he could hear Fogarty's voice, asking for help.

"Go ahead," Akiyo urged.

Tanaka felt as if he had been pushed from behind. Losing balance, he toppled down from the rock, the water parting before him.

"Remain conscious." It was Akiyo's last command before he awakened in a white room. Bob Moyer was standing beside him with a sea of metal tables all around. There was a body on every table, each of them naked but one.

"You've still got some work to do," Moyer said.

"Autopsies?" Tanaka asked, looking down at the covered body.

"Just this one," Moyer answered.

Tanaka looked up again and knew that the bodies on the tables were all of those that he had worked on, faces that he'd thought he had forgotten when, in truth, he remembered each of them. But his feelings were attached to the body directly below him and those feelings made all the difference.

"He's a friend. I can't."

"Then you shouldn't be here," Moyer replied.

Tanaka reached forward and took the sheet between his fingers, hesitating.

"Listen, he's a friend of mine too," Moyer said, handing him a scalpel. "That's why we've got to examine his heart."

Tanaka pulled the sheet slowly across the forehead of the corpse, surprised that the hair was not the corn-yellow color of Fogarty's but thick and dark. He felt relieved.

"That's the stuff, kid," Moyer urged.

Tanaka lowered the sheet another few inches and saw the brown eyes staring up at him. A rush of fear froze his fingers.

"Come on, Joey, you're wasting time." Moyer took the cloth from Tanaka's hand and pulled it from the body.

Tanaka stared down.

"Do you know who that is?" Moyer asked.

It took a few seconds for the shock to dispel. It was not like looking at a reflection in a mirror. It was different, as it always was, without animation.

"It's me," he answered.

"That's right. Now we've got to get inside. Start with a nice lateral incision below the sternum. We want to expose the heart completely."

Tanaka lowered the blade of the scalpel. His hand was trembling. He pressed inwards against the flesh and felt pain.

"I can't do this," he said, pulling back from the table. It wasn't the pain that stopped him, it was the feeling of loneliness, the same feeling that he'd had when he'd looked into the stream.

"You've got to," Moyer insisted. "There's stuff in there we've got to see. Things you love. We've got to get them out."

"I don't want to."

"Then you're not ready," Moyer replied.

Tanaka dropped the scalpel to the floor and turned away from himself.

★ ★ ★

He saw the glint of sunlight through the trees. He was lying on his back, staring upwards and his body was stiff from the cold hard ground. He got up slowly, and rubbed his legs and arms. Akiyo was sitting beside him.

"Did you dream?" she asked.

The dream was very fresh in his mind and he repeated it to her without flaw.

"Strange the projections of the mind," she said. "The mortuary is your domain. Obviously many of the lessons of your life are learned there and much of your karma is resolved by your association with the dead. Another man's dream may have been a playing field or a classroom or even a bank, but you, you learn from the dead. This man Moyer is your ally. If he says you are not ready, then you must listen to him."

"Not ready for what?"

310

"To die for the things that you cherish, the possessions of your heart."

The hollow feeling returned and Tanaka thought of Rachel and Billy. "I'll never be ready for that."

"Then you must never face this enemy."

"Why?"

"Because possessiveness of any sort will be the dust on the mirror. He will see it."

"I'll close my mind to him," Tanaka answered.

"I believe it has already gone too far. I feel the connection has been made." Akiyo shook her head. "Can you bring your friend to me?"

"That's impossible," Tanaka replied.

"I sense danger all around you."

Her words frightened Tanaka.

"Perhaps you should stay here," Akiyo added. "We could continue the purification."

"How long would it take?"

"How long does it take a mind to die?"

"I don't know what you mean," Tanaka answered.

"How long does it take to find the silence?"

He shook his head.

"Silence is the end of thought. Stop thinking."

"Stop thinking. Clean the mirror. I

understand these things but I can't do them. I don't have time to do them," Tanaka answered. He felt trapped. "I feel more vulnerable than when I came here."

"You are mistaking being aware with being vulnerable."

"Awareness isn't going to change things."

"Then turn your back on your friend. Break the connection. Without your energy he will weaken and die. Then, maybe, the dark soul will be satisfied."

"I can't do that."

"In that case, I will pray for you."

"Is that it?" Tanaka asked, angered by her apparent inability to compromise.

"Until you let go of everything, there is nothing more."

"Maybe you've never had a family, a husband or children, maybe you've never had a friend . . . " Tanaka stopped speaking, realising that he was projecting his anger in the wrong direction. "I'm sorry," he said.

"Don't be sorry," she answered. "You are quite right. I have never had those type of attachments and I would not ask anyone to denounce them, unless that person had come to me in your position. I don't know another way."

Tanaka stood up and offered her a hand. She felt weightless as she got to her feet.

"I'm going back now," he said.

Akiyo looked at him and nodded her head. "I'm going to continue my journey."

"I'm sorry." He said it again, then turned and walked away.

He hadn't gone more than a hundred yards when he felt compelled to turn and look behind him. There was nothing other than the barren trees and evergreens, but he sensed another presence, as if he were being watched. He thought of Akiyo. Maybe it wasn't over, maybe this was a test, another step in his process of purification. The longer he stood in silence, the more intense the feeling became until he called her name. There was no answer. He walked back a few paces and called her again. The feeling persisted. Then he saw it. Sitting in the tree, on the top limb. The bird was a black silhouette against the gray sky, its hooked bill pointed down towards him. Tanaka stopped and stared. The bird remained motionless but the sight of it unnerved him. "It's a bird, a vulture or a falcon. That's all. Nothing more," he told himself, but there were other voices now, deep whispering voices of doubt. He pulled the collar of his jacket up tight to his neck and turned back to the path, walking without looking back. The feeling followed him.

18

Tanaka returned to the Retreat, gathered his belongings and thanked Richard James. No questions were asked and he didn't feel like talking. He just wanted to get home. Needed to get home.

The sky was a cold gray as he rode out of the foothills and on to the main roads, listening to the sounds of the bike, aware of every rattle, every shimmy and shake. He felt like a first timer, nervous, as if something was about to happen. Some kind of accident. Before he hit the turnpike he pulled off the road and turned off the engine, trying to pull himself together. What the hell had happened to him back there? The feelings he was having didn't make any logical sense. Was it Akiyo's warning? Or was it the bird, sitting there on the limb of a tree? Where else was a bird supposed to sit? He looked up into the sky, searching for it. What the hell was he doing? Was this the way it had started for Bill? He was paranoid, but why? Why?

The sound of the Harley's engine was reassuring and he forced himself to ride the

314

bike hard, pushing it a little on the corners, cranking the throttle on the straights, defying his fear while at the same time trying to analyse it. Running the past weekend through his mind, over and over again. Coming out at the same place. "Silence is the end of thought. Stop thinking." But he could not stop thinking. About Rachel and Billy and Bill. And Justin Gabriel. He had to face him. He'd always faced his fear in the past. Always.

* * *

Tanaka rode straight to University City and parked in the lot adjacent to the medical building.

There was a message waiting from Warden Simms, confirming his meeting with Justin Gabriel. Gabriel had been specific about the time, three o'clock in the afternoon and Tanaka had agreed to meet Simms at two thirty for a briefing. After that Tanaka phoned Rachel and then Stan Leibowitz. He didn't say anything to either of them about what had happened in the mountains, just that it had gone well and that he was home. Rachel had asked him what he wanted for dinner. It was the first time he'd thought about food since saying goodbye to Richard James.

He called Diane Genero's number before he left the office and got the answering machine but left no message, then he tried Stony Brook. Parnelli was not available but Mary Carpenter came to the phone and reported that Fogarty had received his shock therapy at nine in the morning and was still resting. His condition was about the same. She was the kind of lady who liked to give good news and Tanaka could hear the futility in her voice.

After that he left the medical building and rode to Rittenhouse Square.

"Josef, is that you?" Rachel called as he walked into the apartment.

"I think so," he answered, placing his helmet and gloves on the floor inside the closet and hanging up his jacket. He couldn't shake the feeling of nervousness. It was as if everything was happening for the first time. He felt awkward in his own home, and there was something else. It had something to do with his perception, as if the focus of his attention had been marginally adjusted. He'd noticed it while riding the motorcycle, his eyes seemed to get stuck on things, license plate numbers, people's faces, details.

"Are you OK?" Rachel asked. His voice had sounded weak.

He could hear her footsteps, light against

the carpet and sensed her presence in a way he had never experienced before. She was very soothing; it was as if a calmness was moving towards him.

"Anxious to see you, that's all," he replied, but his own words sounded false to him and he was self-conscious when Rachel appeared from the corridor. He felt misaligned.

"You look beautiful."

She laughed and shook her head. "Maybe you should spend more time in the mountains."

"No, I'm serious," he continued. "Have you lost weight?"

"That's really unkind," she answered, walking towards him. She had put on close to forty pounds with Billy and since his birth hadn't had the time to keep to her strict swimming regimen. However, in the past week, she'd been skipping lunch and eating a meal replacement bar instead.

"Come here," he said, holding his arms out. She did look different or maybe he was just looking objectively, as if his eyeballs had been scrubbed and a few layers of corrosion removed. She was barefoot, wearing a thin silk robe, one of the items she'd picked up shopping in Japan and she had bathed with a fragrant shower gel, giving her body the fresh citrus smell of lemon grass and grapefruit mixed with rosemary.

"I think you really do find me attractive," she said as he held her. She could feel him through his pants. "What did they do to you up there anyway?"

"Oh, it was intense," he replied, rubbing his hands down over the curve of her ass. "Remain conscious." Akiyo's words crept into his mind. He didn't want to remain conscious. He wanted to lose himself in Rachel.

"It's in your hips; you've lost weight from your hips."

"I doubt it."

"Three, maybe four pounds," he insisted.

She broke away from him, walked into the bathroom and stepped on the scales.

"Four pounds exactly," she said. "I'll be damned."

Tanaka stood in the open doorway and studied her.

"I love you." He needed to say the words because at that moment he didn't feel them, at least not in a way that made sense to him.

"I love you, too," Rachel replied, then walked closer to him. "I'm not kidding, are you OK?"

"Sure I'm OK," he replied. "How about Diane, have you heard from her?"

She seemed to study him for a moment before answering.

"A couple of times. She's keeping it together, considering what she must be going through, but nothing's changed with Bill."

"I know. I phoned the hospital."

The apartment had a different feeling to Tanaka. It was difficult to define but he sensed the blunt edge of danger.

"Where's Billy?" he asked.

"Billy's asleep."

Tanaka walked from the bathroom and into the small room next to theirs. Billy was in his crib, lying on his back with his eyes closed and his arms crossed in front of his body. Tanaka leaned over him and watched his chest rise and fall.

"He's slept a lot today and he hasn't been very hungry."

Tanaka reached into the crib and gently placed his hand on Billy's forehead. The child stirred but did not awaken. "He feels good, no fever."

"I know, I've checked him; he's probably just tired out."

"It's not like him to need so much sleep."

Rachel shrugged her shoulders and smiled. "Consider it a temporary blessing. Now, I've got some chicken in the oven and I can boil some vegetables. How does that sound?"

"I'll try," he answered.

"Why? When did you last eat?"

"The day before I left."

Rachel shook her head. "I don't understand."

"I've been fasting. I've got to meet this guy tomorrow and I want to be clean, you know, in the mind."

"You also might want to have enough strength to stand up."

Tanaka smiled. The more he looked at her the better he felt. Familiarity was taking the sensation of danger away.

"Now how about if we sit down and have dinner and you tell me about what happened in the mountains?"

Tanaka glanced back at Billy.

"You sure he's all right?"

"Of course I'm sure he's all right. Joey, what's going on with you?"

"I don't know, I'm feeling a little bit off, that's the only way I can describe it, like I'm here but I'm not here. I feel divided, if that makes any sense." He held out his arms. "Where were we?"

This time they kissed and the feeling of division subsided. He felt love, flowing back and forth between them. "Remain conscious."

"I want to take you to bed," he said.

"What? Before dinner?" she teased.

"Right now."

"You're serious, aren't you?"

"Oh yeah."

Rachel looked in on Billy one more time before entering the bedroom, and by the time she had joined Josef he'd taken off his shirt. "You're covered in bruises." She walked closer to him. "Everywhere." She touched his chest, above his breasts. There was a solid blackened line running across.

He looked down, then touched the mark with his own fingers. It was swollen and tender.

"I thought you were going up there to meditate," she said.

"It's a long story," he replied.

"Well I'd really like to hear it."

He kissed her again, this time very gently, pressing her lips softly to his own, and with the contact came a new rush of feeling and memory. He ended the embrace and began to remove his trousers.

"You've got them all over your legs too," she said.

He looked down and saw that his thighs were covered in scratches and black and blue marks.

"I went mountain climbing," he answered.

"Are you sure you didn't fall off your bike?"

"No, I didn't fall off the bike." Even the question made him feel uncomfortable.

"Hey, you're not my mother. You're Billy's mother. I'm fine."

She looked at him and there was a strange knowing to her eyes. Then she nodded and removed her robe.

"I just wanted to make sure," she said, reaching forward to take him softly in her hand.

"God, that feels good," he whispered.

She sank down and put him in her mouth.

There was a sound from the next room, a cough or a deep breath. Tanaka straightened, listening.

"Shhh — It's OK, OK," she soothed, standing with one hand still wrapped round his cock, pulling him forward as she sat down on the bed and leaned back. He looked down at her. Her pubic hair was only a shade darker than the hair on her head, full and thick, the shape of a diamond with a thin trail running to her navel. The lips of her vagina were pink. "Remain conscious."

She smiled, touching herself, inviting him.

He squatted down and she guided him inside her, sighing as he pushed deep and stopped, controling his urge to movement, kissing her, wrapping his arms around her, breathing with her. She put her legs around him and he lifted up so that her rear did not touch the bed. Supporting her with his hands he began to move, slowly, very slowly, and as he did he closed his eyes. "Remain conscious." It was hard not to give way to the sensation of ecstasy as he felt Rachel merge with and envelop him, their feelings for each other like gravity, drawing them to oneness. It was almost a test to see if a part of him could remain outside, a consciousness separate from the act, an observer, but the sensation of pleasure was too strong. Broken only by Billy's voice. They both opened their eyes at the same time. The child spoke again. "Da-da. Da-da."

"I've got some competition," Rachel said.

Josef used his right hand to draw her closer to him, pulling inward on her hips, forcing their pelvic bones together, then he continued a slow grind. He could tell by her respiration that she was near orgasm.

"Da-da? Da-da?"

Tanaka pressed tighter, pushing his finger into her from behind. Billy? Was Billy all right? He was not sure why he was worried about the child but the feeling gnawed at him.

"Yes. Yes." Rachel's body tensed and bucked and he could feel the contractions inside her. After that she relaxed and he held her for a while, remaining still.

"You didn't come," she said as he withdrew.

"It's Billy, I can't stop thinking about Billy."

"Come on then," she said, getting up and slipping on her robe. "Let's go see him."

He pulled his shorts back on and together they went to the boy's room. It was illuminated by a small, socket-mounted night light and the walls and ceiling were papered to look like a soft blue sky with white billowing clouds and a mobile that hung above the end of the crib, casting a long shadow. Grace Tanaka had sent the mobile from Tokyo. It was a seagull, made by hand of delicate wood and painted white and gold. They had named it Jonathan. A string hung from its belly and Josef had taught his son that if he pulled the string the wings of the bird would open.

Billy was sitting up in his crib. He was staring at the mobile and reaching out towards it with both hands.

"Da-da."

"I'm right here, son," Josef said, lifting Billy from his crib and holding him. The child laughed and grabbed hold of Tanaka's nose.

"I missed you," Tanaka continued, dislodging the tiny fingers. Billy felt warm and smelled of Johnson's powder.

"He just wanted to see his daddy," Rachel said.

"Pret-ty," Billy said, reaching again towards the wooden bird.

"What?" Tanaka asked.

"Pretty," Billy repeated.

"He has a new word," Rachel said. "Beska heard him say it the other day when he was playing with his teddy."

"Pretty," Billy repeated, continuing to reach.

"Yes, pretty," Tanaka answered, stepping towards Jonathan so that Billy could touch the string.

"Gently now, gently."

Billy wrapped his fingers around it and pulled but didn't have the strength to get the wings to move.

"Let Daddy help," Tanaka said, assisting him. The wings opened and closed. "Is that what you wanted to do?"

Billy laughed and tried to pull the string again.

"I think that's exactly what he wanted to do," Rachel said. "In fact I think that Billy will be very happy to help daddy pull the string for the next several hours."

Josef smiled and opened the wings, then let them close.

"Do you feel better now?" Rachel asked.

"I feel a lot better," Tanaka answered. "By the way, earlier, didn't you say something about chicken and vegetables?"

"I thought you were fasting?" she teased.

"I've decided I'm getting too thin."

"Yes, I noticed," she answered. "It will take me about twenty minutes. Do you think your arm will hold out?"

"Pretty," Billy repeated and Josef pulled the string again.

"I'm good for another half-dozen pulls," Tanaka said. "By then I'll try and convince him that Jonathan's tired."

"That makes sense," Rachel replied. She patted him on the seat of his shorts. "Good to have you back." Then walked from the room.

"Good to have you back." That was it. He was feeling less separated, as if the observed and the observer were once again inhabiting the same mind. "Akiyo." He thought of her. Envisioned her walking into the room right now. What would they say to each other? The experience they had shared seemed so alien to the apartment in Rittenhouse Square, and, for a moment, he wondered if it had ever happened at all. It seemed like a dream, a very vivid dream, made real only by the bruises and welts on his body.

"Billy, the bird's tired. I'm going to put you down," he began. Then he saw that Billy was asleep in his arms. He stood a moment, holding the child, experiencing a closeness that was without division, as if his flesh had moulded with the flesh of his son. "Remain conscious." He was conscious only of love.

★ ★ ★

Tanaka ate slowly and sparingly. "I'd forgotten what it's like after a fast," he explained. "It's as if my taste buds have all been dusted off and polished."

"Are you trying to tell me I overcooked the chicken?"

He laughed. "No, but I think my stomach's about a quarter of its usual size." He placed down his knife and fork.

Rachel looked at him carefully. He seemed aloof, not quite there. She'd been feeling it since he'd come in, even during their lovemaking.

"You haven't said anything about your weekend. Did you get what you were after?" she asked.

"What I got felt like a crash course in enlightenment and I think I failed." He could see by her expression that his answer

327

wasn't enough. "I'm sorry, I know I'm being vague but I'm still trying to make sense of it myself."

"Is it going to help you tomorrow?"

Tanaka hesitated.

"With Gabriel?" Rachel added.

The feeling of danger came back in a rush. "I don't know," he replied.

"Are you sure you're not giving this man a little too much credit?"

"What do you mean by that?"

"I mean you may just find a dirty little old convict in there and not Merlin the magician."

"I can't say that would disappoint me," Tanaka answered.

"Are you sure?"

"What's that supposed to mean?" he asked defensively.

"It might mean that Bill is just plain sick. That there's nothing supernatural about it. Maybe you've been hoping there was something more, some mysterious connection, but maybe it doesn't exist."

"Why the hell would I hope for that?"

"Because it would mean you wouldn't be so helpless. You wouldn't have to sit here and let that New York doctor fill him full of drugs. You could feel as if you were doing something."

"Like what?"

"Like whatever it was you did yesterday and the day before. Like going to see this guy tomorrow. I've been thinking about this."

"Yes, I can hear that."

"You're taking this the wrong way. I'm not criticising you."

"Really? Well you could have fooled me."

"Come on, Josef, stop it. Do you think I don't feel for Bill. Do you think I don't know what he's going through?"

The ice melted.

"I don't want to see you get all messed up over this," she continued. "I don't want to see you get obsessed with trying to get to the bottom of something and then find out that there is no bottom. Bill's going to need you, that's for sure, but so do the people where you work and so do Billy and I."

Tanaka sat back in the chair. "You're right, I'm sorry."

"Don't be sorry about trying to help a friend, I respect you for that. That's the kind of man you are, but please, don't let it take you over."

"It won't," he promised.

"OK," she replied.

"It's just that there are so many coincidences

with this thing. It's like a gut feeling I've got."

"You're going to see the guy tomorrow. See how your gut reacts when he's standing in front of you."

"I will."

Rachel reached over and touched the tip of her index finger to his nose. "And whatever you do, don't hit him," she said, getting up from the table and walking to the kitchen. When she returned she had a stack of mail in her hand. "Looks like a letter from your mother and about ten catalogues. Here." She laid the Victoria's Secret Christmas Special on the table. "I wouldn't mind the diamond-studded bra. I think it goes for an even million."

Tanaka laughed and his mood lifted.

★ ★ ★

Tanaka woke up alone in the bed; the room seemed unusually cold and dark, somehow claustrophobic, as if the walls had closed in during the night. He rolled to his side. The bed felt rigid beneath him and he thought he heard the sound of shoes against concrete, walking in his direction, echoing against the tight walls of the hallway. He had a terrible forlorn feeling, a loneliness mixed with regret, a sinking in the pit of his stomach. He was slipping, a part of him dying, wasting away. He closed his eyes and saw another place. There was sunshine there, warmth, white sand and laughing people. And music. Guitars, violins, and a trumpet. Fiesta. It was party time in the other place. Celebration. There was light and there was life. He wanted that life, that energy.

Then he heard the sound of a lock turning, hard and metallic and sat upright, his back pressed against the wall. He could see a figure in the frame of the open door.

"I'm dreaming. I don't want to be disturbed," he said. "Leave me alone." The voice was coming from him but it was not his voice. Not his mind.

"Josef, what did you say?"

A child began to shriek.

"Josef?" Her voice more demanding.

Josef. It was as if he was awakening for the second time, layers of sleep peeling from him like the skin of an onion.

"Rachel." He spoke her name tentatively. "I'm sorry, I must have been dreaming."

"Well if you can dream through that commotion I'm amazed."

Tanaka raised his hand to wipe the last of the sleep from his eyes. He felt sick physically. His stomach upset.

"You didn't hear Billy screaming?" she asked.

"I didn't hear a thing," he answered soberly. Gradually the sensation of nausea was passing, leaving him feeling weak and slightly disoriented.

"He must have had a nightmare. By the time I arrived he'd almost climbed over the side of his crib."

"Here. Let me hold him."

Rachel carried Billy to him but the child began to resist and cry as soon as he was near.

"Come on Billy, stop it," Tanaka said softly, cradling him.

His voice seemed only to agitate the child and the crying escalated.

"I guess he prefers marathoning in the hallway with Mom," Rachel said. "We must have walked a mile up and down."

"Billy, stop it now. It's me. Daddy," Tanaka continued but the child's sobs turned to shrieks.

Rachel took him back and the crying stopped.

"That's right, you're safe." She placed the child down on the carpet and he stood holding tight to her leg. "He still seems frightened," she said.

Josef got out of bed and squatted down

beside him, looking into his face.

"You sure he doesn't have a temperature?" He attempted to lay his hand on Billy's forehead but the child turned his head away and buried his face against Rachel's thigh.

"I checked him earlier and he was fine," she replied. "Maybe he's just angry that you left him for the weekend."

Tanaka reached again to stroke the top of the boy's head. This time Billy turned and bit him on the hand.

"That's enough of that!" Rachel scolded, bending and lifting the little boy level with her face. "You don't do that to your daddy. No. No. No."

The punishment brought on a fresh flood of tears.

"I've never seen him this way," she said.

"Maybe he's getting some new teeth," Tanaka answered, looking down at the indentation. "Looks like a molar." He forced a smile and tried to sound unconcerned but inside his nerves were jangling. "If it keeps up, maybe you ought to call Dan Renzin."

"I will," Rachel replied. Renzin was their pediatrician and a family friend.

By the time Tanaka left the apartment Billy was back in his bed and fast asleep.

19

Tanaka had chosen his clothes carefully, a soft brown leather outer coat over a light cashmere pullover, loosely fitted blue jeans and suede Ralph Lauren shoes. The shoes had thick rubber soles and hardly made a sound against the linoleum-lined floors as he walked easily behind the prison officer through a network of interlocking rooms and corridors towards the segregated housing unit of the building. He had wanted to feel comfortable, neither to be conspicuous nor to be presenting too formal an air to the man he had come to visit. He intended to make no more of Justin Gabriel than was necessary. To attach no emotion to this self-assignment. To carry out an assessment, using his skills as a clinician to take the case and weigh the evidence. As Rachel had said, maybe he was going to meet a tired old convict who at most was sending hate mail and making threats from his prison tomb. Tanaka had come to de-mystify the man, not to aggrandise him and by his de-mystification to disempower him, at least in his own mind.

The corridors narrowed as he moved deeper into the old building and he had the strange sinking feeling of earlier in the morning, as if he was entering a place of no return, a lonely solitary place. He thought of Rachel and Billy, safe and secure behind him, in another world. He pushed them from his mind; he didn't want thoughts of safety and security, of wife and child. "Let go of everything you love." Akiyo's advice had seemed harsh and without human feeling but he'd understood it both as a doctor and as a fighter. An experienced opponent could latch on to emotions, sensing fear and weakness, striking at the time of greatest vulnerability. A good fighter had to know how to shut the door on anger, and passion, and compassion. The same was required in his profession.

He followed the blue-uniformed guard through a final set of doors. Phillip Harrison waited on the other side, standing with an older man who reeked of cigarette smoke and Old Spice aftershave.

"Hello, Josef, how are you?" Harrison asked. They shook hands and Harrison introduced him to Art Weller. Weller smiled but it was a jackal's smile, hungry and suspicious. After that, Tanaka, flanked by Harrison and Weller, began the final walk of fifty yards. The atmosphere in the segregated

335

unit was more somber than in the adjoining parts of the prison. This seemed a place for men without voices, ravaged eyes staring from behind barred doors. The linoleum had ended and Harrison's cleated heels 'click clacked' against the concrete floor and Tanaka felt his first touch of nerves, as if he had suddenly entered enemy territory.

The visitor's room was green, not light and not dark, but somewhere in the middle, like a sickly hospital green, with paint peeling and a circuitry of thick pipes running the length of one side of its ceiling. There was the intermittent sound of water flooding them and a constant dripping from an area of condensation above a joint in the middle.

"Used to be a cell," Weller explained with a glimmer in his eyes and poker face, "but too many prisoners were found hangin' from them sewage pipes." Tanaka wasn't sure if it was supposed to be a joke but nobody laughed. "Here," Weller continued, ushering him to a black plastic chair which had been placed facing a metal table. "Make yourself at home, I'll go fetch the doctor."

Tanaka sat down and Weller walked from the room.

"Asshole," Harrison uttered as the older man's footsteps grew faint in the walkway. "He thinks this little pimp is something special. He'd wipe his ass for him if Gabriel wanted him to."

Tanaka noted the remark and kept quiet. "Words open doors." He wanted everything battened down tight.

"You all right Josef? You don't look well."

"I'm fine," Tanaka answered. The last thing he'd expected from Harrison was to hear that he didn't look well. It was Harrison who didn't look well. His fingernails were bitten to the quick and he seemed to have developed a nervous tick in his right eye. He also seemed to be talking for the sake of talking. Nerves?

"Don't worry, he'll be coming soon," Harrison added.

"Good," Tanaka answered.

"Watch your step with him though, he's tricky," Harrison added.

A moment later Tanaka was staring at Justin Gabriel.

"Dr Tanaka. I'm so grateful that you have come to see me." Gabriel's voice was cultured and gentle, almost sing-song. "Please, remain seated."

Tanaka hadn't even realised that he'd stood halfway up from the chair. He lowered himself back down.

"Please, Art, give us some space," Gabriel

said, motioning towards the bars with manacled hands bearing fingernails so long that they curved inwards like claws. In contrast to his voice and demeanor Gabriel's physical appearance brought to Tanaka's mind some kind of ape or chimpanzee who by a quirk of nature had evolved to become almost a man, but the most extraordinary feature was not the compactness of his muscular body or the coarse hair that sprouted like a hedge from the top of his overalls to form a perfect ring around his neck; it was his eyes. Dark and cunning. Aware like those of a wild animal, yet deep with intelligence and as they pierced Tanaka's he had the sensation of danger. It was not a danger he was familiar with, not quick and violent. It was simply there, within them, calm and insidious.

Tanaka harnessed his feelings, studying the longhaired man who stood in front of him, his head not reaching more than three quarters to the top of the seven foot frame of the door. He was dressed in brown overalls, wearing a pair of rubber 'flip-flops' on his feet, his short toes thick and hairy, his ankles bound by leg irons and his hands cuffed in front of him.

Gabriel walked towards him and stopped a few feet away. He stood still, their eyes meeting, as if he was allowing Tanaka to gain a sense of him and he of Tanaka, then he continued to the table, the top of his head passing a few inches below Tanaka's nose. "He even smells like an animal," Tanaka thought, inhaling the musk. It was not an unclean smell, but sweet and heavy.

Gabriel sat in the chair facing him and his expression changed from neutral to a thin smile. Waiting, welcoming Tanaka's attention while never taking his eyes from his. Harrison and Weller moved to a discreet position against the door of the cell and the rest of the block was quiet; it was as if everyone was waiting.

"My name is Josef Tanaka and I'm the medical examiner for the city of Philadelphia."

"I know who you are," Gabriel replied softly. "You've replaced my old friend, Bob Moyer." The smile never left his lips.

"That's right," Tanaka answered.

Gabriel exhaled and all the features of his face appeared to relax and settle. He looked suddenly young and somehow innocent. His eyes grew warm and inviting, the pupils appearing to contract and dilate in slow undulations causing Tanaka to wonder if he was on some type of medication, a sedative or something.

"Did you come alone?" Gabriel asked.

It was a peculiar question, layered with innuendo.

"Yes," Tanaka replied. It was a lie, but he didn't realise it till the words had left his lips. He was not alone. Bill was with him.

Gabriel sat a little straighter. "Why?"

Tanaka had anticipated the question but Gabriel's tone was so direct as to be disarming. "Why did I come alone, or why did I come?"

"Either," Gabriel replied.

"I came to meet you."

"I'm flattered."

"I'm looking into a series of harassments that apparently preceded one of my recent cases," Tanaka said. He thought he heard Art Weller cough nervously in the background. "The woman's name was Maura Allan."

"Maura Allan?" Gabriel repeated.

"I believe her unmarried name was Maura Rich."

"Of course. She was a patient of mine."

"She also testified against you in a court of law."

"That's true."

"Well a little over two weeks ago she became a patient of mine, at the city morgue."

Gabriel shut his eyes, inhaled and smiled

340

without showing teeth.

"Her husband told me that before her death she'd had a card from you, postmarked from here in Collegeville," Tanaka continued.

Gabriel's eyes opened as he exhaled through his mouth. When he spoke again his voice was lower and softer. "That's entirely possible. I often keep in touch with former patients. Let them know I'm still around. And thinking of them."

"In this particular instance, Mrs Allan's husband has suggested to me that the card was distressing to his late wife and may have aggravated a nervous condition."

"What type of condition would that have been?"

"Before her death she was having trouble sleeping."

"As I recall Maura always had problems with sleep," Gabriel answered.

Tanaka felt as if he was getting nowhere, gaining no sense of the man at all.

"Do you also make telephone calls?"

"When I have permission, certainly."

"Do you make those calls to people who were also involved with putting you in here?" Tanaka asked, his voice hardening.

"My calls are all listed," Gabriel replied.

Tanaka raised his head and glanced quickly at Art Weller. "Maybe you have someone make the other calls for you?"

"I don't feel comfortable with the direction of this conversation," Gabriel said.

"You realise of course that any type of suspicious behavior is going to go against you with regard to your chances of a parole hearing," Tanaka continued. "You'll die in here."

Gabriel's eyes flashed anger. It was what Tanaka had wanted. To open him up.

"You have no idea of what you are getting into, Dr Tanaka."

"Are you threatening me?" Tanaka asked.

"I'm stating a fact."

"In that case, no I don't, but I do have the postcard you sent Maura Allan," he lied. "And I do have a tape from an answering machine in New Mexico with some very peculiar recordings on it. Things about birds and flying — "

"You don't understand do you?" Gabriel asked, lifting his hands from beneath the table. "I am not the one in chains here, you are."

"I don't think so," Tanaka replied. He was gaining confidence. Gabriel seemed shaky.

"That's because you don't understand the dream," Gabriel said.

"Obviously not," Tanaka answered.

"The dream is everything. All that ever

was and all that ever will be. The dream is the eternal now, the connection. Everyone you have ever known, ever seen is a part of your dream and you are a part of theirs. Everything that affects them, affects you. The illusion is that we are separate. In fact we are all one mind, all connected to one vast neurological network. All sharing the same illusion. Once a connection is made, once two people have been in contact, a change in one causes an immediate change in the other, however subtle."

"I see," Tanaka said. He was ready to leave, to write Gabriel off as a crank, a mad man. Once a murderer but now a pest.

"You and I are particularly connected," Gabriel stated.

"I'm sure," Tanaka said condescendingly.

"I have a picture of you from an old newspaper article. I've studied that picture for hours. To get a feel of you. In fact I was thinking of you last night as I drifted off to sleep."

Tanaka began to stand up.

"I believe our minds finally touched early this morning, just as I was waking up. Did you feel it?"

Tanaka shook his head. "I don't think so."

"Don't you remember the music? It was

a mariachi band. Mexico. You were there, in my dream." It was as if it had touched a nerve. Tanaka's mouth tightened and twitched. It wasn't much but it was all Gabriel needed as confirmation. "You see, we are connected. The only difference between us is that I've learned to travel the web, to fly between minds. What's going on with our friend now?" Gabriel continued. "With Mr Fogarty. Is it some type of shock therapy, insulin or electric?"

Tanaka settled back in the chair. There was no one who could have told Gabriel about Bill, particularly about his treatment.

"I feel it in the mornings, always around nine," Gabriel said. "At first I didn't know what it was, you see I'm never ill. Never. And then this terrible sensation in my head, hot and very painful. Made me vomit."

Tanaka couldn't believe what he was hearing. He was searching his mind for a con, a trick.

"After the third day I began to figure it out. It was so regular and my thought patterns were temporarily disoriented in a particular way. Not natural at all. I've seen shock administered but I would never prescribe it. You see I just don't believe in it."

"Do you know I could have you

344

committed?" Tanaka replied, harnessing his feelings.

"Wouldn't it be simpler to act upon your dream?" Gabriel asked.

"I don't know what you're talking about."

"Your dream. My dream. The great dream. The great river. It's all metaphor, nothing more. We define everything that we perceive, every pulse of energy. We run, we swim, we fly, we think we move from place to place. We don't move. It's the mind that moves."

Tanaka shook his head. He wanted to get out of the room. It was time to get clear of this man.

"You dream of the river. You see the bodies," Gabriel's voice flowed. "You know them, because the river is the dream and the dream is the river. One body is asking for release. Let him go. Let him swim free. Let him fly."

Tanaka looked into Gabriel's eyes and saw the mirror, dancing with images from his own mind. He turned away.

Gabriel stopped speaking. He inhaled and exhaled as if to blow his thoughts clear. "I must apologise," he said. "I actually don't speak very often so perhaps when I do I expect the subtleties of my communications to be understood. Allow me to paint a new picture. An infant. A little boy, still unformed. He looks a bit like you, Doctor, although his skin is fair and his eyes are blue."

Tanaka stared across the table.

"The mental membrane that filters energy into thought is not yet developed," Gabriel continued. "His imagination is not yet harnessed to the great collective consciousness that will eventually tell him what's what. He's so incredibly vulnerable. Anything is possible within that mind. Visions of such ecstasy that you and I have long forgotten them, and such terror. Terror that is beyond your imagination. The introduction of a bad energy into that unformed mind could cause permanent damage."

Tanaka could feel a fury building inside him as he glared at Gabriel. He thought of Billy and tried to banish the thought from his mind.

"I can feel him now. He's right in front of me. I can see him. His eyes are angry. Incredibly angry. Such anger is not good for him. It's like an overload to his circuits. They're not sophisticated enough to channel such energy. Do you know that anger is malignant? Causes cancer?"

Billy. Billy with cancer. Tanaka's gut tightened and his mouth went dry. Everything seemed too close, the walls, the ceiling, even the air he was breathing. He felt misaligned and naked, all exposed and visible, too big for the space, his emotions glaring. "Stop it," he warned.

"What is the life of an old tired policeman when compared to the life of your first-born?" Gabriel asked.

"You're a dead man," Tanaka said flatly.

"Pretty," Gabriel whispered. "Pret-ty."

It all broke inside him as he threw himself across the table and gripped Gabriel by the collar of his overalls, both hands clenched, fists tightening against his windpipe.

"You're dead. Dead!" Tanaka shouted, squeezing. Then there was a feeling against his own throat, hard and penetrating. He could hear himself gagging and feel his body losing strength as he was hauled backwards.

"Steady now. Steady," Weller urged, loosening his hold with the baton. "No call for violence here. No need."

"Easy, Josef, easy," Harrison said, putting an arm on Tanaka's shoulder and guiding him back to the far wall of the room. "You gonna be OK now?"

"Yes," Tanaka replied.

"Stay back here with me, Josef. Stay back," Harrison said, while Art Weller led Justin Gabriel to the exit.

Gabriel turned towards Tanaka and lifted

both hands to his throat, clearing it as he rubbed the swollen red area around his adam's apple. Then he looked at him and shook his head sadly. "I'm sure you'll make the right decision," he said.

Tanaka stared at him, completely lost inside.

"When the time comes you'll know what to do," Gabriel added. Then he was gone.

"Don't worry, Josef, if he tries to press charges I'll deny that anything happened in here. Our word against theirs. It won't go anywhere."

Tanaka looked dumbly at Harrison. What the fuck was he talking about?

After that there was silence, no more voices, no shouts or curses, just the eyes of the witnesses in their cages as Tanaka walked with Harrison down the corridor like a condemned man.

He didn't say another word till he was in his car, driving east on Route 73 towards Philadelphia, confused to the point of being dazed. He looked at the cellular phone that sat on the seat beside him. Picking it up he punched in his Rittenhouse Square number. The answering machine caught on the fifth ring and he heard his own voice. He pressed the End button and dialed Rachel's number and her message played down the line.

"Rachel, if you're there, will you pick up the phone? It's me, Josef."

Another few seconds of silence then the bleep.

It was Tuesday. Rachel didn't work on Tuesdays. Maybe she'd been called in on an emergency and Billy was at home with the nanny. He tried her office and was connected to her answering service.

"I'm sorry, Dr Tanaka, Dr Saunders hasn't checked in this afternoon, but if you leave me a number where you can be reached, I'll have her call you."

Tanaka left the number for his cellular phone, then threw it down on the seat beside him. A minute later he pulled off the road and sat with the engine running, thinking of turning around and going back to Graterford. He needed to look into Gabriel's eyes again, to convince himself that this was all impossible. Or maybe he wanted to do something else, maybe he wanted to commit murder. Or to beg?

He felt lost inside, floundering, and desperately, like a man about to drown, he reached for God.

"Help me."

The memory of the mountains returned. Tanaka thought of the stars and the moon, the rhythm of the leaves and of Akiyo. Her words, her wisdom. "Control your thoughts, your emotions. Give him no opening, no place to enter you. Magokura. Pure heart."

She'd been right. He had not been ready.

20

There was a note from Rachel on the dining-room table: '4.30. Billy not well. I've taken him to Dan Renzin. Love, R.'

The note was like a death blow. He sat down in the chair. This was happening. It was really happening. He had allowed Justin Gabriel to touch his thoughts and enter his mind. He had been shown the consequences in advance, dissected the bodies, interviewed the relatives of the victims, seen his best friend broken, but now it was in his house, infecting his own flesh and blood.

Tanaka ran from the apartment and took the stairs to the street. The hospital was fifteen blocks west and he didn't stop till he was through the glass-fronted doors and into the elevator. The pediatrician's office was on the fifth floor and the receptionist was packing up to go home.

"Hello, Dr Tanaka," she said, recognising him.

"My wife and son?" he panted.

"They're with the doctor on the ward."

Tanaka left the office and pushed through the double swing doors that opened to the pediatrics unit. He saw Rachel standing at the end of the long corridor. She was talking to Renzin. They both turned towards him as he approached.

"What's wrong with him?" Tanaka asked.

Rachel looked to Renzin. He was a solidly built man of fifty with a full head of steel gray hair and kind hazel eyes. There was something basic and reassuring about his presence. "I'm not certain what it is right now," he replied. "It may be an allergy, or it may be a virus, the tests aren't back yet, but don't worry, we'll find out."

Tanaka turned to Rachel. "How long has he been sick?"

She was accustomed to her husband's inner calm but now there was a look in his eyes that unsettled her. She sensed panic.

"It started at about three o'clock this afternoon. He seemed to have some kind of seizure, like convulsions," she answered, tightening her emotional reins as her feelings welled.

Tanaka stared at her. Three o'clock.

351

That's when he had been with Gabriel. Black thoughts crawled through his mind; he tried to block them but his efforts served only to give them power.

He turned to Renzin. "Have you given him anything, any medication?"

"I've put him on a monitor, that's about it. I want to make sure his breathing stays regular. I don't want to do anything else till I get his blood work back from the lab. Probably in the morning."

"May I see him?"

Renzin smiled. "Of course you can see him."

They entered a white room that contained several cribs. Billy was lying in the unit closest to the door, on his back with his eyes closed and the monitor attached to his chest. The sight of his son, small and defenseless, was overpowering. "Would you mind leaving me alone with him?" Tanaka asked, stopping a few feet in front of the crib.

"Not at all," Renzin replied, checking the monitor before turning towards the door.

"Do you mind, Rachel?"

She looked at him with a quizzical expression. "Are you all right?" she asked.

"I'd like to be alone with Billy, that's all." His tone was defensive. "Then we'll sit and talk."

Rachel followed Renzin from the room and Tanaka walked to the crib. There was still a part of him in denial, a part that wanted desperately to believe that it was all coincidence, that the world of Justin Gabriel could not possibly be connected to this sleeping boy.

The door closed and Tanaka and his son were alone.

"Billy?" he said softly, reaching down to lay his hand on the child's forehead. He wanted there to be a fever, something tangible, something that a doctor could understand and medicine could put right, but the boy's skin was dry and cool. Then he touched his son's neck, pressing inwards to feel the flutter of a pulse. Billy opened his eyes.

"Your mother said you haven't been feeling well," Tanaka soothed, experiencing hope in the passive gaze, but as the boy's blue eyes focused he began screaming and flailing his tiny fists against his father's hand. The commotion drew Rachel and Renzin back into the room and continued inconsolably till Tanaka, sensing that he was the cause, walked out.

* * *

He stood waiting on the other side of the door for fifteen minutes before Rachel joined him. Her face expressed fear and mistrust.

He avoided her eyes.

"Josef, something's not right with you. I can feel it. I've felt it since you walked in here. What is it? What's the matter?"

"Can we go somewhere and talk. Please."

They walked into the empty visitors' room and sat in the two chairs furthest from the door.

"You know where I was today, don't you?" he began.

She looked puzzled.

"I went to see Justin Gabriel."

"Yes, I know that."

"Well, I think that maybe I've been so involved with Bill Fogarty that I've let certain things get to me that shouldn't have and I need to sit down and find some perspective . . . " He hesitated, looking for a way to say what he felt had to be said.

"Josef, I don't mean to be insensitive, but why are you talking about this now?"

"Gabriel really got to me."

"I don't understand what that has to do with our son."

Guilt flooded Tanaka's eyes and he lowered his head.

"For God's sake, what is it? What the hell's

going on?" she pleaded.

He looked up. "I'm trying to tell you that whatever has been happening to Bill Fogarty could be happening to Billy."

"And what's that?" Her voice was clipped and challenging.

"Gabriel uses people like conduits, one mind linking with another, like some kind of telepathy. He makes them sick."

Rachel stared at him. "Do you actually believe what you're saying?" She sounded skeptical but inside she was frightened by the conviction of his words.

"I think he killed Bob Moyer," Tanaka continued. "And I think he used Phillip Harrison to do it. He gets into people's dreams and the dreams become a kind of reality. It's hard for me to explain."

"I don't understand what you're talking about and I'm not sure that I want to," Rachel answered. It was more than his words that frightened her. Her husband seemed somehow changed, less solid and stable.

"Gabriel's insane and it's the madness that gives him his power. I felt it when I was with him. His mind's got no inhibition. Nothing's impossible. If he can imagine it, it's real. He was trying to get to me, maybe use me to get to Bill and he must have had some information before my visit, personal stuff. He started talking about Billy and — "

"Stop it! Stop it right there." She was scared and her voice was fierce. "I don't want to hear that crap. You got involved with this in order to help your friend and that's fine, but don't bring those ideas in here."

"I may have already done that," he answered.

"I'm warning you." She was as close to hating her husband as she had ever come. "I don't want to hear it."

"I'm sorry," he said.

"You weren't there. You didn't see Billy. I thought he was going to die. His body was all twisted up; he was screaming in pain." She began to cry. "And you're sorry. Well I'm sorry too. I'm sorry you've come in here talking like this. I thought I knew you better; I thought you had more self-control."

Tanaka struggled for words and found none.

"Please," she said, swallowing her tears, "don't ever mention our son's name in the same breath as that man's. Never again."

Tanaka nodded his head and she felt herself softening towards him. She could read the confusion in his face. See that he was lost inside. "Maybe you should go now.

356

I'll take care of Billy. You go and straighten yourself out about this."

"I'm sorry," he repeated.

"So am I."

She watched as he stood up and walked towards the door then listened to his footsteps disappear down the corridor.

21

Tanaka hailed a cab outside the hospital building and stared out at the city as they edged through the evening traffic, across Broad Street and down Walnut towards Rittenhouse Square. The weather was unseasonably mild and there were people everywhere, talking and laughing, walking arm-in-arm. Normal everyday people. He felt like an alien. As if he was infected with a disease that kept him apart from their lives. Lives without complication. Lives that would be lived in the bliss of knowing that things were as they seemed; that a dream was nothing more than a dream. Tanaka was caught somewhere else, somewhere in the shadow land between denial and belief. If he could cross the bridge to one place or the other he would either be cured, or at least capable of fighting; as it was he was in a tortured limbo of uncertainty. Tomorrow? Maybe tomorrow Billy would be well. Maybe Fogarty would recover. A virus, a stress disorder. They were the kinds of things that the people beyond the closed windows of the yellow cab understood, things with medical names and antidotes and cures, things that a doctor would understand. Yet Tanaka had seen the powers of the mind. In Japan, he had meditated in the ice-cold waters of mountain streams, run miles barefoot in the snow, learned to control his breath and channel his emotions before entering the fighting square, to step forward in the face of his fear, channeling his energy. He was a martial artist, and his art had entailed as much mind as body. He believed in the power of the mind. Maybe that was working against him now. Perhaps it had opened a window in his psyche that allowed the seed of doubt to grow. He thought of Phillip Harrison, then of Jim Allan and Barbara Rossi. They believed too and they were infected. Akiyo had spoken of vibratory fields, people linked by thought and energy. He had walked amongst the lepers and contracted the disease. Now he was passing it on. "To Billy. My son, my flesh and blood."

"Is this OK, mister?" The cab driver's voice came from far away. "Looks like a lot of traffic up there, probably be quicker if you walked across the square."

Tanaka paid his fare and stepped out of the car. He felt as if he was running with no place to hide.

* * *

Art Weller and a second guard, an Afro-American who usually worked in the main blocks, walked to cell 25 and stopped as Weller peered through the bars.

Gabriel was in the center of his cell. He was naked and standing in a position that resembled a man riding a horse, his legs taut and his hips pushed forward. It looked as though he was striking the air with his cupped palms, whipping his hands from the sides of his body in a circular motion, exhaling as he extended them, then inhaling as he drew them back. As if he was pulling an invisible ball into his solar plexus.

When Weller had first seen this daily ritual he had assumed it to be some type of martial art, karate or kung fu, but when he had asked about it, the doctor had informed him that the exercises were used to build and control energy, to increase the powers

359

of concentration and awareness. "The act of creation requires a much finer energy than the act of war," he had explained. "I'm a creator, Art, not a soldier. I'm building myself a new dream." Art had never really understood what he'd meant.

Weller watched until Gabriel had completed a set of twenty repetitions of the 'energy ball' exercise.

"Doctor?"

"Yes, Art."

"The warden's given his permission. You've got three minutes."

"Thank you, that's more than enough."

Weller opened the door and they entered the cell, the second guard stopping to block the exit, his hand resting on the butt of his baton, while Weller laid the arm and leg irons on the cot, waiting for Gabriel to climb into his overalls. When he was clothed he walked to the front of Weller and stood like a man about to have his shoes polished.

"Not quite so tight as last time. I don't want my ankles bruised," he said.

Obediently, Weller bent over, fitted the restraints, then loosened them another notch and secured them, before placing the cuffs on Gabriel's wrists. Then he moved with his back to the guard at the door and discreetly slipped a folded sheet of paper containing a telephone number into the right side-pocket of Gabriel's overalls.

★ ★ ★

Tanaka had showered and put on a pair of Levis and a cotton pullover; he was walking to the kitchen for a glass of water when the phone rang. His first thought was of Billy.

"Hello, Josef."

Tanaka recognised the soft insinuating voice and didn't answer.

"You don't have to say a word, I can feel you. The more you resist, the stronger our connection. How's Billy?"

As Tanaka placed the phone down he heard the words, "sweet dreams."

He sat down on the sofa. It was like having a killer in the house, watching him walk free, unable to stop or even touch him. Until the killer found his son's room and entered. "Billy." Tanaka was unable to get the image of the child out of his mind. Lying there in a hospital crib, helpless.

He picked up the phone. A voice inside of him kept saying that he shouldn't make the call, that he should stay clear until his mind was settled but he couldn't hold to it; he needed to know. The ward nurse sounded guarded when he asked as to his son's condition.

"Your wife and Dr Renzin are with him now."

"Why, has something happened?"

"He was having some difficulty breathing," she replied.

"But he's all right?" Tanaka asked, his mind racing.

"I'm sorry. You'll have to talk to the doctor."

"Let me talk to my wife. Put her on," Tanaka demanded.

The phone went dead and Tanaka closed his eyes. "No. No. No," he kept repeating to himself. It was as if he was trapped inside a nightmare, afraid to move as the ground crumbled beneath him. He was falling.

"Josef?" Rachel's voice caught him.

"Is he . . . " He was about to say alive but he couldn't bring himself to it.

"It isn't good. They've put him on a respirator. Josef, where are you?"

"I'm in the apartment."

"I think you should be here."

"I can't come," he answered. It was at that moment that he admitted it to himself. He believed. In Gabriel. In Fogarty. In the secret behind Maura Allan's glassy eyes.

"What?"

"I'm no good to Billy. Not if I come there."

"Your son may be dying," Rachel said slowly, her voice defining each of the words, like an indictment against him.

"I'm going to help him," Tanaka answered.

"God help you," Rachel answered and the phone went silent.

The fury hit a few seconds later, so hard that physical movement was impossible. Tanaka could only sit while it pounded his head and broke his reason. Nothing made sense. He was crazy, as crazy as Bill Fogarty. Bill Fogarty. He thought of him, not as his friend, but as the carrier of a plague, the murderer of his child, the destroyer of his life. In that moment he hated Bill Fogarty.

Tanaka got up and walked to the bedroom. His gun safe was in the lower right side of the closet. He squatted down and tumbled the lock. He owned three handguns, a Colt, a Smith and Wesson .38, and a Glock. He took out the Glock and made sure that the magazine was in place, then he stalked back towards the main room of the apartment, stopping by Billy's door. He looked in at his son's crib. The wooden bird hung above it, moving slightly in the draft from the heat ducts in the upper wall. He pointed the gun at the bird. Justin Gabriel. How could he get back inside the prison, concealing a weapon, through the guards? He lowered the Glock. He didn't need a weapon; he'd break the man's neck with his bare hands. It didn't matter what happened after that, who believed him and who thought he was out of his mind. Nothing mattered but the little boy who belonged in that crib. Absolutely nothing. But would that stop it? Would that stop what Gabriel's mind had conceived and put into motion? Would that stop the energy? "Break the connection with your friend," Akiyo had advised, but it seemed an impossible connection to break.

* * *

Justin Gabriel lay in the darkness of his cell. He was thinking about Josef Tanaka. The man had come to debunk him. He'd seen it in his eyes and felt it in his tone of voice. That had made rapport easier to establish because Tanaka's energy had flowed without the restraint of fear, until he had stepped headlong into the mind trap. Now he was a live conduit to the target.

The process of visualisation was simple. Gabriel lowered his heart beat by reducing his rate of respiration, causing his brain waves to go from the rapid alpha stage to the slower and more rhythmic theta waves of light slumber. He focused his mind on Tanaka, recalling each detail of his face, his fine nose, marred only by what looked like an old fracture, high up on the bridge, his full lips and chiseled jaw, his high, well-defined cheekbones and penetrating brown eyes, his shining black hair; he imagined his frustration and anger, triggered again by the phone call. The anger billowing outwards, forming an aura of red around Tanaka's head, stretching to touch everything that was close to him. He imagined it as a mind virus, a kind of cosmic cancer, spreading and highly infectious. Gabriel knew that Tanaka would do everything in his power to assure that his sickness did not kill his son. Tanaka had courage. Gabriel had sensed it during their meeting, courage and a warrior's pride. And guilt. He had sensed guilt also. A lethal mix, but that was his nature, passionate and protective. The type of man who would take matters into his own hands.

He could see them together. Tanaka and Fogarty. Somewhere desolate. Cold and lonely. There was anger all around them. Incredible anger. A flash of light. An explosion. A new feeling came. It was a sense of complete disorientation, of being lost at a point without reference; there was nothing familiar about the feeling. It was a sick hollow, a bottomless pit. It was death. He could feel death.

★ ★ ★

Tanaka returned to the living room and dialed Stony Brook. Mary Carpenter was still working and Tanaka persuaded her to get Bill Fogarty to the phone.

"You coming to see me?" Fogarty asked. "Sarah's coming tomorrow. Oh, Jesus, I keep doing that. Sarah. Sarah." His words were labored and his speech slightly slurred. "Diane's coming to visit. Not been a lot of fun for her. Don't know why she stays. I couldn't blame her if she went back to New Mexico."

"She's there 'cause she loves you, Bill."

"Yeah, I guess so."

"We all love you, Bill." Even as he said it he felt something else. He felt anger and a tinge of hatred for Fogarty; he suppressed the feelings.

"I'm sorry, Josef. It's just that everything is on the surface. It's hard to describe; it's like all my emotions are wide open, all the time. It's really raw. I've got no control. It must be the drugs. Every five minutes somebody's in here with another handful of pills and a

366

paper cup full of water. I got to be rattling inside."

"I want to talk to you about that."

"What?"

"The drugs."

"I just want to forget about all this and — "

"I know, Bill, I know, but you've got to make me a promise."

"What is it, Josef?" He sounded whipped.

"I want you to stop taking them."

"What?"

"The pills. Hold them in your mouth, spit them out when they leave the room. Just don't swallow them."

"But, Josef, I need them."

"Is anybody listening to you talk, Bill?" Fogarty's voice dropped an octave. "Nobody can hear me."

"No medicine till I get there. Do you understand?"

"I need them," Fogarty answered.

"No you don't."

Fogarty was silent.

"Bill, are you still there?"

"I'm sorry, Josef. Sorry. I told you I'm all strung out. I go off the handle. Why? Is it Parnelli? You don't trust Parnelli?"

"Parnelli's fine. He's doing what he thinks is best. It's just that I've got another idea about what's going on and I need to see you straight. No drugs. Just the two of us."

Hesitation.

"I shouldn't have done this over a telephone," Tanaka said. He could hear Fogarty breathing short, frightened breaths.

"I don't want to be straight any more."

"Just till I get there."

"When?"

Tanaka looked at his watch. It was eight o'clock.

"In the morning, first thing."

"I won't be here."

"Why?"

"I've got shock therapy at nine."

"Where do they take you for that?"

"Downstairs."

"How do you get there?"

"The elevator. Peter and Paul take me."

"Who?"

"Peter and Paul. They're the psychiatric aides."

"How about Parnelli?"

"He came the first week, until I got used to going down. Now he sees me afterwards, when I wake up."

"Nine o'clock in the morning?"

"That's right."

"Don't take your medicine, Bill, and don't say a word to anybody about this call. Not to Diane, not to anybody."

"What's the fuck's going on?"

"You sound better already," Tanaka replied.

"What's going on?" Fogarty repeated.

"Trust me."

There was silence as Tanaka fingered the trigger of the Glock.

"I've got to go now. I'll see you tomorrow. No medicine. Let me hear you say it. No medicine."

"No medicine, I promise."

Tanaka put down the phone. He had the sensation of weight, in his gut, on his shoulders, in the hand that held the gun. It was stifling. He was manipulating the people that he held closest to him, holding back on them, lying to them. He needed clarity yet everything he did felt wrong. It was as if there was no way out of the maze, no correct path.

He phoned the hospital four more times in as many hours and Billy's condition was reported as the same. He didn't ask to speak to Rachel. There was no use in that.

Finally, at three a.m., wearing a brown corduroy suit and carrying a canvas training bag, he walked from his apartment and took the elevator to the underground car park. He had showered a second time and shaved meticulously, anything to effect the outward appearance of the order and cleanliness that he so desperately needed inside.

The expressway was deserted and he traveled at a steady seventy miles an hour towards the entrance to the turnpike, slowing to pay his toll then proceeding north, stopping once in New Jersey to fill the tank, before entering New York State. It was seven o'clock in the morning and the sun was glaring straight into his eyes, causing him nearly to miss the exit sign for Stony Brook. He'd been trying not to think, concentrating on the road, the rhythm of the car, the crackling voices of all night djs and the songs they played. The same songs, over and over again. That was what life was generally all about, repetition, except now, right now. There was no frame of reference for what was happening now.

★ ★ ★

Fogarty lay in his bed and sweated. The pills were underneath his pillow, three of them, tiny and pink but with enough power to hold the lid down tight. He liked it tight lately. No way for anything to get in, no thoughts, nothing. The price he paid was a feeling of loss and of being lost. There was no way home from that place and there was no one

370

there with him. He was all alone, standing in a tower, looking out on to the dead black sea. When he could feel he felt like a coward because he knew that he was running away and he knew that the running would finally kill him. Not like a man, but like a shell of a man, a zombie, wandering the corridors of madness in his cloth slippers and white robe. Still, he was too frightened to shut his eyes. Maybe after the shock treatment he could sleep, maybe after the electricity had burned the sickness from his mind for an hour or two, but it always came back.

He could hear the ward awakening, doors being opened and people speaking, or trying to speak. "A couple of hours. Peter and Paul'll be here," he thought. They'd say, "Hey, Bill, how ya' doin'? Ready for a ride?" After that he'd get a little sleep. And Josef was coming, and Sarah. No, not Sarah. Diane.

★ ★ ★

Looking over, Tanaka could see the hospital on his left, the sun reflecting off its bank of windows. He stayed on the main road and continued to drive for another fifteen minutes. There was a diner up ahead, one of those that looked like a silver house trailer; Tanaka pulled into the lot and parked between a white Chevy pick-up truck and Ford van. He locked the Jeep and went into the diner, bought a *USA Today* from the news rack and sat at the counter, ordering a pot of tea and some wholegrain toast with no butter. He wasn't hungry but he needed to kill an hour and he didn't want to do it in the parking lot of the hospital or beside the road. The tea and toast came and he ate slowly, burying himself in the newspaper and not taking in a word he read.

Twenty minutes later, at about eight o'clock, he paid his bill, returned to his car and phoned the pediatrics ward at University Hospital in Philadelphia.

"This is Dr Tanaka and I'm calling about my son, William Tanaka. He was admitted last night."

"And you are?" As if the nurse hadn't heard him.

"I'm the boy's father," Tanaka answered, with enough bite to get through the crackling line.

"Will you please hold?"

Tanaka died inside as the seconds passed.

"Josef?"

It was a male voice.

"Yes?"

"This is Dan Renzin."

Tanaka's heart was pounding.

"William is stable," Renzin said. "I've taken him off the respirator, but I'm not discounting another seizure."

"Seizure?" Tanaka repeated.

"That's what it looked like to me," Renzin replied. "I want to give him an MRI, see if there's anything there."

'There' meant in his brain. A lesion or tumor.

Tanaka was desperate. "How about the other tests?"

"His blood work was fine."

"Could it be infant death syndrome?"

"No, I don't think it's SIDS. I'm really going to need to do the imaging before I can say anything more, but your wife is on the ward. Do you want to speak — "

"Don't let anything happen to my son. You keep him alive. Do you hear me?" He didn't intend to sound threatening but he did.

"Of course I hear you."

"Sorry, Dan. I know you will. I've got to go now."

He placed the phone down and looked through the windows of the Jeep at the parking lot and at the diner. Traffic had thinned since breakfast. Was anyone watching him? How long had he been sitting out here?

He turned on the ignition. The digital clock read 8:15. He took off his jacket and tossed it into the back seat, then unzipped his canvas bag. The nine-millimeter Glock lay nestled in his folded clothing. He looked at the gun, reckoning that he could do what he needed to do without a weapon, but maybe that was being arrogant. There were two of them and what if things got sloppy? "I can't take a chance," he decided, pulling a white lab coat from the pile of clothing. He slipped it on then opened the glove compartment of the Jeep. There were two laminated identification tags inside. He took one out and pinned it to the lab coat above his heart, then removed a role of surgical tape from the bag and slid it into his pocket.

He drove slowly back to the hospital, arriving there at 8.35. Using the driveway that led to the main part of the building he parked in a small space reserved for doctors. Tanaka had MD plates on the Jeep and he figured they'd buy him the time he was going to need.

The Glock felt cold and hard pressed against the small of his back as he walked, carrying his training bag, into the main entrance of the hospital, past the information desk and to the main elevators which were directly across from the gift shop. It was in fact the first time he'd been on this level of the building but he'd studied the blue and white Visitors Guide until he was familiar with the layout. When he got to the main elevators he pressed the button for Up and waited.

* * *

Fogarty heard the key turn in the lock at 8.45. Then the door opened and Paul entered the room, pushing the gurney in front of him, its wheels squeaking against the linoleum.

"Where's Peter?" Fogarty asked. Usually when they came for him he was halfway out of it already. Now he was nervous.

"Got the flu," Paul answered. "I told him not to take a shot. Damn shot'll give it to you every time." All the while he was talking he was arranging the pillow on the gurney and pulling back the sheet. "You feel like a ride?"

Fogarty was confused. Where was Tanaka? He thought he'd see him before the ECT; there was sure as hell no point in seeing him afterwards. "So you're on your own, huh?" he asked, stalling.

"Yeah. Come on, hop on, we'll be late."

Fogarty didn't like the idea of going down straight. He thought of his pink pills. Probably too late to take them. He looked into Paul's face. "What's your last name, anyway?"

"Kapinsky."

Fogarty climbed slowly from his bed. "You and Peter related?"

"We're brothers. I told you that before."

"I couldn't remember."

The big aide looked hard at Fogarty. "You OK, Bill? You don't seem right today."

"I hate this electric therapy shit," Fogarty answered, noticing a fresh tattoo on the underside of the massive forearm that steadied him as he climbed on to the trolley. A blue and gold eagle flew below a light, flaky scab. "Birds. Fucking birds."

"Another week after this, that's all you got," Paul said, trying to keep it light. Actually, he hated it too, going down. He'd had an operation once, an appendectomy and the trolley ride to the operating room had frightened the hell out of him. Why did the blood and guts part have to be done underground? "Ready?" he asked. Without waiting for an answer he pushed Fogarty towards the open door.

It was a lot different traveling like this, stone sober. For Fogarty it was terrifying.

Knowing what lay ahead.

At first he didn't recognise the man. Standing by the elevator, his head turned away but as the ward nurse closed and locked the door to the unit Tanaka turned towards them. He was wearing a lab coat, just like he did at the medical building. "What's he doing that for?" Fogarty wondered. He was about to sit up and call his friend's name but instinct checked his actions. He watched and waited as Tanaka walked straight towards them, smiling.

"Peter?"

Kapinsky checked the name on Tanaka's coat, "Yes, Dr Saunders." He'd never seen the guy before, if he had he would have remembered him. There weren't many doctors who looked that healthy.

Fogarty was alert now. Dr Saunders? What the hell was Josef doing?

"Where's Paul today?" Tanaka continued.

"He's off sick," Kapinsky answered, relaxing. At least the guy seemed to know his way around. The elevator door opened and there was a moment of hesitation. "Is this the patient who's having the ECT?" Tanaka asked.

Peter Kapinsky nodded and Tanaka read the question in his eyes. He shot a hand in and found the 'Hold' button on the control panel. "Let me help you in with him."

Together they pushed the gurney into the elevator.

Fogarty stared at Tanaka, trying to read him. Something was going down; he just couldn't figure out what it was.

Tanaka pressed the button for the 19th floor. "We're going to take him up to neurosurgery. Dr Parnelli wants Dr Robinson to examine him before the ECT."

"I'm sorry, Doctor, but nobody said anything to me about that. All I know is that this patient is due downstairs at nine o'clock," Kapinsky replied. He knew that some of the doctors had egos the size of houses and he wanted to keep his job, but there was something wrong here. He could feel it. "Dr Saunders, the last thing in the world I want to do is offend you, but could I see your hospital ID?"

"Sure," Tanaka said, knowing that it was time to make his move and deciding not to use the gun. He stepped forward, pretending to reach into his hip pocket. "Here it is," he continued, bringing up his right hand to grab neck high on the lapel of Kapinsky's gown, positioning his outer wrist bone against the aide's windpipe while forcing him into the wall of the elevator. "Push the stop button," he shouted, using his left to secure a grip on Kapinsky's opposite lapel. Then pulling tight he extended his wrist inwards against the man's throat.

By the time the elevator had clunked to a halt, Peter Kapinsky was slumped across Tanaka's shoulder, unconscious.

"You're crazy," Fogarty said, standing up. He seemed in a state of shock.

"Open the bag and get into those clothes as fast as you can," Tanaka ordered. "There're some shoes at the bottom. Put 'em on." He lugged Kapinsky to the gurney and laid him out. "Hurry up, we've only got a few seconds."

"He was a very nice guy," Fogarty mumbled as he dressed.

"Stick this back in the bag," Tanaka said, holding out the gun. By now the ex-cop's head was just emerging through the top of a gray sweat shirt.

"Jesus, man, do you know what the fuck you're doing?"

"Move it," Tanaka urged, pushing the Glock into Fogarty's hand. Then he pulled the role of tape from his pocket and ran a strip across Kapinsky's mouth before using the rest to secure his arms and legs to the gurney. After that Tanaka laid the sheet up and over the aide's face, and positioned him against the side wall of the elevator, out of sight from the door.

"I'm sorry about this, Peter," Fogarty said as the elevator stopped and the door opened. There were two people dressed in street clothes waiting to get in.

"Go ahead, straight through to the lobby," Tanaka said. "I'm right behind you." He turned and looked at the body on the gurney. Kapinsky wasn't moving. "Sorry, folks, they need this one back upstairs," he explained, pressing the button for the 19th floor and stepping into the lobby as the door closed behind him. "There's another one coming."

Fogarty looked weak from behind, his footsteps more a shuffle than a walk and the training suit dwarfed him.

Tanaka caught up quickly and gripped him by the arm. "You're dragging your ass; you look like an old man."

Fogarty squared his shoulders and lifted his feet. Out the door and on to the pavement.

"Over there. The Jeep. Keep moving."

Tanaka pressed his remote and the doors of the car clicked open.

"Get in."

"We just committed a felony," Fogarty said, climbing into the passenger side.

"That's right," Tanaka replied, shutting the door. He walked round the car, took

380

off his lab coat, stuffed it into the gym bag, zipped it and threw it on to the back seat. Then he got in and started the engine. Fogarty panicked. "I'm not going!" He made a grab for the door handle. "I need that place!"

Tanaka reached across and locked his wrist. "It's too late for that now."

Their eyes met.

"You're fucking crazy," Fogarty said.

Tanaka turned and dropped the shift lever into R. "Oh man, oh Jesus, oh man," Fogarty repeated as the Jeep reversed out of the space. Then Fogarty turned once more and looked at the dark towering building. "Christ, I hated it in there." Then he laughed. It was a wild, contagious laugh. A madman's laugh, and Tanaka laughed with him. All the way from the driveway to the main road.

"We've done it now, haven't we?" Fogarty asked, as they turned into the west-bound entrance of the Long Island Expressway. "No way back?" It wasn't really a question. It was an answer.

★ ★ ★

The elevator got to the 19th floor and stopped as Kapinsky struggled to turn his head towards the sound of the opening door. He waited for voices or footsteps. There was nothing. Just the sound of the door closing again and the rumble of cables as he descended to the gynecological unit. Women's voices. He tried to sit up, grunting through the tape, his head hidden beneath the sheet. "Oh my God!" Followed by a shriek. "Ester, we'd better do something, tell somebody. There's a body under there and it's alive!" Fast footsteps, the clank of the closing door and he was going down again.

The door opened a third time and he heard a female voice that he thought he'd heard before. "We've just revamped the maternity unit, why don't we start there today." He strained against the tape and shouted through his closed mouth. The voice responded. "Pardon me; there's something wrong here. Stand back." After that the sheet came down and Kapinsky stared into the face of Ginny Elliot, Stony Brook's PR whiz. Three people stood behind her, one of them shouldering a camcorder with the letters WMEW TV stenciled on it. Kapinsky bellowed again and Elliot pulled the tape from his mouth. "Call security!" he shouted.

The camera was rolling.

22

After the rush of adrenaline died they rode in silence, mulling over the implications of what had just happened.

Tanaka broke the freeze. "How long do you figure before they put a bulletin out on us?"

"Probably been done already."

Tanaka checked the clock. Ten on the nose and they were rounding the shore of Staten Island.

Fogarty was thinking like a cop and it was giving him some clarity for the first time in what felt like eternity. "Whose name's the car registered in?"

"Mine," Tanaka answered.

"How many times have you seen Parnelli?"

"Once."

Fogarty turned and looked at Tanaka. "Let's say Peter Kapinsky, the psychiatric aide, remembers the name Saunders from your tag. They'll run that through the computer first. That'll get us a little time, but as soon as they get him talking and he describes you, Parnelli will put it together.

383

You're not that easy to forget."

"I suppose not," Tanaka answered. He took the exit for the Verrazano Bridge and climbed. At the peak they could see the Statue of Liberty through the right-side window. Another five minutes and they'd be at the entrance to the New Jersey turnpike. He had a touch of paranoia. "Will you hand me my sunglasses, they're in the glove compartment."

Fogarty passed him the bronze-framed Matsudas that Rachel had given him for his birthday.

Tanaka put them on. He felt better, less exposed even though the guy at the toll booth hardly looked at him.

"You could get done for assault if Kapinsky wants to press charges," Fogarty said. "You know that don't you?"

Tanaka placed the ticket in a pocket of the center console and drove on without answering.

"That and the unlawful release of a patient, hell, they could put you inside . . . Probably didn't hurt him much though, and Peter's a pretty good guy; you might be lucky and get off with a fine," Fogarty continued, trying to bait him.

Still Tanaka didn't answer.

"I don't understand, Joey, why'd you do

384

it?" Fogarty asked finally. He'd thought about it and it didn't make sense. They were going to get caught and Tanaka had to realise it. Plus there was another thing. Fogarty wasn't sure he wanted to be out. It had started a week ago, after the ECT. He had begun to surrender to his situation. He felt safe on the ward, with Parnelli, and Peter and Paul. And the drugs, the black sleep. What was he going to do without the drugs? "Why did you break me out?" he asked again.

Tanaka was thinking of his son. It was hard not to be able to own up to Fogarty, to lay it all out, but this wasn't the time or place and in the past hour it hadn't made sense to him either; he was still full of doubt and loaded with guilt, trying to follow his gut but getting confused along the way.

"I didn't think you were going to get well in there," he answered.

"Maybe I can't get well, period."

"I don't buy that."

"It's not happening to you, is it?" There was no edge to his voice, more a resignation, but Tanaka still felt a rush of anger. He wanted to get into it, to open it up but he held back.

"There's somebody I want you to meet," Tanaka said.

"Are you taking me to Stan?"

"No."

"What's the mystery? I figure I've got a right to know where we're going."

"We're going to the mountains."

"What?"

"The Pocono Mountains."

Fogarty leaned back in the seat. "Fuck," he whispered, closing his eyes. He suddenly felt tired, bone tired. He started to drift then jolted awake. "You've got to stop the car."

"I can't stop the car."

"Well I can't stay awake."

"That's OK."

"No, it's not OK," Fogarty snapped. "I need coffee, a lot of coffee."

"Can you wait till I get off the turnpike?"

"I can't wait!"

Tanaka turned and saw the terror in Fogarty's eyes. "Next service area, I promise."

★ ★ ★

Tanaka drove straight into the parking lot and got as close to the restaurant building as he could. "Just a quick in and out," he said, flicking the master switch to unlock the doors.

"I'm not going in," Fogarty said.

Tanaka looked across the seat, trying to

assess him. In the past quarter of an hour Fogarty had seemed agitated. Maybe the drugs were clearing from his system, or maybe he needed sleep.

"Are you sure you have to have this coffee?"

"You don't understand, do you? I can't go to sleep. That's the problem. I've got to stay awake. Yes, I need the coffee."

"OK," Tanaka agreed, turning to get his jacket. "I'll be right back." Before he left the Jeep he picked up his cellular phone and slid it in his pocket.

Tanaka had just walked through the glass doors when Fogarty heard the 'kiaw'. It was coming from above him. He turned to see the seagull swoop down above the trash can that sat on the verge about five feet from the car. Landing on the rim of the container, the bird began to pick at the contents that spilled over the side, its head popping up regularly, eyes darting. Fogarty stared at it. The bird became still. It was watching him. He could see its dark eyes. Was it the bird? The same bird? Was it out there or was it in his head? He pinched the skin on the top of his thigh, hard enough to hurt. He wasn't asleep. Had the goddamn thing come for him? Had Tanaka brought him here on purpose? Maybe he was part of the plan. It made sense. Why else would Tanaka have sprung him from the hospital? Where was he taking him? There was something going on. Fogarty lowered his head. "Think rationally," he told himself. "Josef is my best friend. But where's he taking me?" He could hear the gull pulling at old pieces of cardboard, pecking at the sides of the container. He looked up. The noise stopped. The bird was watching him again. He turned his head. Staring at the door of the restaurant. "Josef. Where's Josef?" The door opened and two people came out. A man and a woman, both of them grossly overweight. The man was wearing sunglasses with big black lenses. He looked in Fogarty's direction and pointed. "What's going on?" The thought was a little more urgent than his last. The man and woman began to walk in his direction. Fogarty hunched down in the seat. When he opened his eyes again they were only yards from him, walking straight towards the Jeep. Undercover cops? Was that a shoulder holster inside the fat man's plaid jacket? Maybe they'd already copped Josef inside. The bird squawked and flew away as the fat man dropped half a hamburger and a few fries into the garbage can. After that the couple walked by the Jeep and headed for a beat-up Toyota which sat in the parking space behind. Fogarty watched them in the rear-view mirror, waiting for them to start their engine. He intended to open his door and make a run for the restaurant.

The couple sat in the car and Fogarty thought the man was watching him. Were they waiting till he made his move? "Kiaw!" The gull returned. It didn't take it long to find the remains of the burger. The Toyota still hadn't started. The bird was eating but it was sitting on the edge of the can. It dropped the meat and stared at Fogarty. Where was Tanaka? "I've been set up." He turned and reached into the back seat, got a hold of the bag, unzipped it and found the Glock. Moving slowly, very slowly, eyes glancing from the rear-view mirror to the trash can and back again. The fat people were talking and the bird was buried in the garbage can. They were getting ready to make their move. He'd hit the bird first, then move on the feds. Get them talking. Find out if Tanaka was part of the set-up. He needed to get the window down for a clean shot. He hit the button and nothing happened. The keys? He looked across at the steering wheel. The keys were gone. He was locked inside. Trapped. Tanaka? They must have got to Tanaka. He was part of it. That's what the cellular phone was all about. They were all in communication. Linked up and ready to pounce. Fogarty pressed the lock release and heard the click as every lock in the car disengaged simultaneously. OK. OK. He'd get out, get to a phone and call Parnelli. They could send an ambulance and bring him some medication. He eased the door open, keeping the weapon tight to his side. Feet touching the ground, eyes on the bird, ears on the sounds coming from behind him. So far, so good. One move from the fucking bird and he'd blast it. An engine coughed to life. He turned. It was the Toyota. They were making their move on him. He'd shoot straight through the windshield.

"Bill?"

He turned the other way. Tanaka was halfway across the parking lot, walking towards him. "What are you doing?" There was gravity in Tanaka's tone.

The Toyota accelerated towards the exit sign.

"I've got your coffee, let's go."

Fogarty looked at the trash bin; the seagull was gone.

"Come on, Bill, get back inside the car," Tanaka continued. It was the way Fogarty was standing; Tanaka couldn't see him completely, the lower part of his body concealed by the hood of the Jeep. He did,

390

however, sense that something wasn't right. "Get back in," he said, stronger this time.

Fogarty felt as if his legs were going, as if reality was disintegrating in front of his eyes. He stuffed the gun in the waistband of the training pants and pulled the top down over it. "If things get bad, at least I'm armed." Even that thought didn't make complete sense. He climbed inside the Jeep and Tanaka joined him a few seconds later.

"What the hell were you doing, Bill?"

"Just stretching my legs, my knee was bothering me."

"Here." Tanaka handed him a paper bag. The large capped cup of black coffee was inside. "Can you handle it on the move?" It didn't matter because he was already starting the engine.

"Yeah. Hey, where's the phone? I thought you took a phone with you. Who were you calling?"

Tanaka backed out of the space and drove towards the On ramp. "The phone's in my pocket. I was calling about Billy. He hasn't been well."

Fogarty thought there was something shifty about Tanaka's tone. Like he was holding something back, or making it up. "What's the matter with him?"

"Some kind of virus; they're not sure."

Fogarty stared at Tanaka's face as he spoke. He couldn't see his eyes behind the sunglasses but he was good at reading voices. Tanaka wasn't being straight with him

"Josef, I want you to turn this car around and take me back to the hospital."

"You know I can't do that."

Fogarty thought of pulling the gun. He imagined pointing it at Tanaka's head, ordering him back to Stony Brook.

"We're both screwed if I do that," Tanaka added.

"I need help," Fogarty said. He was coming off the edge of the paranoia but frightened it would happen again. "I'm falling apart."

"No, you're doing fine. Just keep fighting it." Tanaka's voice was firmer now.

"You don't understand what nearly happened back there," Fogarty said.

"Tell me about it. Talk."

Fogarty told him about the parking lot. He gave him the whole story, the bird, the fat couple. Everything but the gun. He held back on that.

"How long has it been since you've slept?" Tanaka asked.

"Since yesterday," Fogarty answered, sipping the coffee. It was boiling hot and it tasted bitter but the caffeine was getting to him quickly, lifting the veil from his exhaustion, exposing the raw nerves underneath.

"Are you going to be able to hang on for a few more hours?"

"I'm not going to sleep; that's for sure," Fogarty stated.

"OK," Tanaka answered.

"What happens if I'm just plain nuts?" The hand holding the coffee began to tremble. "I mean, look at me now, sitting here quaking. I've got no control over myself."

Tanaka looked over as Fogarty fumbled to get the lid back on the cup, finally snapping it shut. He loved him like a brother and he wanted to tell him the whole story, about Gabriel and his son Billy, but he restrained himself. Akiyo had said that words opened doors and now was not the time for that.

"Let's just keep going. Give this a shot."

"OK," Fogarty answered, straightening up. "But if whatever you've got in mind doesn't work, I want you to do something for me. All right?"

"What's that, Bill?"

"I want you to let me die."

Tanaka looked over and saw Fogarty staring at him. The fire had gone from his eyes; he looked like a hunted animal that had been run to ground.

"You giving up already?"

"I want it to be my choice."

"That's very negative talk."

"I'm serious. I'll try whatever you've got in mind but if it doesn't work I don't want to come back. I've been thinking about it and it isn't fair."

"To who?"

"Diane for one."

"Isn't that her decision?"

"She's got too good a heart to walk out on me."

"Why don't we get where we're going and then discuss this?" Tanaka replied. "We can talk about everything. We need some quiet, some quiet and some peace."

"Yeah, OK, but that's the way it is."

They drove in silence after that and Tanaka had an empty feeling inside him, as if the pressure had been released. Fogarty was going to make it easy. If it came to the crunch, down to Bill or Billy, Josef would only have to step back. Bill Fogarty would do the rest.

They continued on to the Pennsylvania turnpike, following the signs for the Northeast Extension, then off at Allentown. It was the same route that Tanaka had taken less than a week earlier, but this time everything seemed different. The sky had turned gray and foreboding, the trees were barren and a light rain left the highway shiny and slick.

His thoughts returned to that dark cell in Graterford Prison and to the man inside. Nothing to do but think. To learn to use his mind, to concentrate and to project.

23

Phillip Harrison opened the medicine cabinet and took out the dark brown plastic bottle. It was dusty from sitting and the date on the side read 2/12/93. He looked at the prescription label. 'Diazepam 10 mg. One tablet before bedtime.' "One of these should put you to sleep, five of them could kill you." That's what they'd told him at the VA hospital. He'd used them for two years, until his tolerance was so high that it scared the hell out of his wife. He'd take three, bang back a shot of Johnny Walker Black and end up in a twelve-hour coma, which is exactly what he needed at the time. Trouble was he'd be groggy for half a day afterwards and dangerous behind the wheel of their car. Then he'd nearly lost it, driving Patty to the hospital for work. Ran a red light and missed a commuter bus by six inches. After that the dosage dropped and the last sixty pills rotted in their container, carried from Virginia to Philadelphia along with half-emptied bottles of mouthwash and aerosol cans of Right Guard. Unpacked and stuck in the back row of the medicine cabinet behind the dental floss. Until the day after his Uncle Rob's death. He'd taken them down with the intention of using them himself, emptied three into his hand and stared at them. "One of them will put you to sleep, five will kill you." He'd dumped another four out and carried them to the kitchen, placed them on the wood cutting-board, covered them with a paper towel and banged them to dust with the round side of a teaspoon. The powder was fine and white and tasted a little bitter. He'd scraped it off the cutting board with a steak knife, folded it in Handi-Wrap and put it in his pocket.

The next morning the entire packet was served mixed with Justin Gabriel's scrambled eggs, and the bastard had let them sit. Hadn't even taken a bite. Harrison wondered if Gabriel was on to him, maybe he could sense the danger. If that was true the little man had certainly not let it show. He'd continued to treat Harrison in the same indifferent manner, as if the guard's actions were of no consequence. So the game had continued. Twice more Harrison had spiked

Gabriel's food and on both occasions Gabriel had not eaten, but Harrison was determined and not overly concerned with the potential for discovery. Drugs were smuggled in and out of prison all the time. Gabriel's overdose would probably spur an investigation and the guards that worked in the segregated unit would be questioned and that would be the end of it.

"One of these days his appetite will be stronger than his ESP," Harrison thought, pulverising ten of the small yellow tablets. He wrapped them, placed the wrap in his pocket and prayed for mashed potatoes and gravy.

★ ★ ★

Tanaka drove the Jeep into the driveway and parked it beneath the oak tree.

"This is it," he said, looking at the old farmhouse in the distance. "I'll get out and let them know we're here."

"I'll come with you," Fogarty replied, opening the door.

Tanaka put a hand on Fogarty's arm. "Bill, you stay put. These folks don't answer their phone too often and I haven't exactly told them that we're coming."

"How long are you going to be?" Fogarty

asked, his voice anxious. "Last time you left me I nearly lost it."

"Not long."

Tanaka stepped out the car, closed the door and walked to the farmhouse. He could smell the incense as he approached the front door; it was a different smell than last time, not quite so sweet. He knocked.

A woman answered. She was barefoot and stood as tall as Tanaka, with sharp features and closely set eyes, her raven hair nearly as dark as her robe.

"May I help you?" Her voice was gentle.

"I'm looking for Richard James," Tanaka replied.

"Did he know you were coming?"

"I was here in the beginning of the week and he'd invited me back."

"You must be the doctor from Philadelphia."

"Yes, Josef Tanaka." He extended his hand.

"Cassandra." They shook and she smiled graciously. "Richard mentioned you. You were with Akiyo in the mountains?"

"Yes. I don't mean to be rude but I'm very anxious to see Richard again."

"He's not here."

"When do you expect him back?"

"Later tonight, or in the morning."

"How about Akiyo?"

The woman laughed and raised her hands. "She comes and goes."

Tanaka was becoming impatient. "Do you know where she might be now?"

"Probably in the mountains."

"Do you think it would be OK if I left my car there while my friend and I went looking for her?"

Cassandra looked at the Jeep then up at the sky and shook her head. "The weather's turning bad and it gets dark so early this time of year."

"We'll be fine."

"Do you know the trail?"

"Yes."

"Good luck, then. I'll tell Richard you were here."

Tanaka walked back to the car and got in.

"What's going on?" Fogarty asked.

"We're going to take a hike."

"What?"

"We're going to take a hike into the mountains."

"Why?"

"The woman I want you to meet is in the mountains."

"Joey, it's going on four o'clock. It'll be getting dark in another hour."

"I brought warm clothes and a couple of

blankets, and I've got a flashlight."

"Why are we doing this?" Resistance in his tone.

"Because we've got to." Tanaka's voice was sharp and his eyes angry. "Now let's put some warm clothes on and get out of here. There're some thermals in the training bag and some jackets and blankets in the back." He opened the door and stepped out. Fogarty waited till he was behind the car to grab the gym bag. He opened it and pulled out the socks and underwear. Then he placed the bag back behind the seat. When Tanaka came around to his side Fogarty handed him a set of the thermals through the opened window. "I'll change in the car," he said.

Tanaka took off his trousers and pulled the long johns on while Fogarty did the same, keeping the Glock concealed from view and sticking it back inside his waistband when he was through. The heavy socks made the training shoes feel like they almost fit and a quilted ski parka hid the bulge from the gun.

Tanaka locked the car and they walked towards the field at the back of the house.

"That smell," Fogarty said. "I know that smell."

"It's incense, Bill."

"Reminded me of something else," he

400

answered, stopping in the knee-high weeds.

"Come on, Bill," Tanaka urged.

It was nearing dusk when they found the path leading down to the ravine and the ground was slippery.

"I'm so fucking stiff I can hardly walk," Fogarty complained. "My knee feels like it's loaded with broken glass."

"Just keep moving," Tanaka answered. He was edgy now himself, time was slipping and things hadn't worked the way he'd planned. Plus, in the past hour or so he'd begun to feel a real resentment towards Fogarty.

They stayed close together as they descended, moving slowly and it was dark by the time they'd made it to the lip of the ravine.

"What the hell are we doing?" Fogarty asked finally. He was sore and tired and frustrated.

"Looking for somebody."

"Who?"

"Akiyo!" Tanaka shouted her name and his voice echoed. "Akiyo!" He called again. When the echo died there was silence.

"Oh man, what the fuck's going on?" Fogarty complained.

Tanaka switched on the Maglite and pushed the beam into Fogarty's face. "This is it, Bill. Last stop."

Fogarty reached up and shoved the light away from him.

"What's the matter with you?"

Tanaka stood in silence.

"What is it?" Fogarty continued. "You commit a criminal act. Take me out of a place where I was getting help. Drag me here. Fuck with my head. What's your problem?"

"You," Tanaka answered.

"Then why didn't you just leave me where I was?"

"Because I couldn't."

"You're not being straight with me, Josef. You haven't been straight since we left Stony Brook. You're keeping something back."

"And you haven't been straight with me."

Fogarty shook his head. "What are we doing here? Look at us. We're in the middle of nowhere. What are we doing?" Suddenly he felt very cold and very weak.

Tanaka handed him a blanket. "Here. Wrap this around you."

"You're not answering me."

"And you're not answering me," Tanaka countered.

"About what!"

"Justin Gabriel." The name sounded heavy and final, as if it couldn't have been said before. As if it had to have been saved for

402

a time and place from which there was no escape.

"Justin Gabriel," Fogarty repeated, and with it the smell of the room returned, of bodies and death, and something sweet. Fleeting.

"It's time for some truth," Tanaka said.

"I don't know the truth," Fogarty replied.

Tanaka searched the ground till he found the three rocks that had formed the seat he'd used during his visit with Akiyo.

"Sit down, Bill."

Fogarty was hesitant.

"There, on that rock. Sit down."

"Why?"

"Just do it."

Fogarty walked to the rock and sat on it.

"Justin Gabriel." Tanaka said the name again.

"Some little creep I busted about twenty years ago."

"Mac Parkinson."

"Fuck you."

Tanaka suppressed a violent rush of anger. "What happened, Bill? Did you kill him?"

Fogarty glared at him. "You don't know what you're messing with, son!"

"So maybe you ought to tell me."

"I don't remember."

"Did Justin Gabriel kill him?" Tanaka asked.

Fogarty jumped to his feet, took a few steps towards Tanaka and stopped. "He'll never get out. No parole hearing. We're keeping him inside. Do you understand?"

"Who?"

"Justin Gabriel."

"Who's keeping him inside?"

"There're a few of us and we've got some power with the board."

"It's only you, Bill."

"Bullshit!"

"The rest of them are gone."

"Don't play with my head."

"Bob Moyer was the last. He's dead."

"Bob?"

"He had a heart attack."

Fogarty was stunned.

"So did Howard Rossi, and so did Maura Allan. Is that a coincidence?"

Silence.

"You're the only one left. The only one who knows."

"Knows what?"

"The way to Justin Gabriel."

"I don't know what you're talking about. I really don't. You've got to believe that."

"He's inside you, Bill."

"You're not making sense."

404

"He's making you sick."

"I don't believe that."

"What happened to Mac Parkinson?"

Fogarty stared at Tanaka. Standing there, all self-righteous and accusing. Pushing at him, probing old wounds, trying to get into places that he didn't belong, opening up old scars. He felt a rage building.

"You're going to talk to me, Bill, or we're never leaving here. Do you understand? This is it."

"Don't push me."

"How did he get to you, Bill? Was it over the telephone? Was it those crank calls in New Mexico? The ones you wouldn't talk about. Before Diane had the number changed. Did he send you a postcard? Is that when the dreams started?"

"That's my business, not yours."

"You almost lost your badge over that bust, didn't you? How many men did you kill?"

The words crushed him. He lowered his head and sat down on the rock. "I didn't get to kill anybody." His voice was suddenly soft, submissive.

"Mac Parkinson was your partner."

Fogarty held his head in his hands. He felt as if everything inside of him was on display. Every secret.

Tanaka sensed his friend's weakness. Now was the time to open him up, to go in for the kill. It hurt but he knew that it had to be done. There was no gentle compromise.

"What happened to Mac Parkinson?"

Fogarty answered without looking up. "One of the guys from the stakeout shot Mac."

"How did that happen?"

"It was an accident, just an accident." There was a plea buried inside his voice. It said, "Please leave me alone. Please."

"What kind of accident?"

Fogarty's head hurt. The pain was right behind his eyes, pushing out against them. Something was going to give.

"What happened during that bust?" Tanaka asked again.

The door opened and Fogarty could see it. Black wings unfurling against the night, steel talons cutting the sky, ripping down through the fabric of his mind. Everything streaking through the fissure. Those hollow-pitted eyes. Gabriel's eyes. Searching for him. Circling. Hunting him down. The night was caving in around him. He began to cry. "I can't take any more. No more," he sobbed. Reaching down he pulled the Glock from beneath his coat. "You set me up, Josef. Why?" His tears stopped as quickly as they had started.

"That's not true, Bill," Tanaka answered, keeping his eyes on the gun, silently cursing himself for leaving it unguarded yet wondering at the same time if he had wanted it this way. Planned it subconsciously.

"Then what is true?" Fogarty asked, letting the weapon hang to his side, his hand loose on the butt.

Tanaka spoke carefully, measuring every word. "I brought you here because I wanted you to meet someone who would understand your situation in a way that the medical doctors don't. She's a Japanese woman and she comes into these mountains to meditate and to pray. That's why we're here. I wanted you to meet her."

"And Bob? Is he really dead?" They had been so close for so many years. Through so much. Like brothers, flesh and blood.

"Yes."

"And the others?" He was feeling smaller and smaller. Isolated and guilty. If Bob and the others were gone, why should he still be alive? It was the same feeling he'd had all those years ago. After the bust that had gone all wrong and before he'd denied the memory.

"Yes, I told you the truth. They're dead," Tanaka replied.

Fogarty made a sound as if he'd been

slapped on the back. His breath seemed to leave his body all at once. "That's it, then, isn't it? He said he'd get us and he did."

"What do you mean?" Tanaka asked.

"Justin Gabriel. When they took him down. He vowed he'd get to each of us. 'Sweet dreams.' That's what he said. He was some kind of voodoo man. Did you know that? Did you know he could change his shape into a bird and fly?"

"Bill, you can't believe that?"

"I tried not to, but once, just once I saw something. In that room. Mac Parkinson saw it too, just before he died. I did kill Mac." He stopped and trembled, wrestling with something that lived inside him. He couldn't beat it but he could expose it. He needed to confess, to let it out. To share it with his best friend. To witness the shock on Tanaka's face when he learned that Fogarty had been a coward, to suffer his condemnation. He steeled his voice. "No, that's not exactly true. It wasn't my gun and it wasn't my bullet. It was worse than that. You see, Josef, that's the problem. I couldn't pull the trigger. I was too scared to pull the trigger. I was the closest one to it and Mac yelled for me to fire, to kill it, but I just stood there and stared. I was frozen solid. The only thing moving was the piss down my pants' leg."

"What was it that scared you?"

Fogarty closed his eyes. His lips tightened and his head shook.

"What was it, Bill?"

He spoke with his eyes closed. "A bird. It was a goddamn bird." Then his eyes opened and he stared at Tanaka. "But not like any bird you've ever seen. This thing came straight from hell. It was the size of a man, with claws like knife blades. It just kept coming at us. Screeching and shrieking. Like it was laughing. It didn't make any sense what was happening. It was all crazy, out of control. Ricky Cook fired the first shot. Must've been him; he was standing right behind me. The bullet grazed my shoulder and hit the wall. Then somebody cut loose with a shotgun and Mac caught the full load. It tore his head and most of his neck off. There was nothing left but the bones of his spine, jutting up, out of his clothes. Looked liked somebody'd fileted a fish and what was left of it was standing there, pumping blood and jerking around. When he fell, he fell forward, right into me, but I wasn't there. I was in another place, just watching. Like I'd slipped out of my body. I could see it all happening, but I couldn't feel it any more. I was ice cold. Numb. After that everybody was shouting and shooting. Everybody but

409

me. I never got off a shot. Finally there was silence, the most terrible silence I've ever known, and smoke and the smell of sulfur from the guns, and dead bodies. Mac and the rest of them. I was the only one left alive in that room and you know what I did?" Fogarty asked. His eyes had not left Tanaka's but now they were glazed, as if his vision had turned inwards. "I got down on my knees and prayed. Not for them. Not for the guys that died. I prayed for myself. I prayed that the fucking thing didn't come back. I was so scared. I've never been so scared. You see, I didn't know what it was, not till later. Not till they picked him up."

"Picked who up?"

"Justin Gabriel. Stark naked, walking in the street in front of the house. He strolled right up to the cop on the front door and gave himself up. Simple as that."

"I don't follow you."

"Gabriel. That's who it was in the room. It was Gabriel, but he'd taken on the form of a bird. Bob Moyer was the ME; he covered the crime scene. He saw the marks on the guys where the claws had dug into their faces. He found feathers all over the floor. You should have seen the crime stills. Mounds of bodies. And then there was Maura Allan. I remember sitting in a room with her and Howard Rossi and Bob, trying to make the case against Gabriel. 'Do you believe a man can fly?' she kept asking us. 'He's a sorcerer,' she said. 'He can change into a bird.' She told us about the way he could alter his form, his shape, and about the drugs." Fogarty hesitated, his eyes coming back into focus. "That's what kept me on the force. The drugs. Bob testified to Internal Affairs that there had been traces of an hallucinogen in all the bodies; the chemical came from some kind of mushroom grown in Mexico, and that's what had been in the pipe, that and cobra venom. They'd soaked the mushrooms in the venom. We'd all breathed it. That's what caused the numbness and the disorientation. At least that's what the lab boys said. So I wasn't responsible for what happened, besides my gun hadn't been fired and Mac was in charge of the bust. He'd given the order to enter the room, so I was clear. Everywhere but in here," Fogarty said, touching his head. "I'd seen it. They could say all they wanted about hallucinations, cobra venom, and altered states of consciousness, but the bottom line was I'd seen the thing. It got inside of me. That was our case. It was about belief and control, like some kind of mind virus, and by the time it was over we

411

were all infected." Fogarty stopped talking and lifted the gun, looking at it as if it were some foreign object, as if he was wondering how it had ended up in his hand.

"Bill, give me the gun," Tanaka said, walking towards him.

"I told you that if this didn't work out I wasn't going back," Fogarty said, raising the barrel and pressing it beneath his jaw.

* * *

Justin Gabriel waited in the darkness, sitting on his cot in a half lotus posture, his spine straight and his back pressed against the cold wall. He could sense the proximity of his prey. Feel it like a confusion in the center of his stomach, a churning sickness that demanded release. He closed his eyes and thought of the cop, visualised his face. Imagined him lying on the ground, helpless. The sensation in his belly intensified, as if the muscles of his abdomen were bunching to form a fist. Ready to punch out at his enemy. He held tight to the energy and relaxed his mind, visualising the dark sky, the stars and moon, the wind lifting him up, a pillow of air beneath him. He had wings, he could fly. He had the eye of the eagle.

"Bill, you don't want to do that," Tanaka said. "Don't give up now."

Fogarty looked at him and smiled. "I'm tired. More tired than I've ever been in my life. Everything aches, my body, my head. I can't sleep and I can't stay awake. I can't live."

Tanaka thought of Billy and the thought kept him from pleading or rushing forward. He withdrew his hand, watching as Fogarty's finger wrapped round the trigger.

"Thank you for everything, Josef — "

Their eyes met and Tanaka could feel it tightening. It was a sensation in his gut, as if the cord that bound them was being pulled taut, about to break. The feeling contained the past, everything they had been and done together, and it held the future; it held his son. He could feel the fabric of the cord stretching, fiber by fiber.

"Funny when it gets to the end. How fast it's all gone, just a blip, and the only thing that finally matters is relationships, who you've loved, who's loved you back, everything else is bullshit," Fogarty said. "You've been the best friend I've ever had, Josef. You and Diane. I'll miss you." Then he squeezed the trigger, sending the

413

firing mechanism on an oiled ride along the polished joints, its pin digging deep into the cap of the cartridge, exploding as the bullet began its spiraling climb.

24

Tanaka lay motionless on the ground. Stunned, a thin gray line running from the side of his jaw up and over his cheek, furrowing through the hair of his temple. He had not seen Akiyo walk into the clearing but when he looked up she was sitting there, on the rock beside Fogarty.

"I heard the thunder," she said.

He remembered the moment, wrenching the gun from Fogarty's grasp, the roar from the barrel, the bullet grazing his face.

"And then the silence," she added.

It was true. There wasn't a sound. No birds, no wind, nothing. As if the universe was poised and waiting. He sat up and looked at Fogarty, sprawled on his back, his feet together and his arms stretched to his sides. His eyes were open and staring skywards. Tanaka's act had been spontaneous but now the realisation of what he had done was sinking in. By saving his friend from suicide he had committed his own life and the life of his son, but there was a difference to his feelings now and his feelings prior to his act. The ambivalence had disappeared. He was no longer swinging between love and hate. In fact he was empty of emotion, existing in a kind of hollow place, detached from his passion. It was as if he had in that single act crossed an invisible boundary. Maybe Akiyo had always been in this other place, waiting for him. He had a sense of inevitability as he looked from her to his friend. Fogarty's face was without expression. It was only the movement of his chest and lower abdomen as he breathed that testified to the life in his body.

Fogarty was confused. He remembered Tanaka rushing towards him, the impact of their bodies colliding, the explosion from the gun. In that moment of pulling the trigger he had surrendered everything. Past, present and future, all obliterated in one roaring moment. He had wanted to be dead and he wasn't. He wasn't quite alive either. Not in the way he had been before. Something was missing, another layer of protection had been destroyed. He'd held the power in his hands and that power had been taken away from him. What was going to happen now that he had lost the final control? He tried not to think about it. Tried instead to concentrate on the hard cold ground beneath him and the pain in his right wrist. Tanaka must have bent it backwards when he hit him, twisted it. Fucking Tanaka. "That's it. Think about Tanaka. Get angry. Think about the pain in your body. Cold, I'm so cold. Keep it physical. Concentrate on the physical. Think about anything but . . . " The fear came then, like a nausea from the pit of his stomach, spreading outwards into his limbs. "Don't think about that." The more he told himself not to, the stronger it got.

Tanaka watched closely as Fogarty's face appeared to solidify, his mouth tightening as his jaw clenched.

"It is coming," Akiyo said.

With Fogarty's nausea came his memory of the syringe. More than memory it was a craving for the numbing liquid, to slow his heart and close his eyes, to take him below the surface of his mind; he wanted to hide in that familiar blackness. Instead he lay raw and exposed.

"You must be ready," Akiyo said, motioning for Tanaka to join her by Fogarty's side. "He will need you."

Tanaka was uncertain as to what exactly was transpiring but he could see that Fogarty, whose eyes had remained open and fixed on the sky, had begun to tremble and sweat. He crawled forward and knelt next to Akiyo.

At first what Fogarty saw was like a falling star, a streak of light on the edge of darkness, then the light grew brighter as the energy intensified. "Take me down, take me down. I'm ready," he said, staring at the light as it began to spiral and shape.

"Take you where, Billy?" Tanaka asked, trying to establish some connection.

"Please, let's go." Fogarty's voice was insistent. He was talking to Peter and Paul. Willing their strong hands to lift him onto the gurney and wheel him away, to hold him steady while the electrodes were attached, wrapping his mind in an electric cage, burning his fear to ashes. "Now! Now!"

Tanaka searched Fogarty's face. Even in the moonlight he could see that the pupils of his eyes were tightly contracted. He was staring at something. So intensely that Tanaka looked up, following his stare. He saw only the moon above them. "Bill — " He began to speak but Akiyo quieted him with a gesture of her hand. "Be patient," she whispered. "He is traveling to the other place. Soon the crisis will come." Tanaka settled back, resting his hips against his heels, as Akiyo began to chant.

Fogarty closed his eyes. He needed help, protection. The gun. Hard and cold, an extension of himself. A man. A cop. A protector. He could pick up the gun, stand and shoot the thing from the sky. Kill it. He attempted to reach with his hand, straining, his fingers intent on groping for the weapon, but there was no sensation or movement in his limbs; it was as if he had become disconnected from his body. Only his mind was alive. Then it was above him, so close that he could sense rather than see it, like a huge hovering shadow, its wings fanning the fire that spread outwards from his gut. Pounding like the wind. If he could have, he would have clasped his hands over his ears. Anything to stop the sound, but he was powerless as from somewhere inside the wind he heard a woman's voice, repeating the same words, over and over again.

I have wings
I can fly
I have wings
I can fly

He wanted it to stop, the sounds, the voice, all of it, but the membrane that had divided him from what was out there had been torn and opened. Everything was pouring in.

It landed. Heavy, talons sharp and digging into the flesh above his breast, securing their grip. He struggled for breath and as he exhaled the weight increased, the pain with it, like a steel band across his ribs. His heart missed a beat as the band tightened and tightened again.

I have wings
I, I, I

The voice came from another place, a dimension removed from his torment. He tried to concentrate on the voice, to reach it but everything was slipping away. He couldn't hold on.

I have dreams
I can fly
I have dreams
I can fly
I have dreams
I, I, I

He heaved for breath, arched backward, then went rigid as the air rattled from his lungs. Akiyo stopped her chant. "We are losing him," she said.

Now it was Tanaka who took charge. Placing one palm on top of the other he drove his hands down against Fogarty's sternum. "Lift his head, make sure he can breathe.

"Don't quit on me, Bill, don't quit!"

"Help me. Help me." Fogarty could only think the words. It was as if the flesh and bones above his heart had been punctured and a molten liquid was being poured into the cavity, spreading outward from the center, flowing down his left side, causing every muscle to go into a burning spasm as it passed. He forced a last breath before giving in to the pain completely. "Let me go." He pleaded with the eyes that stared into his. Eyes that were so familiar that their presence seemed eternal. "I want to die," he begged. The eyes held him a little while longer, extracting their revenge for his resistance.

There was a cracking sound, like the breaking of a tree limb. After that the pain stopped and he was looking down from the outside. Watching a dark-haired man straddle another man's body, while a squat oriental woman held the fallen man's head in her hands.

"Don't let go, God damn it, don't let go!" The darkhaired man was shouting, slamming his palms into the chest of the body again. "Come back here! Come back!" His words were meaningless. The man he was shouting at was clearly dead. "Come back, Bill, come back."

It was the name that did it. "Bill." His realisation was sudden and shocking. "That's me lying there. Me and Josef. I'm dead. Jesus Christ, I'm dead. Is this real, or am I dreaming? What do I do now?" His thoughts coincided with the feeling that he was being sucked upwards, away from the drama below. Tanaka's voice grew fainter, trailing behind as he began a headlong flight. Picking up speed the air seemed to fold in around him, forming a dark tunnel. Inside, there was sound. Disjointed voices, shouting and crying. He had the feeling that he knew them, the voices, that he had heard each of them before, that their words were important to him. A woman screamed, followed by a child calling for her father. "Daddy. Daddy." There was such loneliness in the child's cry, such abandonment. It merged with the sound of squealing tires and he knew exactly what was coming next. The crash. Metal impacting with metal, windows exploding, the wail of a siren, far away. Then he saw them, just as he had all those years ago. Ann and Sarah, mother and child, his wife and daughter, so young and so frightened, staring at him from behind the windshield of their overturned automobile. "Daddy. Daddy." "Yes, baby I'm coming," he answered, crawling back towards the car across the hot tar of the newly surfaced highway. "Daddy's coming." It exploded before he could reach them. Fire and tears, inside and outside of him. He was pure sorrow, begging forgiveness.

The process of cleansing went on for a long time as episodes from his past life engulfed him then dissipated with a discharge of emotion, each leaving him lighter, more able to fly to the pinpoint of light that he could perceive at the end of the tunnel. There was salvation in the light. He was going to be free. Finally. Just one more thing left to do. One bit of unfinished business. But what was it? Surely he had suffered enough. What sin had been left unatoned? His momentum was decreasing and he was beginning to descend. There was something down there, beneath him. Something he did not want to face. He stared straight at the light and willed himself forward. It was the first time he had been aware of his body. He still had arms and legs but they were not solid; they were simply form and shape, made of air. He tried to run towards the light, then to crawl but he was in a place that was not bound by the laws of the physical universe. He was sinking into the blackness. Visions flashed.

Faces. People he almost knew. On the cusp of some ancient memory he traveled down, lower. He could see it beneath him. Like a ribbon of tar. Water, that's what it was, a dark churning river.

He hit feet first, sliding beneath the surface, flailing his arms and kicking as he was swept up with the current. There were other bodies with him, but they were different to his. Everything had been drained from the others. They had been there longer and were blue and bloated, without faces. He had a face and he could still recall a name. "Bill Fogarty." That's who he was; that's who he had been. He brushed against them as he sped past. "I'm not ready for this. Not ready." Looking up he saw a man staring down at him. It was Tanaka. "Help me," the thought escaped him like a bubble, rising to the surface. Tanaka reached out with his hand.

★ ★ ★

"That's it, Bill, that's it. Come back," Tanaka said, preparing to strike down again against Fogarty's sternum. "You can make it."

★ ★ ★

Fogarty wanted to grasp Tanaka's fingers, to be pulled from the water but the current was strong and he could not quite make his body respond to his desires. He lost the connection to his friend as he traveled on, faster and faster, thoughts, memories, and emotion churning into one free-falling moment. It ended with the most intense pain he had ever known.

★ ★ ★

Tanaka heard the crack and wondered if he had broken one of Fogarty's ribs. It didn't matter. He couldn't stop. He'd lose him if he stopped. "Breathe, breathe," he commanded, pounding down again against his sternum.

★ ★ ★

Fogarty came to on his back. He could see Tanaka above him. He tried to speak but the effort was too much. Something was wrong with his chest. He tried again and managed a groan. "It's all right, Bill, you don't need to talk, just stay with me, stay with me." Was it over? The question had barely formed when he saw it sitting in the tree behind Tanaka's head. He struggled again to speak, to warn Tanaka that it was

424

up there waiting. "Up there," he murmured. Tanaka turned quickly and looked up. His action must have startled the bird because it spread its wings and flew from the branch. That was all Fogarty needed. The fear was back. "It's just a hawk," Tanaka assured, but Fogarty was already struggling violently to stand and run. Tanaka held him down. The second heart attack was quicker and stronger than the first. Fogarty gasped for air, arched backwards, then slammed down hard against the earth.

★ ★ ★

The bird was hovering above him. It would never let him go. Maybe that was his penance, his own personal hell. To die and be reborn over and over again, to suffer without reprieve.

I can fly
I have wings
I, I, I

Tanaka bent forward, cupped his mouth over Fogarty's and blew, filling his lungs before continuing to pump his chest while Akiyo sat back, away from them, and continued to chant.

425

I have wings
I, I, I

★ ★ ★

She could feel the power building inside her,
knew that the change was near. Let the
doctor continue with his Western medicine.
The dying man needed it; he needed all their
medicine.

25

Gabriel sensed the kill. It was always this way,
first the resistance, then the struggle, followed
by the weakening and finally the moment of
surrender when everything opened to him. It
was a strange soft feeling, almost sexual in
its intimacy. It was the time that he could
drop his own defenses and unleash himself
without restraint. He let go completely.

★ ★ ★

Fogarty didn't want to go through it again.
He wanted to surrender, to be done with it.
He wanted to die. He willed it to happen.

"Take me. Finish it, once and for all." The pain started then, but it was no longer a specific pain, it was all over him, inside and out, vibrating like a hot electricity. He prayed it would end quickly and waited for the cracking sound, the sound that would signal his release. He wanted to be detached, to look down from the other place, without the fear and hurt, but it didn't come, it just wouldn't come, and that was the most frightening part of all, the thought of eternal suffering.

It built in waves, escalating until every nerve ending was on fire, and with this crescendo he screamed in silence, unable to connect his mind to his body. Until something began to break up inside of him, prising at his being, cracking his world apart and opening him to a new reality; there was combustion, an explosion of light, and then there were two birds, one white and one black, fighting over him as if he were a piece of meat, ripping and clawing as they tumbled through space.

At first he believed he was witnessing an external phenomenon, but when he closed his eyes the image of the warring birds remained constant. The only thing that changed was the levels of fear and pain. When the white bird was attacking the levels diminished and he realised that what he saw and what he felt were connected. He also realised that the white bird was an ally. It was fighting for him. After that he willed it to victory and as his will evolved he became conscious of the control he had over the action of his mind. He concentrated on the white bird and it became stronger and more delineated while the image of the black bird began to flicker and finally, as he persisted, like a candle's flame, it died, leaving only the white bird in his mind. It was a pure image, untainted by doubt or fear.

So pure that its feathers seemed to be made of light and its eyes were like the blue sky. He stared into them. He wanted to stay, to exist there, in their infinite peace.

"That's it, Bill, that's it." The man's voice broke into his ecstasy and with it he had the sensation of gravity. "You're breathing. You're going to make it." The voice had weight and the weight was bearing down on him while the eyes of the bird became smaller and smaller. He didn't want to let them go; he belonged to them, but he was falling back into time, tumbling through inner space. He didn't want to but he was powerless to resist.

To a room inside his mind. He could hear his own thoughts as if they were voices. "I don't want to be here." He repeated, "I don't want to be here."

There were bodies all around him and the acrid sweet aroma of gunpowder mixed with the poisoned smoke of the psilocybin mushrooms. That's what Bob Moyer had said it had been. Fogarty remembered now. He remembered everything. It had been a battlefield and he was the sole survivor, on his hands and knees, praying. Praying that whatever had happened was over. "Please, God, don't let it come back. Save me, Lord, save me."

When he lifted his head it was standing above him, looking down. Everything seemed exaggerated. Its head was long and wide and covered in brown and black feathers while its bill appeared to be shaped from carved and polished bone. Long arms dangled to its sides and where the feathers ended there were gloves with metal blades sewn into their fabric, replicating talons. The legs were clad in a similar fashion, some type of suit with feathers glued to the cloth, ending at the knee. Beyond that were the muscular calves and bare feet of a man.

Fogarty had never seen it so clearly, and although the old terror echoed inside him he was empowered by this new clarity. It wasn't a bird, nor was it some mythical creature.

It was a man wearing a costume. He stood up. He was much taller and bigger, in fact the bird-man was diminutive. He reached towards it and the bird-man reacted with a swiping movement from his hand. Fogarty blocked and held the arm in check, surprised at his own power and strength, and with this awareness his determination increased. Pieces of his old self were coming back into alignment. He was a man, a policeman, and this was his investigation, the most important investigation of his life. He needed to see the face of his fear. It was going to require courage, clarity and intent but the reward was freedom.

He took hold of the head beneath the jaw. It felt hard between his fingers, some type of cardboard or papier-mâché. He stared at the bony beak and feathered crest. It was a ceremonial ornament, a shaman's mask, nothing more. He lifted it free and dropped it to the floor.

Justin Gabriel stared back at him.

Their eyes locked and time shifted.

★ ★ ★

They were alone, the two of them, in a small concrete room with gray painted walls, a steel toilet and a single cot bed. They were seated

430

opposite one another on the floor, so close that Fogarty could feel the heat from the other man's body.

"You shouldn't be here," Gabriel said. His tone was authoritative.

Fogarty returned his stare. The situation was absurd. This tiny naked man with long hair and terrible breath, staring at him in wonder and telling him he "shouldn't be here".

"Go away," Gabriel ordered.

Fogarty felt anger welling inside him. He understood the feeling. He had never responded well to intimidation, particularly when he had his man dead to rights the way he had this one.

"This is a dream," Gabriel continued.

"Yes I know," Fogarty replied.

"It's my dream and I've got the power," Gabriel insisted, his eyes growing more intense.

Fogarty shook his head. "Not in here you don't. You've got nothing." Prison cells, lock-ups. Interrogations. He was a cop and this was his domain.

"I can change; I can shape. I can fly." Gabriel squared his shoulders and lifted his head. He could feel his heart pumping inside his chest. "I can free myself from this," he said, concentrating on the assemblage point between his eyes. He had to gain control, to make it stop. He had to wake up. His heartbeat accelerated.

Fogarty reached across and touched Gabriel's forehead with the tip of his index finger. "I don't think so. You committed murder. You'll die in here." He pressed inwards.

"Stop it!" Gabriel shouted, grabbing for the finger and finding air. "I said stop!"

Fogarty laughed and as he did he could feel oxygen flood his being, giving him a new equilibrium, pouring fresh life into him. More life than he'd ever felt before. He pressed harder.

"Stop!" Gabriel shouted again, pushing himself back against the wall. Reality seemed to be disintegrating in a jigsaw of distorted images. There was a silver bird flying towards him, or was it a bullet? Had the cop finally fired his gun? He could see it coming, fast and shining, spinning through the air. Headed right for him.

Fogarty maintained the contact. He could see something changing. Gabriel's eyes were hardening with fear, giving way to panic. It was like looking into a darkened mirror, his own face was staring back at him. Clean and strong and the more intently he stared the more pronounced his reflection.

"Stop." The word was clear in his mind as the mirror cracked and the dream ended.

★ ★ ★

Harrison was at the end of the cell block when he heard the scream. It was a retching, curdling noise and it continued for as long as it took him to run the walkway. He stopped at the door of cell 25 and peered through the bars. Gabriel was on the floor curled in a fetal position, gasping for breath and heaving.

Harrison purposely took a long time to open the door and longer still to straddle the small body and flip it over on to its back.

There was a white foam coming from Gabriel's mouth and it seemed, in the darkness, that his eyes were still open. Harrison waited until he was certain that he was no longer breathing, then called for assistance.

As they pulled the blanket up to cover Gabriel's face Harrison noted that his eyes were bloodied, one of them nearly torn from its socket, and there appeared to be a puncture wound in the side of his neck, as if in his death throes he had used his taloned fingernails against himself. His face was swollen and blue.

"Looks like a massive coronary," one of the medics said as they lifted the stretcher.

"Didn't even get a last supper," the other noted.

Harrison turned to see the food tray in the far corner of the room, mushy mashed potatoes piled high on the white plastic plate. Gabriel had never touched them.

Somebody spat at his corpse as they carried it down the walkway and the born again shouted, "Blasphemy will be punished." After that there was only the sound of Harrison's cleated boot heels against the concrete.

26

Fogarty's first perception was that an enormous weight had been lifted from his chest, leaving only the air above and the ground below. He lay still, exhausted, listening to a woman speaking. He focused on her voice.

"It's gone. The sickness is gone," she said.

A man answered, speaking in Japanese. "*Arigato*." Fogarty understood the word; it meant 'thank you'. The man repeated it many times. Until Fogarty recognised the

434

voice. It was Tanaka. Josef Tanaka, his friend. Then looking up he saw the day begin to break, a swirl of reds and golds above the mountain tops, and for a moment he thought he saw a bird, like a dark speck amidst the perfect colors. He felt a tinge of anxiety, a residual bit of emotion from an old memory, but as he raised his hands and rubbed his eyes the fleck of dust dissolved and the sky was clear. After that he lay back and slept, without fear and without dreams. In silence.

★ ★ ★

The sun was rising as Tanaka and Akiyo helped him up the hill. His gray training suit was torn, covered in grass stains and dirt, and his face was scratched and bleeding. In spite of this, he looked victorious. His eyes were clear and he held up his head, smiling.

Richard James welcomed them inside the Retreat and Tanaka headed straight for the back office and the telephone. He dialed the hospital and asked for the pediatric ward. A nurse answered.

"This is Dr Josef Tanaka. May I speak to my wife?"

"I believe she's sleeping," the nurse replied.

"Please, wake her."

It took a few minutes for Rachel to get to the phone and when she did her voice was a mix of hurt and anger. "Josef?"

"Hello, Rachel."

"Where are you?"

"I'm in the mountains," he replied and waited.

"You've got Bill with you, haven't you?"

"How did you know?"

"Because your machine is full of messages from Dr Parnelli, and when Diane got to Stony Brook yesterday they started asking her all kinds of questions. What did you do?"

"That's not important," Tanaka answered. He'd pay the fine, beg forgiveness, whatever it took. But he knew the rules. If Fogarty tested of sound mind, he was free and clear. He wouldn't have to go back. Yesterday seemed inconsequential. "The reason I called is Billy," he said.

He could feel her go tense down the line.

"I want you to know our son is OK," he continued. "It's over. He's well." He had to say the words, even though there was doubt remaining inside him. It was a small nervous feeling, as if something had been left undone, or left unknown. "Trust me, our son is healthy."

He heard her begin to cry. "You don't

436

know that. Oh, don't do this, don't do this now — "

"I do know, and you've got to believe me," he replied firmly. There was no vacillation in his voice but his heart was pounding.

"I don't understand."

"Put the phone down right now. Go and take a look at him. I'll wait."

"Last night he was so sick," she protested.

"He's not sick now," Tanaka reassured. "Trust me, Rachel. Don't be afraid. Go see for yourself. Please."

The phone went silent and Tanaka waited, searching for the peace he had found at the base of the mountain. He thought of Bill. He'd seen it. Seen the sickness driven from his soul, seen him struggle and prevail. He'd felt the healing in himself. He was whole again. Now was the time to believe and to test that belief. He prayed and the silence ended.

Rachel's voice was tentative; she was still wavering beneath a shadow of doubt. "He's standing up in the crib. He looks OK. He's asking for his da-da . . . Josef, what's going on?"

Tanaka exhaled.

"Dan still wants to run a couple more tests," she added.

Tanaka laughed. "Tell Dan to go easy on

the tests; there's nothing wrong with Billy. Nothing at all." He felt lighter, as if the conviction of his words was lifting the final veil of doubt.

"It has something to do with Justin Gabriel, doesn't it?" she asked. "Something to do with what you were talking about the other night?"

The name fell like darkness. "Yes," he answered.

"I couldn't listen to you then. You terrified me. It wasn't just what you were saying, it was the way you were saying it. I've never seen you like that before," Rachel continued.

"I was scared," he replied.

"So was I. Enough to block it from my mind till I heard the news this morning."

Tanaka was suddenly nervous again. He wanted it to be over. Needed it. "What news?"

"Justin Gabriel died last night."

The strange niggling feeling stopped as the fissure of doubt closed completely. He had known. Had felt it at the base of the mountain, participated in its enactment and now intuition had become knowledge.

"How did it happen?"

"It was on the radio and I only caught the tail end of it. They said he'd had a heart attack."

"His dark energy will be reflected. Turning back on him ... " A heart attack. That made sense. Perfect sense. "A heart attack," he repeated softly.

"I can hardly hear you. What did you say?"

He spoke louder. "Do you know where Diane is now?"

"She's back in Amagansett. Worried to death about Bill. What's going on? Is he all right?"

"Bill's fine. Better than ever ... " His words seemed inadequate. "I need to see you. I'll explain everything then. It's too much to get into over a telephone. I just want to get home."

"Well, come on then, we're waiting," Rachel answered. Something had changed. She was feeling it too. There was a peace between them, a sensation of calm and wellbeing. "Hurry up," she added lightly.

Tanaka said goodbye and replaced the phone. He thought for a moment of calling Diane Genero. No, that was Bill's call. After all Bill Fogarty was the cop, and he'd taken down his man. It had always been Bill's call.

THE END

McLEAN AT THE GOLDEN OWL
George Goodchild

Inspector McLean has resigned from Scotland Yard's CID and has opened an office in Wimpole Street. With the help of his able assistant, Tiny, he solves many crimes, including those of kidnapping, murder and poisoning.

KATE WEATHERBY
Anne Goring

Derbyshire, 1849: The Hunter family are the arrogant, powerful masters of Clough Grange. Their feuds are sparked by a generation of guilt, despair and ill-fortune. But their passions are awakened by the arrival of nineteen-year-old Kate Weatherby.

A VENETIAN RECKONING
Donna Leon

When the body of a prominent international lawyer is found in the carriage of an intercity train, Commissario Guido Brunetti begins to dig deeper into the secret lives of the once great and good.

A TASTE FOR DEATH
Peter O'Donnell

Modesty Blaise and Willie Garvin take on impossible odds in the shape of Simon Delicata, the man with a taste for death, and Swordmaster, Wenczel, in a terrifying duel. Finally, in the Sahara desert, the intrepid pair must summon every killing skill to survive.

SEVEN DAYS FROM MIDNIGHT
Rona Randall

In the Comet Theatre, London, seven people have good reason for wanting beautiful Maxine Culver out of the way. Each one has reason to fear her blackmail. But whose shadow is it that lurks in the wings, waiting to silence her once and for all?

QUEEN OF THE ELEPHANTS
Mark Shand

Mark Shand knows about the ways of elephants, but he is no match for the tiny Parbati Barua, the daughter of India's greatest expert on the Asian elephant, the late Prince of Gauripur, who taught her everything. Shand sought out Parbati to take part in a film about the plight of the wild herds today in north-east India.

THE DARKENING LEAF
Caroline Stickland

On storm-tossed Chesil Bank in 1847, the young lovers, Philobeth and Frederick, prevent wreckers mutilating the apparent corpse of a young woman. Discovering she is still alive, Frederick takes her to his grandmother's home. But the rescue is to have violent and far-reaching effects . . .

A WOMAN'S TOUCH
Emma Stirling

When Fenn went to stay on her uncle's farm in Africa, the lovely Helena Starr seemed to resent her — especially when Dr Jason Kemp agreed to Fenn helping in his bush hospital. Though it seemed Jason saw Fenn as little more than a child, her feelings for him were those of a woman.

A DEAD GIVEAWAY
Various Authors

This book offers the perfect opportunity to sample the skills of five of the finest writers of crime fiction — Clare Curzon, Gillian Linscott, Peter Lovesey, Dorothy Simpson and Margaret Yorke.

DOUBLE INDEMNITY — MURDER FOR INSURANCE
Jad Adams

This is a collection of true cases of murderers who insured their victims then killed them — or attempted to. Each tense, compelling account tells a story of cold-blooded plotting and elaborate deception.

THE PEARLS OF COROMANDEL
By Keron Bhattacharya

John Sugden, an ambitious young Oxford graduate, joins the Indian Civil Service in the early 1920s and goes to uphold the British Raj. But he falls in love with a young Hindu girl and finds his loyalties tragically divided.

WHITE HARVEST
Louis Charbonneau

Kathy McNeely, a marine biologist, sets out for Alaska to carry out important research. But when she stumbles upon an illegal ivory poaching operation that is threatening the world's walrus population, she soon realises that she will have to survive more than the harsh elements . . .

TO THE GARDEN ALONE
Eve Ebbett

Widow Frances Morley's short, happy marriage was childless, and in a succession of borders she attempts to build a substitute relationship for the husband and family she does not have. Over all hovers the shadow of the man who terrorized her childhood.

CONTRASTS
Rowan Edwards

Julia had her life beautifully planned — she was building a thriving pottery business as well as sharing her home with her friend Pippa, and having fun owning a goat. But the goat's problems brought the new local vet, Sebastian Trent, into their lives.

MY OLD MAN AND THE SEA
David and Daniel Hays

Some fathers and sons go fishing together. David and Daniel Hays decided to sail a tiny boat seventeen thousand miles to the bottom of the world and back. Together, they weave a story of travel, adventure, and difficult, sometimes terrifying, sailing.

SQUEAKY CLEAN
James Pattinson
An important attribute of a prospective candidate for the United States presidency is not to have any dirt in your background which an eager muckraker can dig up. Senator William S. Gallicauder appeared to fit the bill perfectly. But then a skeleton came rattling out of an English cupboard.

NIGHT MOVES
Alan Scholefield
It was the first case that Macrae and Silver had worked on together. Malcolm Underdown had brutally stabbed to death Edward Craig and had attempted to murder Craig's fiancée, Jane Harrison. He swore he would be back for her. Now, four years later, he has simply walked from the mental hospital. Macrae and Silver must get to him — before he gets to Jane.

GREATEST CAT STORIES
Various Authors
Each story in this collection is chosen to show the cat at its best. James Herriot relates a tale about two of his cats. Stella Whitelaw has written a very funny story about a lion. Other stories provide examples of courageous, clever and lucky cats.

THE HAND OF DEATH
Margaret Yorke

The woman had been raped and murdered. As the police pursue their relentless inquiries, decent, gentle George Fortescue, the typical man-next-door, finds himself accused. While the real killer serenely selects his third victim — and then his fourth . . .

VOW OF FIDELITY
Veronica Black

Sister Joan of the Daughters of Compassion is shocked to discover that three of her former fellow art college students have recently died violently. When another death occurs, Sister Joan realizes that she must pit her wits against a cunning and ruthless killer.

MARY'S CHILD
Irene Carr

Penniless and desperate, Chrissie struggles to support herself as the Victorian years give way to the First World War. Her childhood friends, Ted and Frank, fall hopelessly in love with her. But there is only one man Chrissie loves, and fate and one man bent on revenge are determined to prevent the match . . .

THE SWIFTEST EAGLE
Alice Dwyer-Joyce

This book moves from Scotland to Malaya — before British Raj and now — and then to war-torn Vietnam and Cambodia . . . Virginia meets Gareth casually in the Western Isles, with no inkling of the sacrifice he must make for her.

VICTORIA & ALBERT
Richard Hough

Victoria and Albert had nine children and the family became the archetype of the nineteenth century. But the relationship between the Queen and her Prince Consort was passionate and turbulent; thunderous rows threatened to tear them apart, but always reconciliation and love broke through.

BREEZE: WAIF OF THE WILD
Marie Kelly

Bernard and Marie Kelly swapped their lives in London for a remote farmhouse in Cumbria. But they were to undergo an even more drastic upheaval when a two-day-old fragile roe deer fawn arrived on their doorstep. The knowledge of how to care for her was learned through sleepless nights and anxiety-filled days.

DEAR LAURA
Jean Stubbs

In Victorian London, Mr Theodore Crozier, of Crozier's Toys, succumbed to three grains of morphine. Wimbledon hoped it was suicide — but murder was whispered. Out of the neat cupboards of the Croziers' respectable home tumbled skeleton after skeleton.

MOTHER LOVE
Judith Henry Wall

Karen Billingsly begins to suspect that her son, Chad, has done something unthinkable — something beyond her wildest fears or imaginings. Gradually the terrible truth unfolds, and Karen must decide just how far she should go to protect her son from justice.

JOURNEY TO GUYANA
Margaret Bacon

In celebration of the anniversary of the emancipation of the African slaves in Guyana, the author published an account of her two-year stay there in the 1960s, revealing some fascinating insights into the multi-racial society.

WEDDING NIGHT
Gary Devon

Young actress Callie McKenna believes that Malcolm Rhodes is the man of her dreams. But a dark secret long buried in Malcolm's past is about to turn Callie's passion into terror.

RALPH EDWARDS
OF LONESOME LAKE
Ed Gould

Best known for his almost single-handed rescue of the trumpeter swans from extinction in North America, Ralph Edwards relates other aspects of his long, varied life, including experiences with his missionary parents in India, as a telegraph operator in World War I, and his eventual return to Lonesome Lake.

NEVER FAR FROM NOWHERE
Andrea Levy

Olive and Vivien were born in London to Jamaican parents. Vivien's life becomes a chaotic mix of friendships, youth clubs, skinhead violence, discos and college. But Olive, three years older and her skin a shade darker, has a very different tale to tell . . .

THE UNICORN SUMMER
Rhona Martin

When Joanna Pengerran was a child, she escaped from her murderous stepfather and took refuge among the tinkers. Across her path blunders Angel, a fugitive from prejudice and superstition. It is a meeting destined to disrupt both their lives.

FAMILY REUNIONS
Connie Monk

Claudia and Teddy's three children are now married, and it is a time to draw closer together again, man and wife rather than mother and father. But then their daughter introduces Adrian into the family circle. Young and attractive, Adrian arouses excitement and passion in Claudia that she had never expected to feel again.

SHADOW OF THE MARY CELESTE
Richard Rees

In 1872, the sailing ship *Mary Celeste* left New York. Exactly one month later, she was found abandoned — but completely seaworthy — six hundred miles off the coast of Spain, with no sign of captain or crew. After years of exhaustive research Richard Rees has unravelled the mystery.

PINKMOUNT DRIVE
Jan Webster

Twelve years ago, moving into the splendid new houses of Pinkmount Drive, they had thought the good times would go on forever. Then came the recession that would take its toll on all their lives.

EMMA WATSON
Joan Aiken

It has always been a source of great frustration to Janeites that Jane Austen abandoned THE WATSONS after only seventeen and a half thousand words. Here, Joan Aitken has used Austen's characters, but has made them her own.

THE MAKING OF MOLLY MARCH
Juliet Dymoke

Life is never easy for a workhouse girl, and Molly's is no exception. Yet fate has wider horizons in store for her. Molly finds herself following the drum in the Crimea, where her indomitable courage wins the reluctant admiration of Captain Matthew Hamilton.